Tapestry
of the

World

A Collection of Short Stories

By

Major Ursa

Burlington, Vermont

Onion River Press
47 Maple Street, Suite 214
Burlington, VT 05401

ISBN: 978-1-957184-23-4 Paperback
ISBN: 978-1-957184-24-1 eBook
Library of Congress Control Number: 2023902777

Acknowledgments

It did not take me long to realize that writing a book is not a solitary task. I found I needed a lot of help and support to turn my dream into a reality. I would like to thank my family for their endless patience as I disappeared into my head or spent hours staring at the computer screen. I also want to thank Green Dragon for reading, correcting, and ultimately turning my work into something that actually looked like a book. There are days that he probably worked harder than I did.

I also want to thank my college roommate JJ. Life at the Zoo was a confusing time. Your friendship was a real gift. I regret it took me so long to recognize that fact. When you introduced me to fantasy gaming, you gave my imagination an outlet that has lasted more years than I care to admit. You truly are one of the Best in Blue.

Author's Note

One of the most beautiful forms of ancient art was the tapestry. The creation of a tapestry was a tremendous undertaking. A simple tapestry might take as much as a year or more for a team of weavers. The creation of these masterpieces began long before the first thread was shuttled across the loom.

Tapestries were more than just pictures to hang on a wall to keep the castle warm. They were a medium for telling stories and documenting important historical events. The images that flowed through the story were carefully selected to enhance the story. The tapestry's tale could not only be traced by its images, but also by specific threads that connected key elements of the story.

Weaving a story with words should be done with the same creativity and effort that went into those ancient tapestries. The words should create images in the mind of the reader just as the weaver creates images with thread. Ideas, characters, and even objects are threads that connect different stories and books. Elements of one story become the building blocks for future tales.

I believe that each story should not only weave its own image, it should provide threads that can be traced through other stories to create a world worth exploring. As I began to write my first novel, I discovered I needed the right threads to weave my tale. I paused again and again to find the right color thread. Before I knew it, I had dozens of short and long stories that answered questions about who and what and why. I hope you enjoy the images that define the world that lives in my heart and imagination. Perhaps you will find those threads that run between my stories.

Contents

All Good Things Come with Squirrels

Chapter 1

In the Beginning

The small ogre child slipped quietly to the entrance to the underground chamber. He turned and looked back. He knew his family was different and so was he. But little of it made sense. First there was the light. With this one exception, the Ogre Caverns where his tribe lived were a place of darkness. There were a few places where the moss glowed dimly, but darkness was normal. He did not mind the dark. As with his kin, he could see heat and cool in the ever present dark and there was little he could not see.

But here in the chambers of the Chief was a light. Not the dim glow of moss, but a bright light that hurt the eyes until they could adjust. A light that left him blind when he returned to the darkness where the rest of the tribe lived. The source of the light was a tiny circle of metal that rested in a small niche well above his head. Sometimes Papa covered the niche, but that was mostly for sleep.

Mama told him the light was magic and it would never go out. She had a funny name for it, but he just called it the forever light. Mama made the light with her magic before he was born. And she was the one who gave him the words for light and magic.

The second reason his family was different was the human woman sitting alone in the chamber. She sat on a rock along the wall with

something she called paper. It had lots of squiggly lines on it and the woman liked to look at them a lot. She was the only human in the Ogre Caverns. She was also the only one who saw anything in the squiggly lines. She was the only human in the tribe and she was Mama.

The woman was much larger than he was, but then again so was most everyone else. She was not as large as Papa, nor was she as large as most ogre women. Papa told him that she was the largest human he had ever met. She was strong. She had long dark hair that fell loosely to her shoulders. She had a strong face and bright eyes. But her eyes did not work in the dark like his did.

Mama had many words. More words than anyone in the tribe. Papa said her words made him strong. But that did not make sense to him. But Papa was the strongest in the tribe. It was one of the reasons he was Chief. She told him that words were power and he tried very hard to remember all of the words she gave him. But words were hard to hold and he lost many of her gifts.

He often wondered if she was the reason that he was different from the other young ogres. He was much smaller and was always getting into trouble. But he decided that it had to be his fault because Mama was so good. As he gazed at her across the chamber, he wished that words came out of his mouth like they worked in his head. But sadly, it was not to be.

He raised his voice and spoke. "Mama, ken me go?"

She turned and eyed him as he stood near the darkness. Her mouth made that funny thing she called a smile. On an ogre it meant you looked tasty, but she would not eat him. She put down the paper she was looking at and slowly turned on the rock to face him. She had to use her hands to shift her lame left leg. She seemed to be looking inside him. "Stay out of trouble, my son. No fighting this time."

He started to argue but she cut him off. "No excuses. No fighting."

He nodded. "Okie. Bye Mama."

He turned and crept softly down the corridor. As he left, he heard her mutter, "Guard him please, Mielikki." He paused in the darkness to let his eyes adjust. He pulled out boots from his backpack and put them on. They were not as quiet as his bare feet, but they would hide the warm footprints that would betray his passing. He did not want to be seen today.

He knew the only way not to fight was to not be detected by anybody. The other ogre children thought him small and weak. Weakness was not tolerated in the tribe. The weak were always targets of cruel jokes and beatings. It was the ogre way.

But the boy knew he was not weak. He was small but he had strength like Papa and Mama. The other ogre children had learned early not to attack him one at a time. Now they looked for him in packs. So, he needed to go unseen. This day he planned to explore places he should not be. He wanted to know what was there and why it was forbidden.

He did not understand why these tunnels called to him. He had asked his uncle about them, but Uncle Three Toe had warned him to stay away. Worse, one of his chief tormentors was the son of an Elder that lived along his route.

He finished with his boots. He had already made up his mind, so there was nothing to do but follow his choice. He began to move up the winding tunnel to the next level. There would be no better time. Papa had called for a hunt in the deep dark this day. The tribe needed more food. With so many adults and older youth gone, it was his best chance to go undetected.

He traveled quickly through the tunnels controlled by the tribe. He eventually reached the most risky part of his journey: the tunnel that led past the chambers of several of the Elders. From this point, he could turn on a corridor that led to more ramps heading up. Forbidden ramps that must hold secrets he wanted to learn.

He eyed the corridor carefully. Many adults lived here, but he hoped that most were hunting in the deep passages with Papa. But it only took one to ruin his plan. He eyed the floors and walls looking for warm spots that would indicate the presence of another member of the tribe. Everything seemed to be the uniform cool of an empty passage.

He also listened for any sounds echoing from the chambers along this particular passage, but all was quiet.

Seeing and hearing nothing, he began to creep down the side of the corridor. He made sure to move his feet quickly to prevent leaving warm prints of his own. He passed several chamber openings without notice and approached the corner leading into a new area he wanted to explore. This was the farthest he had ever gotten. He moved faster now with less care. It was his first mistake.

As he was about to turn the corner, he heard the scrape of feet behind him. He looked back to see Thump's two sidekicks grinning at him from the entrance of the last side chamber he had passed. Realizing his danger, he whipped his head back just as a large fist pounded into his stomach. He lost his breath, but had the presence of mind to spin to the side of his attacker.

He looked up to see Thump bent over laughing at him. Without thinking, he backhanded the larger youth in the mouth. Thump spun face first into the wall and fell to the ground.

He turned to run up the passage he had been trying to reach. He only made it a few strides before one large body hit him in the knees and another across the back. The three youths tumbled to the floor and slid to a stop in front of a small side chamber. The smell of dead animals wafted from it. He struggled to his feet but they pinned him against a large boulder outside the chamber.

As always, the beating was painful. He got in a few hard hits, but he was too badly outnumbered. The three larger youth piled on top of him. Thump managed to grab him by the hair. Then Thump hit him again. He bared his tusks, but Thump growled and smashed his head against the stone floor.

As they rose over him, Thump kicked him. "Chief son runt." One of the other boys yelled "Small!" The third added "Short!" They began to chant "Short…. Short…Short!" Then Thump kicked him again and cried out, "Names him Shorty." And the other youth laughed.

Thump pointed to a small opening where they fought. "Put in dere. Stay where prey wait ta bees kilt. He prey." They shoved and kicked him until he was in the room. Then they all grunted and heaved as they moved the boulder across the entrance. Thankfully, it was finally quiet.

He shook his head and climbed to his feet. He felt bruises in a number of places and a large scrape on his cheek where he had slid across the rock. He felt shame at being beaten again, but there was little he could do.

He slowly approached the boulder blocking the entrance and gave it a little shove. It moved easily and he knew he could free himself at any time. But he heard the other youth through the new opening. They were bragging in the corridor. He decided not to press his luck and risk a second beating.

He listened to them for a bit in frustration. He did not like being called Shorty. It was not a good name. He wanted to be called Strong or Brave, not Shorty or Small or Runt.

He began to wander the chamber, but there was not much to it. On one wall he found a small chimney-like crevice leading up. It would be too small for his attackers, but he fit into it with room to spare. With nothing else to do he began to climb.

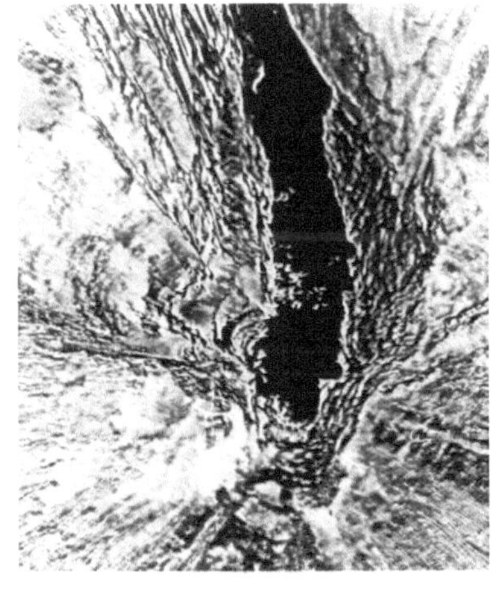

After about fifteen minutes of moving steadily up, he notice light leaking into the chimney from above. "Nudder forever light?" he muttered. He would get it for Mama. He continued to climb and in another ten minutes he crawled into a small roundish chamber tall enough for him to stand.

The chamber was not as bright as the one his family lived in but he could see well enough. The light did not blind him because he had been climbing into it for a while. He blinked a few times and then examined the chamber. The chamber was small. There really was not much to see within it. Just one small rock that could be used as a seat. Like his family's chamber, the light came from a small crevice in the wall. But there was no shining piece of metal here. The light came from beyond.

The boy moved closer to study the crevice. It was about his shoulder height. It was only about as wide as his hand and as long as his foot. He could see that the crevice went in about half the length of his arm. He learned forward and peered within it. On the far side, the crevice opened into a large space. The space beyond seemed to glow even brighter than the light in his own chamber. Stranger still, scents he had never smelled came through the opening on a light breeze.

The young ogre pressed his face to the opening and stared out in wonder. He had never seen a chamber so large before. The first thing he saw was the forever light. But this one was much larger and much brighter. Mama's light was clear and clean. This light had a strange tint to it. It hurt his eyes to stare at if for long. This light seemed to hang in the air without anything to hold it up. It had to be very powerful magic. Even the air was a color he did not know. There were small white things hanging near the forever light that he had no name for.

He turned his attention to the region closer to the ground and saw something taller than an adult ogre standing a stone's throw away. The creature seemed to have many arms and it reached up as if to take down the forever light. But it could not reach. Its arms were covered in tiny things that moved in the breeze. And there were colors. So many colors that all the youth could do was stare.

Then he noticed a small thing move through the air and land on the big thing's arm. It made a noise that was pleasant to hear. He stood and listened and watched. Soon he heard another noise. It was more of a chittering sound. A small rat ran down the tall thing and grabbed a small rock in its mouth and ran back up. The rat was unusual in several ways. Its color was not the same as the rats he knew. And its tail was huge. The tails of the rats he knew were small hairless things. This rat had a large bushy tail that was a different color at the end. Again, he had no words for what he saw.

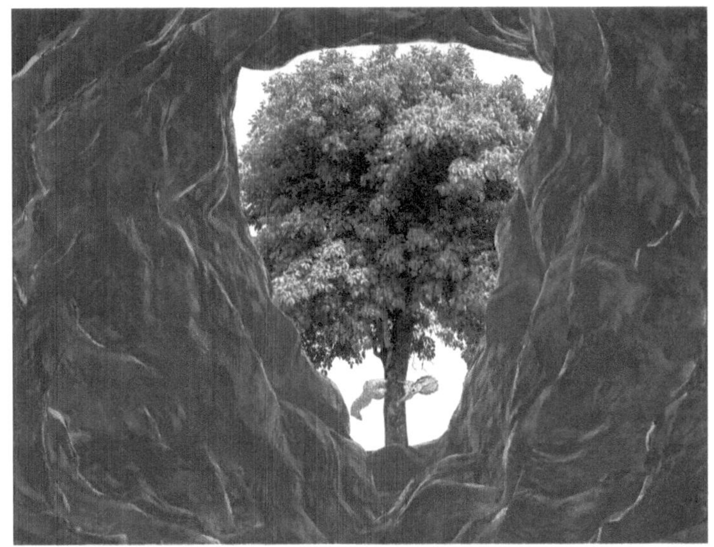

He watched the rat scamper back down and begin to pick up another rock. Then he noticed a second slightly larger rat run from the side and jump on the smaller rat. He growled as he watched them roll around with the larger rat appearing to gain the edge. He wanted to help the little rat and squish the larger attacker. His hands clenched in anger.

Then the smaller rat broke away and ran up the big thing again with the larger rat in pursuit. He whispered encouragement to the smaller rat. Seconds later the larger rat came running back down with the smaller rat doing the chasing. Not fight? He wondered.

They stopped and the chittering noise returned. They did not even fight like the rats he knew. Neither bled from the exchange. Both grabbed a rock in their mouths and climbed back up again.

He continued to stare for a long time. The forever light had moved to where he could not see it. And it began to grow dark. He reached his hand out the crevice and strained to reach down. He felt something with his hand and he closed it before pulling it back inside. As he opened his hand, he found one of the rocks and something soft and flat that was filled with color. So many new things he did not know. But they called to him.

He placed his treasures in a belt pouch and took one last long look through the crevice. Then he climbed back down to the chamber below. To his surprise the boulder no longer blocked his way. He grinned as

he thought about his tormentors searching for him. Then he slipped out
into the passage and headed back to his own chambers on the lower
level.

Chapter 2

Truth and Consequences

He tried to slip back into the family chamber silently and sneak to his mat. Mama was looking at the squiggly lines again. He was almost to the mat when she cleared her throat. "Stop hiding and come here where I can see you."

He hung his head and walked to the rock where she sat. She again struggled but turned to face him. She touched several of his bruises and the scrape on his cheek. "Did you fight again?"

He hung his head and then simply nodded.

She sighed and lifted his chin. "Did you start this one?"

He looked at her and shook his head this time. "No Mama. Too manys."

She looked at him and then hugged him. "Your father will not be pleased. But at least you are not badly hurt this time. Why were you gone so long? It is very late."

He mutely reached into his belt pouch and pulled out the soft thing and the stone. He held them out before her on his hand.

She gasped in surprise and then gently shook him with both her hands. "Where did you get those? Did you leave the caverns? Did you sneak outside?"

He looked confused. "What bees outside?"

She stared at him for what seemed forever. Then she pointed to the floor in front of her. "Sit and tell me where these came from."

He sat and told her of the chimney he had climbed. The words spilled out as never before. The great forever light, and the tall thing and the rats with big tails. His face was a mask of confusion and wonder as he shared his day.

And his mother understood. She began to teach and she gifted him with words. She taught him about the sun and the sky and of clouds. She held the soft thing and told him of trees and leaves and of color. She had him crack the rock. She said it was a nut and she showed him the parts he could eat and the parts to throw away. She spoke of birds and of song. And finally, she told him of squirrels and, most importantly, of playing and fun.

He listened to it all and asked questions. There was much he still did not understand. Color was hard because there was no color in the darkness. But hardest of all was the idea of play and fun. Ogre children learn of power and dominance. Fun did not make much sense. Most of all, he tried to hold on to the words.

And then she hugged him and sent him to his mat to sleep till Papa came home. He dreamed of squirrels that were his friends.

A few hours later he awoke to find Papa shoving him with his booted foot. He rose quickly and faced Papa. Papa growled. "Fight agin. Lose agin." He looked more closely at the bruises and scrape on his face. "Thump gots broke tooth. Youse only scratch. Fair trade fer fight so many same time."

He watched Papa shake his head and turn to Mama. "Tribe name him. Not good name. Call him Shorty."

His heart sank. This would mean many more fights.

Chapter 3

Changing Seasons

His life changed that day in oh so many ways. Papa began to teach
him at each rising. Before he could eat, he had to fight. Papa was not
gentle and many times the lessons hurt. He learned of tooth and claw.
He learned the club and to throw rocks. He learned of swords and axes.
He was allowed to practice with the huge sword his father carried.
This was his favorite. It was much too big for him, but he was strong
and he learned to control it. The blade shined in the forever light. Papa
taught him to use a stone to sharpen the blade. The hilt was plain and
wrapped in leather. There were two heavy pieces of metal, one to each
side of the hilt, that protected his hand. They could be used to catch
an opponent's weapon. He cherished his time with the sword. It felt
right in his hands. Shorty surprised Papa when he was able to use the
weapon equally well in either hand. And he grew stronger.

His new name turned out to be a blessing and a curse. Being named,
he was no longer considered a child. But it also brought much teasing.
Thump and his two companions were a source of trouble. Eventually
the other two were named by the tribe. The first was called Track.
His nose was exceptionally sharp and he was considered very useful
during hunts in the deep tunnels. The second was not as lucky. He just
came to be known as Rock. He was a fairly good shot with throwing

rocks. Shorty knew he was better, though, and secretly thought a rock was about how smart the other ogre was.

Other things changed within the caverns as well. He was given more freedom to travel. But the one corridor was still forbidden to him as to any other but the Chief and the Elders. He did not mind because he was allowed into the prey room. From there he could climb the chimney to the secret chamber above.

When he was not busy training with Papa or hunting with the tribe, he would climb the chimney and watch through the opening. He loved to watch the squirrels most of all. He began to speak to them. His first "Hullo" sent them scurrying up the tree. He did not mind, though, as they soon returned. He tried again more softly and soon they came to accept his voice.

He spoke of many things to the squirrels and they chittered back at him. He told them of his problems and he told them of his dream to climb the tree with them. One day, he reached out and found some nuts. He cracked them and laid the good parts on the lower part of the crevice. He stepped back and watched as the squirrels came and ate his offering.

He went on a long hunt and returned several risings later. As soon as he could, he climbed the chimney to find the world outside had changed. When he looked through the opening, his view of the tree was blocked by something white that he could almost see through. He reached into the opening to feel something cold and hard. He worried that his small friends were trapped somehow, so he punched the thing 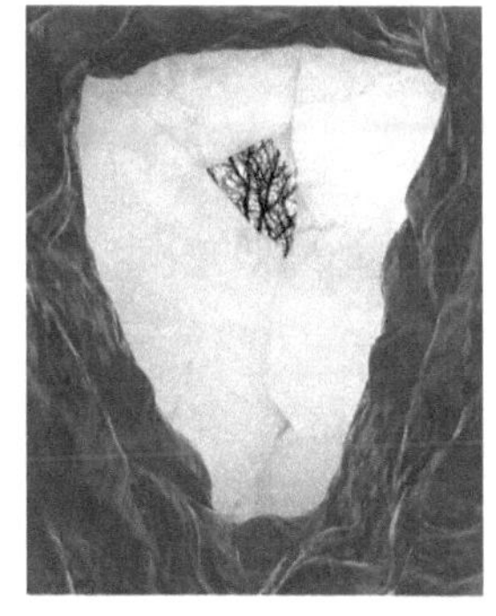 blocking the opening. It shattered, cutting his hand. He cleared the rest of the opening of the white stuff and stared into a world he did not recognize.

The leaves were all gone and the ground was covered with something white. There was more of the white stuff up on the arms of the tree. He did not understand so he reached through the opening to grab a handful of the white stuff. It was soft and cold. He pulled his hand back in and stared at what it held. As he watched, the soft white stuff disappeared from his hand leaving small drops of water. There was no sign of the squirrels on or around the tree. His only friends were gone and he had no idea how to find them.

He came back down the chimney that day lonely and upset. On his way to his chamber, Thump and Rock began to tease him. He grew angry and began to pummel them. When his rage passed, they lay at his feet. Then he saw Tusk, Thump's papa, coming down the corridor. He turned and ran for his own chamber. As he left, he heard Thump yell after him, "No always gonna bees Chief son. Some day gonna bees jus meat."

Shorty returned to his family chamber to find Mama talking to Uncle Three Toe. He stomped in and stood growling softly. His Uncle turned and stared down at him. "Why angry boy?"

He told of his fight with Thump and Rock and finished with pride, "Me strong. More strong den dem. Beats dem muches."

His uncle shook his head. "Strong no make youse bees right." He pointed down at his mangled feet. One foot missing the entire front half and the other was missing the two smallest toes. The foot was smashed flat near where the toes had been. "Attack fuzzface cavern. Me strong. Dem smart. Strong no bees nuf."

Three Toes glanced at Mama before he shuffled out of the chamber.

Mama looked over at him from her seat on the rock. "What is really wrong my son?"

He told her of the missing squirrels and of the white stuff and of the dead tree with no leaves.

She hugged him and laughed softly. Then she made things better with her gift of words. She told him of winter and snow and ice. She spoke of seasons and she promised him spring. She predicted new leaves and the return of the squirrels.

Shorty visited the hidden chamber from time to time, but this thing called spring was slow to come. He watched the snow and the ice grow and then recede. He saw strange lumps form on the arms of the tree. And he heard the strange melody come again with the birds. The leaves came back too. And one day the squirrels returned.

Other changes began to happen. He continued to grow, both larger and stronger. He learned more and more from Papa. But he also found it harder and harder to fit up the chimney. He was growing and he even learned to accept the name Shorty. Soon there were tiny squirrels. Mama called them baby. They would climb up onto the edge of the crack. Shorty would hold out his hand and sometimes they would climb on and let him hold them. He was happy.

Chapter 4

Endings

One day he got stuck in the chimney. He panicked and began to
struggle but despite his strength, it got worse. Eventually, he stopped
and took a deep breath. He relaxed, exhaled and began to wiggle
forward. He made it to the top without any more trouble, but he knew
the truth of it. This would be his last time to visit his friends and it was
not happy.

He spent extra time that day cracking nuts and feeding the
young squirrels. He tried to explain why he could not visit
them again. But they just chittered and chattered like nothing
had changed. But he knew it had. He was growing up. He did
not want to, but he had no choice.

Finally, he said goodbye. The smallest of the squirrels ran
up his arm and sat on his shoulder. It patted his cheek with
its small hand. Then it leapt from his shoulder to the crevice,
ran back through and up the tree. Water leaked from the
corner of his eye. But it was not a tear. He was a warrior
now.

Shorty stood by the chimney and took off his leather armor. He
bundled everything he carried into the armor and dropped the bundle

down the chimney. With a last look at the darkening sky outside the crevice, he began his way slowly down.

He heard voices before he reached the bottom. He turned to see five fully grown ogres blocking his way. He recognized them as the Tribe's Elders. They were waiting for him. One, the leader of the group, was Thump's Papa, Tusk. Shorty did not like Tusk. He was cruel to many in the Tribe. And Shorty thought the one large tooth that stuck out between his lips made him look broken.

Tusk stepped forward and raised a sword. He recognized the blade. It belonged to Papa.

As Shorty looked up, the thief growled out his challenge. "Old Chief dead. Me Chief now. Old Chief fall deep hole hunt."

He growled back. "Papa no fall. Tusk maybeso push." Real anger glowed in Tusk's eyes and he motioned the other four Elders forward.

The others surged forward, grabbing Shorty and pinning his limbs. They tied his arms behind his back and tied a rope from his neck to a hook set high in the wall. He did not struggle. What would be the point? With no Papa and no squirrels, he had no reason to fight.

The new chief put Papa's sword back into its sheath and hung it over his shoulder. Then he looked down at Shorty. "Catched youse. Now kill woman!" At this Shorty began to struggle. But the rope was thick and tied in strong knots. Even his great strength could not break it. They laughed and left the chamber, pushing the large boulder across its entrance.

He sat like that for hours. His mind blank and his hatred growing. Eventually he heard a noise and looked up to see the boulder pushed aside. Uncle Three Toe hobbled in and squatted in front of him.

He looked up hopefully and whispered, "Mama?"

His uncle looked down at the floor and shook his head. "She kilt him. New chief dead. Kill self same time. Big magic. Muches fire. Boom. Chamber fall. All dead."

He looked up and asked, "Me?"

His uncle again shook his head. "Elder pick new chief. New chief say. Maybeso lib, maybeso dies. Not knows."

His uncle moved back to the entrance and looked back. "Strong no make right. Maybe strong ken fix dis time. Maybe so. Maybe no." He hobbled out and the boulder slid back into place.

 He sat there for a bit lost in thought. Then he heard a small chitter from the chimney. He looked over to see a squirrel he did not recognize sitting on its haunches studying him. It came to sit before him and it dropped a nut from its mouth.

He looked at it and whispered, "Me sorry. No hand. No ken opens."

The squirrel sat there for a few heartbeats and then disappeared up the chimney. He sat and thought of Mama and Papa. Even if the new chief did not kill him, where did he belong now? His world was gone.

Then he heard the sound of many small paws scampering out of the chimney. He turned his head to see about a dozen squirrels coming out to climb all over him. Two large squirrels climbed up and sat, one on each of his shoulders. He felt soft fur on his hands as they scurried all around him. He began to hear the sound of chewing and he sat very still.

Sometime later he heard the sound of the large boulder being moved. The squirrels disappeared up the chimney all except the one he had never seen before. It sat on his shoulder and rubbed its head against his cheek. Then it too left him and he was along once more.

Thump entered the chamber with a swagger. Over his shoulder, he could just make out the hilt of Papa's sword. Thump moved forward and both Rock and Track followed him in. Thump leaned over and grinned. "New Chief say me kills youse. Me tells afore dat youse bees meat."

He stared up into Thump's eyes without fear. He would not look away. Thump grew angry and began to growl. Suddenly he threw his head forward, smashing his forehead into Thump's broad nose. Blood spurted and Thump dropped to one knee.

Rock and Track stood paralyzed by the unexpected attack. He rose to his feet and brought a knee up smashing Thump in the face again, sending him sprawling on his back. Shorty began to flex his arm and shoulder muscles. They bulged and the rope began to whine. Then it snapped. His arms came around with pieces of chewed rope still clinging to his wrists.

Track recovered from the shock first and sprang forward. Shorty stepped to the side and released a solid blow into the ribs below Track's left arm. There was the sound of cracking ribs and Track fell to the ground coughing. There was blood on his lips. Shorty shoved Track aside with his foot and reached up behind his neck.

He placed a hand to the rope at his neck and felt where it had been gnawed almost through. He gave a jerk and the rope parted. The snap of the rope seemed to break the spell and Rock came at him with both hands raised.

Shorty stepped forward to meet Rock and they locked hands. Rock grinned confidently and leaned forward using all of his strength and six hundred pounds of weight in an attempt to force the smaller ogre to his knees. But there was no give. Rock strained and the smaller ogre refused to be moved.

Then he whispered, "Me bees Shorty!" He stared up into the face of Rock and with a savage twist reversed the grip, bringing both their arms down low between them. Then he jerked upward. Rock screamed as his arms both snapped.

He turned to see Thump regaining his feet. He drove a fist into Thump's kidney with the force of a war hammer. As Thump fell forward, Shorty pulled Papa's sword from Thump's back. He drew the blade with a snarl of anger and raised it over his head. He intended to kill Thump. He stood like that for a long while as Rock and Track watched helplessly.

And then the anger was gone. He looked down at his foe and his grip on the sword hilt loosened. He thought of his uncle's words, "Strong not make right." He thought of Mama and her many words. Love and Forgive. He did not understand them but he knew this was not her way. He sheathed the sword and walked over to the chimney. He retrieved the bundle and placed it under his arm. He ran his hand over the stones of the chimney and called a soft goodbye.

He turned and walked to the entrance and studied the ogres still lying on the floor. Then he smiled. "Tells Elder Shorty beat all. Tells new Chief small ogre win."

The proud young ogre turned and followed the forbidden corridor. It eventually led to a winding ramp that continued up a long way. It eventually came to an opening. He stepped out into near darkness, but he could tell by the smells that he was outside.

He stared in wonder and saw a pale circle hanging in the dark sky. All around it were many smaller lights that seemed to wink on and off. He wished for Mama. He needed more words. Once again he had none to describe the things that he saw. He had no words for the pain he felt inside at her loss.

He looked for the tree that was the home of his friends. But it was nowhere in sight so he set off to find his squirrels and maybe along the way he could find the words he needed.

Chapter 5

New World and New Beginnings

He sat beneath a large tree with a pile of nuts sitting next to him. He ate a few but mostly fed their contents to the 4 squirrels crawling over and around him. He felt happy. But more than that, for the first time in his life he had no problems or fears. He could do whatever he wanted. He had no words for these new feelings but he knew they were good.

He heard the cry of a large bird of prey and the squirrels darted between his legs and hid. All but the new squirrel who sat unafraid on his shoulder. There was the soft flutter of feathers and he looked up to see the large bird land on a low tree arm. It cocked its head to the side in that strange way birds sometimes do. It seemed to be staring at him and the squirrels around him. 

He raised a hand and shook one large finger at the bird. "No eat dem. Squirrel friend. Goes way. Leave be." Then he ignored the bird and cracked a couple more nuts to feed his friends. A voice came suddenly from above. "Lady of the Wood, I do not believe my eyes. An ogre feeding squirrels?"

He looked up in surprise to see on older human with a long beard. His hair and beard were a light brown with whisps of grey mixed in.

The man was sitting where the bird had been moments before. Shorty scratched his head and asked, "Where bird go?"

The man grinned down at him. "That is a secret. Maybe I will tell you some day. What are you doing, my large friend?"

He looked at the human and tried to decide if the man was stupid. "Feeds squirrel."

The man chuckled. "So I see, but why?"

He shrugged, deciding the man really was not even as smart as an ogre. "Friends. Hungry."

The man slid to the trunk and easily climbed down the tree. He stood watching. "Do you have many friends?"

He thought for a minute. Then he looked down at the squirrels and began to count.

"One…

Two…

Four…

Lots.

He looked back at the man. "Got lots friend."

The man began to laugh again. "I see. And you are very smart too."

Shorty nodded and cracked another nut.

The man squatted down. "I think the Goddess brought me here to find you. May I ask your name?"

Shorty slowly stood up to his full height of nearly eight feet. "Me bees Shorty."

He began to laugh heartily. Shorty had to smile. "Do tell, Shorty. The Goddess is playing with me this day."

He scratched his head and looked at the man. "Goddess? No knowed dat word. What bees Goddess?"

The man studied him. "That is a very long story, my new friend. I would love to tell it to you. Would you like to have more friends?"

Shorty looked down at the shrinking pile of nuts. "Dem eat nuts? Me run out."

The man smiled and waved his hand towards a trail that led down the mountain. "Well, Shorty, I am a druid and I serve the Goddess Mielikki. My job is to protect this area. If you want to learn more, walk with me. And bring your friends. I like squirrels too. And I know a tree with lots of nuts."

Shorty pulled on his backpack and the squirrels clambered up his legs and into the pack. Their heads peeked out as Shorty wandered alongside the man and into the sunshine. The man began to talk. He gave him words.

The Blessed Curse

Chapter 1

Reaching for Freedom

The small boy ran through the forest. His bare feet pounded on the narrow trail. Despite his thick calluses, many things on the forest floor hurt when he stepped on them. But he did not cry, not even when he stepped on something sharp or pointed. He just kept running and dodging the trees.

Running in the forest was nothing like running in the small towns or on the farms where he had been kept for almost as long as he could remember. His memories of the orphanage where he had briefly stayed were fuzzy. He had no bad memories of the orphanage so he considered it to be one of the best parts of his short life.

He also had a vague sense that there was something that came before that time, but it was lost in the haze of pain from his life with the bad people. He never let the bad people make him cry either. To endure the things they did, he forced himself to forget. But always forgetting meant that he lost other memories too. But he still remembered how to run.

He ran on, ignoring the bruises on his feet and the larger ones on his back. He listened for the cries of the dogs. He would not let them catch him or bring him back. He would never go back. He ran on and the forest grew quiet around him.

The trail curved sharply to the right and his foot hit a tree root that stuck up too high in the trail. He stumbled and then fell forward, rolling over several times before crashing hard into the trunk of a tree. The bark was very rough against his bruised back. The boy glanced from the offending root to his bloody foot.

He examined the foot looking for the source of the blood. All of the nails were cracked and splintered. The ragged edge of the nail on his big toe had cut deep into the flesh below it. The blood mixed with the dirt to form a thick mud. Mud was good, it would slow the bleeding. He did not cry. There were worse pains in his world than this. He rose to his feet and faced deeper into the forest. The bays of the dogs sounded somewhere behind him. He ran on.

He wished he could find another stream. Then he could at least fill his belly with water. The hunger would not bother him as much if he could fill up with water. As he ran, he counted back. He had last eaten three days before. The moldy bread had tasted heavenly. It had been worth the beating for stealing it. Better to eat and enjoy it even if he paid for it later. Besides, the bad people had thrown it out. It was not that they needed it, they just did not want him to have it.

The bad people were always starving him. They told him it was because he refused to think the right way. That meant he refused to think their way. They said he needed to admit the wrongs of his ancestors and make amends, but he did not even know who his ancestors were. And why did he need to make amends for things he did not do? So, he went hungry. The hunger did not make him cry though. He ran on.

Sometimes he wanted to remember a time before the bad people. But such longings were frightening. What if things were even worse in that before time? He could not even hang on to details from the orphanage where they had bought him. The bad people had told the cleric at the orphanage that they would care for him. They would give him a better life. They lied. They had made a donation to cover his care while he had been at the orphanage. That was his purchase price. The bad people had made him work for every copper of that donation. But never again. He would not go back. He ran on.

He never understood why the bad people hated him so much. They had so much and he had nothing. They told him that they deserved a better lot in life and somehow he shared responsibility for their pain. He did not understand. He was simply a small boy with no parents. The more they tried to change him, the more stubborn he became. The more stubborn he became, the harder they worked him and the more they beat him. The beatings had not made him cry, and they grew angrier. In the end, he had run.

He heard the sound of the dogs again. They were closer. He wondered why they wanted him back so badly. Why were they still chasing him? Three days since he had jumped from the wagon and run into the trees. He had nothing, but still they chased after him. He was worthless, or so they had told him. "Good for nothing" was their favorite taunt when they beat him. He had nothing to give but his pain and still they came for him. So, he ran on. But he was tired and it hurt to breathe. He would not cry. He kept running, but more slowly.

His breath came in ragged gasps as he heard the dogs getting closer. He wished that he could just disappear. Become nothing. But he did not have that magic in him. Or maybe he could find a cliff to throw himself off of. Then they could never take him back. Dying would not make him cry. It was just another way to run.

He stumbled into a small clearing and was halfway across when he heard a voice behind him. "Who? Whooooo?" He spun around, but there was no one there. "Whooo?" came again from the branches of a tree on the edge of the clearing. He looked up to see a large owl sitting high in the tree staring at him. It did not blink. It was nothing like the barn owls he knew from the farms. This one was huge and it was pure white except for the eyes that seemed to look right through him. "Whooooo?" The bird scared him more than the dogs did. So, he turned breathlessly and ran on.

The trees opened up again into an even larger meadow filled with yellow and white flowers. Strange insects with long tails flew around, darting from flower to flower. Their wings sparkled in the sunlight. The boy moved to the center of the meadow and paused with his hands on his knees. He had no breath left to run, but he would not cry.

He turned back to face his past. He knew the dogs were close. Maybe he could make them kill him. Then he would not have to go back. He never wanted to go back. Two large forms slipped from the trees into the meadow. The dogs had come for him. Pure black and filled with the hate the bad people had taught them. They were called Rotters and they liked to hunt and to hurt. Maybe they would hurt him bad enough that he could not go back. It was another way to run.

He saw a small rock on the ground near his feet. He grabbed it and threw it at the dogs. He missed, but the dogs snarled anyway and began to stalk towards him. The boy let out a primal scream that held all of his hatred and fear. Then, he smiled. Maybe the dogs were the answer to his prayer.

The dogs had only crossed about half the distance to him when they came to a sudden stop. Their snarls changed and somehow sounded even more menacing. They sank to their haunches with their bellies almost on the ground. They bared their sharp teeth. He did not understand what had changed.

There was a loud rumbling noise behind him. It was hard to turn and leave the dogs at his back, but he mustered his courage and spun around. The beast coming from the trees across the meadow was enormous. Even down on all four legs, it was taller than he was. It had a broad face and two small ears. Its pure white coat was out of place in the forest.

As it ambled towards him, it stared first at him and then at the dogs. When its gaze met that of the dogs, it began to growl. The sound was like a vibration running across his skin. He feared the beast and, at the same time, he did not. This was his solution to all his problems. So, he ran. He charged directly at the beast waving his arms and yelling wildly. The beast did not falter.

He reached the beast quickly and screamed in its face. To his shock, it turned its large head and licked his face. It continued on past him. Its fur was incredibly soft as it brushed along his skin. The beast moved toward the dogs and they began to inch backwards, unwilling to face this threat.

The boy spun around to watch as the beast moved ever closer to the dogs. Two men stepped out into the meadow behind the dogs. He recognized them and began to tremble. The first man was the hunter and he carried a large spear. He was the one who tracked all of the runaways. He would bring them back or he would kill them. No one ever seemed to escape him.

The second man was even more frightening. The Master himself had joined this hunt. The Master carried his whip. He knew that whip well for it had marked him many times before. So too had the Rotters. The Master never chased runaways; he just punished them when they were brought back. The boy understood he was in real trouble now.

The white beast continued to move forward. It did not seem concerned about the men or the dogs. The dogs continued to retreat until the Master cracked the whip behind them. He ordered them to attack. They whimpered, but separated and began to move towards the beast.

The beast tracked the movement of the larger dog. The smaller dog sprang from behind, sinking its teeth into the soft white fur. The beast appeared not to notice. The larger dog darted in as well, but the beast struck first with a lightning-fast slap of its front paw. The large dog flew through the air and landed near the tree line. As it staggered to its feet, the boy expected to see blood. But the beast had not used its claws at all. The dog limped into the trees, ignoring the shouted commands of the Master. The beast turned on the smaller dog and it backed away. The boy could suddenly smell urine in the air as the smaller dog turned and fled after its pack mate.

The beast turned to the two men and then rose up on its hind legs. It towered over even the Master who the boy thought was the biggest man in the whole world. The beast began to walk forward on its hind legs. Its front legs began to move in a strange pattern. The grunts coming from its mouth sounded strange, almost as if it was talking to the two men.

The Master grabbed the hunter and shoved him towards the beast. He flicked his whip at the hunter as he backed away from the beast. The hunter raised his spear as if to throw it and the beast suddenly sat on the ground much as a man might have sat. It waived a paw at the trees behind the two men and uttered a long growl.

The trees above the two men began to writhe about. The boy stared in confusion as vines and long tendrils began to lower from the trees. Neither man seemed to notice them until they fell about them and began to tighten. The men began to scream as they were lifted from the ground. They hung suspended below the trees as the vines and branches wound more tightly around them. The boy closed his eyes and began to rub them furiously. This could not be real.

When he stopped rubbing and reopened his eyes, the men still swung beneath the trees, covered in vines except for their faces. What could have caused the trees to attack the bad men like that? The boy looked back at the beast, but the white beast was gone. Standing in its place was a tall, slender man. He had no idea where the beast could have gone.

The new man was strange to behold. He wore clothing the color of spring leaves except for the leather armor on his upper body. He had long, yellow hair so pale that it almost looked white in the sunlight. His hair was pulled back into a loose knot behind his head and he had pointed ears.

The man with the pointed ears stepped around the hunter to stand before the Master. He stared at the Master for a long time as the Master made threats and promised vengeance.

The man with the pointed ears raised a finger and a vine stretched across the Master's mouth, silencing him. "I am F'lar, also known as the Heretic. By edict of the human King, these lands are mine to govern in his name. Return here again and you will face the judgement of the King. If that does not deter you, know that you will also face the judgement of the Lady of the Forest. Her creatures will deliver a far harsher punishment than any King might levy. Lastly, know this: Mielikki has marked the boy. Come near him again and I will personally hunt you down."

The man with the pointed ears turned his back on the bad men and began to walk towards the boy. As he walked, he reached into a bag at his side and pulled out a beautiful red apple. He also pulled a small carving knife out and began to cut slices out of the apple. He tossed the first slice into the trees as he walked.

The boy's eyes tracked the apple slice as it flew into a nearby tree. His mouth began to water and his stomach began to growl and complain. The man raised one eyebrow. "Are you hungry, boy?"

At that moment, his voice failed him. He could only stand and nod while his stomach rumbled with need. The man reached back into the bag and pulled out a second apple. It was as big and beautiful as the first one. The man tossed it through the air and the boy's hands clutched at it as if his life depended on catching it. The boy snagged it and brought it straight to his mouth. He bit deeply. The cool juice ran down his chin and onto his dirty hands. It was heavenly.

The man stood quietly watching him as the apple quickly disappeared. His only movement was to cut another slice of apple and toss it towards the same tree. The boy watched this slice fly through the air greedily as he nibbled on the remains of the core. He glanced back at the man and was forced to drop the core as a another apple flew towards his face. He caught it and took a bite. He was able to control himself with this one and ate it a little slower.

The man's attention shifted from the boy to the tree as he cut and threw a third apple slice at it. The boy had never seen a man talk to a tree before. The conversation seemed very one-sided. The man cocked his head to the side as if considering things. "Yes, I was planning to ask him. No, not yet. Let the boy eat. I will, unless you wish to come out and speak with him yourself."

Even eating slower, the second apple was almost gone. The strange man threw another slice of apple up into the tree. It was strange that they never came down, but he could not see where they went either. The man's eyes turned again to the boy as the second core hit the ground. He asked gently, "Do you have a name, boy?"

The boy summoned his courage and spoke. "They called me Boy when they were being nice. They called me things I did not like most of the time."

The man looked back at the bad men and his face turned grim. "'Boy' is not a good name, but the choosing of a better one is not for them to hear. You have a choice now. You can run and I will not stop you. I will make sure that they cannot follow you or harm you again. Or, you can come with me. I can help you and teach you."

The boy tensed and the man stepped back. "Not that way boy. I do not teach the ways of men or even of elves like myself. I teach the way of the forest and of the Goddess who rules there."

The boy looked at him curiously and a sticky hand made its way unbidden to his ear. "Elf?" The man smiled patiently as he touched one of his pointed ears and nodded.

The boy looked around nervously. "Will I learn of the great beast that was here?"

The elf nodded. "That and much, much more."

The boy looked up at the elf with all the defiance he could muster. "And if I do not like it?"

The elf smiled down at him and began walking away from the bad men. "You will always be free to choose your own path, as I chose mine. The consequences of those choices are forever yours."

The boy watched him head across the meadow, back along the path of the great beast. He glanced back at the bad men and began to hurry to catch up with the elf. As he came nearer, an apple flipped back over the elf's head. The boy caught it happily as the man threw another apple slice into the trees.

Chapter 2

Life is Choices

The elf led him out of the meadow and through the trees. They came to a broad path through the woods. The elf pointed to a rock off to one side where a small pool bubbled up from underground. There were large trees around the pool providing shade to keep the water cool. The boy eagerly drank and rinsed the sticky apple juice from his face and hands. Days of dirt and grime slid from his hands to sink to the bottom of the pool. Life seemed very good with his thirst quenched and a belly full of fruit.

The elf sat upon the rock watching him. "You have made the first of many choices, my young friend. Your life will be filled with them from this day forward. Some will be easy and some will be hard. But all will have consequences."

The boy sat back on the edge of the pool. "Consequences are bad. That is just another word for punishment. If you try to punish me, I will run away. I can run from you too."

The elf sighed and shook his head. "No one is going to punish you, boy, except for yourself. And you do not need to run. You can walk away whenever you choose and no one will chase you or force you to return. You are free."

The boy looked puzzled. "But you said there would be consequences?"

The elf nodded. "Each time you make a choice, it changes you and the world around you. Those changes may be good or bad for you and for the rest of the world. Those changes are the consequences that I speak of. And you must learn that what is good for you may not be good for others or for the world as a whole. And things that are bad for you may make the world a much better place. If you place the needs of the world or others before your own needs, that is a sacrifice, and it is often a good thing."

The boy grinned. "That is easy then. The world is big. It can take care of itself. I will choose what is good for me."

The elf frowned. "That is your option, but you damage yourself more when you try to choose in your own best interests."

The boy looked down, puzzled. "How can that be? How do I hurt myself if I take care of myself?"

The elf stared at him. "If you always choose for yourself first, then you become like those you escaped from. You become one of them. And that means that they have beaten you. Do you truly wish to be like them?"

The boy scowled at him. "I will never be one of them. Never!"

The elf smiled. "Such was my hope when I freed you. I hoped that you could be other than what they tried to make of you. But you must always be wary. You have seen the path of selfishness. It will always call to you and it is an easy road to turn down. The other road takes much courage and effort, but the rewards are worth it. Your life and the lives of others will change for good or ill based on each decision that you make. Consider your choices carefully."

The elf got up and began to walk back to the trail. The boy took another drink and fell in behind him. After a short distance on the trail the elf paused and spoke again. "Another choice lies before you. You may continue to walk behind me as would a servant or a slave. Or, you may walk beside me as an equal worthy of respect. This once I will tell you the consequences of your choice without being asked. If you walk behind me, you set yourself on a path of servitude, never to make your own choices in life. If you chose to walk beside me, you must talk with me. The choice is yours to make." The elf began walking again.

The boy stared at his retreating back. "I can ask what the consequences are?"

The elf appeared to nod as he walked away. "You are free to ask anything. It is how you will learn."

The boy thought for a minute and then ran to catch up. As he came even with the elf he asked, "What must I talk about?"

The elf smiled and met his gaze. "You may choose. What would you like to talk about? Do you have any questions?"

The words bubbled from the boy's mouth before he realized they were there. "What was that huge beast that saved me from the dogs? And where did it go? And how did it make the trees move? I do not understand."

The elf kept his eyes forward as he walked. "The creature you saw is called a bear in your tongue. In the north, they are called Karhu. There are many types of bears. They can be brown or black or even brown with a golden ring about their necks. Some are not much bigger than a man and some are truly huge. The great white one that you met normally lives far to the north. They are called Jaäkarhu. As for where it went, that is a secret that you must pay for. Knowledge is seldom free and what you ask has great value."

The boy walked beside him for a while in silence. "How would I buy this secret? I have no coin to pay for it."

The elf chuckled as he continued down the path. "You would have to work and study. You would have to learn a great many things and learn them well. The only coin that will pay for what you ask is learning. You must decide if the answer is worth your time."

The boy frowned. "The bad people tried to teach me. I did not like it."

The elf nodded. "Maybe they did not teach you things worth knowing. There are some things that are worth learning. The choice is yours now as it was then."

The boy thought a little longer. "Maybe I will learn. I really want to know more about the bears. It licked me." They walked in silence for a bit and then the boy blurted out, "I liked the Karhu. It sounds strong and I want to be strong. I want to protect myself."

The elf too was silent for a bit as if listening to something. He cut another apple slice and threw it into a nearby tree. "For the right creature and maybe for the right person, it is a very good name. The Karhu are fierce. They are great protectors. It is a name that comes with responsibilities."

The boy looked at him curiously "I do not have a name. Can I pick one for myself? Could I pick Karhu?"

The elf rubbed his chin. "Well… We really cannot keep calling you boy. Karhu is a name of power for the Karhu are wise. There would be consequences if you choose such a name."

The boy looked at him eagerly. "What kind of consequences?"

The elf held out his hand and spun in a circle. "The whole world would expect much of one who choose the name Karhu. That person would have to work hard to be strong, to be a protector, and more importantly, to be as wise as the true Karhu. If it was not worked for, the spirit of the Karhu might come to take the name back, and woe to any who anger the Karhu."

The boy looked around him at the many trees. "That sounds like a really big job."

The elf nodded again. "Each choice comes with consequences. Choosing a name has has some of the largest."

The boy stared as his feet as he walked. "Then I will be Karhu. I must learn to be strong and wise."

The elf smiled. "Yes, you must learn. I am happy to meet you, Karhu."

The boy looked up at him. "So, what should I call you?"

The elf paused and turned to face him. He bowed his head. "My name is F'lar. You may call me that, or… you may call me Teacher, for I will teach you if you choose to learn." The elf turned back to the path and cut a final slice from the apple before discarding the core. He tossed it into a nearby tree and muttered, "I am glad you approve."

The boy hesitated for a second. "Teacher, why do you keep throwing away those apple slices. They taste so good. And who do you keep talking to in the trees?"

F'lar handed him another apple as they walked. "That is another secret which you must earn. We will talk about that one after you earn the first secret."

The boy glanced at him nervously. "But where will I stay? I have no home."

F'lar's smile was only in his eyes this time. "Well, Karhu, you could come to live in my home. My wife rules there, so you would have to follow her rules. She is a bit grumpy right now as she is expecting our first child."

Karhu asked, "What are the consequences if I say yes?"

F'lar laughed deeply at that. "That is simple. The Great Karhu would have to take a real bath with soap. He would have to get clean and not smell bad. And then the Great Karhu would have to wear clothes, not rags. He might even have to wear boots on his feet. The most painful part is that you would have to eat her cooking. She is a good mage, but she has no training in the preparation of food. Can you deal with that?"

The boy nodded and they continued on in silence as the boy nibbled on another apple.

Chapter 3

Learning New Things

The boy now known as Karhu came to his new home. There was a Manor House where lived a nice woman with very red hair and green eyes. Her stomach was very swollen and she told him the baby would come soon. Teacher told him that she was a mage and was learning powerful magic. Her name was Jocelynn and she gave him cookies.

There was a plate full of cookies and it sat on a table in the kitchen. He kept sneaking back in to get another when he thought no one was looking. He ate many, many cookies. His stomach began to hurt really bad. Lady Jocelyn was worried that there was something wrong with him. She put him in bed in his new room. Teacher brought in the empty cookie plate and showed it to her. She looked shocked that he finished off all of the cookies. She made a strange noise and left the room.

Teacher just laughed and set the plate on a table where he could see it. He pulled out another cookie from his pouch and placed it on the plate. Karhu did not like looking at the cookie. "Are they poisoned?"

Teacher laughed and tousled his hair before turning to leave the room. "No, they are actually quite good. Best she has ever made in fact."

"Then why does my stomach hurt so bad?" The little boy inside him asked.

Teacher laughed again. "Because you chose to eat too much. There was a consequence to that choice. Now your body is punishing you for making a bad choice." Teacher started to close the door, but paused. "There is a pan under the bed for what comes next. This will not be a fun lesson to learn. And you must empty the pan in the morning so that your room does not smell."

Teacher closed the door and Karhu was alone in the large room with a bed and a dresser and a picture on one wall. The picture was a painting of a strange horse with a horn on its head.

There were other lessons that he chose not to learn right away. One of the hardest was that of being clean. The bad people never made or even let him get clean. He had spent most of his life with dirt crusted on his body. He tried to tell Lady Jocelyn that he could not smell anything bad. But she made him wash anyway. Some days he had to walk back out to the well 3 or 4 times before she would let him join them at the table. What was the point? The dirt just came back anyway.

He struggled with this lesson a lot. Teacher pointed out that he did not have many friends despite all the other children around the Manor House. That did not bother him, though, as he was used to not having friends. There was no such thing as a friend in the orphanage or with the bad people. Trusting was hard.

But he did love his studies out in the forest with Teacher. Tending the trees and the animals there was peaceful. Nothing in the forest hurt him or made him do things he did not want to do. He felt safe there. But he could never seem to get as close to the animals as he wanted. They always seemed to run when he drew near.

When he finally asked Teacher why, Teacher laughed. He could not believe that the animals smelled him and ran away. He yelled at Teacher claiming Teacher was making it all up. Teacher did not get angry though. He smiled and went back to work. Karhu decided to do his own test. He scrubbed really clean one day and put on clean clothes. He slipped out into the forest to where the rabbits had their holes. He moved in among the holes and sat quiet and still. That evening, the rabbits emerged and moved around him. He was even able to touch one.

He began to clean more regularly after that. He still made mistakes and it still did not matter about the other children, but the animals began to accept him and that was important to him.

The day came not too long after his arrival that Lady Jocelyn began to have pains and she retreated to her room. Teacher left him and went to care for her. She made many sounds of pain and Karhu was afraid she was dying. Then there came the sound of a baby crying from within the room. Teacher came out with a tiny baby wrapped in a blanket. He introduced her as Uusi-Alku. Teacher made him wash his hands and then he got to hold the baby.

That day he found another reason to remain clean. He found that he liked holding the baby and talking to it. Uusi never judged him or spoke harshly to him. Her happy noises made him smile and he had a strange need to keep her safe. No bad people would ever take his Uusi. He would make sure of it.

Not far from the Manor House was also a strange building that was not really a building. Teacher called it a Temple and he said it was the heart of the Grove. The four corners of the temple were trees that still lived. He learned later that the trees were oak, willow, ash, and maple. The roof of the Temple was formed by the branches and leaves of the four trees. The leaves of the four trees never changed colors or died in the winter. The trees remained green and alive year-round. Teacher explained that the power of the Goddess Mielikki kept them that way.

The branches and leaves of the four trees were so mixed and tangled together that no sunlight could shine through except in one spot at the center of the temple where a small oak table sat. The table was fairly plain, except that it was also alive. A single branch grew up out of the table. Somehow, this branch bore leaves from all four of the trees. It was beautiful.

It was in the Temple that Karhu and several other youth studied with the Teacher. He was a druid which he explained meant that he was a servant of the Goddess and did her will. She granted him certain powers and spells to aid him in her work. She would do the same for each of the youths if they chose to follow and serve her.

Karhu wanted this power and magic very badly. He thought that if he was strong and had magic, the bad people would never again be able to take him. But sometimes, when he was at peace working in the forest; he wanted the abilities just to care for the trees and animals around him. It was at these times that he felt most like a druid.

Karhu became an initiate and began to study to be a druid too. Some parts were very hard for him. The reading and writing were among the worst of his tasks. Making marks on scrolls or trying to understand what was there already was hard for him. These were things the bad people never taught him.

Working with the plants and creatures of the forest was the easy part. He came to understand each animal and each plant. He knew their needs and their vulnerabilities. There was a peace in the forest that he had not known in all of his life. He did not mind being alone and found that he often lost track of time among the trees. He especially loved the Karhu that lived in the forest. He named each one and would watch as they roamed their domain within the wood.

Two years after he came to the Manor House, on the first day of spring, he was sent to bathe and dress in a pure white robe. He was led into the Temple and given the chance to pledge himself to the Goddess of the Wood. Karhu became a Druid that day. He learned how much more he had to learn. But that was okay, for he had found something that was worth learning, at least to him.

Karhu found that his love of magic was almost as great as his love of the trees and the animals. He spent a great deal of time with Teacher, learning different ways to apply the spells granted him by the Goddess. But he noticed that the Teacher used other spells as well and he asked why the Goddess never granted any of them to him.

Teacher stared out into the forest for a while with a sad expression on his face. "Karhu, the Elves as well as some of the other races are often able to be two things at once. Mage and fighter or either with thief. Our lives are longer and so are our childhoods. It gives us time to master more than one skill. I am both a Druid and a Mage. Some of the spells you see me use are Mage spells like those I have taught Lady Jocelyn. There are a few spells that are a unique mix of the two types of magic. But this mixing of the magic of the Goddess with that of Mages is frowned upon by the Elves. It is one of the reasons I live this far south. It is one reason that I have a human bride."

Karhu stared at him. "What is the other reason?"

Teacher laughed then. "You ask dangerous questions, my young student. My Lady Wife may toss me a fireball if I tell you the wrong thing. But the simple answer is that I love her and admire her spirit. The human King insisted that I tie myself to him by marriage. Of all the maidens from his extended family that I met, only Jocelyn had the strength of character to be more than people saw in her. She did not just want to be Lady of the Manor, she insisted that I teach her magic as well. I too chose to be more than I was allowed. In that way we are an excellent match."

Karhu looked puzzled as his teacher continued. "Someday, young cub, you too may seek a companion. When you do, remember to choose wisely. Choose more than just what the eye can see. Choose with your heart and mind as well."

There were other buildings around the Manor House. It was not a large community, but there was a smith with a dwarf who sometimes allowed him to watch him forge weapons. He even got to make nails once. There were rangers and other druids and merchants. There were even farmers of a sort. They only grew things that were native to the forest. Their crops did not require the precious trees to be cut or the land to be cleared.

But the people who came and went always made him nervous. Karhu was always watching to see if the bad people were around. As he grew, he spent less and less time at the Manor and more time roaming the forest. He always returned to visit with Lady Jocelyn and especially with little Uusi. It was soon after Uusi's fourth birthday that other changes took place. One was that Lady Jocelyn announced that she would have another baby. The second big event was the arrival of the ranger Fensil in the community.

Karhu did not mind Fensil so much as he did the large hunting dog that he kept. The dog was not a Rotter, but it still scared him. He decided that dogs were the one animal he would never like. This dog was a female with strange, almost stripped fur that Teacher called brindle. The dog, Shar, weighed nearly two hundred pounds and Karhu was sure that it could swallow him whole if it ever decided he was tasty.

Lady Jocelyn was getting sick a lot as her baby grew inside her. Karhu thought being pregnant was bad enough, he could not even imagine what it was like to get sick whenever he saw food. Karhu spent more time at the Manor House to keep Uusi company. He did not really mind as she was fun to be around. She pretended all the time and all of her toys had different voices as she made them talk and play with her. She made him laugh. He could not remember any of the kids with the bad people who sounded so smart.

Karhu was eating dinner one night with Teacher and Uusi when Fensil came to ask Teacher for help as Shar had gone missing on their last scouting trip. Fensil was worried about the dog and wanted her back. Secretly, Karhu hoped the huge animal would stay gone. She brought back too many bad memories.

Teacher asked him to stay at the Manor and help Lady Jocelyn with Uusi while he was gone. Teacher took a blanket that Shar slept on and headed out into the forest. It was almost a week before he returned with an angry looking Shar at his side. Shar was more frightening that ever and she even snapped at Fensil. But she obeyed Teacher.

Teacher told Fensil that she was carrying a litter of puppies and that he would have to keep her on a strong leash until they were born. If not, she would run away and rejoin the wolf pack that he had found her with.

Karhu did not particularly like Shar, but he liked the idea of chaining her up even less. It was like she was being held prisoner. When Fensil left with Shar, he asked, "Why chain her up like a prisoner? Why not just let Shar go live with the wolves?"

Teacher's face showed remorse over his decision. "Wolves are one with nature. They mate for life and tend to have litters only when the food sources support a larger pack. Dogs are different. They mate because it is their season. They produce large litters and will grow faster than the region can support. Wild dog packs are dangerous. I wish to prevent this."

Karhu thought on this for a bit. "Won't Shar have more litters after this one?"

Teacher nodded. "Very good question. But there is a spell that I will use once this litter is born. It is not one that I like to use, but it is necessary to preserve the balance. We cannot keep Shar from returning to the pack forever. Once the litter has been delivered, I will cast my spell and we will free her to choose her own path."

The next nine weeks were uncomfortable ones for Karhu. Teacher frequently asked him to come and help with Shar. The dog continued to be surly. Karhu and Teacher were the only ones she would not attack. He spent much of his time caring for the dog and watching over little Uusi who seemed more interested in the coming puppies than in the prospect of a new brother or sister.

The time did pass and he awoke one morning to pounding on his door and the excited screams of Uusi that meant he needed to get up so she could go to see the puppies. Karhu groaned at the thought of more dogs. He was not sure what he had done to earn this consequence. But the Goddess was surely punishing him for some choice he had made. He ate a quick breakfast and went off to Fensil's tent with Uusi.

When they arrived, Teacher was standing outside with a grim look on his face. He explained to Uusi that she should not get too attached to the puppies. Shar had abandoned them as soon as Teacher had freed her. The puppies would not last long without a mother to care for them. Uusi got a determined look on her face and told her father that she would be their mother.

Teacher gave her permission to try and she dragged him around the community gathering supplies. Her first stop was to visit her mother who provided her with a leather bag that could be used to feed small babies. She then went to the small market and demanded all the goat's milk they had. Karhu got to carry a heavy jug of it back to the tent.

Uusi made him help her fill the bag and she began going in to feed each of the six puppies. Karhu waited outside, not wanting to see the animals. Fensil came out of the tent a short time later. "Mother Uusi seems to have it all under control. I will go pay for the goat's milk and make arrangements for more each day. I think Mother Uusi will expect your help each day as well." And so began the next phase of his punishment for crimes he did not know he had committed.

After a week, Uusi finally convinced him to come inside and meet her "children." He decided to go in and see the puppies that she had been talking about non-stop since their birth.

Five of the pups were much like their mother. They were fairly large and were a yellowish tan in color with only slight brindling. Three of them were males and two were females. It was the last of the pups that caught his attention. It was a huge male, half again as large as the other pups. Its feet were enormous. Its coat was also very different from its litter mates. The brindle pattern was more pronounced due to the patterning of the black overcoat and the tan undercoat. The darker back fur was longer and coarser. It almost appeared to be two creatures and not just one.

Karhu unconsciously reached into the basket where the pups lay and began to rub the oversized head of the strange pup. It turned its blind eyes towards him and began to nibble and lick at his fingers. Uusi shoved her feeding bag into his hands and showed him how to hold it so the pup could drink. Karhu fed the large pup two full bags before it fell asleep.

From that day, Uusi delegated the care of the strange pup to him. She made him feed and brush the pup each day. As it grew and began to move about, she showed him how to play with the pup using rope and small balls. Uusi cared for the other five and even had her own favorite, one of the two females. This continued over the weeks and Karhu missed many classes with Teacher as he helped to care for the litter.

Before he knew it, the larger pup was beginning to eat meat prepared for him by Fensil. His pup, or so he had begun to think of it, was much larger and stronger than the others.

Then came the day of another birth. Lady Jocelyn's second child came with much less crying and fewer sounds of pain. This time Teacher brought forth a boy that he presented to Uusi. "This is your brother Metsän Lahja."

Uusi held the baby boy and played with him for a bit. When Teacher took the baby back into its mother, she turned and whispered to Karhu. "The puppies are more fun than a baby brother. I wish we could go play with them." They were not able to return to the puppies until after the naming ceremony the next day.

They entered the tent of Fensil to find two of the male puppies were missing. Karhu breathed a sigh of relief that the large awkward pup that tripped over its own feet was still here in the tent. Uusi demanded to know where the puppies had gone. Fensil took a knee before her. "They are of an age to find new homes. The two males have gone to a caravan master who promised to treat them well and to train them to guard his wagons. I intend to keep two for myself to train as I did Shar."

Uusi looked at the basket and asked, "What of the other two?"

Fensil smiled and picked up the smaller of the female pups that was Uusi's favorite. "Your father has agreed that this is a just reward for all of your hard work. But she must stay within the Temple until your Lady Mother recovers from the birth."

Uusi squealed with joy and gave Fensil a quick hug. Then she grabbed up the pup and carried it out of the tent leaving Karhu behind. Fensil looked at the boy and smiled. "You too have earned a reward. Not just for the care of the pup, but also for your care of Uusi." Karhu started to protest, but Fensil motioned for his silence. "If you wish it, you may have that large scruffy looking pup that cannot seem to walk without tripping. Only the Goddess knows if he will ever grow into those feet."

Karhu's heart sang, but he was still wary of the gift. Remembering the words of Teacher, he asked, "What are the consequences if I keep him?"

At that moment Teacher walked in and replied with a chuckle, "You will have to care for him and feed him. You will have to clean up after him and train him. And most of all, you will have to love him as I think he will love you. And hardest of all, you will have to name him. Choose wisely young Karhu."

Karhu looked from Teacher to Fensil. "I do most of those chores anyway. I will take your gift and give my thanks." He sat down and pulled the pup into his lap. "I name you Beauty for there is no other like you."

Fensil snorted and looked at F'lar. "Your student needs his eyes checked, Master Druid, for that is the ugliest dog I have ever seen. I think none but this boy would have taken him."

F'lar just smiled down at the boy and the dog. "I think he sees to the heart of the matter and the dog. You have let a great prize get away from you, Fensil."

Chapter 4

The Gift of Consequences

Karhu and Beauty became inseparable from that day. For the first time in his life, Karhu became a little boy. He did not shirk his studies or his duties within the forest, but he learned to play and have fun. Many of the games were simple and mindless, but they made him happy. He and Beauty would go deep into the woods to play. Karhu did not want others to see him playing with the dog. He sometimes thought the games were kind of silly for a boy of about fifteen summers. He played with his dog where no one could see or perhaps laugh at his antics.

Being a druid had its advantages too. Each day he asked the Goddess for the spell to speak with animals and each day he used it to speak with Beauty. Even the conversations were childish as the young pup knew few words and most of its concerns were about play and eating. But talking to the dog made him happy. Best of all, Beauty kept all of his secrets and never judged him for the things he said and did. He knew the dog did not understand most of it, but that was okay too.

The boy and dog continued to grow bigger and stronger, especially the dog. Beauty was well over one hundrded pounds by the time he was six months old. Teacher said he would probably outweigh them all when fully grown. Shar had been large even for a mastiff and the pack leader she had mated with had been a truly impressive wolf.

All that mattered to Karhu was that Beauty was his friend. Lady Jocelyn had other ideas though and she reminded Karhu that one of his responsibilities was to train the dog. Teacher made a few suggestions on some things to teach the dog and Lady Jocelyn provided some treats to use to encourage obedience.

Karhu began spending a little time each day working with Beauty to teach him the things Teacher had suggested. Some commands like sit and lie down were fairly easy. Beauty was a smart dog and more importantly, he loved the treats provided by the Lady. His ability to speak with Beauty also helped. Tracking was another skill that Beauty took to naturally. The dog had a wonderful nose and he could track Karhu anywhere. The dog would seek him out by smell and pounce upon him. The game would end with the two wrestling on the ground until the large dog lay across Karhu's body, pinning him to the ground.

Beauty's willingness to work did not extend beyond simple tricks or things the dog considered to be play. The dog wanted to have fun, not work. Karhu tried to teach Beauty to sniff out certain plants and mushrooms that he needed to gather for the community. Beauty told him it was a bad game and refused to cooperate. Karhu grew frustrated as his friend could not be convinced to do anything that the dog did not think of as a game.

Karhu spent a lot of time over the next few days thinking about his problem as he cared for the forest in his area and gathered the medicinal plants he had been asked to find. It made him a little angry that Beauty would not help him when he knew the dog was smart enough to understand the task. He began to think of other ways to solve his problem. There was one spell that he knew the Goddess provided to young Druids, but it was one he had never tried. The animal friendship spell was supposed to allow druids to work with creatures of the forest. He wondered how it would work on Beauty.

He considered the spell for several days. It was not that it was a hard choice, but there was a nagging guilt that he would be taking advantage of his friend. Beauty continued to refuse to play the bad games and in frustration Karhu prayed for the spell one morning. He called the dog to him that morning and Beauty sat before him. As Karhu prepared to cast the spell, he again felt a spark of guilt. He convinced himself that it was his right. The dog was supposed to be there to help him. And besides, the Goddess would not have granted him the spell if it was not okay to use it.

Karhu cast his spell and knew immediately that Beauty had accepted the spell. Beauty had not resisted the magic because the dog trusted him. Again, there was guilt that he had abused the trust of someone he loved. But Karhu pressed ahead and squashed the feeling that this was wrong. To his joy, Beauty cooperated that day and easily searched out the plants that Karhu needed to find. He need only let Beauty sniff a sample and the dog could easily find almost anything.

Karhu's guilt faded over the next few weeks as Beauty learned many more tricks and commands. The dog was as smart as it was large. Karhu came home at night and showed Uusi all the things that he was teaching Beauty. Uusi's Soft Love could not do nearly as many things. Karhu noticed Teacher staring at him as he displayed Beauty's skills. But Karhu did not care. He felt like he had control of things and it was a wonderful feeling.

With Beauty fully trained, Karhu began to think of other things he could do with his magic. He imagined having many pets that he had trained. All of them working to help him in his tasks. But what would be the best animal to befriend next. Karhu again prayed for the animal friendship spell and kept it ready for the next time he encountered a useful animal to befriend.

As Karhu and Beauty were working in a distant part of the grove, Karhu came across a strange set of tracks. The tracks looked like those of a bobcat. But they were too large. They were almost the size of a full-grown cougar. The tracks intrigued him. He thought of all the things he could teach such a cat to do. Karhu called Beauty over to get the scent. Beauty took one sniff and backed away growling. It was obvious the dog did not care for the scent. Karhu used his bond with the dog to force it to track the cat.

It took about an hour but Beauty finally came to a stop about one hundred yards from a large ash tree. Sitting in the lower branches of the tree was the largest bobcat Karhu had ever seen. He eagerly moved forward and stood near the tree. He began his spell but could sense little of the cat on its completion. The cat leapt from the tree and paced over to sit before Karhu. Karhu cast his second prepared spell and attempted to speak to the cat. He told it of his plans for them to be friends. The cat yawned and paced around him once. Then it leapt into the tree and disappeared into the forest. Karhu stared at the tree in surprise. He had been so sure of his success.

Karhu memorized his location so that he could return here the next day to try again. Then he and Beauty completed their duties that day. Karhu slept poorly that night. His dreams were of the cat and the things he could do if he could just ensnare it with his magic. The next day he left the Manor House early with Beauty at his side. He traveled quickly to the ash tree from the day before. To his surprise, the cat sat in the same place.

At his approach, it leapt down and say on the ground in the same spot as the day before. He again cast his spell of friendship. The cat made a soft chuffing noise. For a second, Karhu thought it was laughing at him. But that could not be. Again, Karhu cast his spell to speak with the cat. He tried to tell the cat how strong and beautiful it was. He told it that they would be the best of friends. At his praise, the cat stood and stretched, giving him a view of its powerful body. Then, it turned once more and disappeared into the trees. Karhu did not understand. He could feel the connection when he cast the friendship spell, but it did not seem to affect the cat. Karhu became even more determined that he would claim this beast.

The pattern continued day after day for over a week. The cat was always there in the same tree when Karhu arrived. It would come down so he could cast his spell. Then it would disappear into the trees with the strange chuffing noise echoing behind. One day, he even left without Beauty in his efforts to claim the cat.

When he returned that afternoon, Teacher was waiting for him on the porch of the Manor House. Beside him sat Beauty. The dog's head was resting on Teacher's feet with a sad look in its eyes. Karhu stood before the porch with his eyes downcast. He knew he had let Teacher and Beauty down. Then the defiance rose in him and he raised his eyes prepared to defend himself. "I..."

Teacher cut him off. "Stop. Do not make things worse with words you will regret later. It is time we talk. I have allowed you to struggle with this long enough. It is time for you to listen. Come and sit with me."

Karhu closed his mouth and came to sit on the porch. He sat as far from Teacher as he could. He patted his leg to call Beauty to him but the dog remained where it was staring at him with sad eyes. That brought a stab of pain to his heart.

Teacher looked at him and sighed. "Being a druid is like being part of a family. In a family, each person works and contributes for the good of the family. The things we do for each other are not about ourselves or about what the other person might do for us. It is about helping each member of the family be the best that they can be. Druids work for the good of the world we live in. We serve the Goddess and nature. We serve. Not for the power it brings to us, but for the good of all. Family protects family. Druids protect our world and the Balance. Have you served the Balance young Karhu? Or have you served your own needs?"

Karhu's anger blazed for a moment. "I... I..." Then it faltered as he had no words to answer the question he had been asked.

Teacher met his gaze. "Tell me all that you have done this past two weeks."

Karhu stared down at his hands for a long while, then he began to tell the tale. It was hard. He told of the spells on his friend Beauty. He told of his plans for many animals to be bonded with him. Finally, he told of the cat and his attempts to claim it with his spell.

Teacher nodded. "Would it surprise you to know that I have known of all of this from the beginning? None of this has truly been a secret."

Karhu stared at him in disbelief. "How could you know?"

Teacher chuckled. "First, I am a druid. I have trained many druids before you and I know the mistakes that they make. You are not the first to misuse the gifts you have been given. Second, I too can speak to your friend Beauty here."

Karhu stared accusingly at the dog. "You told on me?"

The dog blinked but Teacher's voice pulled his attention. "No, your friend did not tattle on you. Your friend asked me to help you because he feared you had lost your way."

Karhu's mouth opened but all that came out was, "Oh."

Teacher smiled at that. "Better, young student. The final way that I know is that I also serve the Goddess and the Balance. And sometimes, she speaks to me of her plans and her judgements."

Karhu swallowed hard. "Judgements?"

Teacher reached down to scratch the dog's head. He ignored the question. "Have you forgotten the bad people and what they did to you?" Karhu shook his head no and Teacher continued. "Have you forgotten your vow to not be like them?"

Karhu rose to his feet, secure in his answer. "I AM NOT LIKE THEM!"

Teacher remained calm. "How are your plans for Beauty or the cat or the other creatures you planned to enslave any different than what the bad people did to you? Are your lies and broken promises any better than theirs?"

Karhu stood there with his eyes open wide. Then a single tear leaked from one eye to roll down his cheek. Beauty rose from the floor and padded over to lick the tear away. Karhu, once more the boy running in the woods full of fear, reached out to hug the dog to him.

Teacher rose to his feet. "The Goddess has judged you. She has found you worthy in your heart, but wanting in your thinking. She understands that you are young and that mistakes come easy to one who was so abused in life. Miclikki has set her curse and her blessing on you."

The boy stared at his teacher in fear. "Curse?"

Teacher smiled at him and there was love in his eyes. "Yes boy. Curse. And blessing. The cat will be near you for as long as you live. It will be there to remind you of what you almost became. And the cat is a blessing. For seeing it will remind you that you can still choose to be more than what you once were. The Goddess loves you and does this so that you may choose better next time. The cat is a consequence. For good or ill. You have also been blessed with family who will love you no matter what."

Teacher headed to the door. He paused and looked back as he opened it. "You should come to dinner tonight. The Lady Jocelyn wants all of her children home this evening. Come, Beauty. Karhu needs to forgive himself so that we can forgive him too."

Beauty licked his face one more time and ran inside. Teacher entered and closed the door behind him.

Karhu turned and began to walk. His thoughts were full of loathing for himself. How could he have made so many mistakes? How could he do to Beauty and to the cat what the bad people had done to him? He tried to make slaves of them. Karhu could not understand how any of them could be around him. He was a bad person. He had become what he hated.

Karhu walked a long time, thinking and accusing himself. He judged himself and was deciding on his punishment when he heard a loud snort from the brush behind him. He turned to see a large female boar standing before a bush. He could just make out the smaller shapes of her litter behind her. She was angry and preparing to charge in defense of her babies. Karhu began to back away. But he had no time to climb a tree nor did he have even his staff to fend her off. The boar charged. Karhu saw death approaching him. Then a large tawny form burst from the trees and hit the boar in the flank. The boar tumbled hard to the side and Karhu used the time to climb out of its reach. As the boar circled the tree below him, Karhu notice the cat sitting in another tree not far away. It was licking its fur. The strange chuffing noise came from the beast.

Karhu stared at the cat for a long time until the boar gathered its piglets and moved away. Karhu realized then that despite all that he had done, the Goddess still loved him. She had not cast him aside. She had given him the Blessed Curse. Maybe in time he could forgive himself too. He nodded to the cat and slid down the tree and headed… home? Teacher had said all her children. And now he understood that meant him too. With a smile, he went home for dinner.

Perspectives

Chapter 1

A Bad Day

Serillia lay quietly on her cot. It was nice and warm beneath her blankets. She cracked open one eye to see if was worth climbing out of bed. Her room was a mess, just the way she liked it. A single beam of sunlight pierced the leaves of the tree outside her window to shine into her room. It had a pretty glow as it spotlighted the dirty shirt that she had dropped on the floor last night. Serillia stared at the sunbeam. She began to watch the tiny specks of dust floating around in it. They had it so easy, no rules. They could float anywhere they wanted all day long. She drifted back to sleep as she contemplated life as a speck of dust.

It seemed like only a few heartbeats later that she felt her mother's hand in her hair. "Rillia, time to wake up. You must get to the Temple in time for class. Hurry now." As her mother turned to leave the room, she stepped on the shirt that Serillia had noticed in the beam of sunlight. There was the sound of pottery cracking. It was then that Serillia remembered the bowl of strawberries she had been snacking on the night before.

Her mother frowned and moved the shirt aside with her foot. Her face got a disappointed look on it when she saw the broken bowl and the strawberries that had been left out overnight. "Rillia, how many times must I tell you to clean up your room. And no food in here. It will attract bugs. You are a disaster, my child. Now get out of bed. Get dressed and clean up this mess."

She hated her mother. Always another rule. If mother did not like the way her room looked, then she should not come in here at all. That was a better solution than all the rules. "Do not do this." "You cannot have that." "Go pick up this." None of mother's rules made any sense. She thought mother made up most of them just to have another way to make her miserable.

Her mother's voice echoed from the kitchen. "Hurry up child. I have to get you to the Temple for class. And I cannot be late again. The baker will let me go if I am not there to help with the baking for the afternoon customers. Hurry, child."

Serillia grumbled as she found a mostly clean shirt to pull on. More things that she did not want to do. Classes at the Temple were a waste of time. Why did she need to learn all these things? Reading and making runes was for important people. She was just plain old Rillia. She did not need to learn any of that stuff. History of the lands was stupid. What did it matter what happened a hundred years ago? Those people were all dead. And why should she care about places she would never see? And all the lessons about the Goddess. If the Goddess really cared about her, she would make mother leave her alone so she could sleep a little longer.

Serillia shoved most of the mess under her cot so the room looked neater. Maybe mother would not notice for a few days. She walked into the kitchen hoping for something exciting to eat. Mother took one look at her and sighed. She grabbed a brush and began to brush Serillia hair. It hurt. She swore mother went looking for knots to tug at with the brush. This was one more reason she hated mother so much.

Mother tried to make the whole thing her fault, but she did not believe it. "I try to tell you, Rillia. If you brush your hair and braid it before you go to bed, it will not be full of knots every morning." Her mother quickly braided her hair and tied it off.

Her mother dropped the brush on the table and grabbed a small loaf of bread with some cheese melted into its center. She shoved it into Serillia's hand and gave her a push towards the door. "We must go before I am late." She wondered why her mother loved her job more than she loved her. And why was there never anything good to eat? Bread and cheese was so boring.

Before Serillia could take a bite of the bread, mother grabbed her other hand and dragged her through the streets of the town. Serillia practically had to run to keep up with mother. There was no time to even take a bite. Five streets later, Serillia noticed that they were on the edge of the market. The large trees of the Druid's Temple were visible straight ahead. The baker's building was on the edge of the market to their right.

Mother knelt before her. "I am sorry, child. I do not have time to walk you all the way there. Go straight to the Temple for classes. You are lucky that the Lord F'lar allows all the children to attend classes. Especially girls. I wish I could have gone to classes like you. Now hurry, girl, and stay out of the market. Go." Her mother gave her a quick hug and rushed off towards the baker's building.

She watched her mother rush away and stuck her tongue out at her. One day she would make her own rules. She was 12 now. She was old enough already to tell herself what to do. Mother just liked bossing her around. Serillia began to walk towards the Temple. It was not time for class yet so she was not in a hurry. Besides, the teacher was mean. She liked to make the children miserable. She had too many rules, too. Who cares if the runes were straight or not?

She finally took a bite of her bread and cheese. It was cold now. That was mother's fault. If she had not insisted on pulling her hair, she might have eaten before it got cold and hard. She started to walk past the market, but there were so may colors and things that shined in the sunlight. She decided to ignore mother's stupid rule and go look around. She would learn more here than she ever would from her teacher. And something in the market smelled much better than her breakfast.

Serillia walked down the first line of stalls chewing on another bite. She turned to stare at a beautiful blue dress when someone snatched the bread from her hand and gave her a shove. She stumbled and fell against a table where a

merchant was selling boots. The man grabbed her arm and pulled her away from his table. It hurt.

She jerked her arm from the man's hand and spun to see who had taken her breakfast. She spotted the culprit standing across the aisle with a mouth full of her bread and cheese. The boy wore a dirt-stained tunic and pants. He had a large bruise on one cheek. She recognized him. His name was Thibault. He had stopped coming to class a long time ago.

She hated him. He was mean and he had always acted so much smarter than her and the other smaller kids in the class. He was such a bully, pushing her like that. He had not been a bully back when he came to class, but she still had not liked him. He had always made such perfect runes. The teacher had made everyone else feel bad because they could not make the runes like Thibault.

Serillia stuck her tongue out at him. She stomped past him on her way to the Temple. As she passed him, she whispered, "I hope you choke on it." This was turning out to be a terrible day. First mother was mean and then that nasty boy. And now she had to go to class hungry. She just knew the teacher would be mean to her too.

Serillia entered the grove of trees beside the Temple. There were four boys and five girls already seated before the stump where the teacher sat for lessons. She looked to the side and saw the disapproving face of a stern looking older woman. The woman waved her hand at Serillia as if to hurry her along. "You are late, young lady."

Serillia knew she was no lady and never would be. The teacher was just making fun of her. Classes began as always. A priestess came in and said a blessing over the children. Then, the teacher sat down and read a story about the elves that lived North of the five lakes. The story was boring and Serillia began to doze. Then it was question time. She did not raise her hand because she had not been paying attention. But the teacher called on her anyway. She hated this woman. You had to be a terrible person to make children suffer so. She mumbled something too low to be heard and the teacher shook her head before calling on another student.

They worked on their numbers next. She did not mind that part. She could count real good and she could even add and take away. Next came the lessons about the Goddess and the Balance and the need to care for the forests. More boring stuff to waste her time. There was a break and the class was given something to eat. That was Serillia's favorite part. Especially today since she had lost her breakfast. She was glad that Lord F'lar provided food for all the children.

Class always ended badly though. It always ended with practicing their runes. She cleared the dirt before her and grasped the writing stick firmly in her hand. She hated this part. The teacher told them to write two lines in the dirt about something good in their day. Serillia was at a loss. Her day had been awful so far. What was there to like? She did not like all the stupid things people made her do. She thought for a while and wrote a single line: *My day will be better when I do not have to write more stupid things for stupid teachers!*

The teacher came around the class. She stopped and studied each child's work. Serillia could not wait to see the teachers face when she saw what Serillia had written. But when the mean old woman studied her work, she just smiled. Then she pointed to a rune in the middle. "This one is backwards. You can do better if you try."

Serillia grew angry and stood up. She stared up at the teacher and all of her hatred came rushing out at once. "You should be ashamed to take the Lord's coin to abuse children. You grow rich on our suffering." The woman stepped back in shock. Serillia did not wait to get in trouble. She turned and ran deeper into the grove. She did not look back as she ran.

She did not know how long or how far she ran. But eventually, the sound of the leaves rustling in the soft breeze calmed her enough to stop. She still felt angry. She had no idea what to do with all the feelings and frustration inside her. There was too much for her small body to hold inside. She decided the best thing to do was to go home but had no idea which way home was.

She finally picked a direction and started to walk. There were birds all around and they sang their songs to her, but they were happy songs and she was not ready to stop being mad yet. She saw some nuts sitting on a log beside the trail. She picked them up and threw them into the trees. "Stupid birds!"

 An angry chittering sound rose from the ground behind her. Serillia spun to see a large red squirrel shaking its tiny fist at her and complaining quite loudly. The small rodent crossed its arms and glared at her. She felt a pang of guilt about the nuts but pushed it down. She shook her finger at the squirrel. "That is what happens when you do not put your nuts away."

She tried to turn and stomp away from the squirrel, but found that she could not move. She began to be frightened.

A breeze stirred the leaves around her and a female voice seemed to come from all around her. "So much anger in one so small. And such dislike for the rules that keep our world safe."

Serillia felt as if her thoughts and emotions were being searched as her feelings and memories of the morning came crashing back.

The voice whispered again, "I see. You do not understand the rules or how they protect you. You think them all so arbitrary. You do not understand why people do the things they do."

Serillia wanted to scream at the voice to get out of her head. The voice was right, but she did not like it in her head. Her lips would not move though. She could not draw a breath to scream. Strangely, she did not feel the need to breathe either.

The presence seemed to pause and study her memories. "What you lack, child, is perspective." The voice paused as if to consider. "I know, you do not really understand that word. The simplest explanation I can give is that you only see life through a single window. You miss so much because you have not learned to look through other windows yet. There are so many meanings in life that you have never seen."

The squirrel began its angry chiding again and the voice seemed to listen. "Yes, your nuts are indeed gone. But that is but a small part of her day. She at least felt regret at her action."

Serillia sensed the voice turning its attention back to her. "No child, I am not going to punish you. I think that you need to be given a gift this day. That is a better solution to the problem. Perhaps even a great gift or three."

Serillia's fear began to fade. She liked gifts. Maybe this would turn out good.

The voice began to laugh. "So be it, child. Today you hated three times. So, I will give you three gifts. I give you the gift of three perspectives. What you make of my gifts is up to you, for in the end you must make your own choices and find your own balance in this world."

Serillia's fear returned as her vision went black.

Chapter 2

Hope

Serillia woke up to pain. A boot kicked her in the ribs a second time. A gruff male voice barked at her. "I said get up, boy. I do not have time for your laziness this morning."

She was confused. Boy? That was insulting. She did not look like a boy. She raised her voice and yelled. "I am not a boy, you idiot. Stop being mean." But what came out of her mouth was "Yes, sir. I am sorry, Pa." The voice that spoke the words was not hers.

Serillia tried to reach up and rub her ears. Instead, her hands reached down and pushed her body off the floor. Then they gathered up the thin blanket, folding it before shoving it into a tiny niche in the wall below a window that she did not recognize.

It was still dark outside the window. Where was she and why was she up so early? Then she noticed her reflection on the dirty glass of the window. She did not see herself. The face that stared back at her was that of the boy, Thibault. She did not understand. How could she be Thibault? Then she turned away from the window and scampered out of the small dark room with no furnishings at all. She was following the man who had just kicked her. Serillia tried to stop and back away. But this body did not obey her.

She moved into a dark and dirty kitchen and moved to crouch in a corner out of the way. She watched as the man sliced open a small loaf of bread and placed bacon and cheese inside it. It was then that Serillia realized just how hungry she was. She felt like she had not eaten for days. She hoped the man was going to feed her like mother did. The bacon smelled so good.

The man poured something from a pitcher into a clay mug. She caught the faint scent of the ale that they sold in the market. The man took the loaf and mug and sat on an old chair beside the small table. He began to eat. Serillia felt her mouth water and heard her stomach growl. The man broke off a small piece of the bread and threw it at her. Her hands caught the bread, but they would not bring it to her mouth.

The gruff voice came again. "Better, boy. Self-control is the key to staying alive. Now eat it. It is more than you deserve." Her lands lifted the small piece of bread to her lips and she took a small bite. The bread was dry and hard, but her body craved more. The second bite finished what she realized was her only breakfast.

Serillia's new eyes watched as a tiny piece of bacon bounced off the man's stomach and landed on the floor beneath the table. She felt her body tense. The man finished off the food and then he tipped back the mug and drank it all down. As the man returned the mug to the counter, Serillia's body darted forward and her hand closed over the piece of bacon. She was almost back into the corner when a large hand impacted the side of her face. Scrillia crashed into the wall. Pain consumed her. But her body did not cry out. Only her mind did. The man bent and pried open both hands. But they were empty. Serillia realized with a start that she knew that the bacon was now in a tiny pocket in the sleeve of her shirt. She was not sure where the knowledge came from.

The man released her arms as he shoved her back into the corner. His voice was menacing as he growled, "Do not ever steal from me boy. You cost me enough when your Ma died giving birth to you. I kept you alive all these years despite what you done to her. You owe me. Now you better meet your quota in the market today. I do not care what you have to do to get it, but I expect four silver pieces on the table when I return tonight. Got it?"

Serillia heard Thibault's voice reply, "Yes, sir."

Serillia was not stupid. She finally understood that she was not in control of the body. She could only watch and feel. She was not sure how this had happened, but it had to be the voice that she heard in the forest. Magic. The voice had lied. This was a punishment. It was certainly not a gift. She tried to quiet her thoughts. There had to be something she could do.

As her own thoughts stilled, she realized that she could hear other faint thoughts or maybe they were feelings. They had to be from Thibault. She tried to scream at him, but he did not seem to hear her.

She watched through the boy's eyes as the man left the rundown home and closed the door behind him. She felt hope and determination coming from the boy. She realized that he was determined to do as his father had demanded. The boy actually hoped that if he could steal enough, his father might love him. Serillia wanted to shake her head. It was a crazy idea.

She felt the pangs of hunger again. She had never been that hungry before. Mother had always made sure she had enough food. She did not like this feeling. Thibault brought the tiny piece of bacon to his mouth and savored it. He held it in his mouth until all of the flavor was gone and then he swallowed it. Then he rose and went to the counter where he ate the bread crumbs that his father had left behind. Serillia did not think it helped very much. Then the boy ran his finger around the mug and licked it clean. She thought the taste of the ale was awful. But the boy savored anything he could eat.

The boy slipped out of the house and made his way slowly through the town to the market. They watched the merchants setting up their stalls. There were even a few early customers that came to buy food from the farmers. But the boy held back. She got the feeling that he was waiting till there were more people in the crowded square.

As they watched, a farmer dumped a bushel of apples on the ground. Thibault ran over and began to help pick them all up and return them to the basket. She was surprised that he would do anything so helpful. Then the boy turned and walked away. He turned down another aisle and pulled a small bruised apple from the small pocket in his sleeve.

She had not even noticed their hands placing it there. Thibault ate everything except the seeds. She did not like the feel or taste of the core, but the fruit had relieved some of the ache in their stomach.

Morning business in the market began to pick up. The boy moved into the thicker crowds. She watched through his eyes as the boy's attention focused on a fat merchant moving quickly through the crowd. Thibault moved carefully forward and then tried to cross in front of the big man. His timing was bad and the big man bumped him hard and knocked him into a couple of people shopping across the aisle.

The big man saw the scruffy boy and his hand went immediately to his purse. It was still there so he shook a finger at the boy. "Watch where you are going, street rat." The two men that Thibault had bounced into glared at the fat man. One of them helped the boy to get back to his feet. Serillia wanted to protest when their fingers slipped several coins from the kind man's coat pocket. This time she felt them go into the hidden pocket. She did not understand how he could steal from someone who was kind to him.

They moved on around the market. The boy found a quiet place and pulled the coins from his pocket. She saw a silver and copper coin in their palm. He slid both inside the worn boots he was wearing and they moved on. She felt his hopes rise. He thought his father would be pleased.

Then the boy stopped. His attention was locked on the crowd flowing into the market. She saw a small shape wandering down the aisle staring at the tables. It had something in its hand. She felt the boy's recognition as he stayed just outside the figures view. The boy knew this girl. She knew that he had once hoped they could be friends. That hope was just a weak memory now.

Suddenly the boy lurched forward. One of their hands grabbed the small loaf the girl was holding while the other shoved her into a merchant's table. Her mind was overwhelmed by shock and rage. The girl they had pushed was her. They had stolen her breakfast. How could he? As people turned to stare at the young girl, at her, falling into the table; Thibault managed to lift a small purse from the half open bag of a well-dressed woman.

The boy slid back to the far side of the aisle to watch her. She felt his regret as he realized they could never be friends now. But the feel of the purse in his sleeve brought back the hope. Maybe today would be the day his father told him he had done well.

Their stomach growled again and he took a large bite of her breakfast. As their eyes met those of her body across the aisle, he nodded his thanks. They could not hear the girl's words as they disappeared into the crowd.

She watched as they slid in behind her. The boy followed her as she marched angrily to the grove beside the Temple to go to class. They watched as she entered the class. She felt his longing to go back to class. She realized that he had truly loved learning. He had been filled with such hope to be more than a thief. But that hope too had dwindled. It was still there, but she realized that it was dying in him. The boy moved closer to the grove so they could see inside where the class was gathered.

She thought back on all of the terrible things that had happened to Thibault that day and all of the things he had done to make his father love him. She did not understand how he could feel hope or why he would want to. She realized then that she no longer hated the boy. She felt sorry for him. She did not want his life. It was too terrible.

The leaves of the trees that formed the Temple began to rustle in the wind. There was a chittering noise from one of the Temple trees. She saw a red squirrel staring at her from above the entrance to the grove. She heard the soft female voice in the movement of the leaves. "So, you have gained a new perspective. That is the beginning of true wisdom. I think it is time for another gift." Once again, her vision went dark.

Chapter 3

Charity

Serillia felt her eyes open again. A wave of hope washed over her. Maybe she was herself once more. But the hope faded as a large callused hand came up to wipe the sleep from her eyes. She did not try to control this body as she had the boys. She waited to see what would happen this time. The new body got up and lit a candle. Then it made the bed. They moved next to open the curtains on a tiny window that looked out into an alley. It was still dark outside. Once again, she glimpsed a reflection in the glass of the window.

She was in the body of her mean and selfish teacher. She so did not want to be here. She did not want to go to the school and mistreat the children there. She sat within the prison of the teacher's body and watched as teacher moved out into a hall. The woman entered the next room and picked up a bedpan from beside the bed of an old man who was missing a leg. The teacher took the bedpan and dumped it, rinsed it and returned it to the room.

The teacher's hand dropped to brush the hair from the old man's face. "It is time to wake, father. I will help you clean up before I begin to cook. I have to teach class today." The old man nodded and sat up. The teacher went to a small kitchen and stirred the coals in the fireplace and added several pieces of wood. Then she took a pitcher and bowl and headed back to the old man's room.

They entered to see the old man staring at them with love in his eyes. "You do too much, daughter. You should just let me go. It would make your life easier."

Serillia expected her teacher to agree with the old man. Her teacher must hate having to care for him each day. This man was indeed a burden in her life. Instead, she felt love and joy. "No, father. What would I do without you to keep me company? Your stories fill my heart with joy. My evenings would be so empty without them."

They helped the old man to wash his face and hands. Then they helped him move to an old rocking chair that sat beside a much larger window that faced the street. The teacher patted his arm. "I will bring you breakfast in a bit. I have much to cook this day. Mirtha from down the street has a fever. Her children need to be fed so she can stay in bed and rest. I must cook for my class as well."

Serillia was confused by her teacher's words. The Lord F'lar provided the food for the children. Or at least that is what she had always thought.

Her teacher returned to the kitchen and uncovered a bowl of dough that had been left to rise overnight. She began to knead it and role in out into squares. In some of the loaves she put pieces of fruit that she had cut up. In others she mixed in cheese that she grated with her own hands. She moved a small baking oven into the fire and waited for it to warm up.

By the time all the breads were in the oven, the sun was coming up over the horizon. Serillia felt pain in their fingers and back. Her teacher had worked hard. Serillia recognized some of the food they had made this morning as things she got to eat regularly during their breaks from class. This woman made most of the snacks and treats that the children enjoyed. She could not understand why. The children attended class three days out of every ten. That was a lot of work. Serillia began to question her harsh view of her teacher.

As the first loaves came out of the oven, they put in a second batch. They placed one of the small loaves on a plate and brought it along with a large pewter mug of water to her father. He took them. "Thank you, daughter. You work so hard. I hope it brings you peace."

They kissed the top of the old man's head. "Eat, father. You need your strength. You are the one that taught me that charity is its own reward. I simply do the will of the Goddess Mielikki. I am a pair of her hands in this world."

They began to pack the loaves into two bags. One was large and the second small. They removed the last two loaves from the small oven and left them on the counter to cool. They banked the coals and teacher took the two bags and left her home. She turned and raised her voice as she closed the door. "I must stop in the market on the way home, father. I will see you as soon as I can."

Serillia listened to the thoughts and feelings of her teacher as they walked down the street. The woman was content. She truly did not mind the hard work that she had done that morning. They stopped at a home at the end of the street where her teacher lived. They knocked on the door. A haggard looking man opened the door. Her teacher asked after his wife and then gave him the smaller sack. "Feed the children these. Let her rest today. I will bring dinner as well."

The man thanked her and they turned towards the Temple. Serillia felt the anticipation the woman felt. She was looking forward to seeing her students. Her children of sorts. Serillia began to really question her own beliefs about her teacher. She could not feel any desire to make the children miserable. The woman seemed to think of the children as her own. Serillia was confused.

Serillia sat through the lessons a second time. But this time she shared her teacher's love of what she taught. She saw through her teacher's mind how these thing s might help the children to make better choices. Then it came time to practice writing. She watched herself in the back of the class where she sat with an angry expression on her face. Then there was that mean smile as she sat back from what she had written. Serillia began to dread what was coming.

They moved around the class and she got to see the many small things her classmates wrote about. They were mostly simple things that made them happy. Their simple joys were things she had at home but often did not appreciate. As her teacher came to examine her message, she waited to feel anger or resentment at the mean things she had written.

But those feelings never came. She felt her teacher's pain at what she read. But instead of responding in anger, her teacher simply told her that she had reversed one rune. Serillia felt tears in her eyes as she watched herself yell at the teacher and then run away. She was not sure if the tears were from her teacher's pain or from her own embarrassment at what she had done.

Serillia realized that her teacher had little. She had her time, her knowledge, and some little skill at baking. All the woman had wanted in life was to share these gifts with the children of the class. Serillia saw the memory then of a man and a small babe. She realized they were dead like her own father. She felt sadness as she realized that she and her classmates were the only children teacher had.

She wished that she could hug her teacher and tell her she was sorry. But she could not even share her thoughts to ease the woman's pain.

Once again, she heard the breeze pick up. There was a flash of red through the trees along the path where she had seen herself run. The now familiar voice came again in the rustling of the leaves. "You have gained another perspective on life. It is easier to love those around you when you can see things as they do. Perhaps it is a greater charity to love them even when you do not understand." Once again, Serillia's vision went black.

Chapter 4

Love

Serillia sat in the darkness for what seemed a long time. At least she thought it was sitting. It was hard to tell without a body of her own. She waited. She knew what came next. She had hated three times that day and she had been trapped inside two of the people she had mistreated already. She really did not want to be inside her mother's head. She thought back on the many ways she had disobeyed her mother. She thought about all of the mean things that she said to mother. What if her mother hated her too? She did not want to find out. She knew though that the voice would not let her off that easily.

The darkness around her changed subtly. It went from nothingness to just dark. Serillia felt a mattress beneath her. She became aware of her mother's sleepy thoughts. Mother's hand slid to the far side of the mattress. It was cold and empty. She felt her mother's sadness and her loneliness. Serillia realized that her mother missed father as much as she did. She felt the love that mother still had for father. The strength of that love took her breath away. Well, maybe not that as she did not have a body of her own anymore.

Mother rose slowly and dressed in the darkness. She lit a small lantern on her dresser and began to straighten up her room. Mother turned to the window as the sun began to come up over the horizon. Serillia saw her mother's reflection in the glass. She looked different through mother's eyes. Serillia saw her mother as an old woman who made too many demands on the young girl. The woman in the glass was not old. She was still fairly young. She was beautiful still, or would be if she did not look so tired and run down. Serillia wished she could change that.

Mother took her into the kitchen next. Mother stirred the coals and added a single log to the fire. She understood that Mother was trying to make the wood last as long as possible. It cost so much. As the fireplace began to warm the kitchen, mother placed an old iron pot filled with water in the coals. Mother took down a small loaf of bread and sliced it down the middle. She cut several slices of cheese and placed them in the center of the loaf. The bread went on the rack suspended over the fireplace. Serillia knew the bread would warm there and the cheese would melt. It was her breakfast.

Mother stuck her head into Serillia's room and called for her to awaken before returning to the kitchen to make herself a mug of tea. Mother sat quietly and worried about paying bills while she drank her tea. Serillia had no idea there were so many bills just to take care of two people. Was this where all the money mother got from the baker went?

Mother finished her tea and rinsed out the mug. She went back to Serillia's room. Mother smiled as she stared at Serillia's sleeping form. Serillia was surprised at the protective feelings that washed over her as mother stared at her. Mother carefully crossed the room through the mess. Serillia felt guilty as she knew most of the mess was intentional. She did it because she did not want to follow mother's rules. Mother bent and ran her hand through the dark curls of the girl sleeping on the cot. Serillia felt like she was floating in a sea of love. Despite all she did and all that she said, her mother truly loved her. Serillia compared this with what she had felt between Thibault and his father. She realized just how lucky she was.

Serillia stared through mother's eyes at the young girl. It was confusing thinking of the girl as herself when she was inside mother this way. When the girl was awake and sitting up, mother turned to go. They missed a step and their foot came down on a crumpled shirt. Serillia felt and heard the bowl break under their foot. As mother bent to pick up the shirt and bowl, Serillia felt the sadness. The bowls had been a gift from father. There was only one other left. Serillia wanted to cry, but mother did not.

She expected to feel mother's anger then, but instead there was concern and a bit of fear. Mother turned back to the girl and again Serillia heard the warning about bugs. She was not afraid of bugs. But the images in mother's mind were not of ants and other bugs. In mother's mind there was a rat. A rat that bit and carried diseases. Serillia shuddered at mother's mind pictures. Rats did scare Serillia. Maybe there was a reason for the rules that mother insisted on. She wondered why mother never warned her of rats, only bugs. Then she realized that her mother did not want to scare her.

They took the broken bowl to the kitchen and placed it in the trash pile. Mother made a mental note that she would need to take the trash to the midden on her way to pick her daughter up at the Temple.

Mother turned and Serillia watched herself come into the room. Before them stood a girl with a tangled mess of long curly hair. She felt her mother's frustration. What surprised her was that mother saw beauty in her. Serillia thought she was rather plain. The image mother carried of her in her mind did not match what Serillia saw through mother's eyes. But she really liked the way her mother saw her. She just was not sure she could ever be that girl.

Serillia listened to mother's thoughts as they brushed out the tangles in her hair. Mother winced each time she hit a bad tangle. She had always though mother pulled the tangles as revenge for the things she had done. But there was only regret in her mother's heart. The braid was finished quickly and mother shoved the loaf into her hands. Serillia realized that mother was hungry. All they had that morning was the mug of tea.

They hurried through the town and soon the Temple was in sight. Mother stared at it with longing. Mother wished that she could have attended classes as her daughter did. Mother pushed those thoughts aside and sent Serillia on her way. She was going to be late again and the baker would send her away. They ran down the street and made it to the door just as the Baker was opening it. He grumbled as mother hurried past him. Serillia did not think she liked him. But she decided not to hate him. She did not want to be inside his head next.

Mother worked hard that day. She hauled flour in from the storage room and made batch after batch of dough. The fussy baker would stop by frequently to check the consistency of the dough. By mid-morning, their back was sore from carrying the flour and their hands hurt from kneading the dough. Serillia realized how hard mother worked each day.

Another thing that Serillia noticed that her mother did not, was the baker's assistant. He was not young, but he was not old either. He always had a smile on his face when he looked at mother. He came to help her carry the flour whenever he could. He even got in trouble with the baker once for not letting mother do what she was paid for. Mother was too busy to notice the man though. Serillia decided that she liked this man. He was kind to them.

When the midday rush had ended, the baker set a small pile of silver on the counter. Mother thanked him for his generosity. Serillia thought her mother deserved much more than that. It was so much less than what Serillia had thought mother received. Serillia listened to mother's thoughts as she counted out coins for their rent and for firewood. When she was done, there were two small silver pieces left. Mother tucked the rest of the coins inside her shirt and placed the remaining two in her pocket.

Mother left the baker's business and headed into the market. She kept her hand protectively over the two coins. Mother was truly afraid of thieves and strangers. Serillia realized that this was the reason mother did not want her in the market. She thought back to her encounter with Thibault. Then she thought about the boy's father. Maybe mother had a good reason for her fears. Maybe the rule about staying out of the market made sense too.

Mother stopped at one stall and stared at a dress hanging on the wall. Serillia thought mother would look beautiful in the dress. When the seamstress offered to take it down, mother shook her head and pointed instead to a child's shirt with pretty beads sewn into the shape of a flower. Serillia realized her mother was buying a gift for her. She did not want it. It was beautiful, but she did not deserve it. She could not change mother's mind so she watched as the two women haggled over a price. Finally, mother gave up one of the silver pieces she clutched in her pocket. Mother took the shirt and folded it carefully and tucked it under her arm.

Mother moved into the part of the market where the farmers sold their goods. Mother bargained at each stop to get as much food for them as she could. In the end there were just two copper pieces left. Mother stopped at one final table where there were small baskets of the strawberries that Serillia loved. Mother held out the two coppers she had left. The farmer waved her off. Mother pointed to a basket where several of the berries were bruised. The farmer nodded and mother gave him her last two coins. She took the strawberries and her other purchases and headed home.

Serillia's thoughts began to drift as mother began to put away the food she had bought and placed the beautiful new shirt on Serillia's cot. The woman she had hated was not who she had believed her to be. She did not send her to school to get rid of her for the day. She did it out of love. Everything mother had done that day had been out of love for her. All of the rules that Serillia hated had reasons. They were not just to make her miserable. They were to keep her safe. Why had she never understood that before?

As mother headed back to the temple to pick her up, the leaves again began to rustle in the breeze. Serillia could hear the squirrel chattering somewhere nearby, but she did not see it. The soft voice came to her again. "You could not see the reasons, child, because you did not have the right perspective. Sometimes you must try to look at things from another's perspective. Three gifts I promised. Three gifts you have received." Once again, Serillia's vision went totally dark.

Chapter 5

A New Perspective

Serillia stayed in the darkness for what seemed like forever. She had expected to come back to her own body right away. She wanted to rush home and clean her room. Maybe she could help mother with their dinner. But the black emptiness did not go away. She began to grow frightened. Would she be trapped here forever? After what seemed a very long time to her, Serillia called out softly, "Can I please go home?"

Silence was the only response. She tried again. "Please, Lady.

The feminine voice returned to her. "I am here, child. I have always been here. You had only to call on me."

Serillia whispered, "I want to go home now. To mother."

The voice asked softly, "Do you know me, child?"

Serillia's voice trembled as she replied, "Forest Lady?"

Serillia felt a smile in the voice that answered her. "That name will do. You have the key to go home. You must simply use it."

Serillia shook the head that she did not have. "I do not understand. What is this key?"

The word seemed to echo all around her. "Faith. Faith is the key. Do you believe, child?"

Serillia whispered, "I do."

Then the voice spoke again. "Then let your faith shine in the darkness. Let it be a beacon to light your way home."

Serillia saw a bright light in the darkness. It was golden in color and it was moving towards her. At first, she thought it was a candle, but it did not flicker. As it grew closer, she could see its form. It was a horn. A golden horn. It sat atop the head of a midnight black horse with a grey mane. No, not a horse. A unicorn. It bent close and blew softly in her hair. Serillia realized that she had hair again. She had arms and legs. She was standing beside the unicorn. She reached out tentatively and placed her hand on its side. Its head bobbed up and down and it began to walk her towards another light she could see far ahead.

She walked beside the unicorn and she heard the Lady's voice once more. "Do not judge, child, for those you judge face challenges that you cannot understand. Their perception may be very different from your own. And do not hate. Love those around you even when you do not understand. For love is the greatest gift of all."

———————————————————

Serillia awoke in her room. She stared at the single beam of sunlight that came in through the window. The dust motes danced in it once more. Had it all been a dream? Could any of that have been real? She dismissed it and reached a hand up to rub her eyes. Her hand touched a shirt covered with beads. Serillia sat up and stared at the shirt that mother had bought in the market. It was beautiful. She stared about her room at the mess and she got up and dressed quickly.

She began to sort the things in her room. Dirty clothes went into one pile, trash into another. She even dug the stuff out from under her cot and began to sort it as well. Serillia finally looked up and noticed that her mother was standing in the doorway staring at her. Her face seemed puzzled, but there was a smile on her lips.

"Are you feeling well, Rillia? You came home and went straight to bed yesterday. I was worried you were sick."

She looked up at her mother and suddenly she could feel the love her mother had for her just as she had when she was inside mother's head. She jumped up and ran to hug her mother. "I want to finish cleaning, but I have to go to school today. Is there still time?"

Her mother squeezed her tight. "Of course there is time. You were up much earlier than normal. Tonight, I can help you clean if you would like me too."

Serillia nodded. "I would like that very much." Then her hand went to the beads on the new shirt she wore. "Thank you, mother. I love it. And I love you, too."

She saw the last of the worry fade from her mother's eyes as they held hands and walked to the kitchen to get ready to leave. Serillia took her loaf and walked outside to wait as mother finished banking the coals. She did not take a bite of the loaf yet. She had plans for it today. As she stood waiting, she again heard the chittering of the squirrel.

She looked down towards the ground and watched as it chattered on and swished its red tail from side to side. She broke off a small piece of the loaf. "You caused me a lot of problems yesterday. But I do not hate you. I most definitely do not want to be in your head to learn your perspective." She tossed the small piece of bread to the squirrel. "I am sorry for the nuts though. That was mean of me." The squirrel seemed to nod and it grabbed the bread in its mouth and scampered up a tree."

Mother came out and asked, "Who are you talking to Rillia?"

Serillia pointed up at the squirrel. Her mother chuckled but warned, "Do not get too close child. They do bite."

They held hands as they began to walk through the town. Serillia looked up at her mother. "Mother, sometimes I have a hard time drawing some of the runes well. Can we practice together tonight?"

Her mother's face grew sad. "I was never taught the runes, child. I do not know how."

Serillia smiled. "It is okay. I will show you and we can practice together." Serillia felt a warm glow inside at the joy on her mother's face. Maybe new perspectives were not that hard after all.

When they got to the edge of the market, Serillia pulled her hand away. "I can walk from here, mother. You must not be late for work."

Her mother knelt beside her. "Are you sure, Rillia?"

"I am sure, mother." Then she gave her mother a big hug making sure not to get the bread in her mother's hair. Before she let her mother go, she whispered in her ear, "Remember to say thank you to the nice man who helps you carry the flour."

Her mother leaned back to stare at her in surprise. "What are you…."

But Serillia danced away towards the temple. "Do not forget. Be polite and say thank you."

Serillia spun and watched as her mother turned and walked towards the baker's building with a puzzled look on her face. Serillia laughed in delight then turned to enter the market. This time she was not watching the stalls. She was looking for someone. She headed for the spot where she had watched the morning crowd with Thibault the day before. She spotted him crouched in the same place.

He looked up at her in surprise as she walked up beside him. She broke her loaf into two pieces and held them up side by side. Then she handed him the larger of the two pieces. He took it carefully. "Why? I took your food yesterday. Why are you being nice to me now?"

She took a bite of her half of the loaf and answered as she chewed. "Because you are more hungry than I am. Besides, it is what friends do."

He stopped chewing. "Friends?"

She nodded. "Unless you do not want to be."

He stammered for a second. "No, I would like to be friends."

Serillia pointed to the bruise on his cheek. "Does it still hurt?"

He nodded. His face became sad as he stared down at his feet. "My Pa did not come home last night. I do not think he is ever coming back."

Serillia handed him the rest of her half of the loaf. "Why not?"

He chewed and swallowed another bite. "There is talk in the market. He hurt someone last night. He is running so the Lord F'lar does not punish him." Thibault seemed ready to cry. He sniffed and went on. "He did not come for me though. He just ran."

She studied him for a moment. "What will you do now? Keep stealing?"

He gave her a guilty look but then shrugged. "I do not know what to do."

She smiled. "I know what you can do. Will you trust me?"

At his nod, she grabbed one of his hands and led him back towards the Temple. When they got to the entrance to the grove, she spun to face him. "Promise me you will wait here till I come back. I ask as your friend."

He met her gaze and she saw a little fear in his eyes. But he nodded. "I promise."

Serillia ran inside to see her teacher spreading the fresh snacks out on the table. She ran over and began to help. Her teacher gave her a puzzled look but smiled. Serillia turned to her. "I am sorry that I was mean yesterday. I did not understand."

Teacher looked down at her. "Your apology is accepted child. What did you not understand?"

Serillia laughed. "Many, many things." She motioned for her teacher to come closer and she began to whisper the story of her new friend. She told of his need for a home and someone to love him. Then she led teacher outside. When the boy saw them, he began to back away. Serillia was worried he would run. She called out to him. "You promised."

Thibault stopped and waited, but she could see the fear in his face. She took his hand and lead him over to their teacher. She leaned over and whispered to him. "Let her talk. Listen to her. She really is nice." Then she turned and winked to the teacher before heading back inside.

She watched the entrance closely and smiled when teacher came back in with her hand on the boy's shoulder. He stayed in class until the end.

The day passed quickly and Serillia made several new friends that day. She had never taken the time to ask questions of the other students. She learned that day that they each had a different perspective. It was more fun to learn by asking questions than it was to be in their heads.

At the end of the day, she noticed that Thibault was helping teacher pack up the left-over snacks. They were talking quietly so she decided to go outside to look for mother. She saw mother before she made it out of the gate and she ran to her mother as fast as she could. Serillia gave her mother a hug and began to tell her of her day as they walked home. She remembered to ask mother about her day as well. "Did you thank the nice man for helping you?" Her mother blushed and nodded.

Serillia smiled as the wind rustled the leaves of the trees. She whispered, "Thank you."

The Mushroom War

Chapter 1

In Search of Spores

Unathor Rockwood stared down at the axe haft that he had been polishing for the last two hours. The wood gleamed in the morning light shining through the open window. There was little left to do except to apply the family's secret formula to the wood. Once the spores were rubbed in and allowed to set, the handle would be as hard as stone. It would turn any blade without chipping or shattering. This was his family's legacy and the reason no Forge Master used any other wood when crafting magical hammers or axes.

But sometimes their reputation was more trouble that it was worth. This particular haft was one of those times. It had been commissioned by Forge Master Grundror. Grundror had just finished forging his most sensational achievement of all time, or so he liked to tell anyone who would listen.

The problem was that Grundror was an absolute idiot, even if he was the greatest dwarven smith living in Deephole. All of Deephole was in awe of the Forge Master's latest creation. Grundror had forged a flaming axe head for a dwarven battle axe. Some human had bragged that his flaming sword was the ultimate weapon for slaying trolls. Grundror had decided to prove the human wrong.

Unathor was firmly convinced that any dwarf willing to use the durn thing was an even bigger fool than the smith was. It was a surefire way to become a beardless dwarf in the first few moments of battle. Unathor chuckled at his own humor. He thought his jokes were funny even if no one else did.

Now the Forge Master needed a Rockwood haft that could resist the flames of his ridiculous new toy. Unathor's wife had charged the smith dearly in the contract. But now Unathor had to deal with the Forge Master and his ego. Bah. No amount of coin could compensate him for spending even ten minutes listening to the pompous smith.

It was bad enough that he had to prove the flames would not harm the haft. But the vain arse wanted the wood to have a reddish hue that would complement the color of the flames. The axe was not a dance partner in a fancy gown, it was fer taking heads. Unathor grumbled as he sat down to consider his options.

The Rockwood family had discovered the secret to hardening wood several generations back. The process had allowed them to found the successful town of Rockwood just outside Deephole. The town provided ready access to the oak and hickory that were necessary to their work. The trees thrived here in the low mountains and so did the Rockwood family. The only challenging part of the business was retrieving the spores without anyone discovering how the process worked.

The spores came from a rare fungus that grew on the crowns of the Great Gliomastix mushrooms. The mushrooms could be found in many places in the darkness of the deep caverns below the mountains. But the fungus that produced the critical spores had only been found in three small caverns well to the north of Deephole. The family made three trips a year to the caverns to scrape the fungus from the tall mushrooms. They always came back with a load of their "special" coal to hide the real secret. Many a dwarf was still researching the properties of the coal the Rockwoods simply burned to stay warm through the winter.

The fungus and its spores actually grew in a range of color from yellow to orange to a deep red. So, it was technically possible to rub in spores that would provide the color Grundror desired. The problem was to find the right color without killing the fungus and the spores.

The fungus and the spores that they harvested were bred by the darkness below the mountains. Exposure to light would kill both the precious fungus and spores. Even starlight would cause them both to turn to dust.

The family harvested the spores in the total darkness of the caverns. The spores were even stored in sealed containers in the cellars below their homes. Once exposed to light, the entire process had to be completed within an hour. The container would be opened in a dimly lit room. The spores would be rubbed in carefully to ensure that the entire haft was treated evenly. Then a heavy polishing cloth would be used to work the spores in and warm the wood. If done well, the friction would warm the wood enough to open its pores and allow the spores to sink deep into the wood. It was the perfect combination of art and hard work.

The rub of it, Unathor chuckled again, was that you never knew what color you had until the container was opened for use. The red spores were rare and he had already ruined half of their on-hand supply searching for some. If he was going to meet the terms of his contract, he was going to have to go and find some of the red spores in the caverns himself. The problem was how to do it without destroying all of the fungus within the cavern. It also meant treating the wood in the cavern. And there was the added problem that the light would reveal his presence to every hungry predator near the caverns.

Unathor went to his worktable and pulled out a bag where he kept a single silver coin that had been enchanted with continual light. He opened the pouch and dropped the coin on the worktable. He stared at it wondering how he could control the light. The bright light began to bother his eyes, so he pulled a shield off the wall and lay it over the coin. He paused as an idea came to him. He picked up the shield and turned it over. He stared at the leather straps and reached across the table for a small blade he used to shave imperfections from the wood. He carefully cut at the stiches along one side of the strap. As they came apart, he separated a small section of the folded leather and slid the coin inside. Only a thin edge of the coin stuck out. It was enough light to see with. If he held the shield close to his body, the glow would not spread very far in the cavern. Unathor smiled. He had a plan. It was not a great plan but it would have to do.

Unathor was actually looking forward to the trek through the tunnels. It has been quite some time since his wife had let him travel through them. Too old! He would show her. She was going to give him hell for doing this but it would be even worse if he did not let her know where he had gone. Seeing no another option, Unathor wrote out a note for his wife. She would find it when she came to get him for supper. The good news was that he would be well on his way before she learned where he had gone. As an added bonus, he would miss that boring dinner meeting with the town council tonight. Things were looking up. And when he got back, he could watch her beautiful beard twitch as she expressed her concern for him.

Unathor put the coin back into its bag and placed it in his belt pouch. He found a old backpack and threw in enough hard biscuit and jerky to last several days. He found a waterskin and filled it as well. He tied the shield to the backpack and then he wrapped the haft and several polishing rags in oilskin and tied them to the pack as well. Once it was all packed, he moved to the stand that held his armor. It still fit well, but the process of putting it on was getting harder as the years went by. He eventually got it all on and the straps tightened.

He slid the backpack on and turned to take his weapons from the wall. First came his beloved war hammer. It had a beautiful concave head that would crack the hardest skull. The back side of the head was a curved spike that could be used to rip a shield from an opponent's hand. His favorite part was the spike on the bottom of the haft that could be driven through an enemy's foot. It was a beautiful sight. He slipped it into the holster on the right side of his belt.

Next came his axe. It only had a single blade. It was hard to use a double-bladed axe with the hammer. But it was sharp and he knew from experience that he could cleave straight through a giant's leg with it. He clipped it into the harness on his chest. Now he was truly ready for a relaxing walk through the tunnels.

As Unathor headed for the door, he paused to look around one more time. He noticed the steel helm hanging on a peg by the door. He grabbed it and popped it on his head. Now his wife could not say he was being completely irresponsible. He locked the workshop behind him and headed for the nearest entrance to Deephole. He had a long hike ahead of him. If he was lucky, he would run into trouble on the way. Something he could vent his frustrations on would be nice. One could only hope.

Finder moved silently through the dark tunnels away from the caverns controlled by the Tribe. He could feel the tension seeping out of his body as he moved deeper beneath the mountain that was their home. It would be good to get away. Too many things had changed recently and change was hard for him. He liked things to be predictable. Now the ogres had a new Chief and that was one of the most dangerous changes, for the Tribe must survive.

At least this time the change was a good one. Brawl had not been a good Chief. His brudder Hunter would be much better for the Tribe. But any time there was a new Chief, the other male ogres would be more aggressive until they were sure the new Chief was strong enough.

Finder climbed down a chimney passage and turned towards the south. His mate had asked him to retrieve more of the mushroom that she used to treat the hot sickness in their people. The mushroom that she needed was well to the southwest. The caverns where they grew were close to the region that the fuzzfaces collected rocks in. Normally, Hunter would have come with him in case they ran into the hairy monsters. But Hunter was busy with being Chief. His brudder also had to protect the human female that he had claimed as a prize in their recent battle outside. Finder did not understand why Hunter was so interested in the small thing. Brawl broke it so it seemed to be of little use.

So, instead of hunting food while they traveled to find the mushrooms, Finder did his best to stay out of sight and out of trouble. He heard something scurrying his way up the passage and went to ground behind a rock outcrop. It turned out to be a pair of cave rats about the size of a small ogre child. They would have been good eating, but Finder did not want the sound of battle or the smell of blood to attract larger predators. He watched them pass and moved on. It would take

most of this awake time to get to the caverns he wanted. He picked up
his pace. The darkness was his friend.

———————————

Unathor entered the tunnel where the first and smallest of the caverns
lay. This tunnel ran a long distance to the north. The old dwarf stood
in silence listening. He could hear nothing. The long hairs of his beard
detected no movement of the air that might betray a foe in the tunnel.
Unathor took the shield from his back and slid his left arm through the
straps. The fingers of his right hand slid into the pouch on his belt and
found the coin in its small bag.

Unathor closed his eyes and pulled the coin out exposing the tunnel
to the bright light of dwarven magic. He slowly opened his eyes to
study the way ahead. There was nothing but rock and lichen as far as
he could see. He slid the coin into the strap and the light dimmed as
the coin was covered by leather. He pulled the shield against his body
and began to creep forward. He felt exposed by the glow of the coin on
his chest and stomach. Worse, he could see less in the dim light than
he could normally see in the absolute dark of the tunnels. He moved
carefully ahead the quarter mile to the crack in the rock that marked
the entrance to the mushroom cavern.

He entered the small cavern slowly. He paused again to listen for any
predators that might be waiting within. Unathor knew this cavern was
roughly oval in shape. It was about forty feet to the back wall and
maybe half that across. He turned right and stayed close to the wall as
he began to make a circuit around the cavern.

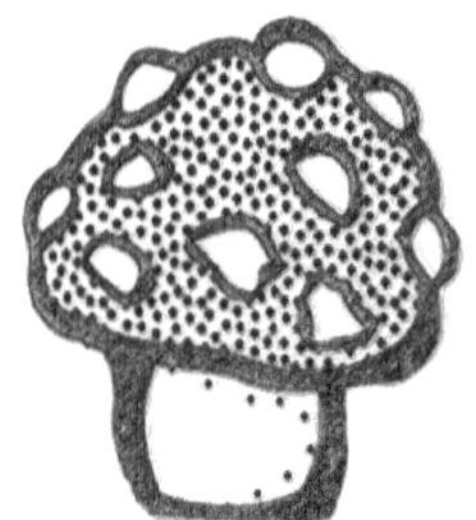

He kept the shield turned towards the outer wall
allowing only a small amount of light to pass
across the crown of each mushroom. Yellow,
Yellow, Yellow, Orange. And so it continued.
Unathor cringed as he passed the tenth mushroom
without finding what he sought. So much of the
precious fungus destroyed to satisfy the vanity of
on idiot smith. On the fourteenth mushroom, he spotted a brilliant red
color growing on the crown of the mushroom.

Unathor quickly propped the shield against the wall allowing only a small circle of light to spread from the coin. He sat on the ground and unrolled the oilskin. He pulled the haft out and lay it across his legs. He reached his bare hand up to the crown of the mushroom and scooped up a handful of the fungus growing there. He began to rub it into the wood with strong knowing fingers. He continued to scoop and rub for almost fifteen minutes, rotating the haft and examining his work in the small circle of light.

When he was satisfied that the haft had a thorough and even coat of the spores, he pushed the shield flat to the floor of the cavern and picked up the first of his polishing cloths. He did not need to see for the rest of the process. Unathor's fingers and hands knew it from years of practice. He began to rub the length of the haft in strong, quick strokes. His hands squeezed the haft as they moved back and forth, increasing the friction of each stroke. He felt the wood warming in his hand. About halfway through the process, he switched to a softer cloth and continued stroking the wood. By the time the hour was done, the wood was hot in his hands.

Unathor placed the wood and the cloths on the oilskin beside him. He reached below the shield to take the coin in his hand. He quickly slid it back into its bag and placed the bag back into his belt pouch. Then he sat and just relaxed knowing that he could soon put Grundror out of his mind. He would take no more contracts from that one.

Unathor stood and began to roll the oilskin around the completed haft and soon had it strapped to his back. He stood and adjusted the backpack so it rested comfortably on his shoulders. He was about to reach for the shield when he heard the soft scuffing of bare feet near the entrance to the cavern. As he watched, a large form came through the dwarf-sized opening and then stood up. Its head almost reached the roof ten feet above the floor of the cavern. He knew immediately that it was an ogre. By the beards of all the dwarven gods, he prayed, may there only be a few of them. One was bad enough. He reached for his hammer as he began to move forward. His boot hit a loose rock, sending it bouncing across the floor. His monstrous foe turned to face the sound.

A harsh whisper filled the cavern. "Fuzzface. Bery bad. Bery, bery bad." Unathor charged forward with a grin on his face. This just might be the fun he had hoped for when leaving his workshop. Hammer in one hand, he pulled the axe from its strap across his chest. But before he could strike, the large figure lunged forward and Unathor felt a spear slam into his breastplate. The rock tip shattered on good dwarven steel. But the shaft of the spear was fashioned from a good hardwood and it hammered into his chest. Unathor flew backward to land on his back.

He heard the ogre whisper, "Uh oh" as it noticed the damage to its weapon. He gave it credit though; the beast came in swinging the shaft like a staff. Unathor rolled to the side as the staff came down hard where he had fallen. He brought his hammer down hard and caught the outside of the ogre's left foot. He felt the powerful blow crush both the flesh and bone of the foot. The ogre grunted in pain.

Unathor spun to the side as he came to his feet thinking to avoid the next blow. Instead, he felt a mighty crack on the back of his head as the shaft slammed into his helm. The helm flew off into the darkness. Unathor staggered, but continued his spin to face the large foe.

The ogre stepped forward again, but it stumbled when its weight came down on its injured foot. Unathor ducked low and brought his axe down on the ogre's right foot. It hit about an inch behind the toes and the blade bounced back hard as the axe went through the foot to strike the rock below it. The ogre screamed in pain. It turned and hobbled back to the entrance and disappeared into the tunnels.

He watched curiously at its strange cadence. He guessed that walking or running with only three toes was probably difficult. He started to laugh, but it came out as a grunt of pain. His head hurt too much to laugh right now. It was time to head home. Unathor moved slowly to the entrance and looked through. He could see the heat from the ogre's tracks turning right and heading north. Good enough. His path lay to the south.

He started to chuckle again, but changed his mind. He would save the humor for when his head hurt a bit less. Unathor turned south and headed back toward Deephole. He was looking forward to a night

in his own bed even if it meant listening to his wife tell him what a
stubborn old fool he was.

<hr>

Finder moved as quickly as he could back towards the tunnels of the
Tribe. Every step was agony but he knew he would die if he stopped
now. He realized that he was leaving a trail back towards his people
and that just would not do. When he reached the edges of ogre
territory, he found a narrow crevice and worked his way inside. He
would have to hope that someone would find him before it was too late.

Chapter 2

Finding a Cure

Alauriel looked down at her notes in frustration. Three more ogre females were now sick with fever and she was fairly certain the young ogress she had just seen was coming down with the same sickness. She had no idea what was causing them to get sick or why it was only the females. But they were not getting better. She was fairly certain that Mielikki's magic would cure the disease, but none of the Tribe's females would consider letting her use "Bad Magic" on them. And there was no way Hunter would order them to allow it.

She had to find another answer. The females had tried their normal remedy for fever, but the mixture made with the spores of mushrooms was not helping. That was the part that had Alauriel confused. Alauriel was fairly certain the mixture they used was similar to a powder that the Temple used to treat wounds that had gone bad. The mixture should work.

Alauriel moved slowly to the ledge where she did most of her work and sat down on the padded rock. She leaned her crutch against the wall. There were two covered bowls sitting on the ledge along with one of her ink bottles that had been cleaned and filled with fresh water. Maker's wife had brought the two covered bowls filled with samples of the mushroom powder that the females mixed with water to make their cure-all.

She slowly uncovered the first sample and examined it. It was a dried powder with an orangish coloring. It was not ground very well, but it seemed usable. She reached in and took a large pinch of the powder and dropped it into the ink bottle. She swirled it around and watched as it eventually dissolved. The bottle grew cold to the touch as the powder dissolved.

She set the bottle down and brought her fingers to her tongue. The bitter taste was as she remembered from when she had been injured in the ogre ambush. It was also similar to what she remembered from the temple. It all seemed to match her memory except for the color. She reached for the elusive memory but could not capture it.

She stared down into the powder and ran her fingers through it. She crushed a few of the larger lumps. She lifted one and noticed that it was beginning to turn from orange to a burnt almost brown color. As she watched, more of the sample began to change. She examined the large lump and it seemed almost dead. She squeezed it and it crumbled to a dust instead of powder. The change seemed to gain speed and within moments, the entire sample was useless. She looked back to the clear ink bottle, but that seemed unchanged. It was still the same orangish color of the original sample.

Alauriel sat lost in thought. Maker's mate never seemed to have a problem with the powder. Why did it break down now? She did not believe the problem was with the powder. But what could be different here in her chamber? She stared around the room and her eyes finally went to the coin sitting on the small ledge high on the wall across her chamber. The continual light spell she had placed on it lit the entire chamber except when it was covered at night. Her chamber was the only one in the Ogre Caverns that had light.

Alauriel rose slowly and took her crutch. She moved slowly to the small ledge and reached carefully up for the coin. She took it and moved back to her seat. She placed the coin on the ledge beside the bowls. She dumped the ruined powder on the edge of her ledge and placed the empty bowl upside down over the coin. The room went dark. Alauriel dumped some of the powder from the covered bow in a pile on her ledge and then recovered the bowl.

Then she lifted the upside-down bowl and allowed light to return to the room. The second sample was a yellowish color. She tasted it and discovered that it was a little less bitter than the orange sample had been. She spread the yellow powder out and watched it. It began to turn brown even faster than the first sample had. It soon deteriorated. She repeated the process several times with similar results. The powder could not survive in light unless it was thoroughly mixed in water.

She knew this was an important detail, but it did not explain why the powder did not cure the fever. She sat again thinking about what she knew. The powder that they had developed at the Temple was not susceptible to light, but it grew in the dim recesses of the forest, not underground. It was constantly exposed to light. Then the image of the mushrooms flashed through her mind. The bright reddish color that normally indicated poison. But on these mushrooms, it meant life for her patients.

She also remembered that the powder that the Temple crafted was even more bitter than the orange mixture. Alauriel wondered if the reddish color grew in the darkness under the mountain. She tasted the mixture from the ink bottle again. Then she opened what was left of the powder. She tasted that as well. It was definitely weaker. The color had to be the answer.

Maker's mate had told her that both samples came from the same cavern. It was a cavern that Three Toes had discovered back when he had been known as Finder. If they could collect some red spores and mix them in water, she believed she could cure the females.

Alauriel sat quietly until her son came home several hours later. "Hullo Mama. Me break nut fer squirrel. Dem eats lots. Bery happy."

Alauriel smiled at the small ogre boy. He was so big by human standards, but her son would never reach the full size of an ogre male. "I am glad your friends are happy, Shorty. But I need your help, my son. Please go get your uncle. Tell him that I need his help."

The boy smiled up at her. "Yes Mama." Then he shot from the room at a run.

Alauriel sat quietly and waited. She knew it would take Three Toes some time to make his way down from his own room to hers. He was doing much better, but would never move with the grace and speed he had before he lost parts of both feet. She felt bad that she no longer had access to the spells that would fully restore his feet. After a time, her son shot back into the room to stand by her side. There was a cough from the darkness outside the chamber.

Alauriel smiled at the politeness of announcing himself when there was no door. "Come inside, my friend. I need your help." Her mate's brother shuffled into the room. He was missing the front half of one foot and the two smaller toes from the other. He came and sat on the ground by her seat and waited.

She looked at him and smiled. "I need your help, old friend, to cure the females who are sick."

He looked at her with concern. "No uses bad magics?"

She shook her head. "No, I want to use the powder that the females use. Do you remember where it comes from?"

He nodded his head. "It no work. Tries it afore."

Alauriel picked up the ink bottle with the orange tinted water. "It does not work because it is the wrong color. It is not strong enough. I need powder that is red. Can you find some for me wherever you get the mushrooms?"

The old ogre looked confused. Alauriel turned and dug in her trunk. She pulled out an old fragment of a torn shirt. It was a bright red. She turned back. "This is the color red. I need the powder to be this color. Can you find some?"

Three Toes shook his head. "No ken do dat."

Alauriel looked puzzled. "Why, my friend? It is very important."

Shorty reached out and touched her arm. "Tunnels dark, Mama. No sees color. Only sees hot an cold. More hots den more ken sees. No bees color in dark place."

Alauriel sat back and thought. She reached out to touch the coin on her ledge. "If I gave you light, could you find it Three Toes?"

Three Toes stared at the light. "Maybeso ken find. Me no touches light. No touches magic."

Shorty touched her arm again. "Me ken helps, Mama. Me carry light."

Alauriel started to protest but Three Toes interrupted her. "Boy ken helps. Me protect. Hides light till gets dere. No let udders sees us dat way. Hopes no fuzzface be dere when go."

Alauriel sighed. She did not want to send her son. But she did not have another option. "How long will you be gone? "

Three Toes tapped his leg for a moment. "Two sleep. Maybeso one mo. Den bees back."

Alauriel knew this was the only way to save the sick femailes. No one else in the tribe would risk using the light or could be trusted to bring her son back safely. She turned back to her trunk and dug out her old waterskin and a small belt pouch. She turned back and looked at Shorty. "Do you have a nut left from feeding your friends?" Shorty placed an acorn on the ledge before her. She gave him the waterskin and sent him to rinse it out and fill it. While she was gone, she cast continual light on the acorn he had given her.

When he returned, she explained things to them both. "When you get to the place with the mushrooms, take out the light and the cloth. Find something as close to this color as you can. Put as much of the red dust as you can into the waterskin. You must do it quickly. Do you understand?" They both nodded and she wrapped the glowing nut in the old red rag and placed both in the pouch. She handed it to Shorty. Then she hugged him and made him promise to stay close to Three Toes and be safe.

As they got ready to leave, Three Toes pointed to several throwing rocks sitting by Shorty's sleeping mat. "Brings. Dark no bees safe all time." Shorty stuck them in the pouch and the two headed out into the tunnels.

There was a brief stop at Three Toes cavern so he could collect his spear and some food supplies. Then the two headed down into the deep tunnels. Three Toes hesitated at the bottom of the first ramp. It had been many years since he had traveled this way as Finder. The path was still clear in his mind, so he led the way, although he traveled much slower than he had years before.

Chapter 3

Captured

Unathor was not a happy dwarf. Getting old was bad enough, but losing his beloved wife was just too much. She had lived a long and, he hoped, happy life. She had passed in her sleep. He had slept there beside her without even realizing that she was gone. That made him angry. He was not sure if he was angry with himself for sleeping through it or angry with her for leaving him alone.

They had placed her in the family crypt that morning. He had returned home that afternoon to a dark and quiet house. He would have welcomed her telling him what an old fool he was over the silence. He had no intention of staying here tonight or sleeping in their bed. It would be too much.

He wandered down to his workshop. There were no projects to complete and nothing to distract him from his memories. He sat staring at the workbench. His eyes focused on the hammer and axe hanging over the bench. With a curse, he got up and stalked over to his armor. He began to put it on. It took a long time to get it all on, but he eventually tightened the last of the straps.

He took both his weapons down and put them in place before he stomped out the door. There was no one to criticize him for taking a long stroll in the darkness. He would find something to vent his anger on. It would not bring her back, but it would definitely make him feel better to beat on something.

Unathor marched through Deephole, ignoring the stares of the many dwarves that knew him. He did not want to hear how sorry they were. Their sorrow was nothing compared to his. He reached the lower levels and turned north. Maybe he could hunt near where the family kept their secret. It was as good a direction as any.

Several days later he was still wandering the tunnels looking for a fight. He had passed the mushroom caverns and figured he was approaching the area controlled by that pesky tribe of ogres. Maybe one of them would fight with him. He passed a ramp down that he had never traveled and continued north. He heard a soft click and felt something sharp hit the back of his neck. Things grew fuzzy and then everything went dark.

Three Toes and his nephew made steady progress through the darkness. They did not meet any trouble along the way to the cavern with the mushrooms. They entered it carefully, but this time it was empty except for the mushrooms.

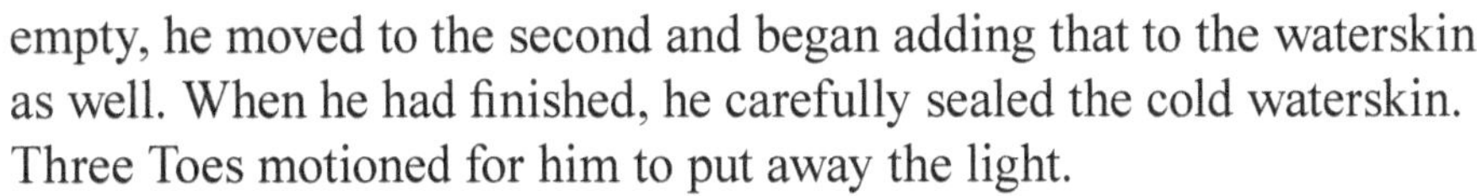

Shorty pulled out the acorn and cloth. He unwrapped the nut and the cavern became fully visible. Many of the mushrooms were as tall as the boy, but he was able to see the colors clearly. There were two mushrooms the color of the cloth that Mama had given him. He moved to the closest one and began scooping the red powder up and putting it into the waterskin. When the first mushroom was empty, he moved to the second and began adding that to the waterskin as well. When he had finished, he carefully sealed the cold waterskin. Three Toes motioned for him to put away the light.

With their mission complete, they headed back into the darkness. Neither noticed that the colors had begun to fade on top of all of the mushrooms in the cavern. They turned back in the direction of the

Ogre Caverns. They passed a ramp heading deeper into the darkness. Three Toes pointed at it. "Neber goes dere. Bad tings lib down dere."

As they continued to retrace their steps, there were several twangs. Both felt something pierce their thick skin. Three Toes crumpled to the tunnel floor and the boy crouched beside him.

—————————————

Unathor woke slowly. His thoughts were muddled and the only thing he was sure of was that his head hurt. The only time he remembered it hurting this much was when that ogre had tried to play stick ball with it. He remembered moving through the tunnels hoping for a fight. Apparently, the fight had not gone very well. The old dwarf rolled to his side in an effort to sit up.

He pressed his hands to the floor to sit up and felt an iron bar across the ground. He shifted his hands and felt a second bar about six inches away. He shoved himself up and smacked the back of his head against another iron bar. This was not good. It took a moment after banging his head for his eyes to focus again. He was in a small iron cage not even big enough to sit up in.

Unathor stared around his prison, hoping to see a way out. The cavern holding his cage was fairly large. There was a faint light coming from numerous bowls scattered around the cavern. From what he could tell the bowls were filled with phosphorescent cave lichen. One side of the chamber had a shimmering curtain of magic across the only exit he could see. His side of the cavern was lined with small cages like the one he was currently in. The other side was lined with larger cages. The final side of the room had several short chains attached to spikes that had been driven into the rock.

Slavers. Unathor recognized the trap he had fallen into. He just was not sure how they had captured him. He would have remembered a battle or even nets no matter how hard they might have cracked his skull. He moved carefully to the front of the cage. There was no door. He examined the sides and top and noticed the hinges on the top rear edge of the cage. But he could not find a lock. He paused to sniff. Magic. He smelled magic. The question was, whose magic was it?

Unathor began to check his body to see what he had for resources. His weapons and backpack were gone. They had even taken his water and ale skins. Thieving bastards. All he had was his belt pouch with a few coins and some jerky in it. He lay back down and partially closed his eyes. Best to learn what he could before they knew he was awake.

Some unknown time later, the shimmering curtain over the exit faded away. A human wearing dirty leather entered the chamber followed by two Drow. The human gestured and a faintly glowing disk floated into the room with two forms on top of it. The Drow grabbed the first form and lifted it into one of the larger cages across the way. Unathor noted that it was an ogre. As they prepared to drop it into the cage, Unathor saw that the creature was missing the front half of one foot. He almost shook his head but refrained himself. It could not be the same ogre, could it? The second form was a smaller ogre. This one was taken to the chains on the back wall and an iron collar was snapped around its neck. There was a click as it locked into place. The little brute was awake but did not struggle as it was secured.

Unathor listened as his captors began to argue with each other in the common tongue.

The first Drow turned on the human. "You promised us good slaves, wizard. So far all you have led us to is a decrepit old dwarf, a crippled ogre, and an ogre child that is obviously a deformed runt. None of these are worth a tenth of what you demand for payment."

The human turned and snarled at the Drow. "Show some patience. That dwarf will know where to find his kin, and so will the ogre. When they wake up, I will get the information we need. I told you to let me deal with them. Both times you had to use those sleep darts on them. I could cancel my own magic. But now we must wait for them to wake up. You will get your slaves and I will get my coin,"

The three slavers walked out and the shimmering field returned across the exit. The disk that had held the ogres slowly faded and was gone.

Unathor continued to lay still watching to see if his captors returned. A small voice suddenly spoke from the back of the room. "Hows come makes beliebe sleepin'? Playin trick?"

Unathor raised his head and stared at the small ogre. "How did you know I was not asleep?"

The youth shrugged. "No makes noise fer sleeps. Youse bery bad dis game."

The old dwarf did his best to sit without banging his head again. "And why are you not asleep like the other ogre? Did the Drow shoot you?"

The boy held out a small dart. "Sticks me wid little ting. No hurt bery much. No bees bed time so no gonna sleeps now."

Unathor stared at the little dart. "Durn cowards. Hiding in shadows and using darts. If I had my hammer, I would show them."

The youth giggled. "Youse bery funny. Bees stuck cage. Hammer an axe udder side funny light wid Uncle tings."

Unathor stared at the young ogre in surprise. "Got a name boy?"

The boy lowered his head. "Gots. No likes. Tribe says me bees name Shorty."

The old dwarf nodded. "I cannot say I would like that name either. Tell me lad, if you did not fall asleep like your uncle, why did you not run away from the Drow?"

The boy stared at him like he was an idiot. "Mama says stay wid uncle. Uncle gos wid elf so me gos too."

Unathor's mouth opened and then he shut it. He had no idea what to say to that. He was trying to decide what question to ask next when the boy spoke again. "Hows come keeps hair on face? Posed bees top a head. Dis hows come Papa calls youse fuzzface?"

Unathor's hands moved to his beard. "This is a beard, boy. All dwarves have them. I am right proud of it." He shook a thick dwarven finger at the boy and continued. "Yer being rude boy. Do you always ask so many impertinent questions?"

Unathor jumped as a deep voice came from the cage across from him. "Him bees askin too muches question all times. Neber bees hush."

The old dwarf looked over to see the large ogre crouched in his much bigger cage. He watched as the creature stuck its nose through the bars and sniffed, once and then again. Its deep voice sounded angry. "Knows youse. Smells afore. Youse takes foot. Breaks udder foot. Makes Finder no more. Now bees Three Toes. No ken helps Tribe no more. Ifn me gets out, me breaks youse."

Unathor began to get riled up as well. "You attacked me ya durn fool ogre! You were in our mushroom cavern. You should have stayed in your own damn tunnels where you belong. You come over here ogre and you will lose more than some toes."

They both paused as a small voice came from the back wall. "Big peoples no bery smart."

The sound of "Shut up, boy!" and "Shuts up!" came in near unison.

The threesome sat in near silence for several hours. The silence was only broken by the occasional threat and the sound of the young boy humming to himself as he tried to build something with small rocks on the cavern floor.

Three Toe noticed a small rock near the back of his cage and picked it up. He leaned out and threw it at the dwarf across the cavern. It was a good throw but the rock was deflected by one of the bars of the dwarf's cage. Unathor picked it up and reached his arm through the bars to throw it back. But the shortness of the cage did not allow him to extend his arm. The rock fell short of the ogre's cage and the two began to argue and threaten each other once more.

The boy finally grew tired of it and stood up. "Big peoples bery, bery no smart." The two adults stopped their arguing and glared at him. The boy continued. "All bees stuck. Maybeso helps each udder den gets way. Den gos home ta Mama."

The boy watched as they both shook their heads and glared at each other. He sighed and looked at his uncle. "Me gos by self den. Tells Mama youse bees bad. Me bees good. Home safe fer Mama wid smelly water."

Three Toes went silent but Unathor could not help himself. "And how do you intend to do that boy? Looks to me like you have a collar and chain around your neck. You are not going anywhere."

The boy ignored him and reached his hand up to the heavy iron collar around his neck. He took a firm grip on each side of his neck. His arms began to strain as he pulled at the collar. He paused and got a better grip and began to pull his hands away from his neck. The metal collar began to stretch and a whining noise filled the cavern. After a few more breaths, the collar snapped and the boy dropped the pieces to the ground.

The dwarf stared at him and then whispered. "By the Dwarf Lord's silver beard, how strong is that boy?"

The older ogre replied simply, "No wants ta knows. Bees bery muches too strong."

Unathor stared at the young ogre. "Maybe we could call a truce."

The boy walked over to his cage and stared at him. "No know dat word. What bees dis truce?"

Unathor ignored him and stared at the boy's uncle across the cavern. "Work together? Fight together against our enemies?" The older ogre nodded once and they both looked to the boy.

Shorty glanced back and forth between them. "Bees friend now?" When they both hesitated, he turned towards the exit.

Unathor sighed heavily. "Yes, we will be friends. I agree."

Three Toes stared down at his feet for and then nodded. "Shorty win. Bees friend."

Shorty smiled and climbed up on the cage next to the one holding the dwarf. He reached down with both hands and grabbed the cage door. He began to pull. The bars did not give. He grabbed a little closer to the front of the cave and heaved again. The sound of straining metal came from a point where the door met the front of the cage. There was a sharp snap and the door of the cage flew up and slammed against the cavern wall. It made a loud clang.

Unathor sighed in relief as he stood up and attempted to stretch out his back and legs. Before he could begin to climb out, the shimmering curtain died and a dark elf came through the entrance with a slender longsword in his hand. His gaze took in the boy and the dwarf. He spoke in a harsh tone. "You might be worth something after all, runt. But the dwarf has outlived his usefulness. Too old to be worth anything anyway."

The Drow moved forward silently. As he neared the cage, his sword darted forward. Unathor tried to dodge but had nowhere to go in the cage. The blade slid into his right shoulder and blood coated the dwarf's breast plate. The Drow drew back his sword to strike again.

Suddenly the youth standing on the empty cage thrust his hand forward. He unclenched his fist, releasing a blinding light that shone from a small acorn still partially wrapped in a red cloth. The Drow raised its empty hand before its eyes and stumbled backwards. As it neared the large cage on the opposite side of the chamber, two large hands shot out to grab both sides of the Drow's head. The huge hands gave a sharp twist to the left. There was a snapping sound and the Drow went limp. The hands opened and the Drow fell to the floor.

Unathor's left hand went to his wounded shoulder. He stared at the caged ogre with a stunned look on his bearded face. "You saved my life. Why?"

Three Toes pointed to the boy. "Him boss. Says friend now."

Unathor just shook his head and slowly climbed from the cage with the help of the very strong youth. Together they pushed one of the smaller empty cages across to the large cage holding the boy's uncle. The youth scampered up to the top of the tall cage to the right of his uncle and began to pull at the door. The older ogre shoved up from below and this lock snapped on the first try.

The youth quickly moved out of the way. The old ogre did not even try to climb out. He simply threw his weight against the front of the cage and toppled it to the ground with a loud metallic crash. Then he crawled out and stood up.

The old dwarf cringed as the cage crashed to the ground. "That will bring the other Drow and the human mage down on us for sure. Could you have made any more noise?"

The old ogre looked around at the other cages. "Maybeso. Ken tries."

Unathor's left hand went to his beard and he tugged on it. With a look of pain, he muttered, "Never mind. Stupid question." He shook his head and carefully led the way from the chamber of cages. The next chamber over was much smaller. In it were three sleeping roles and a small pile of weapons and backpacks. Unathor picked up his hammer. But the pain in his shoulder was too much. He carefully slid the hammer into its holster and scooped up the axe in his left hand. He looked at the backpack he had carried and shook his head. There was no carrying it with his wound. There was a long spear with a stone tip and Unathor moved aside. The older ogre grabbed it. The young ogre bent to pick up a large waterskin. It had a long slit and there was a reddish stain on the ground where something had seeped into the ground.

The boy looked very sad. Unathor could not help himself. He had to ask, "What is wrong boy?"

The boy held up the skin. "Mama needs dis ta makes ogress all betters. Gone now. Mama gonna bees bery sad."

Unathor studied the stain on the ground. "What was in it?"

The boy thought for a moment. "Stuff on mushroom in dat water." He dug into his pouch and pulled out the glowing nut and the rag wrapped around it. "Mushroom bees dis color."

Unathor stared at the red cloth and shook his head. He hated that color ever since he had crafted the haft for that flaming battle axe. "We need to get out of this alive, boy, and then we will talk about your mushroom."

The old dwarf studied his two companions for a moment and then stepped towards the short tunnel into the darkness. "Put that light away and stay close. This could get very bad." As the bright light faded, the old dwarf allowed his eyes to adjust. There were no heat marks on the floor or walls so he moved forward to where the tunnel met a larger cross corridor.

As Unathor stepped into the larger tunnel, he heard whispered words from his left. He felt magic trying to enter his thoughts and control him. "Stupid mage. Dwarves and magic do not go together well." There was also a whisper of movement from the right and Unathor spun that way, bringing his axe up and across. The blade of his axe slapped aside two swords that had been heading for his chest. He began to move his axe in a figure eight pattern as he stepped towards the Drow facing him on that side.

The Drow was fast and Unathor was struggling to keep the two swords at bay. Without his hammer, he was at an extreme disadvantage. The Drow knocked his axe to the side with the short sword in his right hand. Before he could bring the one in his left hand forward, a fist-sized rock caught the Drow in the cheek. The rock hit hard and the Drow stumbled. Before it could recover, Unathor's axe was buried in the side of his neck.

There was a loud grunt from behind him and the dwarf spun to defend himself. He was surprised to see the mage standing there holding a wand. A spear was sunk deep in his belly. The mage shook his head. He whispered from blood flecked lips, "Dwarves and ogres helping each other? Did not see that coming." The mage slid to the ground. The wand fell from his fingers.

Unathor watched the old ogre pull his spear from the mage and wipe the tip clean on the mage's pants. He glanced at the boy and saw him standing there with another rock in his hand. "Nice throw, boy." The youth grinned happily at him.

Unathor reached up and touched his right shoulder. He felt blood again. He would not make it back to Deephole without help. "Help me get home and I will get you the powder you need. Deal?"

The old ogre looked down at the boy. The boy grinned and ran back into the chamber. He returned quickly wearing Unathor's backpack. "What bees way ta go?"

The journey back to Deephole was long and, for the old dwarf, painful. When he was not answering endless questions, he kept trying to come up with a version of the story that did not make him sound like a demented old fool that needed two ogres to keep him safe in the tunnels. In the end, he had nothing. They met the first scouting party about half a day from the gates of Deephole. The guards would not allow the ogres to get any closer. So Unathor wrote out a note and sent it with a runner back to his youngest son.

The cleric in the patrol healed his shoulder which helped almost as much as the food supplies. The two ogres had eaten everything he had packed in the first hour of their journey. Unathor told the patrol leader about the slaving party and where to find them. The patrol was now three more dwarves short as they were sent to recover the remains and any magic items that might be there.

Unathor spent the next two days making sure that there was no problem between the ogres and the remaining members of the patrol. Unfortunately, the boy kept asking his infernal questions. They gave the old dwarf a headache. Why could the boy not understand that things just were what they were?

Chapter 4

Parting Gifts

Unathor woke to a gentle hand on his arm. He looked up to see concern on his youngest son's bearded face. "It is all right boy. I am fine now. The cleric took care of my wound."

His son squatted beside him. "Father, you stumble back almost bled out in the company of two ogres and ordered the guard not to hurt them. That seems far from all right. In fact, there are many that question your mental state right now."

The old dwarf sighed. "Maybe I was in a bad place when I left. I was a bit angry after your mother passed. But it is done. I found my way back from that place with a little help. That crazy ogre boy was a good distraction from my hurt. I will be fine now."

His son stared into his eyes. "What is fine Father? Does it mean there will be no more crazy solo adventures?"

Unathor chuckled. "I think no more adventures at all. They hurt too damn much at my age. Did you bring everything that I asked for?"

His son pointed to a small pile of equipment. A long spear with a heavy steel head, a sealed container, and a small rubber ball lay on the ground behind him. Unathor walked over to the pile and sat down beside the spear. He pulled an etching tool from his belt and began to scribe a small forge and a bearded face onto the spear head.

His son watched his work. "Are you sure Father? Naming an ogre as Dwarf Friend is a bit unusual to say the least."

Unathor grunted. "I will tell you when we are alone. Both stories. But this one was a better friend than most."

The old dwarf stood and picked up the spear. He gestured to his son to bring the other pieces. He walked over to the old ogre and handed him the spear. "This is one of the finest spears I have ever made. The wood will not break. The head is dwarven steel. It will not replace your foot, but it will serve you well." The dwarf pointed to the pictures he had etched on the spear head. "These name you a friend to the dwarves. No dwarf will harm you if you show them this. It is my promise."

Three Toes took the spear. "Muches tanks fer dis. I member we bees friend."

Unathor took the sealed container from his son and tucked it in the backpack the boy still wore. "This is for your Mama. Tell her not to open it in the light. I hope it helps your people get better."

The boy looked at him solemnly. "Tribe says muches tanks fer mushroom." Then he turned and the two ogres began to walk back into the darkness of the tunnels.

Unathor raised his voice. "Wait, boy!" Unathor took the ball from his son and held it before the boy's eyes. "This is for you. You have a great gift, boy. You can see what really needs doing. The right thing. And then you try and do it even when it is hard. That is rare. You need to remember to just be a boy sometimes though. Have fun and just play. Sometimes big people need to figure things out on their own. This is called a ball. My people trade for them from a place far away. Our children play with them. They are special. They bounce." He dropped the ball and it bounced off the ground and came back to his hand. He placed it in the boy's hand.

The youth stared down at the ball and whispered "Magics. Tanks bery muches." He turned with a happy smile and ran to catch up to his uncle who was moving slowly down the tunnel.

The old dwarf smiled as he watched the youth go. His time for exploring and anger was done, but there were other worthwhile things to do in his dotage. His youngest son had a boy that was struggling to find his place in the family. Like him, the boy loved to explore and get into trouble. Maybe it was time to put what years he had left into something worthwhile, like his grandson.

Unathor turned and clapped his son on the shoulder. "Close yer mouth, boy. I will explain it to you some day. Now tell me what trouble your boy has been in lately. I think it is time that he and I became friends."

A Light Shines in the Darkness

Chapter 1

The Blood Rite

Roiland of House DesNurien stood with the wall of the Temple of Strife at his back. This was his first time within the Temple. The sacred Temple was not for lowly males like him. It was reserved for Priestesses and Matron Mothers. But on the night of the Blood Rite, even the most insignificant Drow was welcomed by the Mistress of Pain. Those that survived the Rite would be considered adults. Survival was far from a guarantee though for they were Drow and no one was safe in their world of treachery.

Roiland carefully examined the chamber where he stood. He did not feel like he belonged here. This was the heart of his City and it was filled with corruption. Being here made him uneasy.

The Temple walls were of polished stone that gleamed in the torchlight. They were partially draped in blood red silk that shimmered in the light of the torches. The silk was arranged so that blood appeared to be running down the walls. Across the ceiling were stalactites of various sizes. Each had been carved into the shape of a dagger hanging blade down. There were no seats or even an altar within the Temple. In place of the altar, chains ending in manacles hung from the ceiling. Attached to the wall behind the manacles were three metal plates in the form of large spiders.

Roiland turned his attention to the other occupants of the Temple. He watched and evaluated each of his fellow candidates. He had no illusions of safety this night, but he was determined not to be one of the sacrifices in the coming celebration. Roiland intended to survive the Blood Rite despite the fact that every other candidate considered him to be weak and insignificant. To each of them, he was little better than the humans that they intended to slaughter this night.

Roiland understood the risks he faced in the Rite. He was a lowly male from a very minor House in a small city state on the fringes of the Dark Elf Empire. His House had no powerful allies. The House survived only because eliminating it would bring no real honor to the victor. Those were handicaps enough, but it did not end there. Roiland excelled at neither magic nor the sword. His Matron Mother frequently reminded him he was hardly worth the food he consumed. To her, he was expendable.

If the Blood Rite was not required of all Drow, he would not even be here. His eldest sister had made it clear that she did not expect him to survive the Rite. She assured him that one of the more powerful candidates would bathe in his blood before the Rite was over. His sister had seemed almost excited by the prospect of his demise. Roiland knew his sister had a point. His fellow candidates saw him as either a path to gain prestige or simply as a welcome opportunity to practice betrayal during the Rite.

Roiland had other plans. He fully intended to complete the Rite and he would do it alone. It would be harder for the others to turn on him if he stayed apart. And if they did come for him, he would not go down easily. Roiland's fingers caressed the darts on one side of his belt. He had replaced the normal tips that held the Drow sleep poison with tips forged of the finest steel. If they tried to kill him, they would learn that he was not as defenseless as they believed.

Roiland wished there was some way to avoid the Rite. Unlike the other candidates, he was not looking forward to the senseless slaughter that enflamed the passions of his kind and drove them to the heights of ecstasy. What honor was there in terrorizing innocents? Where was the glory in killing unarmed humans or their children? It seemed such a waste. Bathing in their blood did not excite him. The coming Rite was something to be survived. It was a duty and nothing more.

And when the Rite was over, Roiland would still be insignificant and powerless to choose his own destiny. Most likely, he would be shuffled off into a combat team in the city guard. His life would be spent defending a city that saw no value in his existence. His Matron Mother would not bring him home unless he gained unexpected fame. So be it. Watching for betrayal among strangers hurt less than waiting for it to come from his own family.

Roiland had always hoped for more. He had no idea what that more was though. He was a Drow and this was their way of life. Competition for respect within his House was as fierce as it was between the Houses. He had as little value in his own home as House DesNurien did within the City. His family did not consider him remarkable in any way. He was a seventh child and one without a skill useful to the House.

Roiland had three older sisters that were studying at the Temple to become Priestesses. He had another sister and a brother who were apprenticed to powerful mages. His oldest brother was a master swordsman. The only thing Roiland excelled at was his skill with the hand crossbow. There were none within the City that could match his uncanny accuracy. Sadly, it was a skill that few Drow took seriously.

The tension in the room began to rise as a figure dressed in silk the color of the wall hangings entered the room. The presence of the High Priestess began a stir of activity in the Temple. There were six other males and three females who would join him in the Rite. Two of the females were to become Priestess of the Spider Queen. The third looked to be a mage. Of the males, there appeared to be one mage and five warriors like him. All of them came from powerful houses or had alliances they could call upon. He saw no one he could align himself with or who he could trust to watch his back. He would have to be very careful.

The Blood Rite was the Drow coming-of-age celebration. As ceremonies went, it was fairly simple. The High Priestess would open a portal to a random location somewhere up on the surface. The portal always opened near a human settlement. The young Drow would swarm the settlement to slaughter as many of the residents as possible. With each kill, the Drow would bathe in the blood of their victims. They were to return to the portal before the world above was visited by the orb of fire. Roiland assumed that the only reason that the humans still existed was that Drow bred so slowly. The last Blood Rite for his City had been over fifty years ago.

As Roiland watched, the other candidates began to form into teams. Two groups of three and one of two. Besides himself, only a single Priestess remained without someone to watch her back. Roiland grimaced. Arigans of House Salucifer turned and strode towards him. Roiland understood why none of the others had included her on their team. Her powerful magic was offset by her temper and her reputation for betrayal. She was not one to be trusted and, apparently, she had chosen to ruin his day.

Roiland dropped his eyes respectfully as the Salucifer Priestess stepped before him. Her fingers began to move as she signed, "You will serve me during the Rite. You have been honored."

Roiland nodded. With one hand, he replied, "As you command Priestess. I shall serve."

The vain young Drow studied him. He did not allow the distaste he felt for her to show on his features. Arigans finally smiled and turned to face the front of the Temple. Roiland could only curse his luck. This was a no-win situation. If she decided to kill him, he was in trouble. As long as she did not surprise him, Roiland thought he had a reasonable chance of killing her. But if she did not return from the Rite, her House would make sure he died soon after the Rite ended.

Roiland's musings were interrupted by the sound of a hammer striking the first of three spider-shaped plates at the front of the Temple. A deep tone reverberated through the Temple of Strife. The hammer struck the second spider and a deeper tone began to echo as well. The two tones did not harmonize, nor were they meant to. The vibrations of the two spiders felt like an assault on his senses. Roiland tensed as the hammer struck the third spider. The addition of the third tone assaulted him on a spiritual level. It felt like something had reached inside him to reshape his essence. It was like drowning in corruption. He did not like it. Roiland fought an internal battle to protect who and what he was.

As the tones faded, Roiland took a deep breath. The other Drow in the Temple seemed to find comfort in the disharmony of the tones.

The High Priestess stepped to the center of the room. Her voice rang out as silence followed the tones of the spiders. "Candidates, prepare yourselves. The time of the Blood Rite is upon you. This night you will revel in blood and death and fear. You shall bring terror and pain to the unsuspecting and to the innocent. This is our heritage and our right. This night you shall coat yourselves in the blood of our enemies. For all who dwell upon the surface are our enemies. Let those of the surface world be reminded of our hatred of them. Show them that we can destroy them when and where we choose. Return with their blood upon you and take your place among the Drow."

The High Priestess motioned with her hand and the three plates were struck again. This time as the sound faded away, an oval of pure darkness formed in the center of the chamber. Roiland hesitated as the other three teams ran for the oval and stepped into the darkness where they disappeared from view. Arigans motioned with her mace for him to lead the way. Roiland tried not to tense as he moved swiftly forward and stepped into the portal with his short swords held before him. Roiland's senses were stripped from him. There was neither sight nor sound or even touch. For what seemed an eternity, there was only a cold emptiness. And then he was through.

Roiland emerged from the darkness of the portal into blinding light. Before he could react, his momentum took him into the back of one of the male candidates. Roiland twisted to the side. Something moving fast passed close to his face. Roiland continued to move sideways trying to see through the overwhelming light. There had to be a mistake. Their arrival was supposed to be during the time of darkness when the humans would be most vulnerable.

Roiland began to blink and rub the tears from his eyes. He needed his eyes to adjust so that he could protect himself as much from his own kind as from the humans. Slowly, Roiland began to make out shapes standing before him. He moved back several paces to put more distance between him and the other candidates. They were also beginning to recover and each seemed to realize their vulnerability.

The candidates quickly separated into their teams and the groups moved apart. Each of the candidates began to assess the area around them. Roiland did his best not to recoil when Arigans moved to stand beside him. He kept one eye on her as he began to scan the area. He had no idea what to expect of this strange and very bright world.

 Roiland's eyes traveled first to the source of the light that had so disoriented them on their entry to this world. He needed to understand what danger, if any, that it posed to him. But what he saw puzzled him. It was not the ball of fire that his Matron Mother had warned him about. Suspended above them was a large orb that glowed with a pale light. It hung in a field of lesser lights that seemed to flicker as he stared at them. If this flameless orb gave off such light, what would it be like when the ball of fire became visible?

His attention was drawn to the orb. There appeared to be shapes and shadows on the surface of the glowing orb. He had no idea what the orb was, but he sensed that this was somehow important. There was strength and power here that he did not understand. As he stared at the orb, Roiland became convinced that it was observing him as well. He waited for it to speak, but there was only silence. The silence held a feeling of quiet amusement. Roiland shivered. He sensed that whoever was watching him expected something from him. Whatever he was supposed to do, it was important and he must do it very soon.

Roiland was startled when Arigans pointed off to one side. He saw that they were standing on a rise above a collection of structures. This must be the place where the humans lived. The structures were all quiet and dark. The people that they were to sacrifice this night slept, unaware that death was coming for them. Roiland noted that the two larger teams were already moving towards the human settlement.

Arigans signed for him to follow and she began to run lightly down the slope. Roiland could sense her excitement as she approached her unsuspecting prey. Roiland wished there was another path open to him. He did not want this. Again, he had a strange sensation of being watched. It felt almost as if he were being evaluated and judged.

The human settlement was strange. There were no cavern walls to enclose it. Emptiness seemed to stretch forever beyond its borders. The structures on the edge of the settlement were made of a material that he did not recognize. He only knew that it was warmer than the stone of his subterranean world. He could make out a few larger stone structures towards the center of the settlement.

The candidates ran in silence. When they reached the first structures, the teams began to separate, each heading in different directions so as to not interfere with each other. Their arrival went unnoticed by the residents of this luckless place.

Arigans led him towards the center of the settlement. She seemed focused on the larger structures made of stone. There was an eagerness to her actions that did not set well with him.

Chapter 2

Choices

Roiland could see that Arigans was getting impatient and she began to run ahead of him. Roiland followed behind her as she flashed the hand sign for speed. They soon passed the smaller, less sturdy structures and came to several that were built of stone. She pointed to one of the smaller stone structures and waved him forward. Roiland started to move towards it when she hissed at him and signed one more command. "Young ones. If you find any, bring them to me. Obey or I will destroy you." With that she turned to an even larger structure. She strode with confidence toward its door.

Roiland sighed to himself. He had lost control, or maybe he had only imagined that he had any choices. He wondered if things could get any worse. He moved to the doorway of the structure that Arigans had ordered him to search. As he studied the door mechanism, screams began to echo from around the settlement. It had begun. Apparently, killing alone would not sate his people's appetites. They craved more from their victims. The Rite would not be satisfying without sowing fear and panic among the humans.

Roiland reached out and ran a hand over the surface of the door. He did not recognize the material it was made of. It was hard, but it was much smoother than stone. There was nothing like it in the darkness where the Drow lived. The handle was a simple device and he lifted the lever and the door opened. To his surprise there was a dim light inside. Roiland pulled a hand crossbow into his left hand and pushed the door open with the sword in his right hand.

As he entered. Roiland heard small whimpers. He stepped forward and pushed the door closed behind him. He paused to contemplate the view before him. The dwelling appeared to be one large room. The left wall was dominated by a large fireplace filled with glowing coals. Suspended from a hook was a large pot. The pot still glowed with the heat of the coals below it.

Directly before him in the center of the room rested a table. A long candle sat in the middle of the table. Its light flickered as the door swung closed. Four chairs were scattered haphazardly around the table. On the far side of the room was a large bed. Two small human children huddled on the bed. Before them stood a human female with a small axe. Her grip on the axe was completely wrong for striking at a foe. He wondered who would have taught her to use it that way.

Roiland's attention shifted back to the bed and its occupants. The children were crying. The was a small boy and a slightly older girl. The girl held a small animal in her arms. The beast was covered in short, curly white hair. Roiland had never seen its like. He wondered what it was called.

Roiland stepped forward with his sword out before him. The woman raised the axe, but there was sorrow in her eyes. "Please. Not the children. I beg you."

Roiland paused to consider the words. He recognized the language. He understood the common tongues, but Drow seldom spoke out loud unless addressing a large group. It took him a moment to process the meaning of her words. When he understood her, he was surprised. His people would never have shown weakness by begging. Such words invited violence.

As Roiland looked at the two weapons he held before him and the two helpless children, disgust washed over him. He slid the small crossbow back into its holster. He kept the sword between him and the armed woman. The turmoil of his emotions calmed as he again felt the presence he had detected in the glowing orb. He felt expectation as the silent observer seemed to peer into his thoughts. He was on the verge of something that mattered greatly to the presence. He was not sure why, but he did not want to disappoint it.

Roiland glared at the female and the children. The woman stepped backwards at the hard look on his face. He saw growing fear in her eyes. It made him angry. He did not want or need her fear. His anger faded as he studied the woman. Despite her fear, she would give her life to protect the two children. It would not save them. She seemed to know that. But she would fight him anyway. Roiland suddenly felt respect for her. She had faced her fear and it did not control her. That was true bravery in his eyes.

Roiland realized that he could not kill this woman. Nor could he bring himself to give the children to Arigans. He would not be a part of their deaths. He gestured to the female with his empty hand. She seemed confused. Roiland had to think to find the word he needed. His unpracticed voice sounded harsh to his own ears as he uttered a single word. "Hide."

The human female stared at him for in confusion. Roiland pointed under the bed with his empty hand. "Hide. Now!"

The female stared at him in shock for a moment and then grabbed the boy and shoved him beneath the bed. She tried to get the girl to move as well but the girl would not let go of the small beast.

Roiland placed his sword on the table and gestured for the beast. The woman hesitated and then pried it from the girl and hands. The child began to whimper as the female stepped forward and handed the beast to him. Roiland was amazed at the softness of its hair. He held the beast in one hand and gestured towards the bed again. "Hide."

The female nodded and grabbed the girl. She crawled quickly under the bed, pushing the girl before her. The sound of the crying children came from beneath the bed. Roiland's harsh voice spoke again. "Silence."

He heard the female silencing the children as he picked up his sword one more time. He stared down at the beast he carried. After a moment's contemplation, he stepped around the table and approached the bed. He placed the edge of his sword against the beast's throat and drew the sharp blade across it.

Blood spurted across the bed and onto the wall behind it. Roiland turned the beast so some of the blood ran across the armor on his chest. He smeared more of it on his arms before placing the beast on the bed. The blood quickly stained the bed coverings. Roiland took the coverings and piled them over the dead beast before turning for the door. He knew he had to get out of here before Arigans came to find him.

As he strode across the room, Roiland felt the presence once more. This time, he felt approval instead of judgement. He shook his head knowing that the occupants of this place were still in danger. If the Salucifer Priestess entered this place, they would die despite his efforts and he would die at their side for his actions. He whispered one last warning as he rounded the table. "Be silent. Live."

Roiland suspected he had taken too long as he lifted the latch from the inside. He slowly opened the door extending his sword through the opening. Standing just beyond his swords reach was Arigans. There was blood in her white hair and more running down her face. Her robes were stained in blood. The most frightening aspect of her appearance was the feverish excitement in her eyes. With rapidly moving fingers she asked, "Young ones?"

Roiland shook his head, scattering some of the beast's blood from his neck. "One old one only. It is dead," he signed.

Arigans stared past him into the room. At the sight of the bloody wall, she nodded. Her fingers wove, "Faster next time."

She motioned towards the next large structure near the center of the settlement. Roiland followed her obediently making sure the door swung closed behind him. He wondered what they would find in the next structure. They had almost reached the door when one of the male candidates came running up a large path to the right. There was fear on his face. Arigans turned with a look of anger to glare at him. Her empty hand came up. "Begone. This is my hunting ground."

The male pointed his sword behind him and then quickly signed. "They have a protector. My team is gone. The Priestess and the Mage are dead. It hunts us."

Arigans sneered as her hand came up. "Stupid male. We are Drow. We are the hunters, not the prey. We do no fear!"

The male raised his hand to reply. Roiland caught a flicker in the air behind the male just before a large bolt erupted from the warrior's chest. As the male hit the ground, Roiland could see the fletching from the bolt sticking from the warriors back. For a heartbeat, Roiland marveled that anything could propel so large a bolt with that much force. Then the realization of his own danger sank in.

Roiland turned to see Arigans had already began to run towards the point where they entered the settlement. Roiland raced after her as they retraced their path. By the time they reached the base of the rise, Roiland was several body lengths ahead of the Salucifer Priestess.

Roiland heard Arigans stop and he felt the power of her magic begin to gather behind him. At that instant, a true understanding of his peril came to him. She could not allow him to reach the portal. All knowledge of her fear had to be eliminated. Anyone that knew she had fled from the human settlement had to die here on the surface. Arigans' pride could accept nothing less than his death at her hands.

Roiland threw himself sideways in a roll. A dark bolt of power passed through the space where his body had just been. Roiland began to crabwalk backwards. He needed to put space between himself and the angry Priestess. As her haughty gaze locked on him again, Roiland dropped into a seated position. His left hand pulled his tiny crossbow from its holster. His right hand released the sword and reached for one of the steel-tipped darts on his belt. Could he get off a shot before her next spell?

Roiland slid the dart into his crossbow. He could see hatred in Arigans' expression as she began to weave another spell. Before Roiland could raise his weapon, another of the large bolts struck the backside of Arigans' right shoulder. There was a spray of blood as the head of the bolt erupted from just under her collarbone. The impact spun the Priestess around. The mace dropped from her grasp as she searched for the one who dared to attack her. Roiland was still staring at the fletching protruding from her shoulder when a second bolt passed completely through her neck. Arigans fell, lifeless and bloody, before him.

Roiland glanced up the rise towards the portal in time to see one of the teams rush through it. Roiland's thoughts seemed to accelerate at the thought of dying in this place. His odds of making it up the rise were not good. The unseen archer was very, very good. Even if he did make it to the portal, would House Salucifer let him live with the death of their Priestess? He doubted that they would care that he was not responsible for her death.

That only left him one option. He must run and learn to live here on the surface world. He had no idea if he could survive the coming of the orb of fire. Roiland decided he had a better chance here than he did if he returned through the portal, assuming he could even reach it alive.

Roiland brought up the globe of darkness innate to his kind. He used it to surround himself. He anchored it in place and moved swiftly to the side. He felt the impact of another of those massive bolts where he had anchored the spell. He slipped out the backside of the darkness moving low to the ground. He moved away from both the portal and the settlement as quickly as he could. With the glowing globe before him, Roiland began to run.

Chapter 3

A New Beginning

Roiland melted into the darkness and began to run. One part of him recognized that he was running from death at the hands of the unknown archer. He was also running from a way of life that he disdained. It was a life that would have eventually ended at the hands of his own people.

At the same time, another part of him ran towards a desperate hope that there might be something more. He yearned for the freedom to explore who and what he might become. In this world, one he did not fully comprehend, he could make his own choices and strive to be more than his own people would have let him be. What that might be was only limited by his own willingness to try. His new life was likely to be a lonely existence, but was lowliness any harsher than the lies and betrayal that he had known all his life? He would learn the answer to that question as he explored this new world.

Roiland realized that he needed to know much more about the surface world if he was to make it his home. He began to look, listen, and feel the world around him as he ran. The first thing that came to him was that the air of the surface felt strange. It moved in ways that were foreign to him. Its movements were not constrained by the walls of tunnels. It came and went and sometimes shifted directions. In this world, even the air was free to act as it chose.

The rush of the air made sounds as it moved through the plants that grew here. It carried scents that did not exist in the world he knew. There was the smell of water and of growing things. So many different growing things. Roiland realized he knew nothing of the plants of the surface world or of the creatures that lived here.

As he ran, he noticed the tall plants with the hard round stalks. Their tops were vaguely shaped like mushrooms, but they were not solid. Many of them stretched many body lengths above his head. Their stalks split many times and spread to encompass large areas. Each of the smaller stalks were covered in smaller shapes that fluttered and made a soothing sound as the air rushed past. Some of the tall things had animals living in them. Some of them flew and others that seemed to scurry around as if they were hiding from predators. The creatures of this place announced their presence with a cacophony of noises. Creatures of the world he knew would never have revealed themselves so blatantly.

There were also many smaller plants. There was even one that seemed to cover the ground almost everywhere. It was not a moss or lichen. Roiland wondered if the lessons of his homeland would serve him or hinder him in this place. Would he have the luxury to learn of learning at his own pace? He had no way to judge just how dangerous this world was.

He ran on. He had no idea where he was going so he would have to depend on the presence that was now his only companion. Roiland turned his steps towards the shining orb that still floated above him and he began to follow it. The orb seemed willing to be his guide. It stayed always before him as he ran. He did not know why, but he felt that he could trust in the silent presence.

Roiland passed a few scattered human structures as he ran. Some of the places he crossed had different kinds of plants. These plants seemed to grow in rows. Roiland wondered if the rows of plants might be crops. The Drow had small farms within their underground domain. Most grew mushrooms and fungi that the slaves of the Drow harvested for their masters. He did his best not to damage the crops as he passed through them.

Roiland continued on through the darkness. The last human structure he had seen was now far behind him. There were many more of the tall plants now and he had to wind his way between them. He began to follow what he assumed was an animal track that wove between the taller plants. He ran his fingers across several of them as he ran. Some of the stalks were smooth and others were very rough. He slowed his pace, worried that he might get turned around in the thick growth. The glowing orb that was his only guide was often obscured by the tall plants.

The winding path came to the banks of a stream. He bent to drink and stared down the small waterway. Roiland could see that the glowing orb had sunk low. It now seemed to hover just above the ground. He wondered if it had grown weary while staying ahead of him all this way. A sensation like laugher washed over him.

He considered the glowing orb. His thoughts of it sinking into the ground had amused it. No, not it, but her. The presence was definitely female, he was certain of it. He greeted her formally. "Greetings, Lady, and thank you for your company." Again, there was no reply. The silence continued as it had since he first felt her presence. He smiled ruefully. "Well then, my Lady of Silences. If you will not talk then I shall have to do the talking for both of us." There was a flash of approval but it was quickly followed by a sense of concern.

He turned to look behind him. A new source of light was coming up from the ground. The source of that light seemed to carry hints of color within it. Roiland remembered his Matron Mothers' warning of the burning time and his need to be back through the portal before the orb of fire arrived. He rose and began to move along the stream still following the Lady's Orb. His eyes scanned both sides of the stream seeking shelter, but there was nothing except the tall plants.

Roiland moved back under the shelter of the tall plants as the Lady's Orb sank lower. Soon only the upper half of her orb was visible. Far behind him another orb began to rise above the ground. This orb was yellow and caried heat and much light. The light of the Lady's Orb had been painful when he had first seen it. What was coming would be many times worse. This could only be the Orb of Fire that he had been warned about. Its heat and light ate away the darkness. It overwhelmed his senses.

The cover provided by the tall plants did little to protect Roiland from the orb of fire. He huddled behind on of the larger plants and summoned his globe of darkness once more. He hoped it would provide him with some relief from the assault of the new orb. But the burning orb would not allow it. His darkness was quickly consumed by the light.

He curled into a ball on the ground, wrapped in his dark cloak. The cloak just seemed to absorb the heat from the fire above him. All that he was seemed to be laid bare in the penetrating light. Roiland suffered in silence. Eventually, he crawled to the stream and lay half submerged in the water. That at least drew some of the heat from his body. He had no idea how long the torment lasted, but this orb also began to sink into the ground. Darkness slowly returned.

As darkness once again claimed the land, Roiland hunted. His dart brought down a small furred creature that moved around in one of the tall plants. He was able to start a fire using some of the plants as fuel. The fire gave off more smoke than he liked. He put it out as soon as he had cooked his kill. Roiland knew he needed to be further away from the human settlement before he stopped running. The Lady's Orb was not visible so he followed the flow of the water.

The Lady's Orb eventually rose behind him. He was hesitant to turn back that way so he continued to follow the water. For a time, the Lady's Orb seemed to chase after him as he ran. It did not seem that long before it caught him and moved ahead, of him once more. He let her lead him towards his future.

Roiland traveled this way for two more cycles of the Lady's Orb and the Orb of Fire. The stream grew slightly larger as another small flow joined it on its far side. He used the stream as much as possible to hide his tracks. Roiland continued to search for shelter, but he saw no sign of a cave or any other entrance to the underground. He had to depend on the stream to help him through the periods of heat and light.

Roiland watched the animals of this new world when the Lady's Orb reigned over the land. Many of the creatures seemed to take shelter from the light within the tall plants. Some built nests and others somehow burrowed into the plants themselves. Neither was an option for him. Other creatures burrowed into the soil. Roiland thought this might be his best option. He could not continue to be exposed to the orb of fire.

On the fourth rising of the Lady's Orb, Roiland searched along the sides of the stream until he found an area where the soil was both dry and heavy. He selected a location beneath several of the larger plants so that it would block at least some of the light from above. Having selected a location for his shelter, Roiland returned to the stream to search for a large flat rock to dig with. He found several stones that met his needs and he carried them to the site he had selected.

He spent the next two dark cycles scooping out the earth to create a trench that he could rest in. The work was not easy with only a stone for a tool, but he managed to scoop out an area longer than he was tall. It was two arm lengths across and almost an arm length deep.

Roiland used his sword to cut down a large quantity of the tall, soft plant that seemed to cover much of the ground. He used this to line his trench. As he hunted, Roiland collected a number of the hard stalks that had fallen from the larger plants. He selected a dozen sturdy pieces that were long enough to stretch across his trench. Once he had them placed over the trench, he used some of the dirt from the trench to bury the ends on both sides. Once the heavy soil was packed down, it held the stalks firmly in place.

Roiland agonized over his next step. He needed a layer that would repel water. The only thing he had that was even close to the right size was his cloak. It was an irreplaceable item. In the end, he sacrificed it to cover the top of his shelter. He carefully cut the material with his dagger and then tied it in place over the stalks. Next, he piled more of the soft plants over the cloak. The final layer was spreading the remaining dirt over the top to conceal his work.

His shelter would have horrified most of his kin. Such an undignified hole was beneath them. But he was proud of his work. It was not easy to detect and it kept out most of the light from the orb of fire. The soil was cool to keep the trench comfortable through the time of light.

Roiland lost track of how many dark cycles it took him to finish his shelter. Whenever he took breaks from his work, Roiland explored the area around his camp. Anything that would help him survive he had to learn. He determined which animals tasted good and which ones did not. He did not just hunt the animals, he studied them. They could teach him which plants were safe to eat and which were not. He learned quickly to trust the small furred creatures more than the ones that flew. The small flyers ate many plants that made him sick.

He was content with his new life. He had food, shelter, and water. He had the Lady of Silences to talk to. She never replied, but he felt she listened as he spoke of what was in his heart. It was enough. There was peace in not needing to watch his back. There were few dangers when there was no one around but him.

His one concern through it all had been the Lady of Silences. He had noticed as time went on that her Orb had begun to shrink. By the time his shelter was finished, nearly half of the Lady's Orb was missing. Would she disappear completely? He did not know, but the thought of her absence saddened him.

Chapter 4

The Archer

Roiland woke as the light began to dim outside his shelter. The trench was cool and quiet. He had been on the surface for some time now. He had grown accustomed to the cycle of darkness and light. He wanted for little except companionship. He had the Lady of Silences, but his sense of her had faded as her Orb had continued to disappear a piece at a time. It was as if the darkness was eating away at her light. Her Orb had been little more than a thin crescent when he had entered his shelter to rest. Would there be anything left when he climbed back into the darkness?

Roiland lay within the trench and waited for the last of the light to fade. He was learning to tolerate the light, but he was still more at home in the darkness. Darkness was what he knew. Roiland frowned. Something did not seem right. He listened to the world around him as he waited. He had come to know the calls of most of the creatures that lived nearby. The sounds that he had come to recognize as normal were missing.

He realized that something was wrong. The area along the stream was never quiet unless a predator was nearby. He could not hear even the sounds of the small flying things that sang away the last of the light.

Little he had seen would silence their calls. The only thing he could hear was the soft movement of air through the plants above him.

As true darkness returned, Roiland began to inch forward. He moved with the slow, steady grace of a hunter. His dark hand slid out from under the cover that concealed his trench. He froze at a sound he knew well. The snap of a bowstring releasing assaulted his ears. He tensed when a heavy bolt pierced the ground in the gap between his thumb and the rest of his hand. Roiland suspected that the archer had not missed him. The placement of the bolt had been a warning. Roiland relaxed his muscles and waited.

A gruff voice came from somewhere above. "It might be best if you put your weapons out where I can see them before you come out any further. You puzzle me, Drow. I would like to talk to you without worrying about needing to kill you."

Roiland's hand caressed the large bolt. Its surface was smooth, almost polished. The bolt was strong and heavy. He could not imagine what type of bow could deliver such a projectile with such power and accuracy. He wished to study it and understand it. No, he thought. He desired to touch it and use it. Such a weapon would be a wonder. Roiland withdrew his hand into the shelter of his trench. He grasped the hilt of his short sword and slid it out where it could be seen. He lay it beside the bolt standing out of the ground. His two hand crossbows followed to rest atop the sword blade. Last to join the pile was his dagger.

The voice came again. "Those are interesting little toys. I examined several that came from those that attacked the village. They would require great accuracy to be of much use. Are you that good Drow?"

Roiland considered his response. When he was sure of his word choice, he replied, "My bolts hit only the targets that I choose."

The voice chuckled. "Simple and direct. Your response intrigues me, Drow. The choices we make in life define who we become. You made some unexpected choices in the village. Now come out slowly and carefully. Do not attempt to take your weapons. I would hate to ruin a most interesting discussion before I get the answers I seek. Do not make me put an arrow in you. Climb out and step away from your hideout."

Roiland moved slowly out into the open. He did not reach for any of the weapons as he crawled over them. The crossbows were not loaded anyway. He had little doubt that the archer could place several of his large bolts in him before he could load even one of his crossbows.

Roiland stood and walked three steps away from his weapons before turning to search for the archer. He wondered if finally seeing the archer's bow would be worth his life if the archer decided he did not like the flow of the discussion.

There was a sound from above and to the left. Roiland's eyes traveled up one of the tall plants to a secondary stalk that protruded to the side. An old human sat there with his back leaning against the main stalk. The human's legs were wrapped securely around the horizontal stalk. The human's face was wrinkled and had thin wispy white hair hanging down to the middle of his chest.

In the human's hands was a strange bow. He had expected to see some elaborate crossbow that was large enough to launch the great bolts. Instead, the human held a long, slightly curved length of a material that Roiland did not recognize. He estimated that the bow was at least as long as he was tall. The bow held another of the large bolts. The bolt was at least as long as his arm. The design seemed too simple. And yet, he had seen this bow strike from distances that he could not imagine. What would it be to run his hands along its length? To place a bolt against its string?

His musings were interrupted by the old human's soft laugh. Roiland realized that the old man had been watching him study the bow. "She is impressive, is she not?"

Roiland's eyes did not leave the bow or the bolt pointed at his chest. "It is beautiful. But why 'she'?"

The old man eased the tension on the bow but did not remove the bolt from the string. "Because she claims to be female. Who am I to argue? She is named Oikea Lakko, or True Strike in the common tongue. She is magical and very intelligent. Too smart for me to argue her beliefs."

Roiland's eyes finally shifted from the bow back to the old man's face. "An intelligent bow? Where did you find such a treasure?"

The old man seemed to listen to something that Roiland could not hear. Then his eyes bored into Roilands. "You do not find such things. They select those who wield them with great care. Oikea selected me long ago when I was young and foolish. The previous Archer trained me after the bow informed him that I was to be his successor."

Roiland just nodded, accepting the man's word.

The old man studied Roiland. "I was sent out here by a little girl named Aimée. She sent me to kill you. She says that you are as bad as the others who killed villagers. You killed her lamb and she has sworn vengeance on you."

Roiland's heart sank. He felt guilt even though it has been the only path he could think of to save the children. "The beast seemed the lesser of evils. I regret the child's pain."

The old man seemed surprised by the answer. "Her mother, Renée, asked me to deliver a message to you. She asked me to thank you for her life and especially for the lives of her children. She did not understand why you spared their lives. Frankly, it puzzles me as well, and I do not particularly like things I do not understand."

There was silence for a long time. Roiland did not know what to say. The old man's raspy voice came again. "Why, Drow? Why did you spare them? Many innocents died that night in the village of Mjukr. Your kin butchered them. All but you, Drow. Why were you different?"

Roiland stared up into the old man's eyes. "I came because it is what Drow do. The Blood Rite is expected of us. But… I did not wish it. When the time came, I could not kill them or allow the Priestess to kill them. Especially not with Her watching me."

The old man raised an eyebrow. "Her? Who was watching you? The mother or the little girl?"

Roiland shook his head. "Not the female. It was... The Lady. I cannot explain it. I do not understand it myself."

The old man slowly removed the arrow from the bow and returned
it to his quiver. He turned the bow sideways and lay it across his lap.
Roiland blinked in surprise. What had changed? He made no move for
his weapons. He stood and waited for the old man to judge him.

The old man sighed. "I thought I had been sent there to stop the
slaughter. I am old and I was late. Many had died before I arrived. Now
I am not so sure. Oikea says I was sent to find you. I doubted her. I was
certain it could not be a Drow. I do not know anymore."

Roiland stared up at the old man. "You were sent? Sent by who?
Even the High Priestess did not know where we would emerge on the
surface."

The old man slung the bow across his back and turned to slide down
the tree. When he reached the ground, he faced Roiland. "Long ago, as
a youth, I was Erasmus, a foolish boy seeking adventure. The mistakes
I made cost me someone I loved more than life itself. I should have
died that night too, but the Archer was sent to save me. He taught me.
Eventually, I was reborn as the Archer, Knight of the Lady."

Roiland's voice came out as a whisper. "The Lady?"

Erasmus nodded, and pointed up at the thin crescent hanging above
them. "The Lady of Suffering." His eyes seemed to bore inside
Roiland. "The same Lady that saved you from becoming evil that
night."

Roiland turned his gaze up to contemplate what was left of the Orb.
"I did not know her name. She has never spoken to me. I call her the
Lady of Silences. She is almost gone now."

The old man moved over to stand beside him. "That name suits her as
well as any. She came to me and shared my suffering. So, I called her
the Lady of Suffering. To all she is the Lady. But she is not the rock
that hangs in the sky. That is the moon. It is simply a face that she
turns towards us. Her face may not be visible now, but it will return.
Each month her presence fades and then grows stronger. It never leaves
us. Just as the sun never truly leaves us.

Roiland bowed his head. "There is much that I do not know."

The old man turned and began to walk away. "Then you must choose to learn or choose to stay and live in your hole. You can choose to be more. Gather your things if you wish and come with me. I am old and tired. I am going home."

Roiland moved quickly to sheath his sword and return both crossbows to their holsters. Then he ran after the old human. The old man did not waste time. He began to teach as they walked. His first lessons were language. As they traveled, the old man taught him the names of the plants and animals of this world. He taught him of the things above, the sky and the moon and the stars and the sun. Roiland learned quickly and willingly.

Chapter 5

Rebirth

Roiland sat quietly in the small hunting lodge. The lodge sat in the middle of a vast forest of trees. The old man, Erasmus, was sleeping fitfully in the next room.

Roiland had never realized how short the lifespan of humans was. Erasmus was only a score of years older than he was. Roiland was considered very young for a Drow, but Erasmus was old and his body was failing. The rescue at the village and the long journey to track Roiland had taken a toll on the human. Old age was a concept that Roiland struggled with. Few Drow survived long enough to become old. Not even Matron Mothers.

The old man had kept his word to teach him though. Roiland had learned much in the last two cycles of the moon. He had learned words for many things on the surface world. The old man had done much to prepare Roiland to live out his life in the world he had chosen. Roiland appreciated the knowledge that the old man had given him. But it was the lesson in archery that had truly excited him. The Archer had taken Roiland's raw talent and pushed him beyond anything that Roiland or his people could have imagined.

Roiland's gaze turned to the walls of the room where he sat. On each wall hung different types of bows. The Archer had demanded that he master each of them in turn. Roiland now knew how to not only use each, but how to construct and care for them. He understood which woods to use and how to cure them to create the best weapons possible.

Roiland had started with a light crossbow and graduated quickly up to a heavy crossbow. He had even been given an opportunity to fire a ballista. He had mastered each of these in mere days as they were just larger versions of the hand crossbows he had used for years.

The short bow had taken him almost a full cycle of the moon to truly master. The technique for firing was more complicated with this type of bow. Erasmus had made him take shot after shot until the muscles of his arms and shoulders burned with the effort. Eventually, his body took over from his mind. Once mind and body began to work with the bow instead of against it, his innate talent emerged once more. He had been given the composite bow next and, finally, the longbow.

Oikea was a longbow and Roiland now understood that it was the ultimate tool of an archer. He could not imagine ever using anything else. The arrows of the longbow were heavier and could punch through even the toughest armor. What he loved most was that he could release a dozen arrows in the same time as one shot from the crossbow.

Roiland stood and walked to the longbow that he had been allowed to use. It was one crafted by Erasmus. It was an incredible weapon. But it was not in the same league as the magical bow carried by the Archer. Oikea Lakko still mesmerized him. His fingers wanted to caress its wood. But he would not shame himself or his new teacher by touching the wonderous bow.

Roiland heard the old man cough and then call to him. Roiland rose and went to the door of the old man's room. Erasmus was sitting up in bed, leaning against the wall at its head. "We must talk, Roiland of the Drow. I have shared what knowledge I could with you these past two months. My body is failing and soon you must make a very important choice."

Roiland knelt at the foot of the bed. "What choice is there that I need to make? I have nowhere to go nor anyone else that will accept what I am. My heritage condemns me in this world."

The old man sat up straighter. "Your heritage and your past do not concern me nor do they concern the Lady. It is your future and what you do with it that are of import."

Roiland looked confused. "What choices do I have. Where or what can a Dark Elf become here on the surface world?"

The old man motioned for him to sit on the edge of the bed. "There are things I have not yet told you. I am The Archer, the Knight of the Lady. But I am not the first Archer, nor will I be the last. My teacher was the Archer and before him is a long line of Knights. Each Knight was chosen by Oikea Lakko and then blessed by the Lady. It is how it has been since the time of the Change. One Knight defending the meek and bringing Justice for the oppressed."

Roiland studied the old man. "That sounds like a difficult calling. One that requires much sacrifice."

The old man smiled and for a moment Roiland could see the youth he had been shining brightly in Erasmus' eyes. "It is a calling and one that demands much of the Knight. But it comes with compensation. The Lady and the one she serves are generous. I have never wanted for anything since I became the Archer. You must understand, the rewards are not riches such as a greedy man might desire. The gifts are things that make one truly happy. Gratitude, friendship, hope, and even love. The things that truly matter in this life and the next."

Roiland was silent for a time. "And the cost? I have found that nothing valuable ever comes without a price."

Erasmus gave the Drow a knowing smile. "The price is indeed high. This calling demands that you sacrifice all that you are and all that you have ever been. You must die to self. It is the only way to be reborn into the service of the Light."

Roiland studied the frail old man. "You did this? Why?"

Erasmus spoke with an intensity that Roiland had never heard from the old man. "I did and I have never regretted it. As for why, like you there was little in my past that held any meaning. My past failings were many. I had lost the one that mattered most to me and I wanted to do more than just exist for the rest of my life. I needed hope. The Lady offered me hope and I accepted."

Roiland started to argue, but realized he had no words to argue with. After a moment he asked. "If I choose this path, how do I do this thing you speak of?"

Erasmus gestured towards an oilskin wrapped bundle leaning against the wall. "Oikea Lakko awaits you there. The moon is full this night and the light reflected by the Lady shines brightly. If it is truly your wish to enter her service, take Oikea out into the Light. Unwrap her and take her in your hands."

Roiland eyed the bow warily. A part of him had desired the bow since he had first laid eyes on it. But now he felt a little fear. "And then what, Archer?"

The old man's voice came to him softly, almost as a dying whisper. "Then you must come to terms with what you have been, what you are, and who you might become."

Roiland gazed at the old man. "The Lady will judge me?"

Erasmus shook his head. "No, my friend. It is worse. You will judge yourself."

Roiland nodded and rose to his feet. He slowly reached out and lifted the carefully wrapped bow. His thoughts were racing. Then the old man's voice came to him once more. "Do not fear, Roiland. The road before you is long and its burdens many. Know that they will never be more than you can bear. But your race lives much longer than a human. Think hard before you step onto this path."

Roiland turned and left Erasmus' room. He paused before the door to the lodge. Why was he even considering this? But deep down he knew and he opened the door and stepped out into the darkness. Only it was not truly dark. The light of the Lady's Orb shone brightly. He opened himself to her. There were still no words, but he felt anticipation.

Roiland moved to a tall stump that sat in the middle of the yard. He sat there and gazed up at the Lady's Orb considering his future. He had left his home to escape death. But that was only partially true. He had left his people behind to keep from becoming what they were. He did not wish to be as other Drow. He wanted something more. He suddenly realized that he had other options. Erasmus had given him the knowledge to make his way in this world. If he took up Oikea Lakko, it would really be his choice and not a last resort. His will was still his own.

He stared up into the light shining down on him. The only thing he had ever done that he felt pride in was the night he had spared the woman and her children. He had risked his life to save theirs. The young child hated him for sacrificing the lamb, but he knew that he had done the right thing. Maybe all that mattered was that he knew it was the right choice.

Roiland slowly unwrapped the bow being careful not to touch its polished wood. It was truly beautiful. The soft moonlight seemed to caress its surfaces. The words of the old man echoed through his thoughts. In the end, Roiland understood. He was lost in this world without hope. Existing without was not enough. He wanted, no, he needed something to believe in. He wanted to be a part of something greater than himself.

Roiland turned his eyes up to the Lady's Orb. He whispered, "I choose to serve." He felt approval as he reached out and grasped the bow in his heart-hand. Roiland felt a presence enter his mind and his thoughts. It was not cruel and it was not gentle. Without emotion, it reached deep into his mind and suddenly he was awash in his own memories.

Roiland began to relive his life from his earliest days. Each choice he made came back to him. Each small evil that he had done, each lie that he had told, each piece of selfishness was relived. He was forced to examine each in the light of the Lady's Orb. He also relived each of the good choices that he had made. There were few of those though. The final memory that came to him was the night of the Blood Rite. He watched as the woman crawled under the bed after her children. The memories ended as he watched himself bathe in the blood of the lamb.

Roiland felt numb inside. There was a part of him that burned in shame at the many things that he had done through his life. He tried to tell himself that he had not known the acts were wrong then, but he had known. He told himself that Drow considered the thing he did acceptable. Most were proud of their many slights and betrayals. But the argument did not help. He felt shame. He did not understand where that emotion came from.

A voice spoke softly in his head. *That part of you that feels pain at what you have done is called a conscience.*

Roiland searched for the source of the voice. Then his eyes drifted to the bow that he held in a near death grip. "Oikea? Erasmus said that you were intelligent. He did not say that your spoke to him."

A feminine chuckle echoed through his thoughts. *Yes, I am Oikea Lakko. I chose you I knew you would be willing to serve. You need not speak out loud. I hear your thoughts as they come. All of them."

Roiland shook his head. "That may take some getting used to. Forgive me if I speak for now. What is this conscience? Where did it come from? I have never felt it before."

You were born with it, Archer. And yes, I sense your doubt. But even Drow are born with a conscience. All living beings have one. Sadly, most Drow sacrifice it to the evil that they serve.

Roiland considered the words of the bow. "Is it always so painful?"

*It is a gift and a curse. It can be a guide as you travel through life. It will help you to know right from wrong. It will warn you when your thoughts go where they should not. But you must choose to heed its warnings. As with all living things, it will perish if it is neglected."

Roiland sat silently thinking. He realized that the bow knew all that passed through his mind, but he did not care. Finally, he asked, "What comes next?"

*You must make a choice. You can choose to hang on to all that you were before. If you do, I will return to the previous Archer. Or you can choose to let that part of you pass away."

Roiland closed his eyes. "How could you possibly choose me after what you have seen? I am not worthy. I sense the light in you Oikea. I am filled with darkness and shadow as are all of my kind."

No one is without some darkness and shadow within them. If you allow it, the Light can burn away the darkness and replace it. You have but to accept the light and allow it to flourish within you. Let the Light guide you.

"You make it sound so easy."

The choice is easy. Living it afterwards takes work. Choose with an open heart. Accept the light within you and then serve it.

Roiland opened his eyes and stared up into the soft light washing over him. "I choose to serve, Lady, if you will have me."

The light shining down became brighter. A sense of joy and acceptance washed over him. The light seemed to gather on his skin and then it began to penetrate his pores. Roiland stared at his hands and arms. The light seemed to glow from within him. The bow in his hand also began to gleam with reflected radiance. Roiland felt as if he had been washed clean of all that was his past. There was only the future. He accepted the forgiveness that was offered to him. And then he forgave himself. He would serve the Lady of Silences.

Roiland watched in wonder as the light slowly dimmed. Within moments, everything outside him had returned to normal. The changes were within him. He smiled at the bow gripped in his hand.

Greetings, Archer. I look forward to working with you for a long, long time.

Before Roiland could answer, the door to the lodge swung open. Standing in the doorway was Erasmus. The old man looked different somehow. He stood straighter and seemed less worn. His face seemed somehow younger. Erasmus began to walk across the yard towards him. His step seemed to gain strength as he came closer. Years seemed to melt from his face and his body.

A middle-aged Erasmus smiled down at him. "Greetings to the new Paladin Archer. My thanks for your willingness to accept my duty."

Roiland looked up in surprise. "Paladin? As in holy knight?"

Erasmus nodded. "Search within yourself, young Knight. I suspect you will feel the thirst for law and goodness."

Roiland studied his own feelings and emotions. After a time, he nodded. "I think this is what I have always searched for. I could not find the path to it in the world below. But I thought holy knights used a lance and a sword."

Erasmus shrugged. "Some do. But cannot any, even an archer, reach for truth and justice? Why should any be barred from serving?"

Roiland studied the bow in his hands. "How do I serve? What am I to do?"

Erasmus gestured towards the lodge. "You stay here and continue to learn until you hear Her call. Someday you will find the home that has been prepared for you. You wait for the Lady to call upon you. Then you protect the meek and the downtrodden. You help those who desire peace to find it. You defend the law, and when necessary, you deliver justice."

Roiland raised his eyes to meet those of his teacher. "You will continue to teach me and guide me then?"

Erasmus shook his head but then broke into a beaming smile. "You have Oikea Lakko to teach you the ways of the Light. You have the Lady to be your guide. You have the Light within you now. You also have a conscience to temper your actions. You do not need me anymore, my friend. I go now to the reward promised me long ago. Fear not, Archer. The life ahead of you will be most wonderous indeed."

Roiland sucked in his breath as the glow from above intensified once more. A portal of light appeared across the yard. He watched Erasmus turn and begin to walk towards the portal. Erasmus grew younger with each step. His hair darkened and his frame filled out. Roiland could see the warrior as he had been in his prime. A young woman stepped from the portal. With a cry of joy, she ran to him and threw her arms around his neck. Erasmus clasped her to him. He turned and gave one last look behind him. Roiland saw tears on his teacher's face. But also, happiness. Erasmus scooped the young woman into his arms and stepped through the portal.

Then there was a flash of light and they were gone.

Roiland muttered softly, "I have not known you long, but I shall miss you, old man."

You can do him one final service, Archer. It awaits you inside.

Roiland rose and turned towards the lodge. He slung Oikea across his back and went back through the open door. Inside the bedroom lay Erasmus body. The old man lay peacefully on the bed. There was a smile on his lips even in death. Roiland wrapped the body carefully in the bedding. He went out and found a shovel. There was a grave alongside the lodge. He began to dig a second one beside it.

Chapter 6

The Call

Roiland sat on the stump before the lodge enjoying the breeze and the view of the stars above. He wondered about the twinkling lights.

They are one of many wonderous gifts created to bring beauty into this world.

Roiland smiled at the cryptic answer. It was what he had come to expect from Oikea. He was about to reply when he felt the Lady's presence urging him to move quickly. He felt the need to travel north and east. He rose to his feet and began to run.

*Pace yourself, Archer. We have a long way to go before we serve."

Roiland kept his pace. "If I slow, we may not be there in time."

Have faith, Knight. She has timed her call so that you will be there when you are needed most.

Roiland slowed but kept moving. He traveled through the darkness and into the light of the new day. He no longer feared the burning orb of the sun. The light did not blind him or cause him pain. He continued to travel, taking only a short break beside a stream to refresh himself.

Near midday, he crested a hill and spotted four wagons bunched together in the middle of a narrow track below him. He heard the scream of a woman. He pulled Oikea from his shoulder as he stared down the hill. He could make out the forms of people fighting near the wagons. Roiland pulled an arrow from his quiver and began to run down the hill towards the wagons.

Archer. There is evil nearby. Slow and reach out your senses. Feel the taint of it before you.

Roiland stopped and did as Oikea suggested. The bow guided his thought and showed him how to open himself to this new sense. Oikea was right. He could sense the evil before him. One source behind a tree to the right and another in the bushes more to the left. "It would be better for both of you if you came out," he called to them.

A lanky half-orc stepped out from the trees with a small axe in each of its dirty hands. "You are a long way from home Drow. You should move on. This group is our prize."

Roiland shook his head. "I cannot let you harm these folks. They are under the protection of the Lady."

A human stood up from behind the bushes. He held a bastard sword in his left hand. He raised it above his head, grasping the hilt with both hands.

The orc grinned. "Where is this Lady of yours? We would like to meet her after we dispose of you."

Roiland felt his anger rise at the insult to the Lady.

*Calm yourself, Archer. Anger is not a part of what you are now. Do not let it rule you."

Roiland took a deep, cleansing breath and stepped forward. The half-orc raised one of the axes as if to throw it. The first arrow leapt across the gap between them and took him in the shoulder of his throwing arm. A second arrow pierced the half-orc's thigh before the axe had fallen from his now useless arm. The half-orc fell to the ground.

The human began to run towards him. Roiland's third arrow caught the man in the knee and he fell to the ground clutching the shattered joint.

Roiland quickly verified that neither one would be moving far and then he began to jog towards the wagons.

As he drew close, Roiland paused to study the scene before him. The wagons had apparently carried a group of farmers and their families. There were two men dressed as farmers down on the ground bleeding. There were three armed men moving among the families, shoving people and striking them. Roiland saw one of the men raise a dagger over his head. An elderly woman stood bravely before the man with two young boys behind her.

Roiland's bow came up. He allowed Oikea to make subtle adjustments to his aim. The arrow hit the dagger hand on its way down towards the woman. The man's hand was driven to the side as the arrow went through it and sank into the side of one of the wagons, pinning the hand to the wood.

The other two men spun to face Roiland. Both were armed with blades that appeared to be a cross between a dirk and a short sword. Roiland's bow had another arrow already notched. The two men paused at the sight of the ready bow. "Easy now, Elf. There is enough here to share. If you want one of the women, we do not mind. You can have first pick. There are plenty enough to go around."

Their words caused Roiland's stomach to knot in disgust. He managed to keep his voice level. "Drop your blades. Do not force me to harm you."

The man closest to Roiland smiled. "Durge, he is worried about hurting us. I think he feels sorry for us. Maybe he wants to teach us a better way to live. I do not think he has the stomach to kill us."

The second man lunged towards one of the farmer folks. Roiland's arrow took him in the side. The man screamed as he fell to the ground. Before the first man could move, another arrow was drawn and pointed towards him. He dropped the blade from his hand.

Roiland barked a command at the farmers. "Someone take his weapon! Grab the weapons of the other two as well."

Roiland blinked in surprise. None of the folk from the wagons moved. They all stood as if rooted in fear. Roiland's eyes moved to study the woman that had bravely stood waiting to die at the hand of the first bandit. There were tears in her eyes. Something is wrong, he thought. What am I missing?

Oikea remained silent. Roiland realized that it expected him to find the solution this time. After a moment, Roiland's senses reached out as they had with the two bandits on the hillside. He felt the evil like an irritation on his skin. He focused on the foulness of it. His eyes tracked across the people before him. His eyes settled on a tall man standing with his hand on his daughter's shoulder. No, he sensed innocence and goodness from the child. And fear. The man behind her was filled with darkness like his own kind.

Roiland spun to face the man. He saw a flash as the man pulled a dagger from behind his back. The foul man pulled to child in front of him. Roiland released his bolt at the only target he had left. The arrow slashed between them and the man and the girl flew backwards to land hard on the ground.

A woman screamed, "He shot my Lissa!"

The last uninjured bandit dove for his blade, but the old woman grabbed a shovel from the side of the wagon and brought it down on the back of his head. The man landed face-down on the ground and did not move.

The farmers began to mutter. Roiland heard someone say, "Damn Drow!" But then a small voice came from the ground where the two bodies lay. "I am okay, Mama. He did not hurt me."

The man's body rolled over as a young girl crawled out from beneath it. The girl rose to her feet. The tall man lay with an arrow protruding from his right eye socket. The farmers went silent at the sight.

The old woman with the shovel stared at Roiland. "Why would a Dark Elf save the likes of us? Who are you?"

Roiland stood unsure of himself for a long moment.

You must answer her, Archer.

Roiland met the woman's gaze. "I saved you because the Lady asked it of me. You prayed for justice and it was granted. I am the Archer and I serve the Light."

There was more murmuring from the crowd, but the old woman smiled at him. "I have heard of you, Archer. But I was told that you were an old man and not a Drow. Know that you have our thanks."

Roiland knelt beside the two farmers that had been stabbed. *Place your hands on them and open yourself to the Light.*

Roiland did as he was told. He did not think he could reach the Lady during the daytime, but he asked anyway. "Please help them, Lady." He stared in awe as some light once again shone from beneath his skin. It seemed to flow from his hands over the farmer's wounds. They did not heal completely, but the bleeding stopped and his breathing evened out. Roiland repeated the process with the second farmer. His wound also closed.

The old woman knelt beside the second man. "This is my Jacob. Thank you for giving him back to me. Fool man is too old to be fighting with bandits. But he is a brave one." Her hand reached down to pat Roiland's before moving to caress the man between them.

Roiland stood and pointed back up the hill. "There are two more of them up there on the hillside. They are injured."

The old woman asked quietly from where she knelt, "What do we do with them?"

Roiland was confused at that. He did not know the ways of these people. "Is there a settlement near where they can be judged in accordance with your laws?"

The old woman nodded. "We can do that, but what if they try to escape?"

Roiland turned and began to walk away. "I will be nearby. I will come if you have need of me."

Roiland headed back towards the lodge. He somehow knew that these folk would have no further need of his help. He felt good about his work this day. It was not pride, because he had been forced to kill.

He could not feel pride in that. But there was satisfaction that he had helped others who could not help themselves.

This is why we exists. Oikea Lakko and the Archer. It is our mission.

For the first time since he had taken up the magical bow, Roiland truly felt like the Archer. It was a very good feeling. He understood that there would be many more calls for his service, for he was the Lady's Knight.

The Taste of Fear

I stood secure in all that I had and all that I was. I stared out into a world filled with wants and needs and I found... I found myself wanting. Wanting in faith, wanting in charity, and wanting in love. Oh, I wanted to be wanted and I wanted to be needed. But it was all about my wants and my needs. I wanted to be needed my way. I wanted the needs to be the things I wanted to give. But the world and the people had their own needs and wants. The needs of the world did not fit neatly into my wants. I did not have the power or the right to refashion the world to conform to my own desire. So instead of changing other's lives by my actions, I had to change myself. Maybe, if I can serve real needs, then the help I give might fill the emptiness inside me. Maybe loneliness will recede for a time.

Friar Tully

Chapter 1

Order of the Lawgiver

Tully knelt in prayer before the Altar of the Lawgiver. He was truly thankful for his place in the Temple of Tyr. The work of Tyr was not harsh and going into the City to heal the sick among the poor gave him a sense of self-worth that he never had growing up on his parent's farm. Plowing behind father's ox or even bringing in the harvest had seemed like meaningless drudgery. He had not felt like it served any great purpose.

Besides, it was hungry work. Despite all the food they grew, Tully had always been hungry. There was never a shortage of food in the Temple and Tully's large girth was a testament to how good the food was. It was not like he had totally abandoned his neighbors in the countryside. The Temple sent all of the younger clerics out to care for their needs once each month. Tully always volunteered for that duty. It helped to relieve the guilt over abandoning his family. Every pair of hands was important on a small farm and he knew his father worked much harder now that he was gone.

Tully was lost in his own thoughts when someone cleared their throat right in front of him. He looked up and his face went pale. The Hofgathi stood before him. He was not sure why the caretaker of the

Temple would suddenly take interest in him. Tully swallowed hard and dropped his head again. "Yes, Master, how can I serve you?"

Hofgathi Argnost shook his head and sighed deeply. "How many times must I tell you, Friar Tully? I am not your master. The Lawgiver is our Master. We serve him by serving his people. We uphold the law without showing fear."

Tully bowed his head. "Yes, Hofgathi. May Tyr forgive my ignorance."

Argnost studied the overweight Friar. "I am not sure why the Lawgiver has chosen you for this duty, but I am sure that he sees much that I cannot. Come with me, Tully. We have much to discuss."

An uneasy feeling shot through Tully. There was a bitter taste in his mouth as he felt a moment of fear. Why would the Hofgathi, the Guardian of the Law and the most senior cleric in the Temple, be interested in him? This did not sound promising. He was content with his small place in the world. Change was a bad thing as far as he was concerned. Tully swallowed down the bitter taste and rose to his feet. He followed the Hofgathi into the inner sanctum without another word.

Tully stayed three paces behind the Hofgathi through the inner sanctum to a small office towards the back. Tully knew this to be the Hofgathi's private office. He felt another moment of fear. The same bitter taste nipped at his tongue as he tried to remember what he might have done wrong. Nothing came to mind.

Tully stared around as he entered the room for the first time. He was surprised to see that the office was rather plain. The walls were adorned with old tapestries so faded that the images were no longer visible. There was one threadbare rug in the center of the room. There were only four pieces of furniture in the room. In the rear of the room was an old wooden desk with two straight back chairs, one on each side of the desk. Against the left wall was a small table covered in a sheet. The only luxury in the room was the small window that looked out on the Temple gardens. The room seemed beneath a man of such standing.

Argnost moved to the far side of the desk and sat down on the unpadded chair. He motioned for Tully to sit in the chair before his desk. Tully sat nervously and waited for the lecture. He was sure he was in very deep trouble. He could not clear the bitter taste from his mouth.

Argnost slowly unrolled a scroll and studied it for a while. "You appear to have done well, Friar, although there is little that is remarkable about your performance in the Lawgiver's service." He paused and then nodded. "With the possible exception of your voice in the choir. The director speaks highly of your contribution during feast day services."

Tully was confused. He was not really sure if he had been praised or insulted by the Hofgathi's words. This was not the normal start to a reprimand and he had received more than his share of them. He really did not understand why he was here.

Argnost smiled at the young Friar. He was not sure he had ever been this…. not innocent, but out of touch with the world around him. Young Tully was different from most at the Temple. He had a narrow view of his world. But within that view he lived happily and worked hard.

He wondered if the young Friar even realized that his family had manipulated him into coming to the Temple. As his father had put it, the boy's thinking was not flexible enough to run a farm. He needed a place where the world followed simple and exact rules. Argnost felt momentary guilt that he was about to thrust this young Friar into a role he was not sure the boy could handle. But Tyr had spoken.

Argnost stood and turned to the small window and stared at the garden. "Each morning as I seek guidance and spells from the Lawgiver, I walk that garden. It takes 999 steps to circle the garden. I have always wondered about that number. Do you know why it is not a thousand steps Tully?"

Tully looked confused. "Because your steps are too big, Hofgathi?"

Argnost began to chuckle. "That may be the most insightful answer I have ever been given, my young Friar. But it is not a thousand because it is only 999. Things are what they are and not what we want them to be. The world does not conform to our desires."

Argnost turned to see Tully nod. "Just as you are what you are more than what others want to think you are. And more than what you want to limit yourself to being. This morning as I walked, a large Northern Hawk landed in a tree above my path. It spoke to me, Tully. It told me of Tyr's desire and his plans for you."

Tully's stomach tightened and he tasted the fear more strongly now. "I do not understand. I am just a Friar. I am no one. What could the Lawgiver want of me?"

Argnost smiled again. "He wants all that you can be and I think he expects much of you. But in this instance, he has a mission for you. Two, actually. But the first is a simple a stop along your true journey. Are you willing to serve the Lawgiver, Friar?"

Tully sat for a second as he felt the sweat begin to break out on his body. He prayed that the Hofgathi could not smell the fear that he felt. He forced the fear back into the place where he kept it inside himself and dropped to one knee. "How may I serve him?"

Argnost nodded his approval. "First, you will travel north to the town of Damaclees. It is a small town near the Snowmelt River. There is a problem there. I do not know what it is, but the Messenger of Tyr assured me it would be obvious when the time came for you to deal with it."

Tully nodded as he remained on one knee. "Yes, Hofgathi. And the second task?"

Argnost turned to stare out at the garden again. "That mission is even more peculiar. There is a kingdom north of the river. In it is an elf. This elf is a druid and a mage. Something that I have never heard of before. He faces a peril. His problem involves betrayal and a great evil that should not be allowed in this world. The Lawgiver expects you to protect this elf."

Tully looked up at Argnost. "Protect a druid sir?"

Argnost turned back to face the young Friar. "My understanding was not important to Tyr's messenger. But it would seem that this druid has a roll to play in the Lawgiver's plans. That is enough for me. Is it enough for you, Friar Tully?"

Tully nodded. He fought to keep his fear in check. He would have to have faith that his God knew what he was doing. "How shall I find this druid?"

Argnost shrugged. "I actually asked the Messenger that. He told me Faith."

Tully felt his uneasiness grow.

Argnost walked around the desk and approached the table covered by the sheet. He motioned for Tully to join him. As the young Friar stepped up beside him, he pulled back the sheet. On the table was a shining breastplate with a small sword above where his heart would be. The armor was beautiful and seemed big enough to fit even Tully's chest and stomach.

Beside the armor was a shield painted white with a large silver cross centered upon it. Tully shook his head as he realized it was not a cross, but a sword. It was the symbol of Tyr. The blade of the sword was strange, though, as it did not end in a point, but rather was squared off at the end.

The final item was a small sword in a sheath. Tully studied it. It was the size of a short sword and the sheath seemed a little thicker than normal.

Argnost waved his hand across the equipment. "This is to keep you safe on your journey, Friar. Wear and use it well."

Tully stared down at the equipment in confusion. "Begging your pardon, Hofgathi, but I am forbidden to use edged weapons. Even a sword of the Lawgiver."

Argnost chuckled and reached out to pick up the weapon. "Be at ease, Friar. This is Brjóta." He drew if from its sheath. Instead of a sword blade, what came forth was a solid unsharpened piece of metal. Tully thought it looked like one of the files that father had used to care for the hooves of the oxen. But it was much thicker and the light of the window seemed to make it glow with reflected light.

Argnost slid it back into the sheath. "It is a magical mace, Friar. It only appears to be a sword because we serve Tyr. It is blessed by Tyr and it will serve you best against evil. The greater the evil, the more powerful it will become and the brighter it will glow. Use it well, Friar."

Tully stared down at the equipment. "When am I to make this journey?"

Argnost placed the weapon on the table and turned to clap the young Friar on the shoulder. "In the morning. Most assuredly after breakfast. Eat well."

Tully only nodded. He was not sure he would be able to keep the food down. It seemed more like a last meal for the condemned.

Chapter 2

The Road to Damaclees

Tully was tired and hungry. It had taken nearly ten days to make the trip from the Temple to the small town of Damaclees. Thank the Lawgiver that he had caught a ride in the wagon with that farmer and his wife on the last day. The apples they had shared with him had done little to assuage the growing hunger he felt.

He thought he had packed enough food for his journey, but it had all disappeared in the first several days of his travels. He had stopped briefly in several small towns along the way. There he had healed all who needed Tyr's help. The residents had shared food with him before he moved on. But the relief from hunger was temporary. He had not realized how much energy it took to travel so far on foot. He really missed the meals at the Temple.

He also missed his small cot. Sleeping outside on the hard ground was painful. The only decent sleep he had gotten were the two nights he had been able to sleep in the barns of farmers along the way. He had often slept in the loft as a child so the hay had a familiar feel as he drifted to sleep those nights.

Damaclees was somewhat of a letdown. He had expected to find some sign about his mission here. But there was nothing. He had arrived yesterday. So far, he had settled two disputes and healed four people with minor injuries. Now he was cleaning a young farm woman's foot so he could heal it as well. Was this the problem he had been sent to solve?

Tully stared down at the crushed foot of the young woman who sat before him at the inn. She was very pregnant and he could not understand why she had been milking the cow instead of someone else. And why had the fool woman not paid more attention? She had let the cow stomp on her foot. Tully was sure that at least two toes were broken.

Tully bowed his head and lifted the tiny golden sword that hung from the chain around his neck. He began his prayers for healing. He watched as the golden light of Tyr encompassed the foot. The bloody wound closed and the three middle toes straightened out. The woman thanked him as she got up from the chair. Her husband came forward with an embarrassed look on his face and a small sack in his hand He smiled tentatively. "We have no money to offer the Temple for this healing. I, or we, would like you to have this though, Friar."

Tully accepted the bag and looked inside. There were two small round cheeses and a loaf of bread. Tully realized that this was a generous gift for most small farmers. Like his own family, they did not have a lot of food to spare. "Thank you, Goodman. But the gift is not necessary. The Lawgiver's gifts are given freely."

As Tully tried to hand the sack back, the man shook his head and thrust it back at Tully. "No please, Friar. Keep it. My wife makes a really good cheese. And thanks to you, she will walk again. It is small compensation for what you did. Besides, you will need your strength for what you will do for us on your way north. The whole town is talking about your bravery."

Tully nearly fumbled the sack of food as the young farmer's words sank in. The familiar bitter taste invaded his mouth as he asked, "What feat of bravery are you thinking I will undertake? I must admit that I am a little confused."

The young farmer blinked in surprise. "But... Well, we all sort of assumed that was why you were here. You being a cleric of the Warrior

God and all. Why else would you come all this way except to defeat the barbarians for us? You did say you were going north to the bridge from here. We all figured you would take care of those bandits at the bridge."

Tully's stomach clenched in fear. Of course, that was the reason he was here. The Lawgiver would want bandits stopped. But why him? He was no great warrior priest. Tully turned towards the innkeeper. "Can you tell me a little more? Apparently, I am not as well informed as your town might think."

The innkeeper looked up from polishing the bar and smiled. "From what I have heard, there are three warriors from the mountain barbarian tribe that have come down onto the plains. They apparently followed the Snowmelt River until they found the bridge. Now they are camped there. They challenge everyone that comes by to a fight. If no one fights them, they take all their money and food. Been going on for a month now. None of the local farmers can fight them."

Tully sighed and rubbed his temples. He turned back to see the hopeful expressions on the face of the young farmer and his wife. The woman whispered quietly, "Will you help us, Friar? We need the trade opened back up."

Tully closed his eyes and swallowed his fear back down, again. He locked it tight in that place inside where no one else could find it. Then he opened his eyes and turned to face the farmer and his wife. "Yes, I will go north to the bridge and see what I can do. In exchange, Lady, you must promise to be more careful until your child is born. I will continue north from the bridge and cannot help you again."

The couple smiled and turned to the door. As they left the inn, Tully could hear them yelling excitedly to the others in the street that the Friar really was there to help. Tully headed up the stairs to the room the innkeeper had given him and began to pack his things. He placed the sack of food into his backpack. Once he had his armor on, he headed back down the stairs.

Tully walked up to the bar to thank the innkeeper. He caught sight of himself in the reflecting glass behind the bar. He cut a dashing figure in the new armor with the shield on his arm. It was too bad that he knew inside that it was all a lie. He was not the brave warrior priest that they all thought him to be. Inside he was a cowardly man who feared the world. But he would do this for them despite his fear. At least he would not have to face them again after he failed.

The innkeeper looked up from the keg he was tapping to see Tully standing there. "Leaving now? It will be getting dark when you get to the bridge."

Tully kept his voice even as he replied. "I will stop just short of the bridge. I prefer to arrive just after sunrise. What do I owe you for the room last night?"

The innkeeper shook his head. "You did right by the townsfolk. There is no charge. I will more than make up the cost of a single night if you clear the bridge and bring travelers back this way again. My thanks, Friar."

Tully nodded and turned towards the door. He headed out into the street and turned north. It seemed like most of the town was there to watch him leave. Their hopes that he would make their lives better were written on their faces. He was not sure how he had gotten into this mess. He had only offered to help heal their sick and injured, not to fight their battles for them. He was no more a warrior than they were. He returned a few waves as he walked north out of the town. His stomach churned with the fear he felt, but what could he do other than what they expected him to do?

Tully walked along the road in the late afternoon sun. The road was smooth and wide enough for two wagons to pass. The setting sun was still hot, but there was a gentle breeze that pulled the sweat from his body. He had been walking well over an hour when he began to hear the sound of running water up ahead. He began to look for a place to camp for the night when he noticed a thin ribbon of smoke rising from the side of the road not far ahead. Tully approached slowly to see a lone man sitting beside a small camp fire.

Tully raised his voice to be heard over the sound of the water. "Hello, stranger. Would you mind sharing your fire this night?"

The stranger turned his bearded face to stare at Tully. "Welcome, priest. Would you mind collecting a little extra wood? These old bones do not move like they used to."

Tully moved off into the trees and began to pick up pieces of wood and tree limbs where he could find them. When he had an armload, he headed back to the fire and dumped the load of wood on a small pile beside the old man. Tully took a seat across the fire. He loosened his backpack and set it aside. Then he leaned the shield against it.

Tully sat in silence, occasionally studying the man on the other side of the fire. The old man had a rugged face that was lined with age. He had a beard that covered most of his face. It was hard to tell in the fading light where the blond color ended and the grey began. The man sat silently, studying Tully and smoking an old pipe.

Tully was uncomfortable under the man's stare. Finally, the old man spoke to him in a soft gentle voice. "I would offer you better hospitality, but I had little before the ruffians at the bridge decided to take what was left. I am sorry."

Tully smiled at the words. "Your fire is hospitality enough, kind sir. My thanks for what you offered."

The man smiled. "You seem to be carrying a heavy burden, young priest. Tell me about yourself."

Tully was not sure why, but he began to tell his whole life story. He told of his days on the farm. He told of his need for order and stability. He spoke of how hard it was when routines changed or decisions had to be made. Then he told of his visit to the city and his father's plan to make him responsible for selling the crops each year. He whispered about sneaking away from the inn to join the Temple. He spoke of his joys at serving the Lawgiver. He told the old man about singing on Feast Days, and healing the poor at the market, and he even told of the occasional trips out into the local farming communities to provide spiritual guidance and healing. He told of all the things he loved most.

The old man listened and watched. When Tully began to wind down, the old man asked simply, "So, who do you serve, young Friar? The Lawgiver? The people? Or yourself?"

Tully sat for a moment in stunned silence. "Sir, I am not sure that I understand your questions."

The old man took his pipe into his left hand and pointed at Tully with the stem. "Do you sing in the choir for the glory of Tyr? Or do you sing because it makes you feel good about yourself?"

Tully's mouth worked but he had no answer. The old man continued. "Do you heal the spiritual ills of the poor and destitute that come to the Temple as Tyr demands or do you use the Lawgiver's spells to heal only their bodies because it makes you feel important?"

Tully dropped his head in shame. The old man went on once more. "When you visit the villages, do you take the time to understand their problems and their heartaches or do you simply judge them and preach a message you do not truly understand?"

Tully sat and stared into the fire. The truth of the old man's words brought tears to his eyes as he silently admitted to the crimes of which he had been accused. He wanted to be angry, but there was only sorrow in him. He turned back to the old man to find him smiling softly at him.

The old man took another puff of his pipe. "There is good in you, young Friar. The fact that you feel pain at my words shows that you have a good heart. Your soul might yet find the answers that it seeks."

Tully whispered softly. "What must I do to find these answers?"

The old man chuckled. "Stop seeing the needs of the world through your own eyes. See the needs of others through their eyes. Stop trying to remake the world as you would have it. Accept it as it is and care for it. Stop trying to feel good about what you are doing and simply make sure that those you help feel loved by you. It is not a difficult formula but it is definitely a difficult journey. I think, young Friar, that it is a journey that you would do well traveling."

Tully sat quietly as darkness settled about them. The stars came out and filled the moonless sky.

The old man continued to smoke his pipe. He watched as the young priest tried to come to terms with his past. Then without warning he spoke again. "Tell me, Friar. You are a long way from the safety of your Temple and the life you seemed to cherish. What would bring you all this way to share a fire with a tired old man like me?"

Tully's voice was so soft it was almost drowned out by the sounds of the insects around them. There was sadness in his voice. "Tyr had a mission for me. One I do not understand and one I have no hope of completing."

The old man leaned forward and stared into Tully's eyes. "You seem to have a rather low opinion of your worth, my young friend. If your God chose you for this mission, what makes you think you cannot succeed?"

Tully's voice cracked as he replied. "Because I am not worthy. I cannot be what Tyr needs me to be!"

The old man cocked his head to one side as he looked at Tully. "What is it that you cannot be?"

A single tear rolled down Tully's cheek. "I am not brave. I do not know how to be brave. Tyr is the bravest of the Gods. He sacrificed his right hand to save us all. I cannot be like him."

The old man leaned back. "Because?"

Tully grew sullen. "You wish to shame me. Fine. Because I fear. I fear every day. I fear every change. I fear so much that I can taste it. Do you understand now?"

The old man smiled and then began to chuckle softly. Tully became red with shame and turned his face away. He had not expected the old man to laugh at his fear. But then the old man's quiet voice consumed him. "I do not laugh at your fear, boy. I laugh at your misunderstanding. Do you truly believe that Tyr did not feel fear when he fed his hand to the wolf to save mankind? Do you think the choice was an easy one for him?"

Tully stared at him wide eyed. "He… He is Tyr. How could he be afraid?"

The old man sighed. "He felt fear because he was not a fool. Only a fool does not fear. Fear does not make one less of a man. It is what you do with the fear that makes you what you are."

Tully leaned forward, totally absorbed by the teaching. "I do not understand."

The old man took the pipe from his mouth and set it aside. "A man or a God who places his hand in a wolf's mouth without fear is a fool. He does not understand what it is that he does. Therefore, it is of no consequence. A man or a God who knows fear and can still place his hand in the wolf's mouth. That one is brave. He has conquered his fear. If he does it for himself, then he is selfish although perhaps still brave. If the God or man fears and places his hand in the wolf's mouth to save the world, then he is brave and he is a hero."

Tully stared at him. "Does it matter how much you fear?"

The old man chuckled again. "Yes, my friend, it does. The more you fear, the braver you are if you can stay the course."

They sat in silence for some time before Tully volunteered, "I go tomorrow to face the bandits."

The old man nodded. "I see. Are you afraid of this task?" Tully nodded. "Good, then you are not a fool. But you will do it anyway?"

Tully looked away again. "I will, but I am not sure that I want to."

The old man waved his hand in the direction of Damaclees. "Then do not. Go back to town and return to the life you had."

Tully shook his head. "I cannot."

The old man stared at him sternly. "The Gods have given us free will. They do not take that from us or we would become little more than sheep. If you do this, it must be your choice or it has no meaning. Choose, boy."

Tully stared into the fire for a time. "I choose to seek out the bandits."

The old man picked up his pipe and began to smoke it again. "That is good. And after the bandits?"

Tully pointed vaguely north. "I go to find an elf in another kingdom. I am to protect him from great evil."

The old man nodded again. "Do you fear this journey?"

Tully met his gaze this time. "Yes."

The old man laughed heartily. "Good." Then he rubbed at his stomach. "I have not talked this much in a long, long time boy. Talking sure makes you hungry."

Tully sat up suddenly. "Wait. I have cheese and bread. I forgot. Would you share my food, stranger?"

The old man nodded and Tully pulled the small sack from his backpack. He pulled out a small round of cheese and the loaf of bread. He handed the loaf to the old man. "Please break the bread while I slice us some cheese."

The old man took the loaf from Tully in his left hand. Tully pulled a small knife from his belt to slice the cheese. As Tully finished slicing, he looked up to see the old man place the loaf on his right leg. His right arm came up out of the shadows. The man placed his arm across the loaf of bread to hold it in place. As he broke the loaf in two, Tully realized that his right hand was missing. He handed half the loaf to Tully with his left hand.

Tully absently took the bread as he continued to stare at the old man's right arm. "You… You have no right hand, good sir."

The old man took his own piece of bread into his left hand and then lifted the arm before him. The arm ended at the wrist. The old man laughed and stood up. "You are right, Tully. It is indeed gone. But it was my choice as it was my fear to conquer. And I would do it again. Especially if it meant an enjoyable evening such as this."

Tully fell to his knees. "Lawgiver…." Tully glanced up, but the old man was gone. All that remained was the sweet smell of his pipe. Tully heard a voice that seemed to echo from far away. "Thank you for the bread, my young friend. The farmer's wife really is a good cook."

Chapter 3

Carrying the Word

Tully spent most of the night going between contemplation about his life and prayer. Strangely, he was not tired when the sun came up over the horizon. But he was hungry. He ate some of the bread and cheese and placed the rest back in his backpack. Tully buried the ashes of the fire before putting on his pack and taking up his shield. Tully took a last look around and returned to the road. As he tuned to face the river, he felt the return of his fear. He once more tasted the bitter on his tongue.

Tully began to walk. He wished there had been more time to listen to the old man. There was so much more he wished to understand. Each step towards the bridge seemed more difficult. The familiar bitter taste returned to his mouth, but Tully kept moving. A soft breeze caressed his face and he stopped to listen. On the stillness between breathes of the breeze, Tully heard the old man's voice once more. "Sing for me, Tully. Sing out."

So, Tully began to sing. It was tentative at first but the songs of the Temple soothed him. Tully sang of battles fought and won. He sang of brave heroes and their suffering. He sang of times long past. But mostly he sang of a One-Handed God who chose to save the world from evil. As he sang, the bitter taste in Tully's mouth became sweet.

The fear was still there roiling strong in his stomach, but its taste no longer tormented him.

Tully paused his singing when his feet stepped onto the bridge. It was only then that the he heard the voices behind him. He turned to see three large bearded warriors. Each wore leather armor and bore a warrior's two-headed axe. Tully just listened as they spoke to each other.

"This one is dressed all fancy like some knight."

"But he gots no horse."

"Sings like a song bird. Thought he would never stop."

"He has a sword."

"But is he too afraid to use it."

"These lowlanders are all cowards. We will never demonstrate our prowess here."

"The Wise Woman sent us here so here we will stay."

Tully smiled and bowed to them. "It seems there are three of you and but one of me. But I am here to send you away."

The smaller of the three laughed. "The one of you is bigger than the three of us. How can you fight with so much fat?"

The man closest to Tully called for silence. "We only leave if you defeat us, Man who Sings. But we wish to prove our skill. We will fight with honor, so it shall be one of us at a time you must face. Draw your sword and face me."

Tully placed his hand on Brjóta's hilt. "It is not a sword as I am a cleric of Tyr. It is a mace, and it will serve me. I will fight you unless you are afraid." Tully slid the unusual mace from its scabbard.

The leader stared at the weapon for a moment and then shrugged. He raised his axe in both hands and stepped forward to bring it down in an overhead chop. Tully brought up his shield. The axe hit it and rebounded. A clear, almost perfect note rose from the shield as it was struck. Tully began to sing in tune as the sound rang from the shield.

The words of a feast song consumed him and sweetness caressed his tongue.

Tully stepped forward. Instead of bringing the mace down on the man's unprotected head, Tully drove it forward like a sword into his stomach. The air seemed to explode from the man's lungs and he bent over holding his stomach. Tully brought the hilt of the mace down on the back of the warrior's head, but not hard enough to crack it. The man dropped to his knees.

Tully stepped past the fallen warrior and into the second man in line. Tully drove the shield into the man's face before he could even bring his axe up. A second clear note rang out as the man staggered back. Tully tripped him, knocking him to the ground.

The smaller man darted forward and swung his axe at Tully's right arm. Tully brought the mace across and knocked the axe blade aside. Before the small man could bring the huge axe back around, Tully brought his smaller weapon down hard on the man's hand. There was the crack of breaking bone and the axe fell to the ground.

Tully moved to the side of the bridge and leaned against the wooden rail there. He waited silently as the warriors recovered from the fight. After a time, the leader approached. "You have defeated us, warrior. We will return to our mountain home. But first I must ask, who is this Tyr of whom you sang?"

Tully smiled as a small breeze caressed his face. "I will tell you of Tyr, but only if you allow me to heal the wounds that I gave you and if you share my meal with me."

The second man looked at Tully in astonishment. "You defeated us and you will heal and feed us. What strangeness is this?"

Tully smiled. "It is the way of the Warrior God. It is the command of the Lawgiver himself."

Tully followed the three men to their small camp. Once there he healed their wounds. He pulled out the sack of bread and cheese. There seemed to be much more than he remembered. The four men all ate their fill while Tully shared the songs and stories of Tyr. He spent a week with them teaching them the ways of the Lawgiver. They left to return to their mountain home. They took with them the stories and songs to share with their people. Tully promised to visit them when he completed his mission. It was a frightening promise, but the taste of his fear was sweetness in his mouth. Tully turned to the north. His God had other duties for him.

The Burden of Her Gifts

Chapter 1

Trial by Fur, Feather and Scale

F'lar looked up as the mingled sound of growling, barking, and laughter came through the open window of his study. He rose and walked over to stare out into the morning sun. His eyes were drawn to the stretch of grass in front of his home. A massive dog lay across the squirming body of a young man. He had no need to see the young man's face to know it was his apprentice, Karhu.

The dog had little trouble keeping the young man pinned to the ground. It outweighed the young man by at least 40 pounds. He smiled as he watched them play. The pair were a puzzle that would take a lifetime to figure out. But they suited each other despite the many contradictions in each of them. Their love for each other made them whole as nothing else could have.

He studied the large dog as it once again leapt on the young man knocking him back to the ground. Even to the eyes of a druid, the dog was one of the ugliest creatures the Goddess had ever created. Its sire was the pack leader of a truly impressive wolf pack that lived to the north of his valley. Its dame had been a mastiff owned by one of the local rangers. She had been large even for a mastiff with brindled fur that drew the eye.

If the dog had taken after either parent, it would have been beautiful. Instead, the Goddess had given it a patchwork of mismatched features, colors, and fur. Its coat was a mix of short mastiff fur with longer strands of wolf pelt. Its striped fur contained lines of red, black, and yellow. Its head had the typical blocky shape of the mastiff but its body was the more slender shape of the wolf. Its feet were comically large. F'lar wondered if any but a lonely and abused boy could have loved such a dog. But the boy had somehow seen past the dog's looks to see what lay within. In contrast to its exterior, the animal's spirit was as the boy had named him, Beauty. F'lar could not imagine a braver or more loyal companion than his fosterling's friend.

The young man was in many ways the inverse of the dog. Karhu was a good-looking young man on the outside, something that F'lar's daughter pointed out to him much too frequently. But Karhu had suffered a great deal as a youth. His parents had died when he was young and he had been sent to a small mission orphanage near a very poor village. Life there had not been good and it had just gotten worse for the youth.

He had been taken from the orphanage by slavers. The slavers had treated the small boy badly. Karhu was still haunted by ghosts of his past. F'lar worried that the battered boy inside the young man might never get past those experiences. Still. Karhu had a good heart, but at times his decisions were based on past fears instead of his current situation. He knew the boy had come a long way in the years since F'lar had rescued him, but was it far enough?

F'lar had done all that he could to help the boy heal. He had to have faith in the boy and in the Goddess that Karhu would become both the man and the druid that F'lar saw within him.

F'lar shook his head and put aside his thoughts. It was past time for his foster son to move forward in his studies. It was time to let go of his own fears and trust in the Goddess. Karhu was either ready for his future or he was not. It was not F'lar's place to judge the boy's heart or his dedication. Mielikki would know Karhu's destiny and the role he would play in her service.

F'lar left his office and moved to the front door of his home. He reached down to open the door. There was a smile on his face as he stepped out into the sunshine. He drew in a deep breath of the late spring air. The scent of grass, flowers and trees calmed him. The peace he felt told him that he was making the right decision.

The young man and the dog stopped their roughhousing and rose to their feet. F'lar stepped forward and squatted before the dog. He reached out and gave the scruffy animal a good scratch behind both ears. F'lar uttered a few soft yips and growls as he spoke to the dog. "Go find something interesting to sniff, Beauty. I must speak to your boy for a time."

The dog whined softly and the elf laughed in response. "No, he is not in trouble again. But he does have work to do that you may not help him with. You will have to settle for playing with Uusi for a time." Beauty yipped softly as his tail began to wag furiously. Then the dog turned and trotted around the side of the house, leaving the elf and the man alone.

Karhu stared down at his teacher. "You slip into his tongue so easily that I cannot always follow the conversation. Am I in trouble again?"

F'lar shook his head in response to his son. Both the dog and the young man understood the boy's almost innate ability to find trouble. F'lar's smile grew as he rose to his feet. He gestured to the two chairs resting in the shade of the house. F'lar moved to the closer chair and sat down. He waited until Karhu settled on the other chair. Karhu stared at his foster father. "If I am not in trouble then how may I serve Teacher?"

F'lar met his eyes. "The Summer Solstice is in two days. I believe that it is time, maybe even past time, that you take the Trial of Fur, Feather, and Scale."

Karhu blinked in surprise, then his eyes dropped to his hands as they clenched in his lap. His hands were suddenly sweaty. "I am not sure that I am ready Teacher. I thought I had at least another year to prepare."

F'lar studied the young man carefully. Goddess help them both. He had been waiting for the boy to ask for the trial as most young druids did. But Karhu was content in the safety of his foster parents' home. He would never move beyond that safe little world on his own. This fledgling would need to be pushed from the nest. "Another year to do what Karhu? What will you learn in the next year that you do not already know? It is time to let go of the control you grasp so tightly. Mielikki wants you to become more, to risk more. She wants you to demonstrate your faith in her. For a change, allow her to be in control. You might be surprised at how much easier that makes your life."

They both sat in silence for a time. Karhu fidgeted as he reflected on the meaning of his teacher's words. Finally, he raised his eyes and asked. "What can you tell me about the Trial?"

F'lar answered him softly. "The trial begins at sunset on the Solstice. It will last for 9 days. During that time, you will take the forms of three of her creatures, one each of fur, feather, and scale. You will remain in each form for three days. When the trial is over, you will return to me and tell me your tale."

Karhu shook his head. "That does not seem that difficult. I have studied the beast forms for a long time now. The trial has always seemed ominous. You make it sound easy."

The elf chuckled softly. "That is not the trial my boy, those are just the rules. Your trial will be given to you by the Goddess. Something unique is asked of each initiate. I do not know what she will ask of you, but it will force you to confront your past to prepare you for your future."

The young man paled slightly. "I do not like my past. I prefer to leave it buried." The elf did not answer him. After a time, Karhu continued. "Teacher, you know what I went through. Why would she ask me to confront that again?"

F'lar turned his gaze to the north. "My childhood was not as difficult as yours Karhu. But it was not all pleasant either. In my trial, Mielikki asked me to stand once more against the will of my mother and her people. Despite defeating her once before, I was still afraid of my mother. She was and still is powerful. The Goddess showed me that there were solutions other than power against power. It was liberating to see my mother learn the same lesson. We are still not close, but there is a truce between us now."

Karhu looked surprised. "You have never spoken of your mother to me."

Sorrow showed on the elf's face. "Some pain even I prefer to leave buried. Finish your Trial and I will tell you of my youth."

"Do you have any advice, Teacher?"

"Only that you should choose each of your forms carefully. The forms that you take during your trial will be your most powerful forms for the rest of your life. Choose them wisely."

Karhu studied his teacher. "Teacher, why are your forms all creatures of the far north? I have always wondered."

F'lar's eyes took on a distant look. "My parents were of two powerful Homes. They did not spend much time together. For most of each year, I lived with my Mother. She was of the Jäätikko. In your tongue it means People of the Ice or perhaps Ice Elves. The creatures that I understood best were those that walked the lands of Jäätikko. So, the Ice Bear and the Snow Owl were creatures that I had more time to study."

The young man nodded. "Thank you. May I ask, how will the Goddess let me know what I am to do?"

F'lar shrugged. "I do not know, but She will make it clear to you. Now go say your goodbyes. Uusi will not be happy with you if you do not spend time with her before you leave. Besides, there is little to prepare. You may not bring anything except your courage and your faith on this adventure."

F'lar watched as his son rose and walked away following after his dog. He wondered how Mielikki would bring the boy back to face his past. His mind drifted back to his own trial. That had been a painful confrontation with his mother. But in the end, the guilt he had carried about his own choices had been resolved. He said a silent prayer that the Goddess would find a way to help Karhu find peace.

Two days later, F'lar led his young apprentice south from the Temple. They traveled swiftly through the morning hours. They stopped for lunch beside an old hickory tree. After a quiet meal, F'lar opened a path from the hickory to a place that Karhu did not recognize. The second hickory was much younger. It sat on the edge of small clearing.

F'lar turned to face his apprentice. "You have until sunset to prepare yourself. You must decide by then which of her creatures you will take the form of. Be well my son."

Karhu looked at F'lar nervously. "Teacher, how do I do this? You have explained the process of the transformation, but I have never tried it."

F'lar place a warm hand on the boy's shoulder. He squeezed gently. "You do this through faith, with Her love, and in accordance with Her will. This is a gift that she gives only to those who chose to follow her path. Simply focus on the form you wish to take and ask her blessing."

Karhu looked confused. "No words or gestures? Nothing?"

F'lar gripped his foster son's shoulder harder. "It is not a spell. Simply believe. Remember three days in each form. No more and no less. I do not know which of her minions will visit you, but you must complete the assigned task within the time allotted."

F'lar stepped back and smiled once more. "Go with my blessing. And your mother said to tell you not to get yourself hurt. I will wait for you at home." With that F'lar stepped back and spoke a single word in the language of the Arcane. Then he was gone.

Chapter 2

Feathered Observer

Karhu walked to the base of the hickory tree and sat down. He leaned back against the trunk of the tree. His thoughts returned to the coming trial and the choices he would have to make. He had decided on his first form as soon as Teacher had explained the Trial to him. He wanted to fly. The prospect of flying was as scary as it was exciting. To soar above the earth would give him true freedom. He could escape from anything or anyone simply by taking to the air. That was also the frightening part. What if he made a mistake and crashed? Birds were fragile things. Dying during the Trial was not a great plan. His foster mother would not be pleased.

There were many birds that he could have chosen, but he was not interested in the tiny birds that were little more than prey. He had been prey once before and he never wanted to feel that kind of fear again. At the same time, his fear of making a mistake made him leery of the predators that flew high and fast. In the end, he had chosen the Great Horned Owl. It was a powerful bird that could fight as well as fly great distances. This would be his first form in the Trial.

He considered his options for the second and third phases of what was to come. Karhu knew what furred form he wanted to use. Becoming a karhu, a bear, had been his dream since the day he had been saved from the bad people by a great white bear. That bear had really been Teacher in animal form, but that did not stop the small boy from idolizing the karhu. They were strong and fearless. So unlike the boy that had taken their name for himself. Now he had the opportunity to truly be a karhu and he fully intended to transform into his namesake. His choice would not be the tame brown or black Karhu, he would be the strongest of them, the grizzly. As a grizzly, he would never need to fear again. He just hoped being a grizzly would work well in whatever task the Goddess set for him.

His problem was in choosing a scaled form. Even the venomous snakes he knew were vulnerable. They were slow and nearly defenseless against most flying predators. He did not like feeling vulnerable while stuck in a form for three days. He could not think of any of the scaled folk that could really protect themselves. He would have to wait and see what the Goddess asked of him before deciding.

The sun was getting low in the sky when Karhu opened his eyes and pulled out the jerky and water he had brought along. He knew he would have to eat in his animal forms, but he did not want to start out hungry. He wanted to learn more about flying before he had to hunt for food. When he had finished eating, Karhu wiped his hands on the grass and turned to the hickory. He began to climb until he reached a large branch about ten feet overhead. He thought that his first flight would be easier if he did not need to take off from the ground.

Karhu watched as the sun began to sink below the horizon. It was time. He focused his thoughts on the powerful wings and the sharp talons of the owl. At the same time, he reached towards the Goddess in hope and supplication. Darkness fell. Instead of his vision growing dim, it seemed to sharpen. Every small detail of his surroundings seemed to leap into focus.

His hearing became more acute as well. He could hear the sound of a field mouse scurrying through the grass behind him. His head swiveled to search for the mouse. To his surprise, his head twisted farther than he would have believed possible. He spotted the mouse. It was a nice fat one. Karhu raised his arm to rub his eyes, but he had no arms. What he saw was a strong feathered wing. Karhu could only marvel at the change. The Goddess had blessed him with the form he had desired. He lost all awareness of his surroundings as he studied his new body and the sensations that came with it. There was a light breeze. The small feathers along the surface of his wings told him much more about the flow of the wind than his human senses ever could have.

Karhu's wonder at the transformation was interrupted by a predatory growl from behind him. Without thought, Karhu dropped from the branch and spread his wings. They caught the breeze and it lifted him into the air. He glided across the clearing to land on a sturdy branch high in a new tree. He had flown for the first time. Sadly, he had not had time to enjoy it.

There was a soft chuffing noise coming from the hickory tree he had been forced to flee. Karhu turned back to face the way he had come. His eyes focused on the branch he had just vacated. It was now occupied by an enormous bobcat. The cat was sitting and grooming its fur with a self-satisfied expression on its face. It was his blessed curse and he just knew the cat was laughing at him. How had the stupid cat gotten here anyway?

As he watched, the cat gave its fur a final lick and it leapt gracefully from the branch to the ground below. It padded silently across the clearing and stared up at him. Its voice carried a questioning note as it growled up at him. Karhu could not cast his spell to speak with animals in this form so he had no idea what it was trying to tell him.

The cat turned south and began to walk. After about a dozen steps it stopped and looked back over its shoulder. It growled again, more harshly this time. Karhu dug his talons into the branch in frustration. He had to assume that this was the messenger that the Goddess had sent to lead him to his quest. Of course, she would pick the one creature in the world that loved to torment him. The cat would teach humility as it led him to his task.

Karhu spread his wings and dropped from the branch. His first flight had been instinctive. Driven by fear, he had not thought about what he was doing. This time was different. He had to work hard not to override his body's natural responses to changes in the air flow. As he began to follow it, the cat loped south. Through the early part of the night, the cat kept a slow pace. Karhu had time to become familiar with flying. His confidence grew and he began to fly higher. The cat took as its signal and it began to run south at a much faster pace. They did not slow as the night passed.

Near dawn, Karhu was tired and hungry. It seemed like ages since he had eaten below the hickory tree. The great owl that was Karhu beat its wings and gained more altitude. His keen eyes began to scan the ground below. Karhu detected movement in the tall grasses to the right of this path. His prey became motionless. But it was too late, the shape of the small rabbit was clear to him. He dipped one wing and glided towards it. Karhu forced his thoughts to still and the instincts of the great owl took control.

His wing tips curled in and he dove towards the ground. Just before he struck, the small rabbit broke from the grass at a run. Karhu felt his wings unfurl slightly, adjusting the path of his descent. They unfurled fully just before he struck, slowing him just enough. His talons went deep into the softness of the rabbit. Its small form was crushed beneath him as he hit the ground much harder than he intended. Apparently, there was more to hunting in this form that he realized.

Hunger took over at that point and his sharp beak ripped into his kill. Karhu looked up moments later to see the glowing eyes of the cat watching him. Strong emotions washed through his new body, equal parts fear of the large cat and a desire to defend his kill. Karhu wondered if there was a danger of losing himself in the beast if he stayed too long in this form.

His hunger was quickly satisfied. The body of the owl did not hold much and it seemed incapable of overeating on its own. He flapped his wings and returned to the air. He found a large tree and settled on a wide branch. He watched the cat finish off the rabbit as the sun rose above the horizon. Karhu's talons sank into the wood of the branch and his eyes closed. He slept.

His sleep was not peaceful. There were dreams that all carried a sense of urgency. There was someplace he needed to go and something he must do. But he did not know where or what. At times he dreamed of riding currents of air that pushed him onward. At other times he moved through grass that towered over him. Throughout the dream, he caught glimpses of a young girl with a strange birth mark on her arm. Just before he awoke, the dream changed again. He felt strong and powerful. But those feelings were washed away by fear and panic. Those were the emotions that drove him from sleep into the waking world.

Karhu's eyes fluttered open to see lengthening shadows. The sun was setting once more. It was time to move. He had somewhere to be but he had no idea how much further he would need to travel to get there. He glanced to the ground below the tree. The cat was sitting there staring up at him. The remains of a dead possum lay at its feet. Karhu unfurled his wings and glided to the ground.

He hesitated. Would the cat actually share its kill? Before he could decide what to do, the bobcat turned its back to him and walked away. Karhu hopped closer and began to eat. In addition to some of the flesh, the cat had left the more nutritious parts. Karhu ate the heart first. He ate until he heard the impatient yowl of the cat. He looked up to see it waiting on the trail they had been following. Karhu took to the air once again and followed the cat south.

The second night, the cat set a grueling pace. Karhu was not sure how the cat found the energy to run so far and so fast. Karhu hunted again just before dawn. His meal this time was a pair of field mice. It was enough. He found another wide branch and slept again. His dreams were similar to the first night, but now he sensed danger to the girl. His need to protect her rode him until his eyes fluttered open. The sun was still well above the western horizon. Again, the cat sat below the tree with a fresh kill. Karhu ate ravenously before rising into the sky.

The cat turned east towards a line of hills visible above the trees. It moved more slowly than the night before, staying in the cover of the undergrowth as much as possible. They moved into the hills well before midnight. They had crossed several low hills when the cat came to an abrupt halt near the crest of a hill. It stared into the darkness before them and growled softly.

Light rose from the ground in several locations on the far side of the hill. Sounds drifted to him from the same direction. He rose high into the night sky as a breeze carried him over the small valley beyond the hill. As he drifted forward, Karhu could make out a lone farmhouse and a barn. The area around the buildings was lit by many campfires and torches. Karhu allowed the breeze to carry him closer as he studied the scene below. Arrayed around the farmhouse were a dozen large caravan wagons. Karhu felt uneasy but he did not know why. He was afraid but did not know why.

Karhu circled the farm several times. People gathered around large fires near each of the wagons. It was late but there was a lot of activity around several of the wagons. The scene below seemed hauntingly familiar. Each time he searched his memories, panic rose to disrupt his thoughts. He was certain that these wagons had never visited the Grove before. So why did he feel like he knew them?

Something about the scene below did not make sense. Despite all the activity around near the wagons, the farmhouse was dark and silent. The door was closed and the windows were all shuttered. He did not understand why the cat had led him here. What did this have to do with the girl? Karhu descended towards the barn. He settled on the roof of the barn on the end that allowed him to study the front of the farmhouse. This location also gave him the best view of the three wagons that seemed most active.

The Farmhouse seemed almost vacant so he turned his attention to the three wagons parked in a semi-circle around its front door. Karhu's eyes locked on the wagons. There was a symbol painted on the side of each of them. The great owl went perfectly still. He knew that mark. He had seen it every day as a young boy traveling from place to place with his tormentors. These were the bad people. He prepared to take wing and escape from this place. As he unfurled his wings to flee, a familiar shape walked towards him across the roof of the barn. It was the cat. Some of his fear ebbed away as the cat settled beside him. The panic faded and Karhu suddenly remembered that he had come here to discover what the Goddess was asking of him. He resumed his careful study of the wagons below.

The wagon nearest the farmhouse door was the most elaborate of the group. He recognized it as belonging to the tall man he had called the Master. There were several young girls gathered at a fire near the Master's wagon. They looked to be cooking for him. His ears picked up a clinking sound as the girls moved about. Karhu guessed that they wore chains and shackles to prevent them from running as he had. The Master did not like losing his property.

The second wagon near the farmhouse did not seem familiar, but he knew the third one well. He stared at the wagon until he could make out the shapes of the dogs tied to its side. The one he had called the Hunter still traveled with the Master. Karhu turned his head to eye the cat. His thoughts were still in turmoil at where he had been brought. He could not imagine why the Master would risk getting even this close to Teacher again. F'lar had been very clear about what he would do if he ever encountered the bad people again.

The cat met his gaze. Karhu gave a soft screech as if to ask why he had been brought here. The cat blinked twice and then padded to the far end of the barn where it could see the back of the farmhouse. The owl beat its wings softly and flew to join the cat. There were wagons behind the farmhouse as well. But these were quieter and the bad people there appeared to be sleeping.

They sat with the stillness of predators, watching the rear of the farmhouse. After a time, Karhu heard a light squeak of metal. It would have been hard to hear with human ears. Neither the owl or the cat missed it. The cat's ears were perked forward as it stared into the darkness. It raised a paw as if to gesture towards the farmhouse.

Near the corner of the home, the ground appeared to be rising, leaving a dark opening. It took Karhu's human mind a few moments to realize that a trap door had been hidden below several inches of soil. A small form slipped from the opening to crouch beside the farmhouse. Something even smaller was handed out next. The first form grasped it tightly. Finally, a larger form exited and lowered the trap door.

Without thought, Karhu stretched out his wings and glided across to the edge of the farmhouse roof. Looking down, he could see a woman strapping a baby to her chest. Beside her stood a young girl of about twelve years of age. This was the girl that he had dreamed about. Karhu was certain of it. He thought he understood now the task that the Goddess had set for him. He just wished he knew how she expected him to save the girl and her family. Even if he took on the form of the karhu, he would not be able to fight off all of the bad people. Hunter and his dogs could easily overcome even a full-grown grizzly.

He watched as the woman took the girl's hand and led her into the darkness, staying as far from the wagons and their small fires as she could. Karhu opened his wings and dropped from the roof. He soared silently above the fleeing humans. The woman tried to run quickly, but the young girl stumbled frequently. It was not hard to keep pace with them as an owl, but Karhu knew he would soon be forced to take another form.

Karhu followed the three humans through the remaining hours of darkness. There was something strange about the way the young girl moved. Her mother scanned the darkness around them, looking for danger. The young girl's gaze seemed to be fixed on the ground before her. Even with that she struggled to stay on her feet. Only her mother's firm grip on her hand kept her from falling. Even with the coming of dawn, the girl's movements seemed hesitant as she ran beside her mother.

He stayed near them for most of the morning. Sometimes he flew a bit ahead and rested on a tree until they had passed him. By midday, he was tired and needed food. He knew he could not afford to sleep for long. He prayed that he could find them again after he rested. The woman had been moving mostly north through the night. Hopefully they would not change direction before he awoke.

But before he slept, Karhu had an important decision to make. He must take a new form at sunset. He must take either a furred or scaled form. He knew many furred forms well, but he had never been drawn to the scaled ones. Conversation with snakes and lizards had not been very exciting to a young boy interested in adventure. His lack of interest might cost the girl dearly now.

Karhu did not want to use his furred form yet. It was his most powerful form and the one that gave him the most options. He needed to save it until the girl was truly in danger. Still, he needed to keep up as they fled. Most of the scaled ones he knew were not fast enough. Then Karhu had a thought. He remembered one reptile that was very fast. He just could not know if it had the stamina to keep up with the fleeing humans. He would have to risk it; he could not think of any other options. The owl settled on another wide branch and closed its eyes. He had flown far since the last time he had slept.

Chapter 3

Scaled Persistence

Karhu opened his eyes to see shadows moving across the ground below. The sun was setting and he needed to transform soon. His head rotated from side to side as he scanned for threats. Seeing nothing, he opened his wings and glided to the ground. As he settled in the tall grasses, his thoughts drifted back to his days as a young initiate working in the Grove. He had been in a hurry that day. The fox vixen had delivered her litter and she had promised him that he could see the pups. He had left Beauty with Uusi because the large dog made the fox nervous.

Karhu had been moving swiftly through the trees, not really paying attention to the forest around him. The large black snake was lying on a sun warmed rock soaking in the heat when he broke through the underbrush. His soft boot had landed between its coils. He was ashamed to admit that he had yelled when its head had come up to hiss in displeasure. To this day he was still not sure who was more surprised at that moment, him or the snake.

He had frozen at its warning, waiting for the snake to strike. Its head waivered from side to side as its large eyes seemed to stare right through him. The moment has stretched on as he studied the snake.

Its scales were the deepest black he had ever seen, except for the small white patch beneath its lower jaw. It was scary and yet very beautiful.

Then it had moved. It had literally shot across the clearing away from him. Karhu would have been hard pressed to keep up with it. It crossed the clearing in a heartbeat and disappeared into the brush. He could not comprehend how a creature without legs could move that quickly. He has always intended to ask Teacher about the snake. But he had forgotten in the excitement of seeing the pups.

Karhu's mind focuses on that one brief moment where he had locked gazes with the snake. His mind reached out to the Goddess while visualizing midnight black scales undulating across the clearing. He asked the Goddess to grant him the swift form of the snake. His choice frightened him. This form was vulnerable and he doubted its speed could save him from the bad people. He could only trust in the Goddess and pray that this form would help him to find the girl even if it could not protect her.

He was more aware of the transformation this time. The powerful wings of the owl sank into his body. The feathers melted into soft, supple plates that covered his body. The owl body slimed and softly toppled to the grass. Karhu expected the clarity of his vision to fade as the owl eyes mutated into those of the snake. He was pleasantly surprised that it did not. The snake's sight was different, but it was just as sharp in the evening shadows as the owl's had been.

Karhu's awareness of his new form grew with each passing moment. He marveled at his new body. This form was stronger than he would ever have imagined. The hundreds of muscles in his own form had been replaced by thousands and thousands of muscles hidden within the snake's supple body. He was suddenly sure that the snake had the stamina to catch up to the girl and her mother. Especially with the woman carrying a baby against her chest.

Karhu turned his attention outwards to study his surroundings. He searched for the trail of the girl and her mother. There was grass all around him. It rose above his head and he realized he could see little through the forest of tall grasses. Karhu raised his head above the grass to look about him. The angle was wrong and he still could not see much. Worse, he would not be able to move very fast holding his head above the grass. He feared that he had made a mistake in choosing this form.

Karhu cursed himself for not learning more about snakes or any of the scaled children of the Goddess. He had never found them to be that interesting. His focus had always been on the creatures of fur and feather. He had been content to study them. Now, lives depended on his ability to use this form and he just did not know enough. The girl might to pay the price for his lack of study.

He tried to smell his surroundings hoping that perhaps the snake could follow the scent of the humans. There was nothing. His human nose could detect more than that of the snake. He began to worry. The speed of the snake was useless if he could not track the girl.

Karhu was at a loss. As his mind searched for a solution, his snake tongue shot from between his jaws into the air before him. As it retracted, it pressed against the roof of his mouth. The flood of information about his surroundings almost overwhelmed him. The snake part of him identified plants and small animals and even insects. Some of those scents he tasted reminded him that he would need to eat soon. But not too much, as he did not want his new body to become sluggish.

He tried to move slowly forward so his tongue could sample other scents, but his undulations took him sideways instead of forward. His movements were jerky and lacked rhythm. As he had with the owl, Karhu had to learn to be less controlling. His snake body knew how to move smoothly and swiftly as long as he did not confuse it with unnecessary commands.

Karhu began to glide slowly forward. It grew easier as he thought less about what he was doing. His tongue shot out over and over, bringing tastes back to the roof of his mouth. Then he tasted a scent that alarmed the snake's instincts. It was the scent of humans and they were dangerous. But the part of him that was Karhu knew that this was what he had been searching for. He began to follow their trail while searching for things that he could eat. He managed to catch a caterpillar crawling towards the base of a tree. At another point there was a tiny tree frog low on the trunk of a nearby tree. Thankfully, he did not have to taste either meal. Both were swallowed whole. It was not a lot of food, but it kept him moving through the night.

He guessed it was almost dawn when he finally found the three humans. They were sleeping under the boughs of a spruce tree. They looked exhausted. Since they were sleeping, he moved in closer to study the young girl. He had to be certain that this truly was the girl he had dreamed about. Her clothing was dirty and her shirt was torn. The sleeves of the shirt were not long and he could see something on her arm. He moved closer and raised his upper body so he could study the strange marking on her right forearm.

The birthmark was just as he had dreamed of it. And it was much, much more. To his snake eyes, it seemed to glow in the darkness. It was not just the outline of a tree. It was detailed down to individual branches and leaves. He had never seen a mark like this before. He recognized it as a Hickory tree. As he studied it, he realized that the birthmark was not flat. Branches and leaves created a textured pattern on her skin. If he still had fingers, he swore he would be able to feel the grain of the tree's bark. Mielikki had plans for this young girl. He was certain of it. He just had to make sure that she escaped from the Master.

The sun had risen while he studied the girl. He moved back into the shadows and settled near the trunk of the spruce. With the coming of the sun, the humans began to stir. He watched as the woman sat up and nursed her baby for a time. When the baby appeared satisfied, she woke the young girl and handed the baby to her. The girl sang softly to the baby as her mother pulled two small potatoes from a bag tied to her waist. She also pulled out a tiny knife and began to slice the potatoes into wedges. Karhu could remember a time when a piece of raw potato would have seemed like a feast. He did not miss those days.

The woman held out a hand with several slices of the potato. But the girl did not reach for them. Her mother hissed with an exasperated tone. "Hold out your hand, girl." Karhu watched as the young girl held her hand out in the general direction of her mother. The woman turned the girl's hand over and placed the food in her palm. Karhu suddenly realized that the girl could not see. She was blind. Suddenly the stumbling journey as they fled their home made perfect sense.

The woman began to eat several of the wedges as she studied the area around their camp. Between bites she began to speak to the girl. "We must be on the move soon Annah. Those men will not allow you to escape so easily. Remember girl that you must run if I tell you to. Do not hesitate."

The girl stopped chewing and asked quietly. "Why do they want me, Mama?"

The woman reached over and took the baby back. She placed the last pieces of the potato in the girl's hand. "You have gifts, Annah. Your father moved us out in the middle of nowhere to hide you from those who would have used you."

The girl's head dropped. "My gifts with plants and animals did not save Papa from the fever. What good are they if I could not save him?"

Her mother finished strapping the baby to her chest. She reached across to place a gentle hand on the young girl's knee. "Someday you will understand your gifts, child. Do not doubt that they will serve a purpose somewhere in your future. Now finish your food. We must run again."

The girl placed the last slice of potato in her mouth and got to her knees. Her fingers reached out to stroke the trunk of the spruce and she whispered a thank you to it. As she backed out from beneath the tree, her faced turned towards Karhu. She froze as her eyes seemed to lock on him. It felt like she was staring into his soul. Then she smiled and nodded. He mother reached down and took her hand and pulled her to her feet. They turned north and began to run once more.

Karhu lay there for several long moments, huddled near the base of the spruce tree. The girl could not see. And yet, she had known he was there. Not the snake hiding in the underbrush, but the young druid that was there to help her. He did not understand. Then he shook his head. Understanding was not required. All that mattered was that he kept the girl safe.

He began to follow them once more, but he was slowing down. He had traveled far in this form. His tongue brought him the taste of prey. Karhu turned from the girl's path to chase down a field mouse. After he had swallowed it, his body seemed sluggish. There was a warm rock nearby. Karhu curled himself around it intending to rest for just a bit. When his eyes opened again, it was dark once more.

He slowly uncoiled from around the still warm rock. The food and rest had restored his energy. His snake body was not sore despite the distance he had traveled the previous night. Who would have thought that a sun warmed rock would make such a comfortable bed? Karhu had no problems locating the trail of the girl and her mother. Once he had the taste of them, he began to pursue them at the snake's top speed. He had little doubt that he would catch them again. This form was more capable than he had expected it to be.

It was near to midnight when he detected three new taste-scents. The new trail came from his left and merged with those of the woman and the girl. The new tastes seemed, he struggled for a word to describe what he tasted, fresher. He assumed they were more recent than that of the girl. Two of the new taste-scents were human, but he could not identify the third taste-scent. The snake did not know it.

The third creature seemed to move in strange patterns around the path of the humans. Almost as if it were hunting. The pieces finally came together in Karhu's mind and he knew fear. The Master and the Hunter had come for the girl and her family. They had brought a rotter to track the fugitives. The rotter would be able to scent him too.

Karhu was not sure what to do. How could he hide from the nose of the dog? He would be little more than a quick meal if the dog caught his scent. The snake, no he, would be prey for the rotter. He hated feeling vulnerable this way. And he despised himself for the fear he felt. Karhu lay there in the grass for a long time. Fear of the Master warred within him with his need to save the girl. Memories of the many abuses he had suffered at the hands of the bad people flooded his thoughts. He carried the scars of those abuses on his soul as well as on his body.

The mental image of a glowing hickory tree-shaped birthmark reminded him of the girl. He could not allow the Master to hurt her as he had hurt Karhu. A voice in his mind whispered that he was no longer that small boy. That boy could not defend himself. The small boy had grown into a man. Now he was a druid, an Initiate of the 5th Circle. He would defend the girl. He just needed to find the courage to try.

Karhu began to move forward once more. He had to believe that Mielikki would not send him on a mission he could not complete. He needed to have faith. He began to race through the forest following the fresher trail of the men and dog.

Karhu's sense of time was distorted in his current form. Snakes or owls had little need to measure time other than day and night. It might have been an hour later or maybe two when the snake part of him wanted to turn away from his path. It had tasted the scent of fire. Fire meant danger and death to the snake. But the man within the snake forced it to continue on. Karhu lifted his head above the grass and he could see light flickering through the trees before him. He began to move carefully towards the light.

Karhu paused every few body lengths to raise his head above the grass to study the scene before him. The two men sat around a campfire in the middle of a clearing. The rotter was tied to a tree on the far side of the clearing. The large dog whined and stared in his direction. Karhu realized the dog knew he was there, but it could do little chained up as it was.

He took advantage of his black coloring to slip closer. He stayed in the shadows behind the Master to make sure the firelight did not reflect off of his scales. Karhu was curious about everything he had seen back at the farmhouse. Why was the Master taking such a risk to capture this girl when there were so many orphans in the land that were easier to acquire?

Karhu slithered closer and closer, his soft scales sliding silently over the grass and rocks. He curled behind the Master's backpack and lifted his head to listen to the conversation between the two men. Maybe he could learn something that would help him understand his own role in this hunt.

Hunter sat to the Master's left. He held his spear in both hands with the point down. The Hunter stabbed the tip into the ground between his feet over and over. He appeared nervous. There was resentment in his gruff voice and he complained to the Master. "This is damned foolish, Boss. That druid fella told us what he would do if we come this close to his lands again. Why is one girl worth the risk? I do not fancy facing that white bear again."

Karhu could not see the Master's face as he responded. "Do not be such a coward. That druid is over a week's ride from here. We are not in any danger as long as we catch the girl quickly."

Hunter stabbed his spear deeper into the soil. "That is the problem. The rotter keeps losing the scent. It is not natural. That dog has a good nose. Every time we get close, the trail gets all muddled."

The Master patted the whip tied to his belt. "I will motivate that dog the next time it loses the scent."

Hunter shook his head. "It is not the dog, Boss. I am telling you. It is that girl. Why is she so important?"

The Master spat into the fire. It hissed and there was a brief sizzle. "Do you remember that dark robed priest that showed up in camp a couple weeks back?" The Hunter nodded and the Master continued. "He was a Priest of some god named Set. Offered me a bag of gems to bring him a girl with a tree-shaped birthmark on her arm. Told me right where to find her. With what he offered me, I can buy a keep and pay others to do my slaving for me."

The Hunter sighed. "Them gems are only good if this does not get us killed, Boss. I will do my best to keep the hound on the trail. Just do not get angry and kill this one. I need this one to sire a few litters before I lose it."

Karhu slithered away from the two men and into the darkness. He was more confused than ever. He had never heard of this Set before. And why would a priest of some strange god want a little girl marked by Mielikki? It made no sense. He might never understand what this was all about, but he did know what the Goddess was asking him to do. He had to get to the girl before the two men did.

Karhu went around the camp in a wide circle, staying as far from the rotter as he could. Once again, he found the trail of the small family and he began to follow it. The rest of the night passed quickly as he worked to make up the time he had lost sleeping. Dawn had come and gone by the time he found their campsite. But they had already moved on.

He was exhausted at this point and his body craved food. He searched for something he could eat as he moved slowly along the girl's trail. He managed to catch a beetle, but there was little else to eat. As much as he wanted to keep going, Karhu knew he needed to rest for at least a couple hours. He began to search for a safe place where the rotter might not find him.

Not far past the deserted campsite, he spotted a tree with a depression at its base. He slipped into the depression and curled up. He closed his eyes and fell into a troubled sleep. He dreamed again of the girl. Something was wrong and she was very, very afraid. He understood her fear for he had felt its like many times when he was young. He knew the Master must be close and that knowledge drove him from his dreams.

It well before sunset when he woke and crawled from under the tree. There were several fat caterpillars on the leaves of a nearby bush. He ate them quickly and returned to the place he had last tasted the scent of the girl. Traces of the Master and the Hunter now lay over the trail he had followed. He began to race after them once more. Darkness fell around him as he chased after the two groups.

As he moved swiftly through the grasses and trees, Karhu began to think about the next phase of the Trial. At the next sunset, he would transform into his final form, that of fur. He needed to find the girl and learn the fate of her family before he could make a final decision about which animal he would become. His desire to become a karhu no longer mattered to him as much as the safety of the girl and her family. His choice would depend on what he found when he caught up to them.

The night passed too quickly and he still had not found those he sought. He realized that he was moving slower. This form had been a good choice, but he had pushed it too hard with too little food. He would not be able to go much farther. Karhu pressed on as the sun rose overhead. He no longer had the strength to move fast, but move he did.

Then heard a woman scream from somewhere ahead. "Run Annah! Run!"

Karhu wanted to rush to their aid, but he had nothing left. Besides, this form could not help those he was to protect. They would have to stay safe until sunset. All he could do was learn more and be prepared. He slithered into the underbrush and began to move very carefully towards the voices he heard. He must not be detected by the men or the rotter.

By the time he reached a place where he could watch what was happening, the excitement was over. The woman lay on her side with both her feet and hands tied together. There was a large bruise forming around her left eye. The girl sat leaning against her mother clutching the baby. Anger burned within him, replacing the fear he had felt before. Karhu found a place in a thicket where he could watch everything while remaining safe from the dog.

He watched as the Hunter made a small cookfire and began to prepare a meal. The Master stood over the three captives with a self-satisfied smile on his face. He knelt and briefly examined the birthmark on the girl's arm. "You are about to make me very rich, child. If you were not worth so much, I would make you pay for the chase you led me on."

The Master stood and turned to the Hunter. "Get the food cooking. I want to be on our way back as soon as we have eaten. We came much further north than I intended. I want to be gone before that druid learns what we did."

Karhu lay coiled in the thicket wondering what he should do next. He thought of all the furred warriors that he knew. He would have to fight to free the woman and her children. It would not be an easy fight with the two men and the dog. Only the karhu, the fierce grizzly bear seemed to have a chance. He did not think he could win, but maybe he could do enough damage to let the woman and girl run once more. The snake's eyes closed in exhaustion. Karhu slept without him realizing what he had done.

Chapter 4

Furred Fury

Karhu snapped awake to find the sun low in the sky. He had not intended to fall asleep. But he had and now the camp was deserted. He had lost them again. Soon it would be time for his final transformation and he had no idea where to find the girl. Should he take a form that he knew could track her? He quickly reviewed the furred forms that he knew were good at tracking. In the end, he dismissed them all. Not even the wolf met his needs. None of the good trackers would be able to free the girl from the Master.

Deep inside, Karhu knew that the girl's fate would be decided in battle. It was time that he stood up to the Master. It was time he faced his past. He knew it would not be easy, but he suspected that it was what the Goddess had intended all along. She was not interested in his past; she wanted him to put it aside. Her interests were in his future. A future not burdened by old fears.

There was good news, though. If he was going to make an insane rescue attempt, he might as well do it in the form he had desired since he was a small boy. He would become the mighty karhu. It might not be the white bear that the Hunter feared, but it might be enough to shake the man's confidence.

Karhu's mind drifted back to his last encounter with the Master as a boy. Teacher had saved him using the form of the great white bear, the jääkarhu. The beast had seemed invincible. But he was not Teacher and he had never fought in bear form before. One small spark of hope burned in his heart. Defeating the men and the dog was not required. He only needed to free the girl and her family. That and make sure that the Master could not capture them again.

A sense of peace washed over Karhu as he made his decision. He would be powerful and strong for a time even if it was the last thing he did in this life. What more could he ask for than to die living his dream? He would serve Mielikki in this quest and he would do it gladly.

It was sunset and he turned his thoughts back to the first grizzly that he had met. There were several that roamed the forests near the Grove. In his mind, they were the rulers of the forest and few creatures or men willingly challenged them. Teacher had promised him a treat, taking him deep into the forest to meet an old bear named Metsän Vartija. That day was burned into his memory.

Metsän had been taller on four legs than the twelve-year-old boy that had stared at him in amazement. The bear had been over nine feet tall when it had reared up on its hind legs, It had seemed like a giant. Metsän had been extremely intelligent and the old bear had taught him much about the forest it considered its own. Teacher had asked the old bear to let the young boy touch it. Metsän had agreed on the condition that the boy give his back a good scratch in the places the old bear could not reach.

Karhu's mind relived that time of exploration. It had been late fall and the bear's pelt was getting long and thick. It had been difficult to get his fingers through it. The pelt had been a deep brown with white near the tips. He had marveled at Metsän's heavy muscles, especially the hump between its shoulder blades. The old bear had especially enjoyed being scratched at the base of the hump.

Karhu felt his body begin to shift as his mind relived that long ago day in the forest. The Gift of the Lady came faster this time. His eyes blurred as his perspective changed from just above the ground to several feet above it. He felt his body grow and expand. His incredible sense of taste faded, to be replaced by a sense of smell far beyond that of his human form.

Karhu rose on four legs. It was strange to have legs again. He walked into the human camp. The smell of people was strong and unpleasant to his ursine nose. Then he picked up another scent in the campsite. His lips peeled back in a snarl and his neck fur rose as anger flooded his body. Dog. The part of him that was bear wanted to lash out  at the canine odor. It was too close to the smell of the wolf packs that occasionally attacked bears.

He pushed down his dislike of the smells and began to follow the trail of the humans. They were taking a different route back. Their path drifted a bit to the west as it moved south. He scented water somewhere ahead. The trail was several hours old so Karhu picked up his pace. It did not take him long to reach a stream headed mostly south.

Karhu felt a rumble in his core. He had not eaten well while he had been in snake form. This body was going to demand a lot more food. He moved into the stream and bent his head to drink from the river while he thought about what to eat. There was a flash of silver beneath the water. He raised his muzzle and licked away the excess water. Fish! The thought of a fresh fish or three was appealing. The bears he had observed always made fishing seem so easy.

Karhu waded deeper into the stream and began to stare into the gently flowing water. There was another flash of silver. He swiped at it with his paw. The bear form was fast but the fish was faster. The swipe of his paw sent a spray of water towards the shore but nothing more. He waited patiently for another flash of silver. When it came, he struck again. He felt the fish slide across his paw. Again, only a spray of water hit the shore. Karhu feared he would starve at this rate.

He realized more quickly this time that he needed to depend more on the bear's instincts than his own. Karhu stilled his thoughts and ceded control to his animal form. The bear's hunger took charge at that moment. This time he felt the claws on his paw curl down. When the next flash of silver came, his paw stuck straight down. His claws sank into the fish and pinned it to the stream bed. The fish thrashed against the rocks below as his head dipped beneath the water. His jaws clamped around the fish and he carried it to the bank, where he devoured it quickly. It took three more fish before his massive body felt sated.

He drank deeply once more and then moved back to the trail he had been following. The great bear began to lope along at what felt like an incredible pace. The trail was easy to follow especially with the dog marking its territory at regular intervals. Karhu knew he had a lot of ground to make up, but he kept to a steady pace that would not tire his new form. Daylight seemed to slip away as he closed the distance between them. Near midafternoon, he spotted several berry bushes that he recognized. They had not fully ripened yet, but he did not care. Karhu paused long enough to strip berries and leaves from the bushes. The bear form seemed to relish the bitter juice as his jaws crushed the fruit. His hunger receded once more.

The trail began to veer away from the river before nightfall. Karhu slowed his pace. He knew he was getting close. He continued to follow the trail as the sun set once more. Karhu legs felt the strain of the hours he had been on the move. But he would not rest again. He could not afford to fall behind. He could not afford to let the Master rejoin the wagons before the girl was safe.

Smoke drifted through the forest and Karhu turned his face into the breeze. He followed the smell moving cautiously through the trees, one paw at a time. He came to the edge of a large clearing. A campfire flickered in its center. He could see two forms moving around in the light of the fire. Karhu eased to his belly and began to move away from the tree line. He prayed to the Goddess that his dark coloring would hide him in the shadows. He stopped about halfway across the clearing to examine the area around the fire.

It did not take long to spot several forms lying on the ground near the fire. He was certain that these must be the girl and her family. The two men were busy preparing something to cook over the fire. Karhu recognize a spit but could not tell what creature they were about to cook. Karhu's eyes continued to search the near darkness. He needed to know where the rotter was before trying to free the captives.

He was still searching when a sound came from the trees somewhere behind him. The two men turned to stare in his direction. The Hunter stood with the long spear in his hands. The spear head seemed to glitter in the light of the fire. A second, taller man stepped forward. It was the Master. He seemed to shake something out with his right hand. Karhu's eyes followed that motion. His eyes could not make out what the Master held, but his imagination filled in the details that were hidden in the darkness. The Master had his whip in hand. Time seemed to come to a stop as the fears of a small abused boy washed over him again.

Karhu knew that whip. He had "earned" many beatings with it. The leather was long and braided. Its delicate tip could leave a long, painful stripe along back or a leg. In the Master's hands, it could also leave deep cuts. The tip of the whip was a truly bad dream, but beyond the tip was where the nightmares began. The leather beyond the tip had tiny pieces of metal imbedded in the leather. When one was very, very bad, the Master would move closer so the bits of metal could rip and tear at the skin.

Karhu's muscles tensed in anticipation of the next strike of the whip. He could scarcely breathe. The body of the grizzly was paralyzed by the fears of the boy he had been. How could he face either of these men alone? Then he heard it. A soft feminine voice whispered in the recesses of his mind. "You are not alone, my Karhu. Have faith."

Karhu shook his broad head. He had to keep telling himself that he was no longer that boy. He could cower here in the darkness or he could stop the Master. He had the power to ensure that the two children did not suffer as he had. He would not allow the Master to keep the baby or sell the girl to this priest of Set. He would save them.

Karhu slowly rose to his feet. Even on four legs, the Master did not seem quite as large as his fear had painted him. Before he could step forward, the noise came again from the woods behind him. This time it was accompanied by a growl. Karhu looked back to see the large dog break from the trees towards his rear. He began to spin around but felt the teeth of the dog sink into his rear leg.

Karhu swung his front paw back at the dog. He connected hard against the animal's chest, but not with his claws. The dog flew away into the dark, but it rose to its feet and charged back at him. He heard the Master order Hunter to attack. Karhu was trapped between foes.

Then a tawny shape with glowing eyes darted from the trees and launched itself at the dog. The yowl of a hunting cat mingled with the screams of the dog as the two bodies tumbled across the clearing.

Karhu rose up on his hind legs and turned just as the spear head dug deep into his left shoulder. He raised his head towards the moon and roared out his pain and fury. Without thought, his right paw lashed out at the Hunter with his claws fully extended. He smelled blood as the Hunter stumbled back, both hands trying to cover the deep gashes on his face and the remains of his left ear. Karhu twisted his head to the side and he bit down on the spear shaft, pulling it from his body. It fell from his jaws as he began to walk steadily towards the Master.

The Master stepped forward as well and drew back his arm. As the whip came forward, Karhu raised his injured arm to protect his face. The tip of the whip struck, but there was little pain. His coarse fur kept the tip of the whip from touching his skin. The sting of the cruel weapon could not hurt him. Karhu gave a grunt of pleasure as he continued towards his prey.

Karhu noted with pleasure that the Hunter had turned to flee. His now-bloody shirt was held to his face as he ran from the clearing. He hoped the man would never come this way again. Karhu turned his attention back to the Master as the whip cracked again. He felt the whip impact his fur once more. This time, the metal bits caught in the fur of his chest and side. When the whip was pulled back, Karhu felt fur being torn out, but little else. He roared his fury. The Master stepped back, dropping the whip and reaching for the sword at his waist. Karhu did not hesitate, he dropped to all four legs and charged. He reached the Master before he could bring the sword up to strike.

Karhu's furred bulk knocked the man backwards. The Master stumbled and fell heavily on his back. The angry bear swarmed over him planting one paw to each side of the man's body. The Master was still struggling to bring his sword up when Karhu lowered his head and closed his jaws around the arm with the sword. Karhu shook his head savagely. The Master cried out in pain and dropped the blade. Karhu felt bone snap beneath his powerful jaws.

Karhu released the arm and turned his head to stare into the Master's pale face. Karhu's jaws opened again and he roared his hatred of the man who had hurt him so many times. As he voiced his rage and pain, the acrid scent of the man's fear came to his nose. But that fear was not enough to wash away a child's suffering. Karhu raised his good paw in the air intending to ensure the Master never hurt anyone ever again.

A small body stepped between him and his victim. Karhu felt small hands digging into the fur of his neck. The small form did not have the strength to turn Karhu from his path. But somehow the rage inside him stilled at her touch. He did not strike. As the storm inside him abated, the small girl's voice came to him filled with tears and sadness. "Please no Forest Guardian. Do not kill. It is wrong."

Karhu turned his head from the Master to stare into the eyes of the young girl. His gaze traveled slowly to the tree-shaped birth mark. Then he lowered his head and ran his tongue across her cheek as the Teacher had once done to him. Somehow her tears tasted sweet instead of salty.

The girl stared up into his eyes. Again, he felt like those unseeing eyes had pierced his soul. He lowered his head and licked the remaining tears from her cheeks. The last of Karhu's anger disappeared with the tears. He used his muzzle to push the girl behind him. He sat back, settling on his haunches, and watched as the Master scrambled away from him. The man rose to his feet clutching his bloody arm to his chest. He glanced down at his sword. Karhu growled softly at him and the Master turned and ran. A part of him wished the Master knew who he was. But he realized that it was more important that he knew who he was and not what he might have become if the girl had not interceded. Karhu watched the Master disappear into the darkness. The fear he had carried for so many years left with his tormentor.

Karhu remembered the rotter and turned his head to study the clearing behind him. There was no sign of the dog anywhere. The cat sat on the edge of the firelight. It was grooming itself as if nothing of importance had happened this night. Amusement flowed through the great bear. His blessed curse was still with him. He gave a soft prayer of thanks to Mielikki.

Karhu examined the girl. She was holding the sword awkwardly, using its edge to cut the ropes binding her mother's arms. He listened to her voice as she told her mother that everything would be all right. The bear was her friend and that he had come to save them. Karhu wondered how a blind girl could see so much.

Karhu realized that the battle was over. The girl and her family were safe. The sense of purpose and strength that he had felt during the fight was suddenly gone. In its place there was only pain. His leg hurt where the rotter had bit him. The wound in his shoulder throbbed. He felt blood soaking his fur. The spear had struck deep. He still needed to get the three humans to safety. His wound would slow him down.

Karhu watched as the ropes parted and the woman's arms came free. After a moment, the woman took the sword from her daughter and began to cut her legs free as well. Instead of staying with her mother and the baby, the young girl returned to his side. He felt her small hands exploring him as her soothing voice whispered in his ear. "Oh dear. They hurt you. That just will not do." Karhu watched in amazement as green light the color of spring time began to form on the leaves of the girl's birthmark. The glow flowed down her arm onto her hand. She reached out and pressed the glow into his wounds. Karhu felt the pain leave him. The girl smiled up at him.

Wonder at the young girl's power rose within him. How could one so young possess that much healing? Then he realized she was still talking. "We must go west from here, Mother. The Bear will protect us. I know you are tired and scared, but I know something good is waiting for us. The cat will lead the way. And the Forest Guardian will carry you and Lissa."

Karhu shook his head at the girl's words. He glanced back to where the cat sat. Its head seemed to nod in agreement. Karhu lowered himself to his belly and waited as the girl led her mother over and helped her to sit carefully on his back behind his hump. The girl came and stood beside his head. She urged him to stand. Karhu nudged her with his muzzle until she also climbed to his broad back. Then he slowly rose and began to walk towards the cat. It stopped licking its fur and turned to lead him into the darkness. They crossed the stream heading west. The moon hung over the trees as they traveled deeper into the forest.

Chapter 5

Trial's End

F'lar studied the young man sitting in the chair next to him. Karhu sat idly scratching his large dog's ears. The signs of perpetual vigilance were gone from his face. He seemed at peace for the first time since F'lar had spotted him fleeing through the forest. The Goddess had worked her magic on the boy and F'lar sensed that his foster son had healed many old wounds during his Trial.

F'lar had been worried when Karhu had failed to return after the nine days allotted for the Trial. It had been hard not to go out searching for the boy he had grown to love. He had been forced to wait another week for his son's return. He was not sure if that was due to the will of the Goddess or the willfulness of the boy. His prayers to the Goddess had been answered that morning when a great horned owl had soared in to circle the house several times before landing in the apple tree.

Unlike his wife and daughter, F'lar had given the boy time to clean up and check on his dog before pestering him with endless questions. When Karhu was ready, they had come out to sit in the yard. Karhu had told him the tale of his Trial. Mielikki had pushed the boy hard. Karhu had done well and F'lar sensed that the man she had sent back to him would be a powerful druid. He suspected the Goddess had many more challenges in store for his son.

F'lar cleared his throat. "And what of the young girl, Annah? And her mother and sister?"

A look of awe came across Karhu's face. "The cat led me west for two days. Not long before I was to return to my human form, we reached our destination. We were met by… Teacher, there were three of them. Treants. There was an ash, an oak, and a hickory. They came for the girl and her family. They promised her mother that the three of them would always be safe. They promised to teach the girl to use her gifts."

F'lar nodded. "Did they speak to you?"

Karhu smiled at the memory. "They thanked me and said the Goddess was pleased. They told me to study hard. The Lady has a difficult task for me if I am willing to serve her."

F'lar nodded again and waited for him to continue.

"I asked them about the girl, Teacher. She is special. I wanted to know more about her. All they would say is that Mielikki hopes that she will choose to serve her."

"What happened next?"

Karhu shrugged. "They walked into a mist and were gone. I could not even find their scent. I fell asleep. When I awoke, the cat was still watching over me. Then I started for home."

"Started?"

Karhu looked down sheepishly. "I may have explored my three forms and maybe a few others. I sort of lost track of time."

F'lar laughed softly. "You have done well, my son. In time, there are tasks I will need your help with. But that is well in the future. For now, serve her and take pleasure in the gifts that she has given you."

Karhu frowned as he seemed lost in his own thoughts. "Gift does not mean what I once thought it did, Teacher. Gifts can be complicated. They come with obligations and responsibilities. I would not give up the Lady's Gifts, but I never thought about what accepting them might mean."

F'lar leaned forward and place a hand on his knee. "To those whom much is given, much is expected. It is true of the gifts given by men and those given by the Gods. Know this, my son, the burden of her gifts will never be more than you can bear with her love."

The two sat and watched as the sun set. The sky was painted in a mix of yellow, orange, and red.

Eclipse of the Moon

Chapter 1

Moon Called

The dark elf spun, bringing his short sword up into a high parry before diving to the right. He rolled smoothly over his right shoulder, coming up to one knee to thrust forward. He paused there, studying the position of his blade and then he sighed in disgust. The angle of the blade was slightly off. He would have missed his opponent's heart. At best his thrust would have punctured a lung.

Roiland relaxed and lowered his blade. He had neglected this aspect of his training for far too long. After only an hour of drilling with the sword, his body was drenched in sweat. If he had been facing one of his brethren, he would probably be dead now. He needed to spend less time practicing with his bow and more reclaiming the rest of his skills.

A calm female voice echoed in his mind. *You are the Archer. With me, you have no need of that blade or any other.*

Roiland smiled ruefully at the longbow leaning against the wall of his home. Oikea Lakko was probably the finest bow that had ever been crafted on any world. But one day he might fight a foe that was too close to shoot with the fabulous longbow.

Not probably, Archer. There is no other bow that is my equal. And no foe will get close enough if you do not hesitate when you take your shot.

Roiland decided not to argue with the bow. She tended to win most of their arguments anyway. It was not because she was always right. As often as not, winning the debate was not as important to him as it was to her. It was easier to just let Oikea claim victory in discussions that he did not care about.

He sat back on his haunches. He pulled out a rag and began to polish his sword. It was a good blade forged with excellent steel. But it was not the equal of the short sword he had carried out of the Underdark. Sadly, that blade had not fared well on the surface world. Apparently, Drow tools did not last long in sunlight.

Roiland slid the blade back into its sheath as he rose to his feet. He began to stretch as his muscles cooled down. He was lost in thought when he felt another presence, this one in his heart. There was warm approval. He glanced up at the nearly full moon. He smiled and bowed his head toward the glowing orb. "Good evening, my Lady of Silences." He did not expect a response. She had never spoken to him.

Smiling to himself, he crossed the yard to the small well and drew a bucket of water. He used the water to rinse away the sweat from his exercise. When he was clean, he moved back to sit on the steps of the small lodge. His hand trailed lovingly down the length of the bow before he picked up a piece of cheese from the plate he had prepared before his practice session. It was sharp and he savored the smoky after-taste. His store of the cheese was running low. Erasmus had never shown him how to make it or told him where to get more. He would miss it when it was gone.

As he sat chewing, he felt something change. The warmth and approval of the Lady was still there. But it was now mingled with expectation and need. He stared up at the moon once more. "How may I serve you, Lady?"

There was a brief sense of gratitude and then, as it had on previous quests, he felt the need to be elsewhere. He felt drawn to the north, but the call was still faint and distant. "Somewhere there is one who longs for justice, my Lady. It would seem to be a long journey. Do I have time to prepare?" There were no words in reply. There had been no words in the six years since he had become the Archer. Silence and a sense of agreement was his only answer.

Roiland picked up the plate of cheese and patted his bow before moving inside to pack for the journey. He was not sure why, but he made sure there was extra food in his pack. He even wrapped the cheese in a cloth and tucked it inside. Next, he added his tools for making arrows. He stared around the room at all of the weapons on the wall. Something was missing. His fingers twitched and he reached out for the extra quiver of war arrows. He strapped that to the backpack. He slipped the backpack on and placed his quiver over his right shoulder. There was nothing else he needed.

Roiland walked out the door and picked Oikea up. It was time to leave. He pulled the door closed and latched it. There was a feeling of finality as he heard the latch click. There was something else he needed to do. Roiland walked around the side of the lodge. Before him lay two unmarked graves. He did not really know the woman buried in the grave to the right. But the closer one held his mentor and teacher, Erasmus the Archer.

He walked over and knelt beside the grave. His left hand trailed across the small yellow flowers that grew there. "I am not sure, my old friend, but I think this is goodbye. I owe you my life and so much more. I will try to make you proud."

Roiland smiled sadly and stood. Then he headed north at a light jog. There was no sense of urgency, but there was also not reason to waste time. He felt Oikea's presence in his mind. Wherever they were headed, they would be together in the service of the Lady. Deep down, he sensed that this time was different about this quest. They would be tested this time. He would be tested. He did not mind though. Quests like this allowed him to meet people and he was tired of being alone.

Based on the strength of the call, he knew his journey would be long. He had never been called to travel far from his home before. The task before him was important. What if he failed this time? It was a thought he had never considered before. Was his desire to serve the Lady of Silences strong enough? Was what he had become enough to face this challenge? He was not certain. Oikea's voice whispered to him, *We are enough.*

The nights on the trail passed without incident as he moved steadily north and east. His pace had slowed and at times he almost forgot that he was heading into danger on a mission he knew nothing about. But that was what the Archer existed for. It did not matter where he went. His life as the Archer gave him a sense of purpose that he had not felt among his own kind. He would always choose the uncertainty of this life over the predictability of Drow life. So he continued on. The call of the Lady still held no urgency so he took his time and conserved his strength.

He reached the banks of a large stream after nearly a week's travel . The location was familiar to him. Roiland realized he was not far from where Erasmus, the previous Archer, had run him to ground after the failed Blood Rite of his people. He did not regret the failure of the Rite or his exile from his birthplace. His time on the surface world had been a blessing to him despite his solitude.

Roiland turned from his path and followed the stream east for several hours. Dawn was still hours away when he slipped quietly into the clearing where he had once camped. Something about the place seemed different. He paused and studied his surroundings carefully. The sounds of the night creatures were much as he remembered. Whatever was bothering him was did not trouble them. At first, he was unsure what was out of place. Then he caught the smell of old fire. The smell of wood he had burnt would not have lasted so many years.

Roiland moved forward using all of the skills he had learned as a young Drow in the Underdark. He could sense nothing amiss. He tried to remember how the clearing had looked when he had made it his home. At first, nothing seemed out of place. The plant life had flourished with the stream close by. He almost missed what he was looking for in the darkness. But then he saw it in the brambles on the side of the clearing farthest from the stream.

The lean-to was a work of art. It had been crafted to blend into the brambles. He could have missed it even in full sunlight. He carefully moved closer to study it. The structure was built with a low profile that did not extend above the brambles. It was simple and sturdy. A small stone-lined firepit rested within the brambles but even that seemed almost natural. Soft grasses were piled within the lean-to. There was even a collection of deadwood to restart the fire.

Roiland moved away from the structure without disturbing anything within. He did not know when this place had last been used. The lean-to puzzled him. The location; it was far from the village or even the local farms. The effort that had gone into its construction suggested frequent use. Who would come so far on a regular basis and why? And why the exact clearing that he had once occupied? His thoughts continued to churn but it was a riddle for another time. He had somewhere else to be. The builder of the lean-to would have to take care of themselves.

He turned his back on his memories of the clearing and waded across the stream. His feet began to move faster as he left the small stream behind. It was not long before he was running through the trees, his mind at peace. Thoughts of the past and worries about the future faded with the rhythm of his steps.

It was two nights later when Roiland sensed danger once more. He stood in the darkness, reaching out with the magical senses that the Lady had bestowed on him. Nothing evil stirred in the darkness to his rear. He sensed nothing before him except his quest far to the north. Still, the feeling of danger stayed with him.

Roiland thoughts returned to the lean-to and he wondered again who had built it. Could that person now be on his trail? The Drow began to run once more. As he ran through the night, he searched for a place to meet whoever was tracking him. He wanted their meeting to be on his terms. Then he would learn who would hunt the Archer and why.

Chapter 2

Painful Memories

Roiland's search was frustrating. There was little in this area except trees. What he wanted was a cave or even some boulders, anything that would divert his follower's attention from his own tracks. He considered heading further east. The mountains lay in that direction. But he was not sure he could afford to lose more time.

It was about an hour before dawn when he found what he was looking for. There, on the edge of a small clearing, were two large trees lying one across the other on the ground. He studied the tangle of limbs and trunks. The larger of the two was an old pine. It appeared the weight of the tree had been more than the roots could sustain. It had toppled, wrenching its roots from the soil. As it fell, it must have hit a second, smaller pine. It had fallen too, getting pinned beneath the weight of the larger tree.

The pair now lay with their branches interwoven on the forest floor. The larger tree's trunk was slowly pressing the smaller tree into the soft soil. Nestled in junction of the two trees, obscured by branches and pine boughs, was a hollow. Roiland crouched to peer beneath the branches into the gap under the larger trunk. The opening under the tree was like a small cave just large enough to hold a prone man. He crawled closer to check it out.

There were hoof prints leading in and out of the hollow. Deer tracks. The hollow was empty now, but it was clear that he would not the first to use the trees as a shelter. He placed a finger in several of the tracks. One set was large and the other much smaller. There had been a fawn. He was glad it was no longer here. This would be the perfect bait for whoever was tracking him. He just needed a place where he could conceal himself while he waited.

Roiland turned his back on the fallen trees to study the opposite side of the clearing. There were plenty of trees, but he preferred not to be stuck up a tree if his foe did not take the bait. On the far side of the clearing from where he entered were several bushes that he recognized as having sharp thorns. The bushes should work as cover as long as no one got around behind him.

Roiland took great care to make the hollow look like he lay within it. He took several pine boughs and used them to stuff his cloak so it appeared he was wearing it. He placed two large branches under the cloak to give the appearance of legs. He returned to the tree line to studied the hollow from a distance. Then he moved forward and placed his backpack across the opening to partially block the view of the cloaked form. He inspected his work in the early morning light. He thought it looked like the camp of a tired traveler who had run most of the night. His success would depend on how good his tracker was.

Roiland climbed over the trunk of the larger tree and circled around to the thorn bushes. He did not want to leave any tracks to his hiding place. It took some time to find a position where he could see back along the path that he had used to enter the clearing without exposing himself. In the end, he had to cut away some of the thorns to get a good view. His efforts cost him several deep scratches. Then he lay still and waited, Oikea and a single hunting arrow resting near his hand.

The sun crawled slowly across the sky. Somewhere nearby, he could hear the steady rhythmic tapping of a bird searching for insects in a tree. He had to think for a moment to remember its name. Erasmus had called that bird a woodpecker. Strange name. Several squirrels began to chase each other across the dead trees. They seemed to be enjoying their mindless game. There was a great deal of chattering from the pair.

Then the squirrels went silent. One stood up and seemed to be listening to something. Roiland did not hear anything, but the squirrels suddenly scampered up a tree. Roiland knew better than to discount the senses of the local animals.

He continued to listen for a long time. Even the woodpecker had ceased its melody. The silence of the forest was broken by a single soft click. Roiland tensed. That sound had not been a forest noise. But it was one that he knew from the countless hours of drill that Erasmus had put him through. A crossbow had been spanned. They always made that faint click as the string locked into place. From the tone, he guessed it was a light crossbow.

Roiland reached out with the gifts of the Lady seeking evil. But he sensed nothing in the direction of the sound. That surprised him. Someone intend him harm but their intentions were not evil. What did that mean?

The lone figure was two steps beyond the trees before he noticed it. It blended into the trees as it slowly entered the clearing just to the side of his own route. His tracker was dressed in forest tones that were hard to separate from the nearby trees. The figure's face was hidden within a hooded cloak of mottled greens that hung down to mid-thigh. He might have missed the figure altogether if the lines of the crossbow had not caught his eye. It was loaded with a metal-tipped quarrel. This person wanted to make sure he did not survive.

Roiland watched as the cloaked figure surveyed the two downed trees. Well-made leather boots began to stalk towards the hollow where the two trees met. The boots made almost no sound as they moved across the many dried branches scattered on the ground. His foe had to be a ranger. No one else moved so quietly in the forest. But why would a ranger hunt him like this?

The crossbow never wavered from the cloaked form within the hollow. The ranger shifted position, shifting to find an angle that was not blocked by the backpack sitting at the entrance to the hollow. The figure came closer to his hiding place but its attention was turned towards the hollow.

Roiland waited until the figure had its back fully towards him and then he rose to one knee. His arrow was already notched and he pushed the bow out, holding the arrow at full extension. His movement must not have been as silent as he had thought because the figure before him froze. Roiland spoke calmly. "Please place your crossbow on the ground. Carefully. Then step away from it. I would prefer not to kill you before we can speak."

The cloaked figure seemed to consider its options. Roiland spoke again. "I am the Archer. I will not miss at this range. You need not die this day."

The cloaked form lowered its arms so that the bow pointed to the ground at its feet. Roiland watched as the figure's right hand tightened on the trigger. There was a snap and the quarrel sank to the fletching at the ranger's feet. Then the cloaked figure bent and lay the bow gently on the ground. Roiland studied his opponent. The ranger was short, at least several inches shorter than he was. And they were slender. Elves were slight of frame and he guessed that he was much larger than the person before him.

A female voice came to him. "This campsite was all a lie. It was a good lie, Drow. I fell for it. I should not be so surprised. Your kind are masters of deceit. I should have suspected a trap."

Roiland rose to his feet. The bow in his hands never shifted from the woman's back. "You seem to know a great deal about my people. Why do you hunt me ranger? What have I done to anger you?"

A soft sigh came from the cloaked figure as she turned to face him. The woman's voice was bitter as she spoke. "I have sought your death for years now. A life for a life in payment for your past. I thought the old man at least would kill you. Instead, he decided to take you in and teach you. When he failed me, I became a ranger. I studied hard so that I could take my own revenge."

Understanding began to dawn on Roiland but he wanted to hear more of the ranger's tale. He asked simply, "Revenge? For what offense?"

The figure reached up and lowered the hood. He stared at her face, but there was nothing in her features that he recognized. It had been too long and his memories were of a child. She would be about the right age. Barely an adult. She looked so young. Except for her eyes. They were old. Old and filled with hate. "I swore an oath as a young child to see you dead. You killed my friend. You took the light from my world and you stole the innocence of my youth."

He was sure now that it was the same girl. Could his actions that night have truly affected her so much? She had lost a pet, but he had saved their lives. Her mother had sent her thank you through Erasmus. He could not really understand her hatred or even her extreme need for vengeance. "You accuse me of terrible crimes. I do not remember committing such acts."

The girl sneered. Her voice rose in volume as she accused him. "You destroyed our lives and it was not even worth remembering. Almost seven years ago, you broke into our home. You threatened my mother. Then you killed poor Issi. You cut her throat and painted the walls of our home with her blood. You are a monster. My lamb was innocent." Her voice dropped to a whisper. "Issi was my friend. I loved her. She was all I had left of my father. You took her from me."

Understanding came to Roiland and shame. He had never forgotten that night. He had regretted his actions but killing the animal had been the only way he saw to save the children from his kin. Erasmus had assured him that he had made a good choice, but Roiland had yet to forgive himself. "I am sorry, child, I…"

Her angry outburst interrupted him. "I am not a child. I stopped being a child the night my friend's blood ran under our bed to coat my hands and clothes. I have spent six years training as a ranger to track you down and make you pay for what you did." Then her anger was gone and he could see the uncertainty of youth in her eyes. "I do not understand how you escape justice over and over again. You might as well kill me. If you do not, I will come for you again and again."

A calm, reassuring voice intruded on his thoughts. *Tell her the truth once more. Her heart is either ready to hear it or it is not."

He slowly released the tension on the bow but did not put the arrow away. Then he allowed his own pain to color his words. "The ways of the Drow are indeed evil. The Blood Rite, what we came to your village to complete, is one of their most vile ceremonies. I had little choice but to come. The only time I was allowed to choose was when I came into your home. When I allowed your family to live, I broke every law of Drow society."

The girl seemed unmoved. "What you did was wrong!"

Roiland nodded. "It was wrong, but it was a better option than killing a defenseless woman and two children. The blood of the lamb was the price for saving you, your mother, and your brother. The lamb was slain for the good of many."

The girl shook her head. "You could have stood up to that female elf that came to our door. You did not need to kill Issi."

Roiland sighed. "She was a powerful priestess. I could not have stood against her in a fair fight. She would have killed me."

"No loss there in my opinion."

"You may be right about my death, but then she would have sacrificed your family to her dark goddess." It was then that Roiland finally accepted his own actions and began to forgive himself. "Instead of dying, you and your family lived. You had the chance to make something of your lives as I try to make something of my own. I have learned to make a difference in this world by serving the light. My actions since that night have been my penance for the blood of the lamb."

The girl's expression had not changed. Oikea's voice spoke softly to him. *Her anger is her own burden, not yours, Archer. You have done what you can and now we must go. The Lady calls.*

Roiland gestured with the bow back the way she had come. "I regret the loss of your friend, but I would sacrifice it again to save your family. Go now, the Archer is needed."

She glared at him and then reached for her bow.

"Leave it." He said sharply. "I do not need to be worrying about a bolt in the back."

She turned, back stiff and straight, and headed back the way she had come. "I will find you again. Next time it will turn out differently."

Roiland slipped through the trees following her for a short distance until she broke into a run back the way she had come. He returned to the clearing and gathered up his gear. There would be no sleep for him this day.

He paused over the crossbow and drew his sword to destroy the weapon. It was not a show piece. It was sturdy and well cared for. It was the weapon of a warrior. It did not deserve to be treated harshly. He sheathed his sword and lifted it from the ground. His fingers traced its lines with admiration. When they reached the trigger mechanism, he deftly removed it and dropped it into his pack. Then he drew his dagger and sliced the string. He lay it gently on the trunk of the smaller tree. He was sure she would be back for it.

His heart was heavy as he turned and began to run through the afternoon sun. He was needed somewhere to the north.

Chapter 3

Unholy Crops

Roiland had planned to circle back and check on the young woman. If she was still following him, she might find more trouble than she was prepared to handle. He shook his head at the thought of trying to protect her again. Protecting her had not worked out as he had hoped during the Blood Rite. How had his efforts gone so wrong? Any thoughts he had of making amends would have to wait. For now, he only wanted to be sure that she was not in danger again because of him.

His desire was not to be. A new urgency pulled him forward. Something had changed on the path he was being asked to follow. Lives depended on him. If the young woman chose to follow him, she would have to take care of herself. He said a quick prayer to the Lady to keep her safe.

The next three days passed in a blur of trees and sunlight. He rested for a few hours each night under the light of the Lady's orb. The orb grew smaller each night and so did his connection to her.

Early on the fourth day since his encounter with the woman, Roiland came out of the deep woods. Open fields and farmlands stretched before him. Only a few clumps of trees lay scattered before him. It was beautiful. A fresh breeze blew in his face. It carried just a hint of smoke.

He stood on a small rise overlooking a broad plain. From where he stood, he could see three farms scattered along the banks of a river. There was smoke rising from the closest farmhouse. Strangely, the smoke did not seem to be coming from the large chimney. Roiland sensed trouble. He began to run.

As he got closer, he could make out a scattering of figures around the farmhouse that smoked. He assumed the residents of the three farms were trying to control the fire. Roiland continued to run hoping that he could help.

Something bothered him about the scene before him. The figures moving about the yard did not approach the corner of the farmhouse where the smoke was growing thicker. Roiland slowed his pace and pulled Oikea from over his shoulder. He gripped the bow tightly as he tried to understand what lay before him.

Oikea's voice surged into his mind. It was filled with anger. Her emotions echoed in his head. *Beware, Archer! They are undead.*

He came to an abrupt halt, drawing an arrow. The figures were well within his range, but he hesitated. He wanted a closer look at these creatures. Where had the undead come from? Roiland notched the arrow and began a cautious advance.

He was about a hundred yards from the fence around the property when Oikea again warned him of danger. *To your left, Archer!*

He raised his bow and turned to face the danger. There was nothing there. Then he noticed the ground beginning to churn about 20 feet away. The soil began to bulge up from below. Clumps of dirt and grass flew to the sides. Roiland could see something white moving within the broken earth. A skeletal hand came through the turf. It began to push handfuls of dirt to the side. In moments, a second hand joined it. The rupture in the earth grew larger and the hands were followed by two skeletal arms that planted themselves to either side of the opening.

The arms pressed down and the soil began to surge upward again. Something round and gleaming white began to emerge from the dirt like a festering wound. A skull broke free, followed by a skeletal rib cage. The skeleton sat up and shook the soil from between its bones. There was a clattering sound as its jaw opened and closed several times. Then the skull turned its gaze in Roiland's direction. A red glow began to burn in its eye sockets. For a moment he thought that it was grinning at him. Roiland raised his bow and fired. He did not want whatever looked through those eyes to watch him any longer.

The arrow seemed to strike almost as soon as he released it. There was a bright flash of light. It was like moonlight only much more intense. Bright spots floated before his eyes. He reached up, trying to gently rub them from his vision. He needed to see his foe.

Oikea's voice came to him filled with regret. *My apologies Archer. I should have warned you. My bolts carry the Lady's radiance within them. It is released any time you fire upon the undead, demons, or devils. I was crafted to stand against their evil as you were.*

Roiland acknowledged the apology but his mind was more focused on the dangers around him. He took several steps forward and crouched beside the remains of the skeleton. A fine white powder was all that remained of the skull. The rest of the skeleton's upper body lay in a pile. The bones no longer seemed active or even connected to each other.

He picked up his arrow. The tip was scorched and was partially melted along one edge. It would not fly true until it was smoothed on his whetstone. Repairing it was easier than crafting a new arrow, so he slid it into the quiver with the head pointed up. Then he rose and turned towards the fence around the farmhouse.

Roiland looked at the figures inside the fence. The six figures moving around the farmhouse had not noticed the brief battle or the flash of light. Each seemed to be walking a set route back and forth before the farmhouse door. Nothing within would escape. Roiland glanced next at the fire.

Brambles and loose brush had been piled near the corner of the building and set on fire. The undead in the yard could not have started the blaze. But then who had? The flames now were dancing near the logs of the farmhouse. The lighter colored smoke began to show dark tendrils as the logs began to smolder. The flames had to be dealt with before they spread to the whole farmhouse.

He needed to eliminate the undead in the yard if he was going to deal with the fire. Roiland turned his attention to the figures blocking his way. The three closest to the fence were simple skeletons like the one Oikea had just destroyed. The next one in line seemed to be a zombie. Its flesh was badly deteriorated and all he could tell was that it had once walked on two legs.

It was the last two that disturbed him the most. The forms of a horse and a cow stumbled about closest to the door. The throat of the cow had been torn out and much of its right shoulder had been gnawed away. The white of bone showed within the mangled shoulder. The beast's long tongue hung from slack jaws filled with razor-sharp teeth. The horse was almost as disturbing. Its belly had been opened and its entrails drug across the ground as it walked. Its jaws kept opening and snapping shut with the crack of tooth on tooth.

Roiland had little time to waste if he was going to deal with the fire. He assumed that someone still lived in the farmhouse or he would not have been led here. It was time to get the attention of the creatures within the yard. Roiland repositioned his quiver so he could fire quickly. He raised his bow and sighted down the arrow at the closest skeleton.

Roiland averted his gaze as soon as he released the first shot. The second arrow was already lined up on a skeleton on the far side of the yard when the first flash caused him to blink. Roiland released the second arrow and turned his gaze to check the first target. The chest cavity of the skeleton was gone. The bones of the lower body lay still and the skull sat upon the ground, its teeth still snapping.

Roiland quickly drew and fired at the skull of the third skeleton before checking his second target. The second skeleton had taken a hit high on the back of its spine. Half of its skull was gone and its bones lay scattered on the ground. The third skeleton was no longer moving either.

The zombie was turning towards him as he raised his bow again. It took two arrows this time. The first sank deep into its stomach. Dust and burned flesh fell at its feet, but the flash had little other effect. Roiland placed a second arrow in the center of its face. The body fell motionless to the grass.

Roiland had no illusions of success though. Both of the larger undead were now moving slowly but steadily towards him. He began to give ground, backing slowly away from the fence as he released shaft after shaft. The bright flashes left gaping holes In both undead. But they kept coming for him. There was a feral gleam in their dead eyes.

The bulk of the cow slammed into the fence. It held for the moment. Roiland shifted his aim slightly. His next shaft struck the exposed bone in the cow creature's shoulder. It stumbled and went down, bouncing from a fence post. The post began to lean outward. The cow still struggled, but it could not rise on three legs.

The horse creature tried to use the cow's body to climb over the fence. But one of the loops of entrail hanging from its belly caught on the cow's rear hoof. As it struggled to pull free, Roiland sent an arrow between its snapping jaws. When his vision cleared, the front of the horse's head was just gone. He sent a final arrow into the exposed brain. The body of the horse creature stumbled backwards and fell to the ground. Its body did not twitch.

Roiland's gaze shot towards the farmhouse as one of the window shutters snapped closed. Moments later the door swung open and a man followed by a young boy rushed out with shovels in hand. Both paused at the sight of the Dark Elf standing by the fence.

Roiland yelled at them, "Take care of the fire! I will guard your backs."

He watched as the two moved to the fire and began to shovel dirt onto the flames. Roiland reached for another arrow. He moved back to the fence and stared down at the cow that still tried to reach him. He took careful aim and placed his next shot in its eye. The cow creature stopped struggling.

Again, he reached for another arrow. The quiver was over half empty. His concerns about the quiver were interrupted as a pulse of warning came from Oikea. The battle was not over yet. He turned to survey the area beyond the fence.

There was not much cover on this side of the fence. Just a couple of spruce trees off to his left. He turned his head so that the trees were barely in his peripheral vision and waited. He sensed the movement there more than saw it. One of the shadows beneath the trees became darker and more pronounced. Roiland gripped Oikea and slowly rotated to face the threat.

A shadow slowly detached itself from the base of the trees. At first, he thought it was a large dog made of shadow. But as it drew closer, he could see that it moved on two legs, hunched over at the waist. One hand came down from time to time to keep it upright. The grass seemed to wither wherever that hand came down. The second hand was pulled in tight to its chest.

The creature was fast, but it paused halfway to him. Its gaze met his and Roiland felt the coldness of fear. He could not afford to let this evil get away. He held his shot as the creature darted forward once more. He waited till it was no more than a dozen yards away when he released his first shot. His eyes closed before the flash, but his hands release a second and third arrow along the creature's path.

The creature howled in frustration as each shaft struck home. Roiland was not sure the creature felt pain. But he sensed its anger at being denied the prey it hungered for. He reopened his eyes to see it dragging itself away from him. He edged closer and placed a final arrow in the back of its head. It lay still upon the ground. He still felt the power of the creature's gaze. He felt its coldness wrapping around his heart until the familiar voice of Oikea broke the spell. *Fire Archer. Burn them all, especially this one. If you do not, they might rise again.*

An older male voice spoke from behind him. "Thank you, stranger. Between the undead and those orcs that set the fire, we were in real trouble."

Roiland turned and smiled at the man. The young boy blurted out a question before he could speak. "Pa, is that a real Drow? He has pointy ears."

The man spoke softly. "Hush, Josh. He saved our lives. Does not matter who or what he is."

Roiland looked at them carefully. "Yes, I am a Drow. Do not judge my kin by my actions. They are evil. Is there anyone alive in the other two farms?"

The man shook his head. "They left over a week ago for the village north of here. They figured that fat Friar would keep them safe from the undead."

"Why did you stay behind?"

A look of sadness came over the man's face. "My wife is sick, real bad. She has a fever. I could not move her and I will not leave her. I may lose her still. The fever will not break and the herbs are not working."

Roiland asked. "Is she inside?" At the man's nod, he continued, "Take me to her. Then we must burn these creatures. Josh. Please collect my arrows but do not touch the tips or the bodies. I even want the broken ones. I will need all the arrows I can repair."

The man waved for his son to get started and then led Roiland into the dim interior of the house. The main room was quite large, bigger than his entire lodge. The odor of human and animal waste filled the room. To his surprise, a horse was tied to the far wall near a shuttered window. The man led him to a small side room. A bed took up most of the space within the room. A woman lay there wrapped in blankets. She shivered despite the sweat that soaked her hair.

Roiland knelt beside her and pulled the quilt away. With a soft prayer to the Lady of Silences, he placed one hand on her chest and another on her forehead. A pale white glow emanated from his hands as he closed his eyes and gave his thanks. The glow strengthened and spread to envelop the body of the woman. As the glow faded, her shivering stopped.

He opened his eyes and smiled down at the woman before pulling the quilt back up to cover her once more. He rose and turned to see the farmer staring at him in shock. The farmer spoke hesitantly. "You are Drow and yet you wield the power of a Paladin. I do no pretend to understand but you have my thanks once more." There were tears in his eyes.

Roiland was embarrassed by the look on the farmer's face. "I take no credit for saving your wife. I am a servant, nothing more. I am satisfied with that role. And if that service helped your wife, then we can both be thankful for it."

Roiland reached out and squeezed the man's shoulder before leaving the small room. He paused before heading outside and took up an armload of wood from beside the hearth. He carried it outside and began to stack it over the body of the zombie. The farmer watched him from the doorway and then disappeared inside his home.

He returned moments later leading the horse by its halter. "Take what wood we have. There is more split and piled behind the house. I will bring what I can from my neighbor's homes. It will take a lot of wood to burn the horse and cow."

Several hours later, seven large fires burned around the farmstead. Each gave off black, foul-smelling smoke. Roiland knelt by a smaller fire that he used to cleanse the tips of the arrows he had used. He briefly ran each arrowhead through the flames. A small puff of black smoke rose from each as the remains of the undead burned away.

Roiland spoke without looking up from his work. "You mentioned orcs earlier. Are they the ones summoning the undead?"

The farmer seemed to hesitate. "I do not think so. They seemed to be watching the attack, not participating in it. They did not come close except to start the blaze when we refused to come out."

Roiland was thoughtful as he began to repair an arrow before returning it to his quiver. Of the twenty five he had carried in that quiver, twelve were beyond repair. He carefully removed the fletching from each ruined shaft. He would need the feathers to make replacements. "What did the undead do when the orcs entered the yard?"

The response came from the boy this time. "It was like the dead things did not see them. It was mighty strange." The boy paused for a moment and then added. "My friend Orne has a bow and lots of arrows. His are not as nice as yours. He only fire-hardens the tips. I could go get some of them if you want."

Roiland nodded. "Please. I will need many arrows if there are more undead." He waited until the boy was gone before asking, "What of this village? Did the priest there destroy the undead? Did the village survive?"

The famer came and knelt beside him. "No, the Friar could not stop the undead. Most there are dead. One family came through a few days ago. They had a farm outside of the village. They say the Friar has some folks hold up in his Chapel. I do not know if they still live or not."

Roiland asked softly. "Could he have held them off this long?"

The farmer looked troubled. "I am not sure. The Friar is powerful. Follows the Lawgiver. But he is old. He has at least as much faith as he does appetite. If anyone can hold on, it might be him."

Oikea spoke softly to him. *Our destination is set, Archer. We must aid the Friar in his battle. The dead must be sent back to their graves."

Roiland nodded to himself and spoke as gently as he could to the farmer. "You know more undead will come for you. You must take your family and flee."

The man began to argue, "I cannot leave my wife behind."

Roiland cut him off. "Your wife will wake in the morning. She will need food and she will need to ride your horse. But she will be fit to travel. Get them away from here. I will do what I can to save those in the village."

He watched the farmer look around at his home and his crops. He understood how much he as asking the man to sacrifice. The farmer looked up at his son returning from the neighbor's home. A determined look came over his face and he nodded.

Roiland gave him directions to the village that his people had attacked during the Blood Rite. As an afterthought, he also gave directions to the lodge explaining that it was isolated but safe. And maybe Erasmus would enjoy the company.

Roiland accepted two quivers of crude arrows from the boy. With Oikea's magic, they might do for a single shot. Then he rose. "I will stand guard until you leave in the morning. Rest peacefully. Neither orc nor undead shall harm you this night."

The farmer thanked him once more before leading his son inside and latching the door. Roiland walked from bonfire to bonfire making sure that the undead remains were thoroughly charred. When he was sure that none would reanimate, he found a comfortable place to sit. He spread his tools before him and began to inspect the hunting arrows. The work kept his hands busy and talking with his bow would keep his mind alert through the dark hours of the night.

Chapter 4

The Faithful

Tully stared around the Chapel of the Lawgiver. Besides himself, there were barely a score of people sheltering here. As far as he knew, they were the only survivors. So few considering that the village had been home to nearly a hundred men, women, and children. He wished he could have saved more. But they had been a stubborn lot and did not want to flee their nice homes and good lives.

He had done what he could for them. There were limits to what a man of nearly seventy winters could do. He rested his hands on his portly stomach as he gazed around the room. Fear and defeat were etched into every face. Despite their lack of faith, he was confident that Tyr would send help.

Tully raised his voice and sang a single line from his favorite song from his days in the Temple of Tyr. His voice had not faded over the years. The rich tenor rang out clearly, "Blessed are you that weep and mourn, for one day you shall laugh."

A young farmer sitting beside his wife and two daughters looked up at Tully with anger in his eyes. Tully's mind searched for the man's name. Ah yes, Billup. The man's voice was accusing as he voiced everyone's fears. "Laughter, Friar? We are surrounded by evil with no way out.

Even your abundant supply of food is gone now. What is it we should laugh at? We either get eaten by those dead monsters or we get turned into one of them. How will there be this happy ending that you sing of?"

The old Friar pitched his words so that everyone could hear. "The Lawgiver has heard your prayers. He has promised to answer your plea. Have faith. Your cry for justice will not go unanswered."

There was muttering around the single room of the Chapel. There was little more he could do to calm their fears. Tully motioned for the young man standing near the alter to join him as he headed into a small alcove in the side wall. Tully stood beside the rack holding his armor. His fingers caressed its links. It had served him well since his days as a young acolyte.

Tully smiled as the young man joined him. Thomas was the third son of a local merchant. The boy had no interest in his father's business or any other position the village merchants had to offer. The boy did not yet realize that Tyr had called him to serve. The boy frequently snuck away from his father's store to attend services. He would hide in the back of the chapel hoping not to be noticed. But Thomas had a beautiful baritone voice. The boy could not stop himself from joining in the songs and there was no hiding that voice.

Tully understood the calling that Thomas felt. He had spoken several times to the boy's father about making him an acolyte. The man had refused. He wanted better for his son than being a poor village priest. Now Thomas' father had refused to abandon his store. Now the rich merchant was one of the undead walking the streets of the village. Thomas was free to choose his own path in life and he had come to the Chapel. The boy was barely eighteen, but he had a good heart and Tully was certain he would grow strong in the service of Tyr.

Tully tugged at the chainmail hanging on the rack before him. "Help me get this on, Thomas. I am getting a bit too old to be doing this without help."

Thomas looked at the armor and shook his head. "It will not fit you, Friar. It has been two years since you last wore it. It was tight then and you have, well, umm, you have grown since then."

Tully let out a tremendous belly laugh at the boy's response. More mutterings came from the group in the Chapel. Tully ignored them. "Boys like you grow, Thomas. Old men like me just get fatter. I was a big lad when I was your age. The armor fit then. I have gotten much bigger over the years and the armor has always fit. I will admit that it does feel snug some times. Trust in Tyr. It is magic and it will fit this time too. Help me please, Thomas."

It took some work, but the mail eventually slid down over Tully's large frame. It felt heavier than he remembered, but he was getting old. Tully strapped his weapon belt around his large waist. He had needed larger belts over the years. Thomas asked quietly. "How can you carry a sword, Friar? I thought priests were not allowed to use edged weapons."

Tully reached down and grasped the hilt of the weapon and drew it from the scabbard. Instead of a sword, what came out of the sheath was a strangely shaped mace that looked more like a large hoof file than a weapon. "This is Brjóta. It is a mace not a sword. It is a powerful weapon in the hands of a follower of Tyr."

Thomas studied the mace closely but was careful not to touch it. When his eyes finally turned to meet Tully's gaze, the Friar sheathed his weapon. "Do you remember my instructions, Thomas?"

Thomas nodded. "Yes, Friar Tully. But I do not understand why you cannot take them to the Temple of Tyr yourself. I can get a wagon. It would be wonderful to take you and see the Temple at your side."

Tully smiled sadly. "It would be my pleasure to take you south to meet the Hofgathi." Tully paused at the boy's confused look. "The Bishop of the Temple of Tyr. But I am old and I am tired. The evil that we face will not just go away, Thomas. It must be defeated; I suspect that task will not be an easy one. Many sacrifices will be required along the way."

Thomas looked ready to argue but Tully placed a hand on his shoulder. "We will see what the will of the Lawgiver brings us, Thomas. If I am not able to travel, I charge you to make sure that my weapon, armor, and shield get to the Hofgathi. Now go watch through the shutters while I pray."

Thomas sighed in resignation and turned to do as Tully had asked. Tully did not move to the alter. He knelt on the cold stone floor of the alcove and prayed before the symbol of his God that still shone on his shield.

Roiland had debated their next move with Oikea as he worked on the arrows. It was not that he disagreed with his very opinionated bow, but he wanted to clarify his own thinking. They could rush to the defense of the villagers and their Friar, or they could try to eliminate the source of the undead. Roiland was fairly certain that the village was just another place to be subdued like the three farms had been. In the end he went along with Oikea's desire to save the survivors of the village. Maybe this Friar could provide a better understanding about the source of the undead plague or even the role of the orcs.

The farmer had given him directions to the village before departing with his wife and son. Roiland had watched them disappear to the south before he turned to follow the trail north. He had not been sure what to expect, but he was pleasantly surprised to find he was following a wide, well-beaten path. The farmer had assured him the village was no more than a half day's journey. The path eventually became a road smooth enough for carts and small wagons. He passed several other farms scattered along the way, but each was empty and desolate. Even the farm animals were missing.

The call of the Lady became stronger as he got closer to the village. He set to a brisk pace, but his fatigue was growing. He began to wonder if the farmer had underestimated the distance to the village. His distraction was almost his undoing. Near one of the farms, two small undead creatures burst from a field in his direction. Oikea warned him in time to bring them down with a single arrow each.

He did not have time to burn these bodies so he drew his sword to dismember them before moving on. Oikea's power had destroyed most of the small forms. What remained was too deformed to tell what the creatures had been in life. He carefully hacked what was left into small pieces and then plunges his blade into the earth to clean it. The attack cleared his mind which was good. The village was coming into view.

It was mid-afternoon when he caught sight of the buildings up ahead. The time for speed was past and now Roiland needed to scout the area carefully before getting too close. He wanted to discover what he faced before he was forced to fight. He moved back and forth across the road, checking the areas to both sides. Surprisingly, there were no undead outside the village. It was as if whoever controlled the undead welcomed more victims. Considering what he had faced at the farmstead, only a fool would willing enter the village. Oikea seemed offended by his thoughts. The bow had chastised him for his bad attitude.

Despite seeing no undead on his approach, Roiland had continued his cautious approach. It was about an hour before dusk by the time he was close enough to study the what was within the village. Despite the growing darkness, he could see no lights anywhere along the main road. Dark, but not empty. The streets were occupied by dozens of figures shuffling back and forth. Many of them were clustered around one building near the center of town. All of the figures seemed to be paying more attention to that one building than they were the entrance to the village. He did not think any of them paid the slightest attention to the cluster of trees where he hid.

 The figures he could see moved with the same slow almost jerky movements of the undead at the farm. They were different, some large and some small, some on two lets and others on four. It was almost as if any available corpse was used. It would not be safe to be caught on the streets of this village after dark.

Roiland turned his attention from the undead to the buildings. Unlike the village closer to his lodge, these buildings were all very similar in design and shape. Each was a one floor wooden structures with a flat roof. The buildings were all rectangular with the shorter side facing the road. The windows all appeared to have sturdy shutters. The buildings were not all the same size, but they were similar enough that he suspected they had all been built about the same time.

He began to study them more closely before the light could fade any further. Most of the buildings he could see were not closed up. Doors swung open and none the windows shutters were closed. Had so many been caught by surprise? Roiland thought he saw movement in one or two open doorways. Was this what had become of the residents? He would not be able to take refuge inside.

The only building that seemed a little different was one near the center of the street. A small rock wall sat before it and Roiland thought he saw a bell hanging over it. Could that be the chapel that he was searching for? The question was how to get there without fighting all of the undead along the way.

There did not seem to be a good approach that did not leave him exposed to anything hiding within the buildings. He needed to sneak past as many of them as he could. He was about to sneak around to check out the backside of the structures when he had a thought. He looked carefully at the gaps between the buildings. Again, everything was fairly uniform, From his position he guessed most were about eight to ten feet apart. He could leap across those gaps, moving from rooftop to rooftop. As long as none of the undead could climb, reaching the center of the village should be easy.

Roiland studied the closest structure. It appeared to be a home. The roof was the same height as its neighbor, it just was not as wide or as deep. There were no ladders leading up to the roof on the outside the home, but he thought he saw a way up. There was one large window on the side of the house closest to him. The heavy shutters were still open and he thought the window ledge was wide enough to stand on. If he could get there undetected, he should be able to get to the roof.

He would need a distraction though. There were two undead close to the building he was planning to climb. He was certain they would notice him before he could get to the roof. Roiland considered just destroying the two undead, but would the flash of Oikea's magic bring more undead his way? He decided to target something further down the street. If luck was with him, his shots would attract all of the undead away from this end of the village. A large shape lumbered back and forth across the street about three buildings down. He thought it was another horse creature. It should be an easy target.

There was a flowering bush just a bit closer to the home he intended to climb. Roiland took advantage of the growing shadows to slink in behind the bush. He pulled two of his own arrows from his quiver.

Gauging the position and speed of the large undead, he raised his bow and fired both arrows in rapid succession.

Then he crouched low and waited. In the dim light, the two flashes lit up the street. Roiland stayed crouched low until he heard movement. Another breath and he raised his head, hoping. The two undead that had been in front of the closest building had their back to him as they moved away down the street. Roiland grinned and ran silently to the side of the house.

Roiland slung his bow as he ran. He thought he heard movement from the open doorway to the home. He did not pause to see if it was his imagination or if another undead waited inside. When he reached the window, Roiland untied the right shutter from the wall. Both shutters were heavy, designed to protect the home from storm or attack. Brackets to hold locking bars were mounted both low and high on the inside of each shutter.

Roiland paused to study the dim interior through the window. He could make out a large fireplace and a brick oven sitting beside it. There was no sign of movement within the kitchen. Empty was good and Roiland gave the bracket on the right shutter a sharp tug. There was no give in it, so he used the shutters and the brackets to haul himself up onto the ledge. Once he was perched on the ledge, Roiland rose slowly to his feet.

The upper frame of the window was just above his eye level. He estimated it was another four feet to edge of the roof. Roiland studied the two shutters. He would need the one he had untied to be almost closed so he could use the four brackets to climb. The locking bars would have made a great ladder, but they were somewhere in the kitchen. He could not risk searching for them. Roiland spent several minutes trying to step into the brackets of the right shutter, but it kept swinging open each time he tried to climb. Somehow, he needed to wedge it into the position he needed.

Seeing no other option, he drew his dagger and drove it into the frame just below the upper hinge. The shutter stopped each time it hit the dagger, but he would not be able to retrieve it once he was on the roof. Roiland placed his toe in the lower bracket on his left and carefully climbed to the top of the left shutter. The smooth walls did not make the climb easy, but he soon stood with the tips of his toes resting on the top edge of the left shutter. He stood close to the hinge, but the wood groaned under the strain of his weight. He could see over the edge of the roof now and thankfully it was empty.

Keeping his body close to the wall, Roiland quickly moved both hands up to grip the edge of the roof. There was a finger length lip all around the edge of the roof that provided a solid handhold. The shutter below him was beginning to sag. He had to move quickly. Roiland bent his knees and then thrust upward. He felt the shutter rip from the wall. But his weight had already transferred to arms honed by years of longbow practice. The shutter clattered noisily to the ground as he pulled his upper body over the edge of the roof. A simple twist to the side brought his legs up as well.

He was worried about the noise the shutter had made so he crawled to the front edge of the home to examine the streets below. The sun was gone and the half moon was just coming up over the horizon. But it was enough for him to get a sense of the chaos in the street.

Both of his arrows had struck the horse creature. One had taken it in the neck leaving a blackened hole. The second had struck its right foreleg. The leg was just gone. The creature lay on the ground struggling to rise once more. Other undead creatures were darting forward, sinking in their teeth ad ripping out large chunks of flesh. The undead horse kept trying to twist its neck to snap at its attackers.

Roiland felt bile rise in his throat as he surveyed the scene. He retreated from the edge of the roof so he would not have to watch it any more. He had the distraction he needed, now it was time to move further into the village. He eyed the next rooftop. It appeared to be empty. He spoke softly to Oikea. "Are the rooftops safe to travel?"

Oikea assured him that she detected nothing above the street level. With that, he backed to the edge of the roof he had just climbed. Taking Oikea in one hand, he placed the toe of one boot against the lip of the roof. He surged towards the far edge of the roof. He leaped just before the edge and sailed through the air. His lead foot slipped as it came down on the roof. He managed to toss his bow towards the middle of the roof just before his body hit the rooftop and rolled.

He rolled several times before coming to an abrupt stop against something hard. His hand went to his back. He would have been badly bruised if not for his leather armor. Roiland climbed to his feet and retrieved his bow. Then he turned to examine the object he had hit. A large wooden plank lay in the center of the roof.

He bent and ran his fingers over the plank. The wood was thick enough to hold his weight and it was long enough to span the gap between the buildings. He looked over at the rising moon with a grin. "My thanks for your blessing, Lady. This will make things much easier."

Tully sang softly to his God as he knelt in the alcove. He considered the battle before him. The taste of his fear was not in his mouth this night. It was strange to know his time had come and not fear it. In many ways, he welcomed the sacrifice he was about to make. He was truly tired. Tired of the pain that came with simple things like sleep. Tired of cajoling people who knew how they should treat each other but would not. And some days, he was even too tired to eat. He was ready to join Tyr.

Tully chuckled. Since the day he had been sent north from the great Temple, he had been in one hopeless fight after another. Each time he had somehow survived. Now look at him, he was old. Adventurers were not supposed to die of old age. Where was the glory in that? He shook his head. No, he chose to go as he had lived, fighting and singing as Tyr had asked him to so long ago. He wondered what that strange elven druid would think of his choice. Then again, F'lar was still a young elf. Could he even understand?

His musings were interrupted by a soft gasp from near the shutters at the front of the Chapel. "What is it, Thomas?"

The boy stammered. "I… I do not know, Friar. There were two bright flashes of light and one of the undead is writhing on the ground. I cannot tell what happened."

Tully smiled. The help that Tyr had promised him had arrived. "Stand by the door, Thomas. Unbar it and open it when I tell you."

Roiland crouched on the roof of the building across the street from the bell. The building behind the bell appeared to be a small temple of some kind. The window shutters were all sealed. There were at least twenty undead of different types wandering around the building. None seemed willing to approach the building too closely. He muttered softly as he watched them. "I bet they would be more than happy to eat a lone Drow if he was foolish enough to get caught down there." Whether he liked the odds or not, part of his quest waited for him inside. He just had to hope whoever was in there was willing to let him in.

Roiland laid out his quivers on the roof before him. He had thirty seven of his own arrows remaining and another twenty four of the simple hunting arrows. It was enough to get him to the door, but he doubted it would be enough to get them all out of the village. There were too many undead for that to work out. His mind kept evaluating and discarding plans. Oikea's voice came into his thoughts. *Have faith, Archer. She would not burden you with a task beyond our abilities.*

Roiland nodded. He returned the two quivers with his own arrows to his belt. Raising Oikea, his right hand reached for the hunting arrows as he selected his first target.

———————————————

Thomas stood staring at the Friar like he had lost his mind. "Open the door?"

Tully walked over and gently pushed Thomas toward the barred door. "At my signal, remove the bars and open the door. Have faith, my boy. And be sure to close and bar it quickly after our guest arrives."

The boy looked pale and uncertain. "Are you sure, Friar?"

Tully patted him reassuringly on the back as he moved past the boy to stare out the slots in the shuttered window. Tully's human eyes could not make out the undead moving around on the dark streets. But he could sense their evil and their hunger as they wandered around the sanctuary that Tyr had provided them.

There was muttering behind his back as he stared out into the darkness. Tully understood that the people were afraid, but he knew that the road to their salvation would require them to face their fears. He muttered softly as he watched. "Blessed are the poor in spirit."

Something seemed to explode right in front of the Chapel. The light of a thousand moons bathed the street. Tully had to turn is eyes away as the first flash assaulted his eyes. He could not tell what their rescuer was using for a weapon, but it seemed quite effective. He felt the points of evil disappearing one by one. None seemed to require more than two of the bright flashes before its stain was wiped from his awareness. When he sensed an opening on the street before the door, Tully told Thomas. "Get the door open now! Quickly, Thomas!"

The boy moved to obey. Tully felt something that burned with internal light drop from the roof across the way. He heard nothing as their rescuer landed on the ground. Thomas had barely lifted the latch on the door when something or someone hit it, driving it open.

There were multiple gasps of shock and one woman actually screamed. Tully looked up to see a dark form standing in the doorway. One of the men yelled, "Drow!" The sweet taste of fear flooded his mouth. Tully quickly pushed his fear aside. The external trappings did not matter, only the goodness that shone within. Tully sensed the goodness in this being.

The Dark Elf spun and slammed the door closed. He took the first bar from the stunned Thomas and placed it back across the door. Thomas recovered quickly sliding the second bar into place as well.

Tully stepped forward and held out his hand. "Welcome, my friend. I have been waiting for your arrival. I am Tully and I am Friar of this small Chapel."

The Drow stepped forward and his strong hand clasped Tully's wrist in a warrior greeting. "Greetings, Friar. I am the Archer, Knight of the Lady of Silences. She has sent me to aid you anyway that I can." Roiland's eyes assessed the people within the Chapel. "I am not sure how we will get this many people through the undead though. There are many of them wandering the streets still."

Tully smiled as he squeezed the wrist of the Archer. "Fear not, Archer. Tyr has a plan. With your help, all will be well."

Roiland released the priest's arm and stepped back. 'I would love to hear more of this plan."

Tully motioned for the elf to follow as he led the way back to the small alcove where his armor had been stored. As they walked around the perimeter of the Chapel, Tully could feel the hard stares of his small congregation. There were whispers as well. He hoped the Drow would not take offense.

When they reached the relative privacy of the alcove, Tully turned and studied his new ally. "Do I call you Archer? Or is there a name that you go by?"

Roiland smiled. "I am called many things much worse than that. Archer is fine or you may use my name, Roiland."

Tully glanced at the people sitting on the benches. "Forgive their rudeness, Roiland. They are afraid. So many of their nightmares have come to life recently. A Drow in their midst, even one filled with light and honor, is a bit much for them to handle at the moment."

Roiland stared down at the floor for a moment and then raised his eye to meet the priest's. "My kind have more than earned the fear and hatred of your people. Someday, maybe someone will see more than just a Drow when they look at me. Do not worry, Friar. I will not let their fears interfere with my mission here."

Tully relaxed at his words. "Thank you, Roiland. Tell me please, what do you know of the evil we face?"

Roiland shrugged. "Undead rising from their graves and not just around your village. There are also the orcs. I am not sure how they fit into things. But they are connected somehow to the undead."

Tully considered his words and then continued. "A new power has risen in this region. It is located somewhere to the east near the mountains. Those lands are or were the home of a large tribe of orcs."

"Are the orcs responsible for the undead?"

Tully shook his head. "I do not think so. I believe the orcs are victims in this power just like the people of my village. It is strange how the undead seem to just rise. It is almost as if some magical artifact is animating them. Whether this new power in the mountains control the artifact or is in league with it, I do not know."

Roiland gestured to the building around them. "Your faith is strong enough to keep them from entering this place. Can you go on the offensive and destroy the undead in the village?"

Tully let the frustration he felt show in his response. "Skeletons, zombies, and ghouls are not normally problem. But something ancient and powerful rose with them. It is an evil that I believe was defeated long ago. The same magic that spawned the minor undead somehow freed it from its bonds."

"What is it that we face?"

Tully turned his gaze to stare at the sword embossed on his shield. "A master vampire. It defiles the streets of my village. There are records in my residence of one that was supposed to have been destroyed hundreds of years ago. I believe it has returned and it is not alone. This time it has two powerful minions that fight beside it. Shades. I can defeat the vampire. But then the people here will be vulnerable to the shades. That is why I need your help."

The Friar's subtle message did not escape Roiland's notice. "I take it you expect to die killing this vampire? That is a high price to pay."

Tully's response carried conviction and strength. "Without sacrifice, there can be no love, Roiland. I think you might understand that better than I do."

His words sank into the dark elf's soul. It was a simple message that he had understood for years but had never been able to voice. Roiland nodded as his hand tightened about the riser of his bow. Oikea whispered to him. *Listen to him, Archer. His faith is strong. We cannot defeat them without his aid." Roiland looked up to see surprise on the Friar's face.

Tully sputtered. "She speaks to you?"

Roiland's eyes widened. "You heard Oikea?"

Tully shook his head. "More sensed than heard. Such a marvel. Is she responsible for the magic that destroyed the undead?" Roiland nodded and Tully continued, "Good. We have need of such wonderful magic. Truth be told, I was not sure how we could prevail. Your bow changes many things."

Roiland lowered his voice. "Is your sacrifice truly needed? I might be able to weaken this vampire with a few arrows."

At Roiland's look of concern, Tully chuckled. "I am old, elf. Old as elves cannot understand. I should have died in battle decades ago. I think the Lawgiver stashed me here in this isolated village for just this purpose. I serve his will in this. We will succeed as long as you can do as I ask."

"How can I serve you then, noble priest?"

Tully's hand dropped to his waist and his fingers caressed the hilt of Brjóta. "Our foes have not seen the power of your bow. He will see the destruction you caused but he will not understand the threat you pose. You must not reveal what you are capable of until I tell you to."

Roiland looked confused. "So, I am to watch you fight and die?"

"No, you just need to be patient. Simply hold your fire until after I have drawn my mace. Then I need you to deal with the two shades. Their ability to fly puts them beyond my reach. But your bow has no such limits."

"Why not place a few arrows into the vampire before you attack it? I can shift to the shades after an arrow or two."

Tully's voice took on the tone of a teacher lecturing a classroom of novices. "Master vampires are old and powerful. They have the ability to turn into mist and simply fade away. To defeat them in combat, that ability must be neutralized."

"And how will you block its power?"

Tully wrapped his fingers around the hilt of his mace. "Brjóta's light with take that power and many others from him including his ability to drain life from us. But it will not prevent him from using his claws and other natural weapons."

Roiland studied the old priest. "I will do as you ask, Friar. Do not ask me to let you die needlessly." Roiland was about to say more when Oikea's voice whispered to him once more. *Leave him his honor, Archer. He fully understands the sacrifice he is about to make. He looks forward to meeting his God. Respect his choice."

Roiland nodded and then asked. "When will we do this, Friar?"

Tully smiled. "An hour before dawn. That will give my flock a full day to head south. They must leave their homes. Someday, I hope they can return."

Tully turned then and began to tell those in the chapel what to do when the battle was over. He warned them not to try to return to their homes for anything. "Your homes are a trap. There will be undead around hiding in them still. The Archer will not be able to protect you if you scatter. Get out of here and head south. It is the only way to survive."

Billup stood and began to argue. "But if you win this fight, we can take back our homes."

Tully frowned in response. "More undead will come, Billup. This was but the first battle and the war will need to be won before you can return. I am sorry."

The people looked uncertain, but they all nodded their understanding. Tully went back to the alter and picked up an old, faded backpack from behind it. He handed the pack to Thomas. "Place the chainmail and mace in here for your journey. The shield you will have to carry." Tully turned towards the door and then paused. "There is a loaf of bread in that pack, Thomas. Save it. If you meet a bearded man on your journey, share a meal with him. You will not regret it."

The boy looked at him in confusion. "Friar, I do not understand. What bearded man? Who are you talking about?"

Tully reached out and squeezed the boy's shoulder. "Do not worry, Thomas. I did not understand either those many years ago. Just remember to let him break the bread. You will not regret it."

Roiland watched as the old Friar returned to the alcove and knelt to pray. After a time, Tully rose and moved to the door. He lifted the first of the two bars from its brackets. "It is time, Archer." Roiland stepped up behind him with his bow and an arrow. "How will I see the Shades?"

Tully slid the second bar free and set it aside. His hand gripped the latch on the door. "Brjóta's light will reveal them to you. Do not miss, Archer."

Roiland nodded and watched as the old priest opened the door. Tully's great girth seemed to fill the doorway, but then he squeezed through. Roiland heard his voice begin to sing. Softly at first but with rising power and belief. The rich tenor seemed to carry through the dark streets.

You shall stand before the powers of hell

With death at your side

Know that I am with you through it all

Be not afraid

I go before you always

Come, follow me and I will give you rest

Roiland had never heard the song before, but it settled his nerves. He followed the old Friar out into a street filled with death. The door of the Chapel slammed shut behind him.

A harsh, nasally voice interrupted before Tully could begin the next verse of his song. "Why must you plague me with your pathetic hymns? Do they really inspire you, Friar? They seem little more than a wistful hope that your one-armed god will arrive in time to save you. But alas, he is not here. He cannot help you and neither can the fool that stands behind you. Know this, Friar, you will both serve me before this night is through."

Tully stepped to the middle of the street and faced the voice. He seemed almost jovial as he replied. "My apologies. I selected that one just for this occasion. It is such an old song. I thought it might bring back fond memories of times long gone when you were still human."

The form stepped closer. "Do not play the fool, priest. It is beneath you."

Tully seemed to consider the figure's words. "Perhaps. But I have lived long enough to earn a bit of foolishness now and then. In any event, it is high time we met and ended this standoff. I am too old to play such games night after night."

Roiland concentrated on his night vision. But all he could make out was a man-sized shape that was cold. Very, very cold. The harsh voice continued. "He who controls the stone is not happy at the devastation you have wrought this night, Friar. I was told to make you pay for your actions."

Roiland felt eyes studying him for a moment and then the voice continued. "Interesting. A priest of the light stands with a Drow at his back. Was this your work or his, Friar? It matters not, you shall both make excellent replacements."

The old Friar's belly laugh echoed from the buildings around them. "No, no. That just will not do. I have another engagement with the Lawgiver in the morning. I asked him if I could bring a small token of my respect to our meeting. He suggested that I might consider bringing a lost soul along with me. As it is always my pleasure to serve Tyr, I thought I might bring you along. Your judgement is so very long overdue."

Roiland was still focused on the dark form before him. He was unprepared when Tully drew his mace from its sheath. He had to close his eyes at the sudden burst of light from directly in front of him. He heard a hiss of anger from the voice that had spoken from the darkness. As his eyes cleared, Roiland could make out a man standing just a few yards away.

Except, what stood there was not truly a man anymore. Blood red eyes glowed in the light of the mace. The creature had a fair face, but its skin was pale white. Long fangs protruded from blood red lips. Its hair and brows were a dark color somewhere between brown and black.

It was dressed in a fine linen shirt and trousers. The clothing should have indicated wealth and power, but the effect was ruined by the poor fit of each piece. They seemed to hang on the creature's body almost as if they had been borrowed from a much a larger man. Neither shirt sleeve appeared to be buttoned and pale fingers with long black nails protruded from just below the open ends.

The vampire raised a hand before its face, shielding its eyes from the light emanating from the mace. The sleeve fell away as Roiland watched. The creature's skin seemed to wither slightly in the light of the Friar's weapon. Tully advanced a step with his mace held high.

The vampire retreated a step. "Perhaps I will allow another the pleasure of taking your life, Friar. I find that I do not like your glowing toy overmuch." The creature waved its arm dismissively and then just stood there. A look of outrage crept across its face. "What have you done, foul priest? How have you blocked my powers? I should be…"

Tully interrupted the rant. "Tsk, tsk. I imagine that was a bit of a shock. Archer, please keep the shades from interfering."

Roiland smiled and drew an arrow. The old Friar had courage and a surprising way with words. He wondered if his sermons were as entertaining as his battle humor.

Tully paused for a second as he positioned his shield to face the vampire. "Where was I? Oh yes. You were lamenting the fact that you could not just leave our little chat. Disappointing was it not? You should be well away by now, escaping justice once more. But that would have been rude as I have so much that I want us to experience this night. I planned this for weeks. First, we shall stand together before the Lawgiver to receive his justice."

Tully paused to gauge the vampire's reaction. Roiland could feel the hatred rising from the creature. Then Tully went on. "Not an exciting prospect for you? Since that idea seems to disturb you... Perhaps we should go with another venue. Trial by combat perhaps? Simply defeat me and you may go and do as you wish."

The vampire remained silent as it studied the Friar. Tully began to hum the melody to his earlier song. Then the vampire nodded. "Very well. You are merely a mortal, too old and fat to be much of a threat. I have fed well on the people of this place. Let us see how strong your faith really is, Friar."

The light from the mace seemed to flare outward. It created a globe of light forty feet in every direction. Nothing within the lit area cast a shadow, not even the Friar's great bulk. Roiland stood within the sphere. He watched and waited. The evil that rolled off the vampire over-whelmed his magical senses. He would have to depend on eyesight and his own reflexes. He smiled. He was the Archer.

As Roiland watched, the two combatants began to circle each other. There were occasional pulses of darkness along the edges of the light. Each time, the darkness appeared right behind the Friar. Roiland brought the arrow against the string of his bow. His hunt had begun.

Tully moved with ease despite his age. There was a look of serenity in the old man's eyes that gave Roiland confidence. The Friar knew something that his opponent did not and it was evident in his smile. Roiland hissed in surprise when the vampire finally moved. It was fast. It crossed the distance to Tully in the blink of an eye and struck hard with the claws of its right hand.

Tully seemed to anticipate the strike as he shifted his shield to intercept the blow. The claws stuck the shield hard. The shield emitted a musical tone at the impact that seemed in perfect harmony with the Friar's humming. The mace darted forward, but the vampire was already several steps away.

The vampire darted forward once again. This time it threw its body against the shield. Tully staggered back a step but then began to swing his mace in a complicated attack pattern. Roiland recognized the skill in Tully's attacks. But his blows were always just a bit too slow. The vampire was never there when the mace arrived.

Roiland pretended to be caught up in the fight. But his eyes continued to scan the borders of the light. A shadow slid into the circle of light. It disappeared as quickly as it came. Roiland sensed something and spun to see another shadow racing towards his own back. His arrow met it before it covered even half the gap between him and the darkness. Light erupted at the impact, burning away a chunk of his attacker. There was a screech of fury as the shade retreated into the darkness. The shape that left the light was noticeably smaller.

The vampire hissed in anger. "Am I the next target, Priest? Is this the way you plan to win our battle?"

Tully moved again to close the gap between them. "No. Unlike you, I will not dishonor Tyr with treachery. The Archer will not harm you. But Brjóta will. Come let us finish this. I am tired and it is time for me to go home."

The vampire surged forward once more. It launched strike after strike. Many hit the shield and a few connected with the chainmail. None seemed able to penetrate the Friar's armor. Tully also swung again and again, each strike still a fraction behind the movements of the vampire. Tully was beginning to wheeze as he tried to suck in enough air to fill his lungs.

Roiland continued to spin in place countering the moves of the two shades. One came just a little too far into the circle of light. It was struck by an arrow before it could retreat. Light blossomed on the edge of darkness as the second shade became a little smaller.

The harsh whine of metal came from behind Roiland. He spun to see the vampire's claws digging furrows across Tully's shield. Metal and paint peeled away until the vampire's claws reached the cross shaped sword at its center. At the contact, Roiland caught the acrid scent of burnt flesh. The vampire snapped its hand back with a cry of pain.

The vampire slowed its attacks, avoiding the center of the shield. It began to mock Tully. "You are old and pathetic, priest. So tired. Getting slower and slower. I will feast on your soul, fat friar. Soon enough you will feel the coldness of my touch and then, I will taste your essence."

Tully simply chuckled at the taunt. "Do you truly want to taste my essence? It may surprise you. Come, I will give you the taste you desire."

Roiland watched in shock as the vampire slammed its entire body into the shield a second time. The smell of burnt flesh became stronger. But Tully was knocked to one knee by the impact. Smoke rose from where its body pressed against the symbol of Tyr, but the vampire was beyond caring. The shield was canted sideways as Tully tried to regain his feet.

The vampire howled in delight as it reached past the shield to sink its sharp, black claws into Tully's forearm.

The vampire's look of satisfaction turned to one of confusion. "I cannot draw your life force, Friar. You are not human?"

Tully grinned up at the vampire as blood dripped from his shield arm. "I did promise you a taste of my soul. I am a man of my word, evil one."

Roiland swore there was a brief flash of golden light, but it was gone before he could be sure. The vampire screamed and ripped its hand free from Tully's arm. There was more blood. The scream was still echoing from the surrounding buildings when the two shades darted in from different directions. They ignored him as they hurled towards the helpless Friar.

Roiland raised his bow. Oikea did not miss. The arrows flew fast and true. The shades both came to a complete stop as the bursts of lights bounced between them. They tried to retreat, but the barrage never slowed. Roiland did not realize that they had ceased to exist until his arrows streamed into the darkness to impact buildings on both sides of the street.

Roiland spun back to check on Tully. His heart sank. Tully's shield arm hung limp. The wonderous shield did not rise to save him when the vampire leapt at him. It grabbed the Friar with one clawed hand on each shoulder. Its head darted forward and its fangs sank into the junction of Tully's shoulder and neck. Roiland stared as blood ran down the Friar's chest. He raised his bow, but Tully turned his head. Roiland saw reproach in his eyes.

He lowered his bow to fire, but he would dishonor the Friar by interfering. The vampire began to suck noisily at the wound. Roiland shuddered. The vile creature pulled its head back and licked at its bloody lips. "You are tasty, Friar, and there is so much blood within your fat body."

Tully smiled then. Roiland could see satisfaction and triumph on his face. His right arm rose up between his body and that of the vampire. Roiland saw the long flat head pass between the vampire's outstretched arms. The head continued upwards driving it through the vampire's lower jaw. The light of the mace exploded outwards and then there was darkness.

Roiland came to when the boy, Thomas, pour water on his lips. He licked at the water greedily. His mouth was very dry. He looked around. The sun was coming over the horizon. Roiland stood with Thomas' help. The bodies were all gone. Only he and Thomas remained on the street.

Roiland shook his head. The only proof that the fight had happened were the clothes of the vampire and his own damaged arrows. He crouched beside the vampire's clothes. Ash and dust spilled from them. Nothing else remained.

Tully was also gone. Roiland glanced around looking for any sign of the Friar. Resting on the small stone wall beside the bell were Tully's armor and sheathed mace. The shield leaned against the wall below the bell. The gouges in the shield were gone as if the shield had not been damaged. Its paint was unblemished. Thomas came forward with the faded backpack and began to load the chainmail and mace into it. Tears ran down the boy's cheeks.

Roiland spent the next while getting the people within the chapel headed south towards safety. Several begged to retrieve heirlooms from their homes, but Roiland refused each request. He would not let them waste the Friar's sacrifice. They did not like it, but fear made them comply. They were soon headed from the village.

They had not gone far when Roiland came to a stop. Thomas looked at him nervously. "You will keep us safe, Sir Archer? Please?"

Roiland smiled encouragingly. "No, Thomas. My mission is not yet done. Your Friar must be avenged. That which brought the undead to your village must face justice. It must be dealt with. That is my responsibility. Yours is to lead that lot south."

Thomas looked pleadingly at him. "What should I do?"

Roiland pointed to the south. "Do what your Friar told you to do. He was a wise man. His words will see you on your way."

Roiland stood there as the young boy turned to follow the villagers south. The boy was taking his first steps towards becoming a man. Roiland wished him well. Maybe the boy would meet Tully's bearded man. It would make the old Friar happy.

Chapter 5

A Choice

Roiland watched the villagers until they were out of sight. The last to disappear through the trees was Thomas. The boy turned and waved and then he was gone. Guilt ate at him for leaving them to make their way alone. But he knew he was not meant to share their road. He must follow a different path, one he suspected would be far harsher.

With a sigh, he turned east and headed towards the mountains. According to the Friar, the source of the undead lay in that direction. Stopping the undead was the best way to protect Thomas and his people. Besides, the Lady's call was still strong. Someone needed his help.

He crossed a wide clearing. The morning sun was warm on his face. He yawned. He could barely remember the last time he had slept. Had it been two days or three? More than the traveling, it was the two battles that had taken a toll on him. Oikea's presence surrounded him. *You must rest, Archer. You will be no good to those who need you without sleep. The call of the Lady can wait until morning.*

Roiland knew he was being foolish, but the cause of Tully's death lay ahead. He stubbornly continued on until midday before admitting that the bow was right. He needed rest and time to prepare for the next fight.

He searched the nearby trees until he found one with a large branch well above the ground. None of the undead so far could climb and the shades were gone. He should be safe up there. He carefully climbed up to the branch and tied himself to it. Slipping an arm between the string and the riser, Roiland settled his bow across his chest. "Please wake me if any undead approach, my friend. I would not be caught unaware."

Of course, Archer. Rest and I will watch.

Roiland woke sometime in the night. He was stiff from the hard branch but he did feel rested. He settled back against the trunk of the tree and ate the last of the cheese he had brought from the lodge. When it was gone, he began to sort through the damaged arrows that he had saved. His fingers slid up each shaft deciding which would still fly true. Most would take more time to fix than he could spare.

The work took little thought. His fingers knew by feel which arrows could be salvaged quickly. The rest were left on the branch before him. After they were sorted, he pulled out his tools and began to work each shaft. The sun was once more visible over the horizon when he finished. Eleven arrows sat in his quiver. He prayed that they would be enough.

He slid down the tree into the shadows of the forest floor and stretched until he could move without pain. Shouldering his pack, he continued on. He walked steadily, much of his route was a up a gentle incline. The mountains were visible as he passed through clearing after clearing. But the forest was eerily silent. He had seen no animals all morning, not even a squirrel. He wondered what waited for him in the days ahead.

The sun had not quite reached its zenith two days later when he caught the scent of meat cooking over an open flame. His belly gurgled at the rich scent. The food he had packed was gone and he had seen nothing to hunt since leaving the village. He had no idea who waited ahead, but they had food and that was enough to draw him closer.

He moved cautiously forward until he reached the edge of a clearing. A figure sat comfortably near the center. Roiland's eyes went first to the stick in the figure's hand. Several long strips of meat adorned the stick as it hung in the air over dancing flames.

Roiland put aside his hunger and turned his gaze to the one holding the stick.

Sitting near the small fire was an orc. He was no expert on orcs, but Roiland guessed him to be no more than seventeen. Thrust into the ground beside him was a large spear. It would take strength to wield a spear that size. He drew an arrow and lay it across his bow. Perhaps this warrior could be convinced to explain how the orcs fit into the puzzle of the undead. And if Roiland asked nice, maybe he would share his food.

Roiland stepped into the clearing with his bow ready. The orc looked up as he came into view. He might be young. But the orc was big and muscular. Definitely a warrior. The youth made no move to rise or reach for his spear. Instead, he motioned for Roiland to join him at the fire.

Roiland stood for a moment, baffled. He realized suddenly that the orc had been waiting. Waiting for him. How had it known where to find him? He was in trouble if his enemies could anticipate him like this. He needed knowledge and before him sat a ready source of it.

Roiland decided to sit. That should at least get him something to eat. He moved to the opposite side of the fire and sat. Oikea rested on his lap beside the arrow. The young orc carefully pulled a strip of hot meat from the stick and offered the rest to Roiland. "It is pheasant. Only birds still remain in this land," the orc said.

Roiland accepted the stick. He sniffed the meat before taking a small piece to taste. It was good. "Why are you here, warrior? A lone orc in this region would be easy prey. Especially for the undead."

The orc cocked his head to the side and studied the Drow. "I was sent here by my new Chief to find you. I am supposed to bring you to the Lord of this land."

Roiland took another bite while he considered his words. "Why you? Why would your chief risk a warrior in his prime? Even if I did not kill you, the undead here hunger for the flesh of the living."

The young orc sat straighter at the compliment. "I am Bruhurst, son of the last Chief. I am…" He seemed to stumble over the next word. "Expendable. And the Lord has directed the undead to ignore the Orc for now. He has a use for us."

"Who is this this Lord of yours, Bruhurst?"

The young orc bristled. "He is not our Lord. At least he was not until my father was killed in the challenge. The Lord of this land is Yökutu, first hatchling of Mustasurma, the Dark Destroyer."

Roiland puzzled over the names for a moment. "Hatchling?"

Bruhurst met his gaze. "The Lord is a black dragon. Not an old one, but one that controls great magic. He is the one that animates the dead. He commands them. The Orc cannot stop him. He sends our honored dead to slay us."

Roiland did not allow the concern he felt to show on his face. Even a young dragon would be difficult for a single Archer to defeat. He did not have enough arrows to fight a prolonged battle against a dragon, let alone one that controlled an army of undead. "What does this Dragon Lord want with me?"

Bruhurst looked suddenly unsure of himself. "He wishes to parley. And then he expects you to surrender yourself and your wonderful bow to him."

There was a spike of anger from Oikea. But Roiland just laughed at the orc's words. "Why should I speak with this dragon? I do not intend to give myself up and I will never give him my bow. He will find that taking it from me will not be an easy task."

Bruhurst looked down at the meat he had been eating. His face had a sour expression as he shook his head. Tossing the meat into the fire, he growled, "There is no honor in what I must tell you now. But I have been ordered by my Chief to tell you. There is a hostage. It will die if you do not speak with the Lord."

Roiland's laughter died. "I see. Then I will speak to this Lord of the land. But I will not accept his terms. More than a single hostage will die if I do."

The orc shrugged. "You seem honorable for an elf, so I will tell you that the Lord has no honor. He is evil and his deals are often hard to refuse. He will leave you no choice. He does not even allow an honorable death to his enemies. Our spirits cannot stand before Gruumsh while our bodies still walk this land."

Roiland did not understand the orc's faith, but he at least understood the desire for a clean death over an eternity of undeath. "I will come with you, Bruhurst, to meet this Lord."

Bruhurst motioned for the elf to finish the meat. Roiland needed no encouragement; he ate quickly while the young orc buried the fire. Then they rose and Bruhurst led the way from the clearing. He took Roiland to a small game trail that led north east. The orc broke into a jog and Roiland followed. As they ran on, the trail became wider and more well-traveled. Roiland wondered if this was a path toward the orc village or to the dragon's lair.

His question was answered several hours later as the trees opened up to a view of a large wooden palisade resting atop a hill. The structure was in ruins. The palisade sagged in many places and there were blackened holes in the walls where something had eaten through the wood. The structures he could make out within the walls did not look to be in much better condition.

Bruhurst came to a stop once they were well clear of the trees. He stood as if waiting. Roiland used the opportunity to study what was left of the orc's home. A short time later, two horns began to sound from within the remains of the palisade. The two gates began to open. They were each being pushed by a squad of orcs. As the gates swung wide, the orcs formed two lines, standing shoulder to shoulder at attention.

Roiland sucked in a breath. A large black head broke the plane of the gates. Its face and head were covered with layers of shiny black scales. Three azure horns curved forward from the top of its head. The beast was at least fifteen feet high at the crest of its head.

Roiland did not realize he was on the verge of fleeing until a quiet voice whispered to him. *I am with you, Archer. What you feel is called dragon fear. It is a magical attack. It will pass.*

Roiland forced down his rising panic. This was a parley. The battle would come later. He watched as the beast strode through the gate. The scales on its chest were a charcoal grey and all of the scales on its body looked large and thick. The dragon was at least forty feet long including its tail. It curled up on the ground before the gate and waited. It did not seem concerned about Roiland or his bow.

Bruhurst led him up the hill. As they neared its crest, the young orc went down to one knee. Roiland smiled as he noted that the young warrior did not bow his head or avert his eyes. The boy had courage. Roiland would not display any less.

Before he could speak, the dragon opened its mouth in a large yawn. Roiland saw two rows of razor-sharp teeth. The dragon spoke and Roiland could smell rot on its breath. "How unexpected that the protector of this land is a Drow. Your kind's reputation is as dark as that of my own. No matter though. I am Yōkutu, sired by Mustasurma. I rule the lands west of the mountains. My sire rules those to the east. Your interference in our plans has angered us."

Roiland understood that he could not afford to show weakness before this creature. Power was the only thing it would respect. "Your displeasure is of little concern. Perhaps you should return across the mountains where it is safer."

The dragon began to chuckle. Spittle dripped from its jaws and the ground before it began to smoke. "I do like you, Drow. You have courage. You stand alone before me and issue threats. It is quite amusing."

Roiland wondered if he could convince the wyrm that he led a force of Drow warriors. "My people will not…"

The dragon hissed angrily. "Do not insult me with feeble lies. My captive has already assured me that you are an outcast. The last of your kind in this land. Perhaps you can serve me and save yourself a great deal of pain and suffering."

Roiland lifted his bow a few inches. "I serve the Lady of Silences. My knee will not bend to you."

The dragon stared at him for a time. "I sense the righteousness you hold so tightly. My sire has faced paladins before. He has taught me the weakness of your kind. Your honor is always your undoing." The dragon raised a clawed forearm and motioned towards the gate. "Bring it."

Roiland watched the gate as a large figure stepped out of it with something that struggled thrown over its shoulder. The figure was an orc, but one almost half again as large as the other orcs standing beside the gate. It was much bigger than Bruhurst. Its skin had many warts and scaley patches. Roiland had no clue as to its origin.

The large orc dumped something, no, someone on the ground before the dragon. It was human. Its feet and arms were tied tightly and a large sack had been placed over its head. Roiland tensed. The forest green clothing was familiar. Surely the girl had not been foolish enough to follow him this far? The dragon smiled. "Perhaps you will surrender to save the life of one that you care for?"

Roiland tried to deny it. "If that is who I think it is, she tried to kill me in my sleep. I owe her nothing."

The dragon nodded and the orc removed the sack from the human's head.

It was the girl. She had bruises and a few scrapes on her face that had not been there when she had entered his ambush, but it was her.

The dragon hissed in delight. "So, you do recognize her. If she means so little to you then you do not mind if I eat her while you watch?"

Roiland had no answer for the beast. He whispered softly, "Oikea?"

The strong presence of the Oikea washed through him. *We cannot let her die like this, Archer. I do not like this bargain, but we cannot defeat the dragon and a village full of orcs. If we fight, she will die."

Roiland met the young woman's hate filled eyes. Her voice sounded dry and harsh. "Once again you will escape me, Drow. My blood as well as the blood of my lamb shall stain your soul forever."

Roiland did not break eye contact with the girl. "What are your terms, dragon?"

The dragon laughed. "You surrender yourself to me and I get that lovely bow for my hoard. Simple and direct."

Roiland watched the growing surprise in the girl's face. "In return, you will swear before the Lady of Silences that you will let the woman go. She is not to be harmed by you, the orcs, or your undead. Swear it!"

The dragon's laughter stopped. "I sense power in this Lady of yours. Curious. But so be it. I can afford to be generous. You have my oath. The girl goes free. That useless orc that brought you here can escort her from my lands."

Roiland gripped his bow tightly for a heartbeat. Oikea's voice came to him. It had a strange tone this time. Her words had magic in them. *We will serve together again, Archer. Stay strong until then. We have much to accomplish still.*

Roiland knelt to place his bow on the ground. "Cut her free."

The dragon smiled broadly. "Of course, little Drow." It gestured and the huge orc pulled a dagger and sliced the roped binding her arms and legs. As the young woman moved slowly but made it to her feet. Roiland lay Oikea on the ground and stood up.

The young woman limped towards him with a confused look on her face. She stood before him and asked "Why? Why would you do this?"

Roiland shrugged. "Perhaps I do owe you. Or, as an old priest recently told me, 'without sacrifice there would be no love in this world.' Go. Live, love, and hate no more."

She stared at him and then nodded. Bruhurst came forward and took her arm. As he led her away, she whispered, "I forgive you."

Roiland smiled as he turned towards the dragon. The big orc now had a large hammer in his hand. "Do I kill the elf now?"

The dragon considered the question and then shook its head. "I think not. You will need many slaves to dig in the mines across the mountain. Let him learn how useful honor is to a slave. Make him dig for my ancestor's bones."

Roiland was forced to his knees. His arms were twisted painfully behind his back. He felt them being bound tightly. The dragon gave a sharp order. "Bring me the bow."

Roiland smiled in satisfaction as he watched an orc reach for Oikea. Its screamed as its hand touched the bow. The screams did not stop until it fell lifeless to the ground near Oikea.

Roiland was staring up at what remained of the Lady's orb when the girl's hood was placed over his head, blocking her light from his view. The sound of the dragon's voice came through the sack. "Most interesting. An even better prize than I expected. Wrap it in leather and then bring it to me."

Hopelessness battled with the power of Oikea's promise to him as he was led slowly away. He whispered softly, "I hope you have a plan, my Lady."

Oikea Lakko – Bow of Justice

Beautifully carved bow made of golden-brown rosewood. Running through the wood are numerous reddish streaks that accent the curves of the bow. Etched in the bow and inlaid with silver are four symbols representing the phases of the moon.

Oikea Lakko is a Holy Paladin weapon of high intelligence and ego. The bow is female and her alignment is Lawful Good. Any evil being that touches her takes 3d6 damage per round. Oikea provides +3 to hit and damage. Arrows fired from Oikea can hit and damage creature that require magic to hit up to +3. Undead creatures struck by an arrow from Oikea take an additional 1d10 of radiance damage. Demons, devils, and fiends take an additional 2d10 radiance damage.

Oikea Lakko detects evil within a range of 60 yards.

Oikea Lakko is not an artifact but it is a unique weapon that is carried and used by the Archer, the Knight of the Lady of Silences. When carried by the archer, Oikea provides +3 to all saving throws by the Archer and any of the Archer's allies within 20 feet. The archer gains a saving throw of 20 for all spells even those that do not normally have a save. Additionally, Oikea can cast Bless twice per day.

Brjóta

At first sight, this weapon appears to be a short sword resting within an ornate scabbard. Unlike the sheath, the hilt is of a simple, serviceable design. It is wrapped in leather that shows the sweat stains of frequent use. When drawn from the scabbard, the weapon is revealed to be a strangely shaped mace. It is fashioned of a solid bar of metal. It is 2 feet in length and nearly 3 inches wide. The bar is nearly an inch thick. It is vaguely reminiscent of the large rasp sometimes used to work on the hooves of horses.

Brjóta is a blessed weapon of the God Tyr also known as the Lawgiver. It gives +3 to hit and damage. Against undead and creatures of the lower planes, it is a +5 weapon. Brjóta can only be used by clerics or paladins of the Lawgiver. In their hands, Brjóta radiates blessed light in the presence of undead or creatures of the lower plains. The light becomes brighter the more powerful the creature. Brjóta protects the bearer from energy drains. Undead and creatures of the lower plains may not use innate powers while within its blessed light.

Foretold

Chapter 1

Change in Plans

Alauriel Armonen sat on a stone bench below a massive oak tree. The oak was adorned with large clusters of mistletoe that seemed to live in harmony with the tree, sharing space on many of its branches with the tree's natural foliage. The tree flourished in a small garden outside the High Temple of the Goddess Mielikki. Alauriel's eyes wandered around the garden. Everything in it seemed at peace, except for her own thoughts and emotions.

Alauriel's gaze returned to the equine form standing before her. It stared patiently back at her as she tried to come to grips with her swirling thoughts. She muttered more to herself than anyone else, "But I truly do not understand. The Ceremony of Initiation is today. Why now?"

Her musings were interrupted by an impatient chittering from above her head. Her eyes followed the powerful neck of the magnificent creature upward. She admired its glossy black coat and the long charcoal mane that adorned its neck. She took in its broad face and milk white eyes. Finally, her gaze lifted to the top of its head, crowned by a long, golden horn. Sitting there with its bushy tail wrapped

around the horn was a small reddish-brown squirrel. It chittered again impatiently.

Alauriel returned the squirrel's glare. "I understand it is Her wish. What I do not understand is why we spent the last year preparing for me to take over as High Priestess only to change course less than an hour before the Ceremony."

The squirrel began to wave its small arms as it chattered on, but the unicorn interrupted it with a soft nicker and shake of its head. The squirrel quickly grasped the horn in both its tiny hands and stomped its small foot petulantly on the unicorn's head.

Alauriel looked from one to the other. "I do the will of the Goddess; I just wish to understand this path that is set before me."

The unicorn bent its head low and the small squirrel protested as its perch shifted again. The unicorn rubbed its soft cheek against Alauriel's and blew softly into her hair. She turned her head into its neck and raised her arms to hug it to her. She nodded.

At that moment, someone rustled the ivy at the entrance to the garden. Alauriel said softly, "Come."

An initiate stepped into the garden and gasped at the sight of the other occupants. "Ma... My pardon, Priestess and Great Ones. I did not know."

Alauriel smiled and waved a hand. "There is no need to apologize. How may I serve?"

The initiate looked flustered, but continued. "The Arch Druid says that it is time. The sun is near its zenith. He bids you come, my Lady."

Alauriel sighed and shook her head. "Please tell him that there is no longer a rush. I will be there to explain in a few moments. But I must first say goodbye to my guests."

The initiate bowed and left. Alauriel turned to the messengers and asked. 'Will more be explained to me? I am not sure I understand how to accomplish this task."

The squirrel chirped and leapt onto a branch of the oak tree. Looking back, it chittered once more before disappearing into the mistletoe and leaves. The unicorn stood for a moment longer touching its nose to the palm of her hand. It raised its head and blew softly again. It stared deep into her eyes and Alauriel relaxed. Silence held sway for as long as Alauriel gazed into the Unicorn's eyes. With a last shake of its head, the servant of the Goddess turned and faded into the trees.

Alauriel took a steadying breath and then blew it out. She rose to her feet and walked over to a small pool and stared down. In her right hand, she held a sprig of mistletoe. The image that stared back at her was that of a tall woman standing well over six feet tall. The hands were rough from work and the arms and shoulders were almost muscular. She reached up and tucked the mistletoe into her long dark hair which fell loosely past her shoulders.

She shook her head and turned towards the ivy that marked the boundary of the garden. She moved to the entrance and looked back along the path taken by the unicorn. She whispered to it, "Faith is believing and acting, even when your path is dark and full of peril. Your will be done, Goddess."

She left the Garden to behold the Temple itself. It was not a traditional temple in the eyes of most folk of the land, but it served the druids and those of her faith well. There were no walls or pillars to mark its boundaries. Instead, four giant trees were placed in a square. They spaced fifty feet apart to mark the four corners of the Temple. The trees were Oak, Ash, Hickory, and Willow. Each was a perfect specimen of its kind reaching up two hundred feet in height.

The branches of the four came together and intertwined to form a roof over the Temple. The main branches that reached inside all looked to be polished to a high sheen. They were each engraved with pictures of every plant and animal imaginable. Despite the polished look and the engravings, the branches were alive and vibrant. They were covered with leaves and clusters of mistletoe. The leaf types were so intermingled that it was hard to tell which tree each belonged to.

In the center of the temple sat a simple oaken table. But even here was a sense of majesty and life. The table's life was evident in a single living branch that grew from its center. The branch was adorned by leaves from all four trees and a small sprig of mistletoe.

Standing before the table was an ancient man with a long grey beard and a simple linen robe. He held a five foot staff in his hand topped with a single living leaf. The shaft of the staff had the shapes of many creatures carved into it. Despite his apparent age, he stood tall and straight with eyes that blazed with vitality.

He looked at her with concern as she entered the Temple. He paced slowly forward to meet her and bowed. "Welcome, Priestess Alauriel. It seems a bit late for second thoughts. This alignment comes but once a year."

Alauriel took a cleansing breath and then nodded. "I apologize, Arch Druid Kristophé, but it would seem that the Goddess has other plans for my future."

Kristophé leaned thoughtfully on his staff. "You have worked for this for a long time, Alauriel and I fear I am too old and tired to train another. What has changed?"

She looked down and whispered, "I had a visitation. The unicorn and that foul tempered squirrel came to me in the garden during my meditation."

He looked up at her and sighed. "One of them is to be expected on such an occasion, but seldom do they both come together. Their message must have been of some importance. Are you at liberty to share the Lady's message?"

She hung her head, frowning. "This was a little overwhelming. They told me that I was needed elsewhere. They said I would never return. It frightened me."

He went still. "A mission that you will not survive?"

She again shook her head. "Not the way you mean. It is one that will take my whole life if I understood it correctly."

A small bird suddenly darted between them and around them several times before settling on a branch overhead. It was a sparrow with a pure white neck and underbelly. It looked down at Kristophé and chirped. The ancient druid leaned his head to the side in a bird-like manner and listened. To Alauriel's surprise, he responded in a simple song-like trill. The bird joined in and the melody of their two voices brought a sad smile to Alauriel's face. Then the bird sat quietly and watched.

Kristophé stared at her intently for a few moments. "That explained very little other than to let me know that I am not to meddle." He chuckled softly. "Apparently even Arch Druids are not privy to all the Goddess' secrets. I know not if I can clear anything up for you, Priestess. But I can be a set of ears if you wish."

Alauriel looked into the canopy above trying to order her thoughts. "There is one coming. I am to find him and shepherd him until it is time."

Kristophé motioned to the entrance behind her and several acolytes entered to place chairs for them to sit on. After they had left, he motioned her to a chair and sat himself. "Who is coming? A divine being? A demigod? What type of power is entering our world?"

She sighed and continued, "No, nothing like that. This one is mortal. As I understood it, we as mortals have chosen time and again to follow the wrong path. This time we must choose a better path on our own. This one is to be something or someone that none would expect much of. He must choose to right many wrongs and face many challenges without the aid of the Goddess. And the races must choose to follow his lead. The words were very vague. He will have advisors like me, but the Goddess will not intervene directly."

Kristophé nodded. "Most prophesies are vague. How are you to shepherd him? And until it is time for what?"

She looked exasperated. "I do not know." She smiled sardonically. "It will be revealed to me when the time is right."

He nodded. "How will you know him?"

She absently waved a hand. "The squirrel said I would just know. But if I really needed a clue, his eyes would be a pale forest green. Not much help I fear."

Kristophé smiled softly at her. "It will be when it is time. What else did they tell you?"

Alauriel grimaced. "They asked me to leave with a group of pilgrims heading to the southern lands in two weeks' time. I should prepare and say my farewells." She growled in frustration and then paused and looked confused. "I asked how I was supposed to do this, and the stallion said I must…." She paused for several long seconds and then simply said, "Love."

The old druid glanced up at the bird above him. "Never make it easy, do you, Lady? So, an act of faith it must be. Any words of wisdom my feathered friend?" The bird turned its back on him.

Alauriel looked up suddenly. "The squirrel said one other thing before it left. But it made no sense. He said that we should know that the Heretic has the Lady's favor. Who is the Heretic?"

Kristophé sat in silence staring into the sunshine outside the Temple. "He is an elf who is no longer an elf. His people have never forgiven him his choices. They cast him out. So be it. I am not an elf and if the Lady favors him then I will listen to his words." He turned his attention back to her and asked. "How can I serve you, Priestess?"

She laughed softly. "Tell me what to do. Or, short of that, I need a wagon and horses to travel with the caravan. I also would like copies of any prophesies that might pertain to take with me. And maybe some ink and parchment to keep notes on."

He smiled again and leaned forward to place a hand on her shoulder. "The wagon and two guards are yours. We will make copies of what we can find and get you that as well. As for what to do, follow your heart. It is all I have for you."

They sat in silence as the sun passed its zenith and traveled across the sky.

Chapter 2

The Road to Destiny

Alauriel sat in her tent near the garden and wrote neatly and precisely on the first of the blank scrolls she had been provided.

None of the prophesies I have reviewed so far have been much help. I see no connection in any of them to the task I have been given. I am not sure, but this might be a new prophesy. If so, then I have little to guide me. The only common theme that I have seen in all of the prophesies that I have read is the concept of personal choice. Free will is not taken from us. The prophesy simply predicts a fork in the path of time. What choice we make is not within the prophesies. At most there are vague references to the consequences of one path or the other. The choice is always left up to us.

That means I can walk away from this. But can I? How much of what I believe in depends on the choices I make every day? The forests may continue, but the peoples of this land may not. If I truly have faith in the Goddess, then I must act on that faith.

The Goddess teaches that all are part of the Balance. None of the mortal races are truly evil. There are great evils in our world. The mortal races can choose to turn away from them or bow down to them. These evil beings or Gods use the forms we wear to sew conflict

She sprinkled drying agent on the ink and let it set as she packed her ink and quill into the trunk she had been given. She rolled the scroll and placed it inside as well. Then she hefted her pack and headed outside. Two initiates hurried into the tent to take the trunk to her wagon.

She wandered through the garden towards the Temple and stopped again at the pool. As she looked down, she wondered who this woman was and who she would be in the days and years to come. She bent and splashed the water to disrupt her image. Her future was unknown. She had only faith. Alauriel rose and left the garden.

Sitting before the Temple was a worn caravan wagon. It was pulled by two solid looking draft horses. Sitting in the front bench was a scruffy-looking older man. He had a friendly smile and he tipped his faded cap to her. Alauriel knew she would like this man. Sitting on a horse to the right of the wagon, was a younger man in chainmail. There was a longsword in a scabbard on the saddle. He nodded politely and began to check his gear.

Kristophé was waiting for her as well and he stepped forward to greet her. "I bid you fair journey, Priestess. I will miss your company here at the Temple. The man in the wagon is Lukas. He is an experienced driver and a good shot with the crossbow hidden behind him. The warrior on the horse is Devon. He is young, but a steady hand. Both volunteered to escort you to your destination."

She gave the old druid a brief hug, her words momentarily stuck in her throat. She stepped back and smiled. "Thank you, Kristophé, for all your help. And thank you, Devon and Lukas, for your help as well."

Kristophé moved to the wagon and helped her climb up. "There are provisions and water for several weeks of travel before you will need resort to hunting or magic to replenish your supplies. Good luck."

Lukas made sure she was settled and helped her place her pack behind the bench. Then he turned the wagon and headed out of the forest. Within an hour they had joined up with the caravan heading south.

The first several days were warm, but not too hot. The sun felt good and the trails they followed were in good shape. Lukas assured her this would continue until they reached the crossing point for the Great Sea River. Alauriel chatted occasionally with Lukas or Devon as they traveled, but mostly she kept to her own thoughts of the future.

On the afternoon of the third day, Alauriel noticed the sound of water off to her right. She began to catch glimpses of the river through the trees. The caravan had shifted its heading to the east and was picking up the pace. Lukas cracked the reins above the horses as he coaxed more speed from them. He raised his voice to be heard over the noise of the fast-moving wagon. "There is a good crossing point not far from here. The Caravan Master wants to be there before the tides go out in the Great Sea. That will give the horses time to rest before we cross this evening."

Alauriel looked puzzled. "The Great Sea is a long way from here. Why would the tides there affect us?"

Lukas grinned and winked at her. "Wait, m'Lady. It will be a spectacular sight."

In less than an hour, the wagons were pulled up into a tight cluster along the edge of the river. At this point, the river bed was wide and the banks were almost non-existent. But the water seemed deep for the wagons to safely cross. Lukas pointed at the water. "Watch closely."

Alauriel stared in wonder as the water began to move much faster on its way downstream. The current became faster and the water level began to drop. She could not imagine trying to get the wagons across without the wagons all being swept away. She looked to Lukas. "What is happening?"

Lukas calmly examined the river. "When the tide is in on the coast of the Great Sea, it flows calmly up the river. The higher water levels slow the current and make the river much deeper. Deep water is hard to cross. As the tide goes out, the water begins to escape into the sea. The river water that has been trapped by the tide begins to move downstream rapidly, creating the swift current you see now. Fast water is dangerous. At low tide, there is a short period where the water is at its lowest and the current slows once more. This is when we want to cross. The Caravan Master knows his business."

Alauriel sat and watched the turbulent water. Lukas touched her elbow and pointed ahead and Alauriel noticed the Caravan Master was riding down the line of wagons speaking briefly at each. When he reached her wagon, he paused. "Greetings, Priestess. We were happy to have you join us. I apologize for not coming to greet you sooner, but the first days out are busy getting people organized."

Alauriel smiled. "No need to trouble yourself, good sir. We are a late addition and we do not want to be a burden. If any are injured or sick, feel free to call on me for assistance. And please, call me Alauriel."

He smiled. "Thank you, Alauriel. That is a kind offer. We will not move on until early evening. The lead wagon will raise a green flag when the current slows enough for us to cross. Until then I suggest you rest and get some food."

Alauriel thanked him as he rode on. Then she and Lukas climbed down from the wagon and stretched their legs. Standing felt very good after a day on the wagon. Devon rode up and dismounted. The two men watered all three horses and fed them a little grain. They allowed the horses to graze on the lush grasses nearby. She stood watching the river. She had heard of it before but had never come this way. It was a breath-taking sight.

When the green flag went up, Lukas and Alauriel climbed back into the wagon. Devon tied his horse behind the wagon and took up a position near the two draft horses. The crossing went smoothly as Lukas held the reins and Devon occasionally redirected the horses to better footing. Alauriel stared at the water flowing gently past. It amazed her that the river had so many personalities. Fast and dangerous to slow and deep. It felt alive.

All of the wagons crossed without incident and they made camp on the far side of the river. One of the scouts brought down a young moose in the forest.

Several of the men went out to butcher it and bring the meat back to the camp. They celebrated that night overcoming the first obstacle of their journey. The people of the caravan came together and feasted that night. There were many songs and much laughter. For a time, Alauriel was at peace.

The days that followed turned into a week, then two. The only excitement was healing the broken arm of a young boy. He had been wrestling with his brother and fell from the back of the wagon. Time past slowly as the caravan creeped steadily south. The trees and rivers of this new land kept the wagons to less than ten miles each day.

On the fifteenth day since the crossing, the Caravan Master called for an early stop near a fork in the small trail they followed. That afternoon, there was a meeting of the heads of each of the wagons. Alauriel went with Lukas more for something to do than anything else. The Caravan Master climbed one of the taller wagons and stood on the bench so he could be clearly seen and heard by all. "My scouts report that the eastern side of this mountain chain is being lashed by storms from the Great Sea. The rains have not reached this far north yet, but there is a great deal of rain and mud south of here."

He paused for a minute as the people began to murmur their concerns. He called for quiet before continuing. "We are going to be making a course change tomorrow. I have traveled the western side of these mountains and the route flows through a large valley that contains a long deep lake. The disadvantage of this route is that we cannot resupply at the settlements along the coast. The water is plentiful and clean there. There is also plenty of game. We may lose a few days going in this direction, but that is better than losing a few wagons to the mud. Does anyone have any questions?"

A young woman raised her hand and asked if the area was safe. The Caravan Master nodded. "We have never seen orcs or other dangerous tribes in this area. Surprising, since the region seems fertile enough. But it is an open area with mountains on both sides of the lake. Not all of our scouts are back from the eastern side of the mountains yet. Those that have will begin moving west tonight. The rest should be back with us within a couple days. We will start without them so I can get these mountains between us and the worst of the weather."

There was some quiet discussion but most seemed to accept the news. As they walked back Lukas, politely asked, "Are you okay with the new route, Lady?"

She nodded. "All I know is that I am to travel with these folk. I know not if my destination is the same as theirs."

Lukas nodded and they returned to the wagon. After a light dinner that evening, Alauriel climbed inside the wagon to sleep while Lukas and Devon slept beneath the wagon as was their norm.

And so, the caravan turned southwest and entered a low pass. On the far side it sloped down into a broad valley. It was a pleasant sight to behold. It was filled with groves of maple and pine trees and she occasionally saw stands of apple trees growing wild.

The caravan stayed close to the mountains on the first day so she had a good view of the lake. It was indeed quite long and narrow. The green of vegetation could be seen all along the distant shore. The lake was dotted with small islands. One chain looked like stepping stones across the northern end of the lake. It was a beautiful place. But for some reason she felt uneasy.

Chapter 3

Conflicted

Hunter stood at the back of the large underground chamber where the Elders held council. His pale green eyes watched as the Elders and warriors jostled for position before the council stone. The tribe's Chief had called a council of war. Nearly forty adult male ogres in their prime were working themselves into a frenzy. As they approached the point where they were beginning to fight amongst themselves, there was a roar that shook the room. All turned to look at their leader as he stepped onto the council stone.

The Chief growled out his warnings about the humans who had invaded their lands the previous day. He predicted the hardships the tribe would suffer when the humans settled in their lands. He stirred their ire as he demanded the humans be chased out or, better yet, wiped out. As the overly aggressive males reached a fever pitch, he ordered an attack as soon as the warriors could prepare. They were to destroy the invaders and protect the tribe.

Hunter just did not understand any of it. The humans were outside. The tribe lived under the mountains. Outside was forbidden except to the Chief, Elders, and a few who gathered food like him. From what he had heard, the humans had not slowed their travel through the valley above. They did not appear to be staying. So, there was no threat to anything except to the Chief's pride.

Hunter sighed. He had not liked Brawl even before he became Chief. He liked him even less as the Chief. Brawl seemed more concerned with his own wants than with the good of the tribe. Brawl not only never led a hunt, he seldom even participated in hunting for their food. But the Chief always demanded first choice of the meat brought in. He claimed it was his right.

Hunter shook his head. He was missing the planning and he needed to know just how badly this attack was being planned. He quickly came to understand that the tribe would descend on the humans in a few hours when the bright thing was at its highest. The Chief boasted that they would come down from the round top mountain and crush the humans.

Hunter growled in disbelief. The bright time was not their friend. It would blind their warriors more than the humans who lived outside. If he was Chief, they would strike in the dark when their senses were superior. Then again, if he was Chief, they would not attack at all. There was nothing to gain from killing the humans except maybe a horse or two to eat. And the tribe could not afford the loss of many warriors. The tribe had too many enemies in the deep tunnels to worry about. Strength was important to survival.

As the warriors all began to boast of the kills they would make, Hunter slipped into the forbidden tunnel and headed for outside. His eyes at least would be ready before the stupid battle began.

Alauriel woke before dawn that morning. She still felt uneasy about the day to come. There was no danger she could detect, but she decided to trust her instincts and prepare for trouble. She began by moving off alone to pray to the Goddess. In addition to spells of healing, she asked for the most potent battle spells she knew. Then she returned to the wagon and climbed inside. She opened a trunk and pulled out her chainmail, shield, helm, and mace. She pulled the armor on over her clothing and took her seat on the bench with her mace and shield at her side.

Lukas and Devon were getting the horses in their hitch before the wagon. Devon's mount was already saddled. They looked carefully at her armor and Lukas raised an eyebrow. She looked down in embarrassment.

Devon was more direct. "Something we should know about, Lady?"

Again, she blushed. "Nothing I can explain, Devon. I just do not like the feel of this day. Call it a bad case of nerves."

Both men nodded. But when Lukas climbed to the bench beside her, he took a moment to check his crossbow and placed a pair of bolts on the bench between them.

The caravan began to move out an hour after the sun crested the mountains. The sun was pleasantly warm and the slopes were covered with trees all the way to their rocky peaks. Most were not that high but had steep inclines. The only notable exception to this was a single rounded peak just off their path a few hours ahead.

———————————————————

Hunter squatted outside, eating some berries that grew on bushes near the entrance. He only ate of the bushes that the animals did. He avoided those eaten by the flyers. Those often gave stomach pain. These were good though. They were filled with juice that was very sweet.

Hunter could see the large things that carried the humans well down the slope. Their tops were large and white and visible from a long way away. As he ate, he watched them move along the edges of the mountains. Their path avoided the wet spots and the deeper steam crossings. If not for the danger posed by his tribe, he would have approved of their path.

The humans grew closer as the warriors began to spill out of the tunnels. Most came out and had to cover their eyes. The bright thing blinded them. He wondered how many of them he could have killed before they even knew he was there? Probably all of them with little risk of harm. There was an angry rumble in his chest at the stupidity of it all. Even when they could finally uncover their eyes, the warriors continued to blink and wipe away water.

The Chief called the warriors to him and pointed to the humans approaching. He then gestured to the trees that came alongside their path. He growled and headed down the slope with the tribe fast upon his heels.

––––––––––––––––––––

Alauriel watched as the caravan moved ever southward. The feeling of uneasiness was growing but she had no clue as to why. This valley seemed unoccupied and peaceful. She had sent Devon ahead to help scout for danger. He had checked in several times but had seen nothing of note.

Towards midday the caravan began to roll past the round mountain top. The Caravan Master had promised there was a good place to break for a meal about an hour south. Their resting place would be along a small stream he knew of. The first three wagons had crested a small rise near the round top and were headed down the back side. As the fourth wagon reached the crest, there was a bestial bellow from the tree line about seventy five yards away. A large rock sailed out and hit the fifth wagon, caving in the side panel.

Horses and people began to scream. The wagon drivers lashed their horses and angled away from the trees as they hurried to get past whatever was attacking. Alauriel cautiously stood and stared in the direction of the trees, but she could not make anything out with the bouncing of the rushing wagon. She did make out the horses of the caravan scouts moving to intercept the attack. She also saw Devon spurring his horse towards them.

Alauriel sat and waited for Devon. She watched him rein in and spin his horse as they came alongside. He stayed between the wagon and the trees but matched pace. He glanced at Lukas and then at Alauriel.

"Ogres. A lot of them. Even with their mage, twelve scouts will not slow them for long. We need to turn and make a run for the valley. With luck, we can outrun them."

Lukas pulled out a horse whip and raised it to lash the horses for a run. Alauriel placed a restraining hand on his arm. "No, Lukas. You must let me off first."

Lukas shook his head and stared at her. "Lady are you insane? He said ogres. Not one but many. We run or we die."

Alauriel shuddered as a dozen or more gigantic figures erupted from the trees hitting the damaged wagon and the one behind it. Neither had been able to adjust their course and speed fast enough. The damaged wagon was flipped almost immediately and the viscous creatures began striking at anything that moved. Another dozen or so were headed toward the cluster of scouts charging from the front of the caravan. The remaining group, at least a dozen more, turned towards the rear of the caravan.

Alauriel raised her voice to be heard over the sounds of the wagons and the carnage. "I will not run. I serve the Lady of the Forest and the Balance. If I do nothing, then many will die. Let me down, Lukas. Now! Then you may go."

Lukas face reddened. He turned and locked gazes with Devon. The young warrior nodded as he drew his sword. Lukas sighed and pulled hard on the reins. The wagon lurched to a stop and Lukas set the brake. "No, Priestess. Our duty is to protect you. If you fight, we stand beside you. Tell us your will."

Alauriel stood on the now still wagon. "Kill any who get close and pray." She turned towards the group heading her way. Let us see if they know fear." She began casting.

———————————————

Hunter stood back and watched as the Chief shoved and ordered the warriors into groups. The Chief ordered one group to hit the middle of the line of humans. He sent another smaller group towards the riders. This was the most dangerous fight to be in. Hunter noticed the group had several of the males who frequently disagreed with their Chief.

Hunter suspected this was Brawl's way of eliminating future threats. Brawl joined the largest of the groups in attacking the human's rear. Hunter followed along to see if Brawl would actually fight this day.

The attack began with a large rock hammering into the side of one of the things the humans rode. The center group was among the humans quickly. It was little more than butchery as the humans were quickly overwhelmed. A flash of light from the direction of the riders caught Hunter's eye. Whatever it had been, it had cut through the charging group of his kin. One ogre lay face down and two others were on their knees. "Hates magics," Hunter muttered.

Most of the things near the rear had turned aside and were fleeing towards the big water. Several males had broken off to give chase. The rest of the group was headed towards a lone thing that had come to a stop. It appeared it was going to fight. Hunter thought this unexpected move showed courage even if it was not very smart.

Hunter noticed that the Chief had come to a stop well behind the rest of the charging ogres. He had one of the younger males beside him to guard his back. Hunter's curiosity brought his gaze back to the lone thing. He was curious what it would do with two hands of his people charging towards it.

He quickly assessed the human threat. The battle seemed very one-sided. There were but three humans. One on a horse and two on the thing. One of the two rose to stand high and vulnerable above the battlefield. The human began to shout and gesture. Hunter's skin crawled as he recognized magic about to be used. He waited to see what would befall his people. As the human fell silent, fire rained down from the sky catching the front half of the group charging towards their foes.

When the smoke cleared, a full hand of his people were simply gone. Several others who had been close behind were slapping at flames burning in their clothing and hair.

Despite his dislike of magic, Hunter began to move forward. This foe interested him and he wanted a closer look. Hunter's eyes were locked on the human who made the magic as he edged ever closer to the thing. With half their number gone so suddenly, the group came to a stop. Several looked back to the Chief for guidance. Brawl was a good twenty yards to their rear screaming for them to attack.

Hunter continued to close. He winced as another of his kin fell to the ground a few feet to his right. Hunter could see blood oozing from two chest wounds on the dying male. Both had small sticks jutting from the wounds. Hunter recognized them as the same weapon used by the fuzzface warriors in the deep tunnels. Hunter was not overly surprised to see two ogres turn and run. Both ignored the Chief's shouted commands to return to the fight.

The Chief and his guard began to advance cautiously. Brawl shoved the smaller ogre in front of him. Hunter had a clear view of the human standing high on the thing. He suddenly realized it was a human female. She must be extraordinary to lead such a successful defense with just two warriors against almost a third of his tribe.

Hunter noted that the ogre protecting the chief took one of the deadly sticks in its stomach. The warrior went to his knees clutching at the wood that had penetrated its body. As it tried to pull the stick out, its hands were quickly coated in blood. The Chief stepped past the wounded warrior and threw a large stone. Hunter watched with a flicker of admiration as the stone flew true. It connected with the human who now rested on one knee beside the thing. The stone seemed to blast through the human's body and slammed into the thing's side. The remains of the human did not move.

Hunter stared at the female atop the thing as a strange desire overcame him. He wished to know more about these humans. Especially the brave ones. He decided he would claim the female as his prize. He would understand what drove her to make such a reckless stand. Hunter began to run.

The rider saw him and charged. Hunter grinned. "Brave little human." Hunter pulled the great sword from over his shoulder and prepared to meet the charge. As the human rode in, Hunter brought his sword up and blocked a deadly slash at his neck. The block nearly unseated the human and he struggled to control his horse. Hunter did not wait for the horse and rider to recover; he spun and punched the horse. The horse dropped onto its side. The human somehow leapt clear.

The rider's leap got him free of the falling animal, but he landed hard, striking the back of his head. The rider did not move. Hunter knelt and examined the human. It was not dead, but there was no sign of consciousness. He picked up the human's sword but it was too small and he dropped it. The human was still unconscious. Hunter raised his sword for the kill but then paused. "Coward die sleepin, not brave." Hunter sliced the saddle strap and pulled the horse blanket over the human's head to hide him and then turned away.

Alauriel saw Lukas get hit by a large rock thrown with tremendous force. His death was a shock, but she maintained her focus. She had but two flame strikes and she could not miscast this last one. As she released the magic, she turned to see Devon's horse go down. She whispered a prayer for both of the good men who fought beside her. She smiled in satisfaction as the second spell struck three more ogres. This left the rock thrower and the one that had cut down Devon. She grabbed her mace as she jumped down from the wagon.

Alauriel glanced backwards in satisfaction as she saw seven wagons making haste down the hillside and away from the ambush. Two ogres who had been chasing them had already given up and turned back. This might not end well for three of them, but their sacrifice had saved lives. She could die with that knowledge.

Alauriel had just turned back to find her two remaining attackers when her world exploded in pain. Something impacted her left leg and it felt as if the bones were shattered into countless pieces. She felt herself flying through the air and then everything went dark.

———————————————

Hunter stood above the fallen warrior and watched the human female as she surveyed the battle field. He had a clear view of her as she turned to watch the rest of her tribe get away. She protected them as a good chief should. The human had long, dark hair that blew freely in the light breeze. She was large for a human although not quite the size of a female ogre. There was an aura about her that he did not understand. Females within the tribe were not so bold. They were controlled by the males in the tribe and beaten for any infraction. They had no spirit left.

This human had spirit. She did not fear even death. No, she fought and she killed. She was a prize to be won. This one would be a worthy companion or even a mate, not that she would ever consider such as him. His thoughts were interrupted as the Chief launched another rock that caught the human female in the leg knocking her to the ground.

Hunter charged forward as he saw the Chief run forward to the female's body. Brawl roared in triumph as he raised his huge club high over the helpless human's head.

Chapter 4

Challenges

Hunter came to a stop about twenty feet behind his Chief. He unknowingly still gripped his sword in his right hand. His voice came out in a low threatening tone that seemed to close the distance between them. "Brawl no kill!"

The Chief spun around and bared his sharp tusks at Hunter. "Not Brawl. Chief now. Youse no tells Chief! Youse do what Chief tells."

Hunter sighed as he noted the human female had been forgotten for the moment. He had to keep Brawl's attention so that he would not kill the female. Hunter stared down at the human for a second and then spoke with authority, "No! Not do. Hunter take dis human. Claim prize. Dis one mine. Rest Chief ken keeps. Female mine."

The Chief laughed at Hunter. "What good dis ting? Weak. Broke. Me helps youse. Kills it dead."

Hunter shook his head and raised the fist with his sword. "No kill. Hunter no lets youse."

The Chief grinned and motioned Hunter closer. "Chief claim kill. Claim human fer war prize. Me kill. Me Chief, me make rule. Chief strongest. Bestus. Chief pick afor all. Hunter weak. Fraid. No gets prize"

Hunter bristled at being called weak. He took a step closer. He realized he was tired of being pushed around and bullied by Brawl. "True Chief no take bestus. True Chief feed tribe afore. True Chief not hides. No make udder warrior dies. True Chief brave not fraid. Brawl bad Chief."

As Hunter spoke his voice grew more certain and was filled with a passion he had not felt in a very long time. Somehow this was more than just saving the female warrior.

Other males from the tribe had begun to cluster around. The humans were either dead or had fled from the battle. Brawl glanced nervously at the audience that was beginning to form and raised his club menacingly. "Youse want bees Chief. Den knowed da rule. Challenge den die. Hunter fraid me."

Hunter hesitated. He did not want to be Chief. How did saving the human female turn into a battle for control of the tribe? He did not wish to be responsible for the tribe, but he knew that Brawl was not a good Chief. The tribe would die under his rule and too many had died already this day.

Hunter glanced around, looking for any other options. He noticed that most of the middle attack team was close now. They were watching the conflict with growing eagerness. Hunter tensed as he felt a presence at his back. Then he heard the quiet voice of the Elder called Maker. "What do, Hunter?"

Hunter did not fear Maker. Maker's interests were always for the good of the Tribe. He was skilled at creating tools for the Tribe. He could form many things out of bone and rock that the Tribe needed to survive.

The Chief laughed at Hunter's hesitation. "Who fraid now? Know me strong. Me punish youse. Run way. No comes back ta Tribe."

Hunter's head snapped back around and he stared angrily at Brawl. He heard Maker speaking from behind him. "Youse knowed da rule, Hunter. No like den challenge. Strongest rule. What Hunter choose?"

Brawl laughed and turned back toward the woman at his feet.

Hunter's hesitation dissipated. His sword slashed through the air between them, making Brawl spin back to face him. Hunter's voice rang out across the hillside, "Me challenge!"

Brawl shook his head in surprise. Maker moved forward to stand between them. "Bees no rule. Fights. Kills. Win bees Chief. Lose bees dead."

Maker moved to stand over the human female. He noted with surprise that she still lived. Her fate would be decided by the victor of this battle. At Maker's signal, the remaining males made a rough circle. Hunter and Brawl entered and faced each other. Brawl held his massive wooden club with two hands. Hunter knew the wood was as hard as steel. The end of the club was stained a reddish color from the blood of those Brawl had killed with it. Hunter raised his great sword but also slid a dagger from his left boot.

Hunter began to slowly circle to his left hoping to limit Brawl's natural swing with the large club. Brawl simply ignored the move and charged straight at Hunter. Brawl was still several steps away when he brought the club up and leapt forward, driving the tip of the club straight down at Hunter's head.

Hunter took a half step back with his right foot to brace himself. His sword swept before his face, blocking from left to right. The blade caught the club while it was still above Hunter's head, pushing it to the right. As the two weapons collided, Hunter side-stepped to the left and the club buried its head deep in the mountain soil.

Hunter continued moving to the left, unable to take advantage as Brawl pulled his club free. Hunter flexed his right hand on the sword's hilt. The power of Brawl's blow had almost cost him his grip on the sword. Hunter knew he was strong for an ogre, but that club was trouble.

Hunter went on the offensive with a series of lunges and quick retreats. He was able to keep Brawl off balance, but he could not get his blade past the blocking club. The other warriors were beginning to call for blood. Hunter knew he needed to end this quickly. He needed a decisive victory or the other males would see him as weak.

Brawl began circling to his left. Hunter followed that movement unsure what the change in tactics meant. Brawl stepped back and twisted quickly to the side. The club swung downward, catching a rock sticking up from the ground. The rock shattered, sending up a spray of shards. The fragments flew at Hunter. Most missed or bounced off Hunter's armor. One large chunk cut a shallow slice in Hunter's thigh. He felt a trickle of blood down his leg.

The circle of warriors began to hoot showing approval. Brawl laughed and asked, "Blood come. Youse gibe up?"

Hunter ignored Brawl's question and the taunting noises from the other warriors. He reversed his grip on his dagger as he stood watching Brawl's attention waver as he preened at the compliments of the other males. Brawl looked over at Maker yelling that he would be there soon for the female. As Brawl locked eyes with the Elder, Hunter sprang forward.

As with each of his previous attacks, Hunter's lunge led with his great sword extended towards Brawl's heart. Brawl's attention shifted back and he brought the club across knocking the sword point aside. Hunter moved his sword with the force of the blow, caring only that he kept his grip. Unlike his previous attacks, Hunter did not pull back after the initial lunge. Instead, he moved swiftly past Brawl's left side. Hunter struck with the knife in his left hand as he surged past Brawl. The attack was so swift that it went unnoticed by even the seasoned warriors within the tribe.

Hunter continued well past Brawl almost to the circle of his kin before he spun back to face his opponent. Brawl seemed disoriented at first as Hunter was not where he had expected him to be. Brawl began to spin around to track Hunter when his left leg nearly buckled.

The jeers of the warriors began to fade as they watch Brawl struggle to keep his feet. Their voices went silent as Brawl's hand went to the back of his left thigh. His fingers curled around the hilt of Hunter's dagger and came away red. Brawl grasped the dagger again and gave a tug, but it was buried to the hilt in the back of his leg.

There was murmuring all around the circle as the males came to understand the severity of the wound. Brawl's face flushed with anger as he grasped the hilt and ripped the dagger from the wound. Blood began to flow freely down the leg. He looked at the blood on the blade and threw the dagger behind him. It clattered and bounced to land near Maker. The older ogre bent and picked it up. He stuck it in his belt as he waited to see who would be Chief.

Hunter met Brawl's gaze. His face betrayed no sign of mockery.

"Gibes up? Bees not Tribe. Goes far way, neber comes back!"

Brawl seemed to consider it for a second and then he charged Hunter. His gait was uneven as blood continued to run heavily down his leg. Halfway across the gap between them, Brawl threw his club at Hunter's chest. Hunter went to a knee leaning far to the right. Despite his efforts, the handle of the club glanced off Hunter's left shoulder. His arm went numb at the impact. Hunter brought his blade back around as he began to rise. Brawl leapt before he could regain his feet.

Brawl's leap was awkward, but the full weight of his huge body hit Hunter before he could stand. The earth shook as the two ogres crashed to the ground. Brawl landed on top of Hunter with his hands clawing at Hunters face and chest. Brawl's mouth was open wide, exposing his large tusks as the angry Chief bent to rip out Hunter's throat.

Hunter landed on his back with his sword arm pinned beneath Brawl's bulk. He had managed to get his left arm up and his forearm across Brawl's neck. He had little feeling left in his arm, but it was all he had to keep Brawl from his neck. Hunter tried to work his right hand free. He grabbed and pulled, but Brawl weighed too much.

The two behemoths thrashed, Brawl clawed and snapped. Their combined growls were deafening. Brawl used weight and brute strength to lean ever closer to Hunter's neck, his huge tusks reaching for the thin layer of flesh protecting Hunter's artery. Hunter's left arm began to tremble with the strain as he tried to pull his right hand free.

The murmurs of the warriors grew as they waited for the inevitable end. Then Hunter's arm gave way and Brawl's head snapped forward. Both bodies seemed to tremble as blood pooled around them. Both combatants went still. Silence returned as neither rose from the ground. There were no shouts of triumph.

The warriors became uneasy. The death of both could unsettle the tribe for a long time. Maker began to ease forward to check on the two when an excited cry went up from several of the males. Brawl began to rise from the ground. Maker's sigh turned into a gasp as the body suddenly rolled to its side and lay still. Hunter raised his head and then slowly sat up. He kicked at the body beside him and it flopped over on its back.

As the body settled to the ground, a large gash came into view running from the center of Brawl's abdomen to his left hip. There was a wider opening in the center of the gash. Long ropes of entrails hung from the hole in the center of the gash. Hunter rose slowly to his feet. As he stood, he grasped the hilt of the sword lying on the ground beside him in his bloody right hand. Small pieces of flesh hung from several of his fingers.

Hunter stood unsteadily for several minutes as the Tribe watched their new Chief for signs of weakness. Hunter's left hand went up to his neck and wiped away the blood. There were teeth marks there, but none appeared deep. Hunter turned to Maker and growled softly, but his words carried clearly to the assembled members of the Tribe. "Brawl no more. Dead. Hunter Chief. Any want challenge?"

Maker bowed his head and then looked up with a wry smile. "Good have new Chief. Udder not bery smart." Maker stepped forward, returning the new Chief's dagger. Hunter accepted the blade then began to turn slowly in a circle meeting the gaze of each of the males around him. As their eyes locked, each male nodded its head in acceptance of his rule. Then the tribe began to disperse. Discussion of the challenge and bragging over the recent battle seemed to dominate all of their thoughts.

Hunter turned to look at the only battle group not accounted for. He located them quickly. They were in a cluster around the bodies of several dead horses and, he assumed, humans. The remaining riders were gone. But they had done their job allowing the things to escape with the remaining humans. They had fought bravely. By hunter's count, the Tribe had lost at least a hand of warriors from that group as well. Only the center group had not been badly hurt. This was not good for his Tribe. He realized suddenly that it really was his Tribe now.

Hunter stepped over the human female and made his claim apparent to the other warriors. They began to rummage through the things made of wood. Hunter growled at the first to begin to destroy the thing belonging to the human female.

Maker walked over to a tree along the edge of the wood and began to cut some branches free. He walked over and faced Hunter. "Maybe die. Hurt bad."

Hunter shook his head. "Warrior female. Her fight."

Maker started to kneel beside her but stopped at a warning snarl from Hunter. "Help Chief. No hurt."

Hunter grew silent and nodded. Maker knelt and placed the sticks to each side of the shattered leg. He pulled some small vines from a pouch and began to tie the leg into place using the sticks to keep it straight. When he finished, he rose. "What Chief say do?"

Hunter flinched at the new name and turned to stare at the thing. The two horses were still tied to it and both were stamping nervously at the nearness of the ogres. Hunter pointed at it. "Bring close tunnel. Leave dere. Kill horse. Feed Females. Feed Kid. Warriors eat udder horse. Finds prize udder kill."

Maker nodded and then asked, "What do wid thing?"

Hunter stared at it. "Take all from thing to Chief chamber fer. Den thing be fer Maker."

Maker nodded his understanding and then smiled. "Much good wood." Then he pointed to the round pieces the thing sat upon. "Must learn dat. Maybe help all."

Hunter sheathed his blade. He then bent and carefully picked the human warrior up and carried her back to the tunnels.

Maker asked a final question. "Chief move to Brawl chamber? Bees near Elders?"

Hunter looked down and shook his head. "Dis one safe where am. No so manys dere."

Maker raised an eyebrow and asked, "Kill Brawl mate. Kill kid? Makes safe."

Hunter growled at this. "Nuf dead. No kill. Live. Grow." Hunter turned and walked away.

Maker shook his head. "Muches danger me Chief."

———————————

Devon regained consciousness slowly. He could not see anything, but he was warm. It took a moment for him to realize that his face was covered by something that smelled strongly of horse sweat. His body hurt everywhere, but nothing seemed broken. He lifted a hand and pushed aside what appeared to be a horse blanket. He touched the back of his head and felt a painful knot.

Devon sat up slowly and looked around him. The night was cool. The sky was clear and there was enough moon to see that the caravan was gone. What was left of his horse was scattered a few yards away. He got up slowly and began to walk around.

The remains of three wagons were easy to find. But they had been picked over and there wasn't much to see. The wagon the Priestess had shared with Lukas was nowhere to be seen. He hoped that they had survived.

Devon returned to the blanket and picked it up. Smelly or not, it would keep him warm in the mountain air. As he picked it up, he was surprised to see his sword lying under it. He retrieved it gratefully. Next, he found the remains of his saddle and saddle bags. The bags were ripped open, but there was some hard biscuit left in a side pocket wrapped in oilskin. He checked his waterskin and it was still mostly full. He had supplies to sustain him and a weapon to defend himself.

Devon examined the ground one more time. He wasn't much of a tracker let alone at night. With the area so trampled by the battle, he had no hope of figuring anything out. He turned south and began to move slowly. The Caravan Master had promised a stream an hour's ride south. He should be able to make that at least.

He walked into the night, happy to be alive.

Chapter 5

A Time of Healing

Hunter stared down at the human female. She still lived despite his handling of her. Carrying her this far had been bad enough. But getting the armor off and the things underneath had have hurt her even more. His large clumsy hands were not good at gentle tasks. Some of the things she wore had to be torn to remove them. He saved the scraps, unsure if they would be useful or not. Mostly he dipped the soft scraps in water and used them to clean her.

Long ago, he had chosen this set of chambers because water from the underground stream seeped into a side chamber and drained out through a crevice in the floor of the same chamber. If he blocked the exit hole, it formed a small pool. The water went from cool to cold as time passed, but there was enough of it to meet his needs. The stream was also useful for disposing of waste as the water carried everything down into the dark. When too much water fell outside, he might have a small problem. But that was a rare event and the advantage of having his own water supply was more than worth it.

Maker had given Hunter several small bowls made from the skulls of deep dwellers. They had been gifts to the new Chief. Hunter believed Maker wanted to help him with the human although he was not sure why. He was thankful no matter what his reason was.

Hunter used the bowls to carry water to clean her wounds and clean her body. He dribbled water into her mouth from time to time. On the second rising, he noticed that the leg was growing warm to his touch. He went to speak with Maker's mate. She gave him a powder to mix with the water. It was made from certain underground mushrooms that the female said would help. Hunter thanked her.

He was unsure if the mushrooms would be safe for a human so he did not give it to her right away. Within a short time, she began to sweat and thrash. Hunter mixed the powder in her water and lifted her head so she could swallow. She choked a bit at first and then swallowed some of the mixture. Hunter covered her with extra skins when she seemed to shiver from the cold. After a bit she seemed to settle down into a deeper sleep.

Hunter sat and watched.

She continued to breathe.

And he whispered for her to fight.

––––––––––––––––––

Alauriel woke to a world of darkness and pain. There was no hint of light, not even starlight above. She wondered if she was blind. Worse, her leg felt as if it was on fire. She almost could not breath it hurt so bad. Her throat and mouth were so dry that her cry of pain came out as a croak.

Suddenly, a large and gentle hand lifted her head. It held something to her lips and she tasted water. She drank deeply. The water had a strange bitter taste, but she did not care and drank her fill.

She turned her head towards the hand that supported it. She stared into two large eyes of the palest green she had ever seen. The eyes seemed to glow from within and they were the only thing visible to her. If it was not a fever dream then at least she was not blind.

Her head was lowered to a padded surface. Her thoughts began to swirl. Green eyes. Why were they important? What did it mean? And then she slipped into a dream filled sleep where unicorns and squirrels swirled around her asking questions which she could not answer.

Hunter smiled down at the female. She had opened her eyes and had drunk deeply. Better still, she had met his gaze without screaming. He did not know if she could see him or not, but it was a good start.

It was the sixth rising since he had brought her here. The small amount of horse he had eaten was not going to keep him going. The female would need to eat as well. As she fell into a deep sleep, he sent a messenger asking Maker to visit.

Maker showed up a short time later and Hunter asked him to watch over the female so he could hunt. Hunter rushed through the tunnels heading up, towards outside. It was dark outside when he reached the surface. He wasted no time moving through the trees in search of prey.

He soon saw several deer in a meadow. He threw two rocks in rapid succession, hitting a young male hard enough to knock it down. He rushed forward as it struggled to rise. He thrust his sword into its chest and the beast dropped at his feet. Hunter quickly ate his fill of the raw meat. He cut a number of large strips of the meat and wrapped them in the animal's pelt on the side away from its fur. He rose to return and then paused. He stared down at the carcass thinking of his friend Maker. Then he drew out his sword and cut the head from the deer. He replaced his sword and grabbed the head by its short horns to carry it back as a gift.

Hunter ignored the few tribe members who asked questions of him on his return. He hurried back down to his chambers dropping the deer head by the entrance. He thanked the Elder and told him to take the head with his thanks.

Hunter resumed his watch over the female. Maker walked to the entrance of his Chief's chamber and turned to study him. There was something that drew him to this young ogre that now ruled his Tribe. Hunter gave him hope. He took the deer head with him, debating what he could do with such small horns.

Hunter kept his vigil for another two risings. The woman woke from time to time. Hunter would give her water with the mixture in it. He also would chew pieces of the meat until they were very soft. He would feed these pieces to her. She fought him, but he insisted and she swallowed a few small bites. Each time she would drift back to sleep. Hunter pulled over a spare sleeping mat and fell asleep as well. He had done what he could.

She continued to breathe.

He waited with a hunter's patience.

––––––––––––––––––

Alauriel continued to slip between the haze of pain and dream-filled sleep. Each time she woke there was water to drink. It had a funny taste that she thought she recognized as a fever medicine. But she could not be sure.

Once, she was not sure if it was the third or the hundredth time she woke, something that tasted like raw meat was placed in her mouth. She tried to spit it out but the large hands were firm. She swallowed it and her stomach felt better. She accepted several more bites and then more to drink. She slept again.

The next time she woke, she heard the sounds of heavy breathing from somewhere in the darkness. Her head was still fuzzy, but she could think a bit more clearly. She could not find her mistletoe or anything else. She came to realize she was naked and lying on some kind of mat with soft furs piled on her. Her body felt clean and that was all she could ask for at the moment.

Alauriel knew she needed more than just time to heal and recover. Her thoughts were too muddled for a major casting, but she thought she could cast a minor spell of healing. She gathered her wits and as the pain ebbed for a moment, she took a clearing breath and released the magic she held inside. She placed her hands on her injured leg and saw an emerald glow pass from her fingers into the leg. The pain eased and she drifted back to sleep.

––––––––––––––––––

Hunter awoke feeling a prickle on his skin. He sensed danger, but only the female was in the chamber with him. He was not sure what had woken him. The female was sleeping peacefully. He touched the leg and the unnatural warmth was gone. He sighed and lay back down to sleep. He would need to hunt again soon.

———————————————

Alauriel woke sometime later feeling more refreshed. Her mind was clearer and the pain was tolerable. She took a deep breath and pushed herself into a sitting position. It hurt and took most of her remaining energy. She sat and breathed deeply until the pain subsided.

She touched her left hip gently. It was tender and probably bruised. It was hard to tell without light. There was a crude splint of what felt like tree branches and vine tied to her leg. It was simple, but it had kept her leg straight while she was brought to wherever she currently was being held.

Alauriel picked at the knots and managed to untie the two upper vines. She could not reach the rest. She sucked in her breath as she touched the leg. Her flesh felt soft. She probed the leg as much as the pain would allow, but it was too swollen to tell how badly the leg was damaged. Her memory of being injured was fuzzy. Her last clear memory was of casting her spells in battle. Then nothing. She wondered if she would ever walk again.

Alauriel considered the spells she still had memorized. Most were spells to aid others in battle or defensive spells. But she did have a second spell for light wounds and one for more serious ones. She had given up the spells that could have restored the leg in favor of the flame strikes. As she thought of the battle, she just hoped that most of the caravan got away. She had no memory of the end of the battle.

Alauriel silently debated which of the two healing spells to cast. She wasn't sure she could maintain enough concentration for the more powerful spell. She opted to use the second minor healing. Again, she concentrated and the emerald glow began in her hands and spread to her leg. As it seeped into her flesh, she felt the pain recede to a dull ache.

Alauriel sat back and relaxed. Then she jumped when a deep voice came from several feet to her left. "Magic bad. Why do?" She looked towards the voice to see those same glowing green eyes staring at her from the darkness. They had not been a dream.

Hunter watched the female struggle into a sitting position. He was tempted to help her, but he decided that a warrior like her would not want to appear weak. He watched as she began to remove the protection Maker had put on her leg.

He tensed as the glow grew between her fingers and spread to her leg. He felt the same prickly feeling run across his skin. He spoke softly to her in the tongue of the humans. "Magic bad. Why do?"

She made a startled noise but then turned to bravely look him in the eyes. He smiled at her courage. She replied, "Some magic is good. This will help me to heal."

He shook his head. "No like magics. Tribe no like. No do."

He heard her sigh and then she asked, "Water?"

Hunter moved beside her and brought the mushroom water to her lips. She took a small sip and pushed it away. "No, please. Is there clean water? I need to think."

Hunter understood some of her words but not all. But he knew clean water. He rose and went into the side chamber. He rinsed the bowl and brought it back with fresh water. She drank it all quickly.

She handed him back the bowl and asked, "Light? I want to see. Please."

Hunter shook his head. When she did not react, he placed a hand before her face. He realized she could not see him. He spoke softly. "Light bees outside. No light dis place. Outside bees up."

The female went silent for a time then asked, "Is there anything to eat? Food?"

Hunter picked up the rest of the deer and sniffed it. It did not smell bad yet. "Need hunt fresh meat."

The female hesitated then asked, "Can you cook it this time? Or maybe some fruit?"

Hunter thought for a moment. "What bees cook? What fruit bees? Not know dem word."

The female sighed again. "Fire? Put the meat over fire for a while. And fruit, umm, round things that grow on trees and bushes."

Hunter considered her words with a deep frown. "Burns meat? No can eat den." Hunter scratched his head then added, "Fruit. Dat be food fer animal and little thing go in air. Me know dat. Fruit good word."

Hunter encouraged her to eat a few bites of the deer meat then he eased her back down onto the mat. "Sleep. Me hunt." He turned and headed into the passages. He met many of the tribe on his way out to hunt. There were questions and things that required the Chief. He answered everyone he could and finally made it to the tunnels headed outside.

———————————————

Alauriel lay back thinking as she heard her captor leave the room. When it had been silent a while, she allowed a small cry of fear and loss to escape into the dark and lonely room.

She understood now that she was being held by the ogres that had attacked the caravan. She had never heard of ogres taking prisoners and she wondered what this meant for her. At the same time, it was a strange captivity. The one with the green eyes did not treat her like a prisoner.

The more she thought about her situation, the less it all made sense. She had been cared for. Her wounds were tended. She had been kept clean. She had not been left in her own waste. Even her hair was not too dirty. She had been fed and given water and medicine. She also remembered the gentle touch when she had rested.

As her thoughts wandered, she suddenly remembered why the pale green eyes mattered. The words of the Squirrel came back to her. She would know the one she sought by his forest green eyes. Was this the one she was to Shepard? She groaned and looked up. "Lady of the Forest, what have you gotten me into this time?"

Chapter 6

Learning New Ways

Alauriel woke at her captor's return. He presented her with fresh meat and a bag of some type of berry. The berries were bitter, but they were more appealing than the raw meat. She forced herself to eat some of the meat as her body needed it to repair itself.

When she asked to relieve herself and clean up, he carried her to a side chamber and set her down. He placed her hands in the water and showed her where it came down the wall and where it drained out. He also showed her how to block the exit point to form a small pool. Then he left the chamber.

The water was cold mountain runoff. After she took care of her necessities, she blocked up the drain and took a short and very cold bath. It felt good to clean herself. Her leg still ached, but she could deal with it. She was about to call for help when she realized she had no name for her captor. "Hello? Are you there?"

He returned immediately. She sought his eyes in the darkness and asked, "What do I call you? Do you have a name?"

He stood quietly and she began to wonder if he had understood her. Then a deep, soft voice replied, "Name bees Hunter. Who bees you?"

She smiled to herself. Hunter. A simple name but descriptive. It seemed to capture the essence of who he was. "I am called Alauriel."

He was silent and then began to imitate her. "Al or el? Allor? Bees hard. Big name fer little warrior."

Alauriel looked at him sharply. "I am no warrior."

The sound of his mocking laughter filled the small side chamber. "A lor el fight many ogre. Kills many. Fight Chief. Youse protect yer tribe. Yes, bery muches warrior."

Alauriel was silent as she considered his words. "I guess I did. So where is your Chief now?"

Hunter grunted. "Me kill Brawl ta sabe youse. Me new Chief. No likes."

She pondered his words as he moved over and gently scooped her up. He carried her back to the mat and set her down. He brought another bowl of water and placed the sack with the berries in her lap.

As she ate, she began to think about her future. There were things she needed or at least wanted. Clothing was high on the list. The cave was warm enough but even in the perpetual darkness, she did not want to be naked before her captor. So, she asked, "where are my things that I had on? The things I wore when you brought me here."

He grunted softly and rose to walk across the room. He returned after a moment and squatted before her. Hunter placed her chainmail across her uninjured leg. He placed her belt on top of the mail. Her mace and belt pouch were still attached to the belt. She was surprised that he returned her mace to her. What kind of captor would arm a prisoner? Next, he placed a pile of cloth in her hands. "Broke. Hard gets off."

Her armor and padding were fine. Her shield had apparently been left on the battlefield. The shirt had no buttons left. Otherwise, it was in reasonable shape. Unable to undo the buttons, he must have just pulled it apart. Her pants had been shredded. Some places appeared to have been cut and many others torn apart at the seams. Her undergarments had also been cut from her. Many of the rags were bunched up and smelled bad.

Hunter reached out a single large finger to touch the cloth. "Soft. Use ta clean youse. Not wat hurt more."

Alauriel nodded at his reasoning.

She put the shirt on as it at least provided some covering. Then he took her hand and gently placed the necklace she had worn with her Mistletoe into her hand. The chain was broken, but her Holy Symbol was not. Did he realize the power he had placed back into her hands? She did not know.

She started to speak then stopped and simply said, "Thank you."

He just grunted in response and helped her place her things beside the mat. Then he moved away in the darkness and left her to her thoughts.

Time began to pass in a strange rhythm to her. She would sleep, wake, eat, bathe and try to communicate with Hunter. It took several risings, but he finally seemed to get her name at least close. He would leave for short periods to meet with his tribe. But always somewhere else. She asked about why no others came here. Hunter replied simply, "Protect youse."

She found Hunter was brighter than she had expected. He learned new words easily, but clung to the speech patterns of his people. He had an understanding of things that surprised her at times.

Hunter went in search of food regularly. His diet was mostly raw meat and it seldom lasted long before going bad. The trips were growing longer as her health improved. She tried not to anger Hunter by using magic, but it was hard to resist. She did not understand his dislike of it, but it seemed the one rule he was not flexible about. Still, she did use his trips to try to reach the Goddess and ask for spells. During his first long trip, she prayed for spells to heal critical wounds and one to fully heal her leg. But the connection to the Goddess seemed weak here below the earth.

She understood that the weakness was within herself. She missed the forests and the open air. She missed the smells of growing things and the breezes in her face. Without the connection to nature, she did not feel complete and her more powerful magics were not available to her.

During the second hunting trip, she cast her more powerful healing spell. She knew it helped, but the leg would still not bear her weight. When Hunter returned, he sniffed around the chamber but never said anything to her. She was sure he knew, but was kind enough to ignore her breach of his trust.

More than anything, Alauriel missed the light. She told herself if she could only see, then she might be able to deal with the sense of being trapped here. There were spells that she could use to create light, but she had not prayed for those as they were not needed in the sunlight of the upper world.

Her other option for light would be a trip outside. It frustrated her that Hunter would not take her outside. He had outlawed access to the outside even to the food-gatherers. They hunted in the deeper tunnels now. She was outraged when he explained that the rule was partially her fault. She felt little guilt when he explained that the tribe had lost to many in the battle. Most of the deaths were as a result of her spells. He would not risk making the Tribe more vulnerable.

Without access to the outdoors and the wilds, she had no chance to regain her more powerful spells. But she had to believe that the Goddess would answer her prayers for the less powerful spells. But she would have to convince Hunter to allow her to use her magic.

Alauriel woke when Hunter began moving around. She got his help into the room with the water and cleaned herself up. She got comfortable on the mat and thanked him when he brought a bowl of fresh water and another for her needs.

After he left, she sat in silence for quite a while. Then she drew forth her Mistletoe and held it before her in both hands. She focused on the Goddess and brought forth her memories of the forest and the flowers. She thought of the Temple and its gardens. And in her mind an image of the black unicorn stallion formed.

The image stared into her eyes and at last it nickered. She swore she heard it speak. "Have faith, Daughter." She felt some of her magic return to her. Her less powerful spells were returned to her memory, including a few she had not thought to ask for. Her success excited her. The spells she had received to made her feel a little more whole. She just needed to find a way to convince Hunter that magic was not all bad.

While she waited for Hunter to return, she pulled over the belt that sat on top of her armor. She opened the pouch hanging from it to see what it contained. Her flint and steel were there and a brush and a spoon. It also contained a small blade that she occasionally used when cleaning wounds. Lastly, she found a small silver coin.

The coin was a surprise. It was the perfect receptacle for her continual light spell. She longed to cast the light spell the Goddess had granted her, but she held back. Hunter had shown trust in her. She was reluctant to use "bad magics" without asking his permission first. She put her coin away and lay back with her Mistletoe at hand to await his return.

She awoke when Hunter returned. He entered the room growling softly and stomped into the side chamber to clean himself. Then he came out and gently lifted her to take her in to see to her needs. She asked as he picked her up, "What is wrong?"

He placed her on the ground near the water and turned to leave. "Kid come hunt. Learns. Get bite bad. Maybe gots cuts hand off."

As he carried her back to her mat she whispered softly. "I can save his hand."

She felt him shake his head as he set her down. "Magics bad. No use. Bad."

She heard a note of uncertainty in his voice. "If I save his hand, is that so bad?"

Hunter did not respond, so she asked another question. "Do your people have no magic? No Mages or Shamen?"

She heard him suck in a breath. "Gods no hear ogre. Ogre no hears dem back. Bees ogre magi. Dem bery bad. Hurt Tribe. Hurt all. Must kills dem."

Alauriel continued softly, "I promise not to hurt the Tribe."

Hunter sat in silence for a long time. "How youse do dis?"

Alauriel thought for a moment. "I would need to see the hand. Then I need to touch it. The good magic will save it."

Hunter grunted in satisfaction. "No Light. No work den. Bees good."

Alauriel smiled. "I can make the light if you allow." He started to growl. "Only if Chief say yes," she added carefully.

He again was silent. "Ifn light bad, makes go way?"

She agreed and he thought for a while longer. "Show light."

Alauriel pulled her coin back out and placed it on the mat before her. She again took hold of the Mistletoe and held it above the coin. She closed her eyes and visualized the light. She warned him. "Close your eyes. This will be bright like outside." Then she called upon her magic and released it into the coin.

The glow began softly and continued to grow. After so long in the darkness, it stung her eyes even through her eyelids. She heard Hunter growl louder. She reached down and placed her hand over the coin, blocking some of the light. She opened her eyes to look around her for the first time.

The first thing that she saw was Hunter sitting on a nearby mat with his hands over his eyes. Tears leaked from them as they tried to adjust to the sudden light. She studied the creature… no, person, before her.

Hunter was tall. Sitting, he towered over her seated form. She had to guess that he was at least eight and a half feet tall. Unlike some of the ogres that had attacked her, he had a thinner, almost wiry frame. His face was plain with strong simple features. His hair was dark and long in the back. And he had those green eyes that seemed to see everything. He was not good looking but he was far from ugly.

Hunter reached towards her with his palm held open for the coin. Alauriel realized that this was a true act of bravery on his part as he only knew magic could hurt and maim. She placed the coin on his palm and looked into his face.

Hunter forced himself to stare at the coin. Then, he closed his palm smothering the light. After a moment, he opened it again. He began opening and closing his hand almost like a child with a new toy. Hunter handed it back. "Not bad. Dis tool. Be like sword. Ken use, not use."

Alauriel sighed in relief. Then she glanced around the room and noticed a small ledge high on one wall. She pointed. "Can you place it up there?"

Hunter stood and took the coin. He placed it upon the small ledge and the light illuminated the room. Alauriel had her first good look at the roughhewn chamber that she was confined to. It was spacious but plain. There was another ledge over in one corner. Beside it sat a small boulder that could almost be used as a chair. Along the wall beside it was her trunk and backpack.

She stared accusingly at Hunter. "I asked for my things. You did not tell me they were here. Why?" She pointed at the trunk and then tugged her buttonless shirt more tightly about her. "Why did you make me wear this when I had more clothes?"

Hunter stared at her blankly. "You no ask dat."

Alauriel turned on Hunter with anger in her eyes. "I asked when you brought me these things." She pointed to the armor, belt, and torn clothing.

Hunter shook his head. "Ask tings on youse." Hunter gestures at the chest. "Dat bees wid big ting fer ride. Not same."

Alauriel started to argue, but then stopped herself. She realized that Hunter and his people were very literal. It was something she would have to adjust to. Despite how much they had learned of communicating with each other, Hunter did not use the common tongue the same way she did. More importantly, Hunter's people did not have possessions the way humans did. She doubted he even had any spare clothing. She sighed and asked, "Can I have the wooden box before you bring the child here?"

Hunter shrugged and walked to the trunk and easily lifted it and brought it to her. She opened it and rummaged inside, bringing out a new set of clothes. It embarrassed her that she needed his help to get dressed, but she was glad to have a full set of clothes on.

She looked at Hunter and asked, "Where is this child? A boy I assume? Let me see if I can save the hand."

Hunter hesitated and then disappeared into the darkness. He returned after a time dragging an ogre youth by the arm. Alauriel had no way to estimate the age of the boy but the top of his head did not quite reach Hunter's shoulder. The boy seemed to be very afraid. She glanced up at Hunter. "What is his name?"

Hunter looked at her puzzled. "Still be boy. Tribe no name. Him no ready fer name."

Alauriel started to ask what he meant, but realized this was a lesson in ogre ways for another day. She reached for the boy's bandaged hand, but the child tried to pull away. His frightened voice came out in a rush. "No Chief. No take hand. No cuts wid sword." The boy desperately tugged his arm, but Hunter's grip was firm.

Alauriel raised her voice. "We will not hurt you."

The youth stared at her with almost the same fear he had for Hunter. But only almost. Hunter pushed the boy to the floor before her. Alauriel gently removed the bloody pelt from around the boy's hand. The bite mark was bad. The smallest finger was gone and several others were obviously broken. Most of the skin from the back of his hand was peeled away in strips. The dried blood there was caked with dirt.

Alauriel looked at Hunter and asked for clean water. Hunter released the boy who started to scoot away. Hunter growled menacingly and the boy froze where he was. Hunter disappeared into the side chamber and returned with the larger bowl filled with water. He placed it before her.

Alauriel placed the hand into the bowl and began to clean away the dirt and dried blood. As the hand lay soaking, she motioned to Hunter. He caught her meaning and grasped the boy's arm at the wrist. The boy let out a whimper that rose in volume as she straightened the broken fingers. Finally, she had Hunter pull the arm from the water so it could begin to dry.

Alauriel reached for the broken chain that held her mistletoe and began to chant in a low murmur. As the emerald glow gatherer about her hands, the boy began to struggle in earnest. She ignored his cry of terror and reached out to touch the hand. This was the strongest healing spell that she had and she was not sure it would be enough to mend the damage. Her fingers traced the broken fingers first and left trails of green that sank into the hand. Then her touch moved to the torn skin and allowed the last of the magic to close those wounds as well. She bent to examine the results of the Goddess' gift.

The skin on the back of the hand was whole. It was still red and did not have the toughness or calluses of the other hand. The missing finger was still gone, but the stump was fully healed over. From the way the boy was clenching his fist, Alauriel assumed that the bones had knit as well. She looked up to Hunter for his approval.

Hunter lifted the hand and sniffed it. He poked at the finger stump with the index finger of his other hand.

Alauriel shook her head. "I cannot bring the finger back. But the hand should work as before."

The youth flexed his hand. He seemed surprised. He looked at her and asked, "Magics? No posed do magics."

Hunter grabbed the youth roughly by the neck. "No talk magics. Ifn talk, she takes magic back. Den me takes hand."

Alauriel started to protest but Hunter glared at her. She went quiet. The youth pulled away and Hunter allowed him to escape his grasp. The boy backed to the darkened tunnel. He stared from her to his Chief to the glowing coin high up the wall. "No tells. He turned and fled into the darkness.

Hunter shook his head. "He tells. Maybes no so many."

Alauriel looked at him curiously. "Why not tell?"

Hunter glared at her for a moment then sighed. "Protect youse. No let Tribe hurt. Dem no likes magics. Maybe wants kill."

Alauriel shivered at his words and remained silent.

Life within the Caverns took on a new rhythm after that. The coin with the continual light spell was covered for sleep and left uncovered when they woke. A form of day and night returned to her life. The underground seemed less oppressive to her now. She was allowed to use her magic again, but carefully, so as not to upset the Tribe or Hunter.

Time passed and Hunter watched.

She continued to breathe.

Hunter waited for something he did not have words for.

Chapter 7

New Faces

Alauriel woke one rising with an energy she had not felt since her days at the Temple. Hunter uncovered the coin and light shown through the room. Then he helped her into what she now called the bathing room. When she finished, she called to him for help.

She asked him to settle her on the rock near the ledge. He brought her some nuts and berries and a bowl of water. Then he left to take care of the Tribe. She turned on the rock and opened her trunk. Inside she found what she sought. Her inks were still intact. The blank scrolls were there to make notes on. And more importantly, the copies of the prophesy scrolls were all there.

She had many plans for the morning and it passed in a blur. She began by writing a short summary of all that she had learned of the ogres and the tribe. She closed with her speculation about Hunter and his green eyes. As the ink dried, she took out one of the prophesy scrolls and began to reread it. She wondered if her discovery of the ogres and a Chieftain that seemed larger than life would give her any new insights.

At midday, Hunter returned. He helped her to the bathing room and then back to her seat. Upon it now rested a thick fur pelt folded several times for her comfort. She fingered it and looked over stare at Hunter.

He shrugged. "Cave Bear no needs. Bees dead."

She raised an eyebrow and he turned away. 'It get me way."

Hunter offered her some meat and she waved it away. He studied her
for a moment and then left to meet with the Elders. When he was gone,
her thoughts returned to her magic. She had prayed today for a spell
that she had never had much use for. Food and water were plentiful
in the Temple. She had never had need to create it with magic before.
She placed an empty bowl before her on the large ledge. She held her
mistletoe in her hand and began to gather her magic. She had no clear
intentions as she began to cast, she simply thought of nutritious food
that was cooked. Almost anything would be better than more raw
meat.

As the glow of the spell dissipated, she noted that the water bowl was
full. Beside it lay three small loaves. Each small loaf was a different
color. She wondered what the colors indicated. She had green, a brown
that was almost black, and whitish one. She picked up the green one
first and took a bit. It tasted of a mix of fruit and vegetable. She smiled
and finished it. Then she placed the other two aside for later.

Alauriel pulled out the next scroll and began to read. Soon she lost all
thought of her surroundings or the passage of time. She jumped when
Hunter softly touched her shoulder. "Alert little warrior. Not all bees
friend dis place."

————————————————

Alauriel had day and night back, but the passing of weeks and months
was lost to her. The only clue she had to the true passage of time was
when the stream water began to get colder. It became uncomfortable to
bathe. Most risings, she felt content with her life. She still had no idea
of what the Goddess planned for her but she was willing to wait. Time
had little meaning and she came to measure it as Hunter did. Events of
importance became her timeline.

One of these events began when Hunter returned from a meeting with
the Elders before she had even finished eating her breakfast. Hunter
came into the chamber and began pacing. He glanced from her to the
darkness of the tunnel nervously. When she could stand his pacing no

more, she asked, "What is upsetting you so Hunter? You act like we are in danger."

Hunter hesitated. "Youse meet me friend. Nudder ogre. Bees kay?"

She spun to face him. "Is there danger?"

Hunter shook his head. Alauriel smiled. "Then I would love to meet your friend."

Hunter sighed in relief and then blurted out, "Maker want ta see magic light. Wants ask muches. Keeps ask ifn ken come. "

Alauriel laughed softly. "So where is your friend?"

Hunter coughed and a much older-looking ogre entered the room. He stared for a long time at the light shining from the coin. Then he wandered over and smiled at her. His attempt to smile was a bit disturbing as he bared his large tusks and sharp teeth.

Hunter looked from one to the other then spoke carefully. "Dis be Maker. Tribe Elder." He reached towards Alauriel. "Dis Al or iel, me little warrior."

Maker presented her with a bowl made from the skull of a large beast she could not name. It was polished to intense shine and she thanked him for his gift. Then the questions began. Maker was curious about many things in the outside world. He was very intelligent and also very proud of his creations.

Before she knew it, she was growing hungry and tired. The visit had been a wonderful break from her routine. She offered Maker one of her magic loaves. He sniffed it and looked puzzled. Alauriel realized that the food she created did not really have a scent. She did not rely much on her nose. He broke off a piece and nibbled at it. He politely handed the rest of the loaf back with a warning. "Dat meat old. Bad. Make sick. No eats."

Alauriel chuckled as she realized that some differences between ogres and humans would always exist. Hunter had not been impressed with her food either.

The two males ate some of Hunter's meat and talked for a bit about the Tribe while she listened in. Eventually, Maker left with a promise to return.

It was a special day for her in several ways. She made a new friend and had a good time. More importantly, Hunter and Maker had spoken freely about the Tribe and she believed they might let her help them.

____

Maker continued to visit from time to time. He was always a welcome distraction. His questions were often humorous to her and added laughter to her life. It was not that his questions were foolish, but he had made a lot of strange assumptions based on his limited exposure to the outside world. The simple joy he expressed at solving his many mysteries was truly remarkable.

Once, he came with a large wagon wheel and a head filled with questions. Alauriel was saddened by the thought that this came from her caravan. But the caravan seemed a distant past to her now. She spent that day explaining the idea of a wheel and of a wagon. She did her best to help Maker understand that other races just could not carry massive loads the way the ogres did.

She taught him many words that day. She had to disappoint him on his most important questions. She had no idea how the craftsmen formed the wheels. She could not tell him how to curve the wood. Maker did not seem to mind as he had a plan to shape a wheel out of stone.

____

Another day that stood out in her memory was the day she met Hunter's brother. A messenger had arrived while they were eating dinner and Hunter had hurried out with his sword on his shoulder. He did not return that night. When he did show up the next morning, he was very upset and had blood on his leather. He quickly helped her to the bathing room and then picked her up to carry her to her padded rock. She had never seen him so rattled before. Placing a hand on his cheek, she asked, "Please Hunter, what is wrong?"

Hunter turned his head away, refusing to meet her eyes. He seemed ashamed but she had no clue what made him this way. As he went to place her on her seat, she grasped him tight and refused to be put down. She spoke softly. "Tell me, Hunter. Let me help."

His reply came out as a hoarse whisper. "Need magics."

Alauriel's breath caught in her throat. He had always tolerated her use of magic but had never asked for it. Even the boy that she had healed had been at her urging. She gently turned his face back towards her. "How can I help you, Hunter? What is it you need?"

The words seemed to tumble from him. "Brudder. Old me. Hurt. Fuzzface hurts bad. Die maybe. Need youse magics."

Alauriel touched the Mistletoe hanging from the chain Maker had patched for her. "Where is he?"

Without hesitation, Hunter turned and almost ran from the chamber with her in his arms. She tried to get him to stop so she could grab the coin, but he refused with a mutter about dangerous.

He headed through a maze of tunnels and she was lost again in the darkness. She sensed they were heading further down into the earth and it worried her. But she chose to trust Hunter.

After a time, they entered a small crevice. Hunter barely fit inside. He placed her gently on the ground. She heard the ragged breathing of another and reached out. She felt blindly along the leg of another large form. She guessed it was an ogre. She could not see what was wrong but the smell of blood was strong in her nose.

Hunter stepped back. "Me guard. Maybe fuzzface come." Then he seemed to remember she could not see. "Foots bery bad. Muches blood.

Alauriel focused her attention to the form beside her. Her hands flowed down the leg until she felt the heel of a foot. It was wet with blood. She gently traced the bottom of the foot, ignoring the blood and dirt. As she passed the arch of the foot, everything else was gone. She moved her fingers back and sucked in her breath harshly. The front half of the foot was missing. Blood continued to flow freely. She realized the severity of the wound and wondered how this person was still alive. She did not hesitate but immediately cast her spell for serious wounds. In the emerald glow of the spell, she could see that the cut was remarkable clean with no ragged edges. Whatever had done this was very sharp and very powerful.

Her spell closed the wound, but she knew more would be needed. She had one more spell for serious wounds and another for lighter wounds. She felt around for the second leg in case there was more bleeding there. She found it and quickly moved down towards the foot. There was blood on this foot and she could not be sure if it came from the other foot or not. She traced the outline of this foot until she reached the toes. At least the front half of this good was still there. She quickly checked for all five toes.

Alauriel winced when she felt the outside of the foot. The two smallest toes were as thin as parchment. Every bit of flesh in them had been pulverized. What kind of force would it take to flatten them so that even the bone was crushed? She whispered to Hunter, explaining that she could not save the two toes. They needed to come off before she healed him or they would cause him problems in the future. Hunter grunted and knelt beside her. His only comment was a whispered "Dem gone?" before he stood back up.

Alauriel regretted not having her spells of Heal or Restoration. There had been a time when she could have fully restored both feet. Then again, she would not need to be carried everywhere if she had those spells. Alauriel cast her last healing for serous wounds on the second foot. Then she used her light wounds spell on the first foot to repair it further. The breathing of the unseen ogre seemed less labored. She could only hope.

Hunter scooped her up and ran back to their chamber as soon as she was done. He left her on her rock with a bowl of water to clean with. Then he was gone again. She washed away the blood and dirt and sat thinking about Hunter's brother. She realized she was hungry and took one of the greenish loaves to eat. She thought briefly of what it had cost Hunter to ask for her help. She sighed and waited a long time.

Hunter eventually struggled into the chamber with his brother slung over his shoulder. The second ogre was slightly smaller than Hunter and looked very pale. Hunter placed him on his own sleeping mat and then dragged it over beside her rock.

Alauriel had no more spells of healing until she slept again, but she had tended the sick and wounded often enough to know their needs. She slid from the rock to the mat and began to check the ogre's injuries. She had Hunter bring more water and also the rags from her original clothing. They were clean now and she used them to clean the dirt and blood from her patient. She directed Hunter to give him something to drink.

Hunter watched over his brother that night while Alauriel rested. The next day she sought the Goddess to renew her magic. When she finished her prayers, she turned to examine her patient. There was a definite resemblance between her patient and Hunter. She looked at Hunter. "What do I call him?"

Hunter struggled to find a human term for the ogre's name. "He find way."

Alauriel thought for a second. "Wayfinder? Maybe just Finder?"

Hunter thought for a moment and said, "Finder. But no talk so good."

Alauriel slid over to the sleeping ogre carefully. She looked at the half foot and decided it was doing better. She turned to examine the other foot. She did not think that she could do more for either foot, but the rest of his body had suffered from blood loss. She sought the goddess again and cast another healing for serious wounds. She figured it could not hurt.

She glanced up at Hunter, "What could have done this?"

Hunter squatted beside her and looked at his brother's feet. He pointed to the foot that was missing the entire front half. "Axe. Bery strong fuzzface. Maybe so big axe." He then looked at the other food and nodded to himself. "Hammer. Very strong. Maybe same fuzzface."

Alauriel remembered hearing that word in the darkness of the tunnels. "What kind of monster is a fuzzface?"

Hunter looked up at her. "Bery scary. Can be bery many." He held a hand up about a foot over Alauriel's head as she sat there. "Dis big. Fat. Strong. Much hair on face. Live udder cavern. Like break rocks."

Realization began to dawn on her. Alauriel looked at him. "Oh my. Do you mean dwarves?"

Hunter shrugged. "Fuzzface. Dem no like ogre. Be mean."

Alauriel shook her head, wondering what the dwarf's side of the story might be. She asked Hunter to help her to her mat. It had been a long and stressful rising and she needed sleep. As Hunter turned to head back to his brother's side, she caught his hand. "Get as much water into him as you can. If he wakes and will eat, lots of that meat you like so much." He nodded and she lay down and dozed off.

Alauriel awoke sometime later to find Finder was up and about and eating anything edible in the chamber. She could not believe that he was hobbling about as if he had not nearly died. She shook her head and muttered, "Ogres."

As Hunter had warned, he did not speak much of the common tongue. He spoke seldom but seemed friendly enough. By the time for dinner, he was waddling back towards his own chamber and mate.

Hunter's brother visited frequently after that but was no longer able to scout the deeper tunnels. He became known as Three Toe to the Tribe and Finder was no more.

Chapter 8

Dangerous New Lives

With Maker and Three Toe available to watch her, Hunter began to hunt more frequently in the deeper tunnels. He not only sought food, but seemed to be marking the boundaries between the ogre tunnels and those mined by the dwarves. Alauriel wondered if these dwarves were from Deephole. If so, what could have drawn them so far north of their home tunnels.

It was during one of these trips that things went bad. Hunter had been gone for two sleeps already and she was getting tired. Maker had devised a crutch that allowed her to move around the chamber slowly. She was at least able to bathe and relieve herself without help. Alauriel had chased Maker back to his mate. He had been hanging around the entire time Hunter was gone and she needed a break.

She had finished her dinner and was putting away her scrolls when she heard voices in the tunnel outside. She did not expect Maker back until he had slept. She turned to see who was coming hoping it was Hunter.

Instead, she saw two young ogres standing in the entrance to her chamber. The first and smaller was the youth who was missing a finger. The second was larger and more menacing. Both were blinking in the bright light.

The youth she had healed pointed at her and then held out a hand. "Sees. Wins bet. Chief gots human fer pet." The larger youth slapped his hand aside and started to come closer.

The smaller youth tried to hold his companion back. "No. Chief bees mad. Pay den go."

The older youth grabbed him and tossed him into the wall on the far side of the tunnel. "No pay. Me play. Runs way afore me beats youse."

The smaller youth stepped back into the light and looked at her with fear, then disappeared into the dark.

Alauriel also felt fear. Th second youth was young but was at least a half foot taller than her and he had two good legs. She reached into the trunk and lifted her mace from under her chainmail. She used the crutch to struggle to her feet.

The youth eyed the mace and grinned. He began to walk slowly forward. Alauriel raised her voice trying to infuse a tone of command into it. "Leave!"

The youth darted forward and she swung at his head. Her balance was wrong with the crutch and he caught her by the wrist and began to squeeze. She struggled but lost her grip on the mace. She screamed.

That was when the storm broke within the chamber. Hunter just seemed to appear and his dagger was against the youth's throat. A thin red line appeared and a single drop of blood began to run down towards the youth's chest. The youth froze except for the hand that held Alauriel's arm. The hand relaxed and she pulled her arm free. Alauriel stumbled back and dropped over the padded rock.

As soon as she was out of the youth's reach, Hunter dropped the dragger and grabbed the youth by the throat, throwing him towards the entrance to the chamber. The youth crashed to the floor and tried to rise. Hunter gave him no time. He followed and as the youth's head came back up, Hunter backhanded him. He hit the wall hard and slid down to the floor.

Hunter turned to face her. Alauriel had never seen such anger on his face before. It was frightening. But despite the anger, he gently righted her on her seat. His hand brushed her cheek. Then he turned to face the youth who had begun to crawl towards the imagined safety of the dark tunnel. Hunter's sword appeared in his hand as he stalked after the youth.

The youth looked back to see the sword and his face went pale. He rolled onto his back begging, "No Chief. No kill. Only game. No kill."

Hunter, stood over the youth and raised the sword. There was no mercy in him.

Alauriel finally found her voice. "Please no, Hunter. He is just a boy. Please do not kill him."

The sword paused in the air over the youth. Hunter's hand vibrated as he struggled for control. His eyes blinked several times. He emitted a low growl filled with rage. Alauriel whispered, "Please, my Chief."

Hunter stepped back and he pointed into the darkness with the sword. His voice promised death as he hissed. "Go. Next come. Kills. Go fast!"

The youth scrambled into the darkness, not bothering to rise. The sound of running feet echoed down the tunnel.

There was silence as Hunter stood there staring into the dark. When he turned, his face was a mask of stone. But his eyes still burned with anger. "Boy maybe kills. Maybe do udder bad tings. Where bees magic? Kill many save youse tribe. Hows come no kills dat one?"

Alauriel studied his face and the fist still clenching his sword. She realized she did not fear his anger. "I promised my Chief no bad magic. Only good magic."

Hunter grunted and then tossed his sword onto his sleeping mat. "Chief very no smart."

Hunter came and stood over her. He bent down and picked up the mace and handed it to her. "No mo miss. Hits hard."

She placed the mace in the trunk along with the scroll she had been reading. "I will try, my Chief."

He picked her up and carried her to the bathing room and stood guard outside the opening till she was finished. He covered the light while he waited. When he came back, he picked her up and carried her to her mat.

She touched his cheek and asked, "Would you have killed him?" She felt his head nod. "But the tribe needs all to live. You work to save all of them."

He growled as he lowered her to her mat. "Protect youse. Den Protect Tribe. All times you afore Tribe."

She sucked in a breath then released it. Before he could stand, she kissed his cheek.

He stayed bent beside her. "Youse bite?"

Alauriel began to giggle and the last of the tension left her. "Not a bite. It is called a kiss."

He sounded puzzled as he walked to his mat. "Neber gots kiss afore. Maybe likes."

Alauriel lay on her mat for a long time just thinking. She listened to Hunter. It was a long time before he lay down. Even longer until his breathing slid into a rhythm she recognized as sleep. She thought back to the sudden attack in what she now considered her home. She should be afraid or at least upset. But she was not. Hunter had come. He had protected her and now she knew he would defend her even against his own tribe.

Alauriel considered her situation. Why was it that she did not feel trapped here? She was stuck under a mountain with those she was raised to think of as monsters. Even if she could get to the surface, she could not travel on her bad leg. Here, she felt that she had a purpose even though she really did not understand it yet. But she would someday.

Alauriel stared into the darkness. She was lonely. She realized that she had been alone for a long time, even before coming here. Candidates for High Priestess did not have time for friends.

But here in this chamber, she had several good friends. Maker and Three Toe were good to her and valued her as a person. And then there was Hunter. He made no demands of her. He took care of her. She did not understand why. He could have eaten her or worse. But he had not.

She stared across the darkness to where the sound of his breathing came in steady cadence. Maybe she did not have to be alone at all.

Alauriel sat up and began to slide off her mat and across the floor. She found Hunter's mat and slid onto it. She lay down beside him and placed her head on his arm. He tensed for a moment and then relaxed. Alauriel drifted off to sleep.

Hunter lay there for a bit and listened.

She kept breathing.

He relaxed. She was safe now.

———————————

Things began to change again within the chamber. It was more than just the changes in their personal relationship. Hunter was teaching her more and more about her Tribe and how things worked. He began to seek her opinion about problems the Tribe faced.

Hunter left on long trips less often now. He began bringing the other Elders down at different times to meet her. One rising, she asked Maker about the changes. He stared at her curiously. "All know bees Chief Mate. No bees prey. Bees Tribe."

Alauriel flinched at the term "Mate." She was not ready to be anyone's mate. She thought she understood his meaning though. These were a simple and direct people. Their names and titles defined their role within the tribe. And she was now part of the Tribe, no longer an outsider.

She tried to support Hunter and meet the expectations of the Tribe, especially the Elders. Alauriel did not like all of the Elders, but she came to understand that these were the strongest and most capable males in the Tribe. Hunter needed their cooperation and especially their respect. So, she did her best not to judge them.

She wondered why she never met any of the Tribe's females. Three Toe explained in his broken common that the ogre females did not enjoy the same freedom's that women in her world did. They were kept and controlled. Women could be fought over. Most were not badly treated. Many were even cherished by their mates. But there were exceptions. Sadly, Tribe Law did not allow the Chief to interfere. Alauriel was a challenge to their ways and not all the Elders were happy about that.

The work of the Tribe began to replace Alauriel's time studying her scrolls. She was convinced that none of the old prophesies applied anyway. She emersed herself in Hunter's world and time passed quickly. Although she stopped her research Alauriel made sure she continued to make short notes in the scroll she used as a journal. She hoped someday to return it to the Temple Archives as a record of her quest.

Alauriel was not sure how many risings had come and gone when she awoke one morning feeling unwell. She made herself eat a little from one of her loaves but regretted it immediately. She barely made it to the bathing room before her stomach rejected all that she had eaten. She felt better after a nap and the day went well. But the pattern continued over the next several risings. She found that there were smells that upset her stomach and she had to ask Hunter to keep his meat outside of their chamber. She was beginning to worry.

Alauriel woke late on the fifth day after she fell ill. Hunter had already left the chamber. She was just resting when the realization hit her. She carried Hunter's child. Her initial shock soon turned to fear. She had no one to help her while she carried this child, let alone to birth it. Then she thought of Hunter and realized how big this child would probably be. She began to panic.

Alauriel was beside herself. She knew of herbs that would kill the child and save her life. But this was her baby and Hunter's. It deserved life and she could not kill one not yet born. To do such evil would damage her soul and place a barrier between the Goddess and herself. The Goddess might forgive her, but she would never forgive herself.

There had to be a solution if she could just figure it out. She felt lost in her own fears. Her musings were interrupted by the sound of someone coughing in the darkness. She turned to see Three Toe standing by the entrance.

Alauriel waved for him to come over. He sat on the floor near her rock and cocked his head to the side as he studied her. His broad nose twitched as he took in the scent of her. Then he smiled.

She looked at him and actually growled. "What are you smiling for?"

He continued to smile. "Hunter kid come."

She crossed her arms and glared. "How do you know that?"

Three Toe touched his nose. "Smells. Hunter gonna smells too."

Alauriel began to cry. "I am too small to carry his child. It will die. I will die. I don't know how to do this."

Three Toe reached across to pat her on the shoulder. "Find way, Little Warrior."

Three Toe spent the rest of the rising just sitting there smiling. Alauriel wanted to smack him on the head with her mace. His happy face was annoying, but his presence did help her to calm down and think. She pulled out an unused scroll and began to write down the things she knew about birthings and the things she might need. As a Priestess, she had been called upon to help women before. But casting spells on herself during the process was not going to work.

Hunter returned late that rising and Three Toe left as soon as he arrived. Hunter walked up to her and bent to rub his cheek along hers. He took a deep breath and went still. She stepped back to see him studying her.

She sighed in frustration. "I guess the secret is out?"

He gave her a puzzled look then shook his head. "Ken hab dis kid? Alauriel not so big."

Her breath caught in her throat. She had not expected him to go straight to the heart of her fears. When she could breathe again, she looked up at him. "I do not know, Hunter." Her tears began to flow again. Hunter picked her up and just held her.

Several risings later, Alauriel had the beginnings of a plan. It would take a lot of preparation. But she felt she had a chance. She broke the news to Hunter.

He looked at her and asked, "How do dis ting? Not want lose youse. Magics helps?"

Alauriel smiled up at him. "I will not tell you everything yet. You will not like it. It is magic of a sort."

Alauriel began to tell Hunter the things that she would need. He scratched his head. "Much outside." She agreed and urged him to begin.

When Maker next visited, Alauriel told him of all the bowls that she would need. She described each and used her hands to indicate size. Maker agreed, but only if he could watch her as she worked.

The materials and plants she needed took Hunter many trips outside to find and bring to her. Sometimes they were the wrong plant and she would describe them again before his next hunting trip. He was thorough and eventually she had everything that she needed. Maker also took some time to get everything she required crafted. The hardest item was coming up with something she could boil in. Bone would not survive the heat.

While Hunter and Maker gathered her supplies, Alauriel studied her notes and began to pull the recipes for the potions she would make from memory. She could only hope that they were correct. Much depended on her memory which seemed to come and go with her moods.

Alauriel's pregnancy became apparent much sooner than she expected. She worried about how much time she had to make this work. Worse, could she carry the baby inside her long enough that it could develop? If its birth was too early, it might not survive.

By her best guess, she was four months into the pregnancy before they had everything they needed except for a pot to cook in. She and Maker tried one skull that was thicker that the others. But it blackened and cracked long before a single batch could be finished. Maker tried other ideas, but either the material was too porous or it could not take the heat. Alauriel knew they were running out of time.

The solution came from a surprising source. Three Toe had watched them fail over and over. One morning he entered the chamber with a satisfied smile. His normal unsteady gate was even worse as his hands were both behind his back.

Alauriel studied him from her padded rock. "Hello old friend. What are you hiding?"

His grin grew even bigger and he brought his left hand from behind his back. It contained a small shield. "Makes fire dere."

Alauriel studied it and then patted his leg. "Thank you, Three Toe. That might work very well."

The Three toe pulled his other hand out. He held a bowl-shaped helm in it. "Cooks stuffs dere." He said proudly.

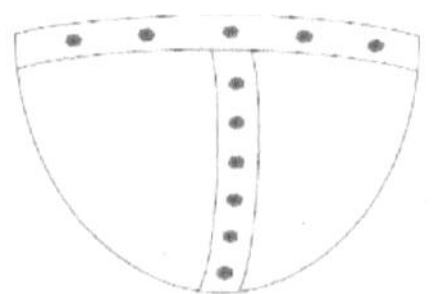

Maker took the helm and examined it. "Maybe not burn."

Three Toe took the helm from Maker. "Yes, no burn. Magics. Fuzzface makes."

Maker began to smile as well. "Work den."

Alauriel got slowly to her feet and gave Three Toe a hug. "Such a gift. My thanks."

Three toe simply patted her head. "Little warrior finded way"

From there, Alauriel began to cook her brews. The first few either did not heal the small cuts she made on her arms or healed too slow. She adjusted her formulas and kept cooking until she had eight potions that she trusted stored in bone jars. She had used a lot of time in the process and she was now too large to move comfortably.

When Hunter returned to eat with her, she asked Hunter to sit and talk with her. She laid out her plan slowly and carefully so he would understand.

"No do!" Hunter growled at her.

Alauriel held his large hand. "It is the only way, my Chief. The baby is already too large to get out of my body. We must make a way out for it. Be brave my Chief."

Hunter bared his teeth. "Brave bery not smart." He reached back to his belt and laid his dagger on the table between them. He then reached out to touch her swollen belly. "Ifn cut dere, kid die. Youse die. Belly cut bad."

Alauriel let go of his hand. She pushed the dagger aside and brought out the small healer's blade from her trunk. "This blade is for wounds. It will not cut deep enough to hurt the baby. It will work."

Hunter left his hand on her stomach. "Much blood cuts dere. Youse bees dead."

Alauriel shook her head and pointed to the potions she had labored on for so long. "Not if you are quick. Take the baby out fast. These bottles hold good magic. It will save the baby and me. We must do this when we next rise."

Hunter stood up and began to pace the chamber. "No like dis. Bery not smart."

Hunter continued to argue until she grew tired. Alauriel finally reminded him that the only other option was to lose them both during the birth. Hunter had no other plan. He had to trust in her. Alauriel stood next to him. "When we next wake it will be time. The magic will not last. It must be soon."

Hunter growled softly and covered the light. Then he carried her to their mat. She slept that night warm and safe beside him.

He did not sleep. He listened to her breathe and he felt fear.

Alauriel settled herself on her old sleeping mat and raised her knees. She knew this was going to hurt but had no way to dull the pain. She hung her Mistletoe about her neck and gathered her magic. She cast a blessing upon herself and Hunter. Then she told him to begin.

The tiny healer's blade looked impossibly small in Hunter's large hand. He had a lot of experience skinning and cleaning his prey, but he hated the idea of cutting into his mate. She had used something to mark where he was to cut. She had even shown him how far in to push the blade. He had cleaned his hands with some bad-smelling plant she had him bring back. He did not like this plan.

He heard his mate finish her prayer and say please. He shook his head and muttered, "Bery, bery not smart." And then he began to cut.

———————————————

Alauriel became aware sometime later with Hunter's arm behind her back. He was holding a bowl to her lips and urging her to swallow. She did and the pain eased. She drifted off.

Alauriel woke again. She was alone on the mat but there was a bone jar beside her. She reached for it and drank. She felt the pain fade and her mind began to focus. She glanced at the ledge. Only three jars remained. She turned to see Hunter holding a large baby and a bowl. He seemed lost as to how to make it drink. The baby's eyes were closed and its breathing was labored. Alauriel held out her arms. "Bring them to me. Quickly."

As Hunter lay the baby beside her, Alauriel realized that the mat was covered in her blood. She ignored the mess as she dipped a finger into the potion and placed her finger in the baby's mouth. It began to suck. She continued to let it suckle the potion as she examined it. It was a boy. Her son. She guessed he was the size of a two-year-old human child.

As she finished getting the potion into her son, he began to breathe more easily. He turned his head and opened its eyes. They were an even paler green than Hunter's. And they glowed even brighter than his father's. Alauriel closed her eyes as a single tear ran down her cheek. She finally understood the Stallion's words. Love was the path. The word was easier than the journey, but she would not fail.

Alauriel sat again at her seat with quill in hand.

Both the baby and I are well. The potions and my spells have healed most everything. His lungs are doing better. Between carrying so large a child and the need to take him out, I do not think I can carry another child. But that may also be a blessing as I barely survived this child. I would love to name my son, but Hunter insists that the name must come from the Tribe when he is older. For now, we are well. My duty to shepherd this one through life will be my pleasure. The Lady's Blessing is on me. I have no clue what the future will bring for any of us. Nor do I care. For now, I am happy.

Alauriel Armonen

Epilogue

14 Years Later

Alauriel wandered the chamber slowly, using the crutch Maker had made for her so long ago. Her leg pained her more and more with each passing year. She kept moving despite the pain. The feeling that trouble was coming bothered her more than the leg. Nothing obvious was wrong but she could not shake the feeling. Maybe it was too quiet. As she limped across the room, she mentally reviewed all that had happened lately.

As always, there were complaints among the Elders. Elder was a risky job these days in the Tribe. Despite how well the clan was doing, someone always wanted more power. Challenges were more frequent and more deadly. She could think of no one in the Tribe that was foolish enough to challenge Hunter yet. Her husband was deadlier now than ever before. His work with their son had sharpened his own skills. The boy would be a great leader someday.

She missed the old days when her friend Maker had been a strong voice among the Elders. But Maker had been pushed aside a long time ago. He had been challenged by a much younger warrior and had lost. At least her magic had kept him alive after the fight. But even her magic could not save him from age. He was gone now and she missed her friend.

She wondered how long it would be till someone did challenge her mate. She had never truly understood human politics. The drive for power over others made little sense to her. She knew that the male ogres had an even greater need for power. Hunter had made them safe. Their territory was secure and food was always available. But many of the males, especially the younger ones, wanted battle and conquest. They seemed to crave it. Someday, they would reject the peace Hunter had given them.

Alauriel studied the chamber she called home. Shorty, her son with Hunter, was not around. He had not been around much for months. She hoped he was safe up with his friends the squirrels. She smiled at the thought of her powerful young son sitting and cracking nuts for a bunch of squirrels. It made him happy and he had been in less trouble with other young ogres since finding the small crevice that let him see outside.

So, her son was out and that was not the problem. Hunter was also out. There had been rumors of something moving about in the deep tunnels claimed by the Tribe. Hunter was leading a party to investigate. He should not be at risk, although she wished he had let someone else track down the threat. But that was not his way.

Alauriel sighed and visited the bathing room before covering the continual light coin that still lit their chamber. Then she lay down alone on the mat she shared with Hunter. She tossed and turned unable to get her bad leg into a good position. It took some time before she fell into a fitful sleep.

Alauriel began to dream almost immediately. The dream was strange in that it was so lifelike and yet surreal. She traveled the dark tunnels of her world, but she could see as if it were fully daylight under the earth. She could even see colors in this dream and that too was not normal. And, she could walk without pain or crutch. She did not even limp.

She turned a corner and before her sat a reddish squirrel with a white tuft at the end of its tail. At that moment she understood that this was more a vision than a dream. The squirrel chittered at her before running ahead. She began to follow as it urged her to move faster.

She followed the squirrel to an overlook where a powerful black unicorn stood looking down. She moved up beside it and it dropped its head to point below with its golden horn. As she looked more closely, she could see her mate Hunter moving along a narrow path beside a deep drop. Hunter moved carefully. His head seemed to dart around as he checked for tracks and watched the rocks around him for danger. He had his great sword in his right hand. The left held a long dagger that he used to poke at the ground.

Alauriel saw movement ahead of Hunter. She tried to call out a warning to him, but found she could not speak. The squirrel, who had climbed up to the Stallion's back, chittered angrily at her.

Alauriel turned her head back to watch Hunter. He approached the place where she had seen movement and stopped. Another large figure she recognized stepped out before Hunter and swung a large club at his head. Alauriel had a vague memory of that club, but could not place it.

Hunter stepped deftly back and the club passed harmlessly in front of him. Before him stood an ogre with a large tusk protruding from the left side of his mouth. She recognized him as one of the newer Elders. He was called Tusk. She knew little about him other than Hunter did not like him. Hunter had refused to bring him to their chamber. Hunter said Tusk was bad, just like his father. But he refused to tell her any more.

Alauriel focused back on Hunter as he began to speak. "Tusk fraid fair challenge? Hide in dark ta kills Chief."

Tusk roared and swung the large club at Hunter again. Hunter blocked the blow. Alauriel noticed the club seemed to have a reddish tint to its tip.

Tusk attacked again and again, but hunter's sword seemed to anticipate each strike, blocking easily. Hunter laughed and mocked Tusk. "Papa Brawl better wid club den youse. Kilt him. Maybe so kilt you long go."

Tusk shook his head growling. "Die old one. Tribe want new Chief."

Tusk continued his attacks, but it was apparent that Hunter was just toying with him. Tusk stepped forward making a desperate swing. Hunter stooped low bringing his sword in to strike the club near Tusk's hands. Tusk lost his grip and the club sailed into the darkness to vanish below.

Hunter stepped forward to kill his foe when Tusk screamed, "Kills!" A figure rose from behind a large rock above and to Hunter's rear. Its arm flashed and a spear suddenly appeared in Hunter's lower back. Alauriel recognized the one who threw the spear as Tusk's son Thump. Thump was one of Shorty's chief tormentors.

Hunter took another step forward before dropping to a knee. The sword fell from his hand and he reached back to grab for the spear. He looked up with contempt at Tusk. "Cheats. No be Chief ifn two fights. Challenge be Tribe way."

Tusk grinned as he stepped forward. "Who tell me cheat? Youse bees dead. Body bees gone"

Hunter leaned forward to strike with his dagger. But his injury slowed him and Tusk stepped back. Alauriel realized his great strength was failing. Tusk caught his hand and held it firmly and he looked down on Hunter. "Gets eben. Hunter kills Brawl. Tusk son Brawl an Thump son Tusk kills youse."

Alauriel watched Thump climb down and moved behind Hunter. He grasped the spear and used it to force Hunter over the edge. Alauriel watched her mate disappear into the darkness.

Alauriel turned her face into the unicorn's shoulder and let her tears fall. After a time, the Stallion blew softly into her hair as it had once before. She turned to look into its eye and then, she woke.

Alauriel lay on the mat for long moments, breathing in the scent of her mate. Hunter was gone. She knew that now. They would come for her and her son next. She only had a short time to prepare if she was to save her son. She had no plan to save herself. Hunter's little warrior would make them pay.

Alauriel rose and found her Mistletoe. It had never faded despite the years or the lack of sunlight. Mielikki was still with her. She began to pray, asking for the magic she needed to save her son. For the first time since she arrived here, the lack of the forest around her did not matter.

Only her need mattered. The Goddess heard her plea and that was enough.

She made her way to the bathing room and then uncovered the coin, letting light fill the room. She opened the trunk and struggled into her chainmail. It was a bit snug after all these years, but it would do for one last fight. She hung her mace on her belt and her Mistletoe around her neck. Then she pulled out her scroll and added one last entry to her journal.

My Chief is gone. Hunter has been murdered. They will come for me next. The Lady has granted me the power to save our son. If only I can be strong enough. I do not know his destiny. I can only hope that the world does not judge him by his appearance, but by his heart. Hunter and I have taught him all we can. He has great love inside him. And he has a fierce need to protect even the smallest. Lady help us, especially the squirrels. I can only hope that this makes its way back to the Temple. Maybe there are those who can guide my son when I am gone. Mielikki bless him as she has blessed me. I do not regret never being High Priestess. This life has been enough for me.

Alauriel Armonen

As soon as the ink was dry, Alauriel rolled the scroll and placed it upon the ledge she used for a desk. She then took an old dwarven helm that she used to make portions and placed it over the scroll. She placed a rock on the helm to hold it in place. It was all she could do to protect the scroll. She left the chest open. The remaining scrolls could perish with her.

Alauriel sat to consider the four spells that the goddess had given her. The first was a powerful spell of healing that would restore her leg. She thought about the spell and realized its purpose. She was not bound to this path. The Goddess reminded her that she was still free to choose. She could literally walk away. But without her son. The choice was easy. She would fight as she had lived with Hunter, crippled in body but not in spirit.

The second spell was simple as well. It was a glyph spell that would allow her to create a magical trap. One that would allow her to release the power of her flame strike before Tusk could kill her. She knew that the spell would also consume her as well. Her goal was not to survive, but to prevent Tusk from harming her son. She had work to do.

Alauriel pulled the last of her ink and her remaining quills out of the trunk and set them on the ground at her feet. She slid from the rock and began to write on the rock floor before her seat. She took her time casting first the glyph spells and then placing the power of the flame strike spell within the wards of the glyph. By the time she finished, she was stiff and sore. She struggled back onto the rock. The mark at her feet brought a smile to her face. "Let them come."

She had time left so she considered the final powerful spell that she had been granted. It was not normally a clerical spell. The druids of her order seemed to favor it though. She had always considered death to be the doorway to joining her Goddess, this spell brought a renewed existence in this world not the next. As she thought of her son, she suddenly smiled and cast the spell upon herself.

She sat and waited. She continued to breathe, but Hunter was gone.

At long last she heard a disturbance in the tunnels leading down to her chamber. Tusk stomped into the room holding Hunter's sword in his hand. It was in a strange scabbard, but it was Hunter's sword. Tusk stared about blindly for a while as his eyes adjusted to the light. She waited patiently. She was in no hurry.

When he turned towards her, Alauriel rose and met his gaze. He grinned down at her. "Hunter dead. Me Chief."

Alauriel stared at him coldly. "You are no Chief. Even with two of you, you had to kill him from behind. Afraid to face him. You are a coward."

Tusk stared at her in surprise. She glared back at him. "Yes, I know the truth and so will the Tribe."

Tusk smiled wickedly. "No, Witch. Me rip out throat. No tell. Dead."

Tusk stepped forward confidently, not even reaching for the sword. This was a puny thing and he would end it this night. Alauriel grinned at him and dropped her crutch to the floor. She pulled her mace up and waited. As Tusk's large hands closed about her neck, Alauriel pulled her lame leg backwards, erasing the ward that withheld the power of her spell.

Fire exploded through the ceiling and rained down throughout the chamber. The ceiling stones shattered and charred as they fell. The rock at the two combatants' feet began to melt. The woman and the ogre were consumed by the flames. When it ended, the chamber was empty except for fallen rock, smoke, a puddle of metal high on the wall that continued to glow brightly, and an old helm covered in debris.

———————————————

Sometime later an old ogre limped into the room and began to dig through the rubble. He moved slowly as half of one foot was missing. The other appeared to be missing two toes. He began near the source of the light and cleared his way across the chamber. After a time, he uncovered a large sword in a scabbard that lay beneath a large stone. He leaned it against the wall near the entrance.

He continued to dig but there was no sign of bodies. As he turned back towards the entrance, a young ogre warrior stomped into the chamber knocking the older ogre onto a pile of smoking rock. The older one looked up from where he had fallen and spoke simply. "Gone, Thump. Dead. Nuttin bees dere."

The youth grabbed the sword and disappeared into the darkness of the tunnel. "Elder make new Chief. Den me kill Shorty. Him fault."

The old crippled ogre got to his feet. As he took a last look at the chamber, he saw a flash of red. Suddenly there was a small squirrel chittering at him from over by the ledge where his human friend used to sit. Its small hands pushed at the helm he had given her.

The old one looked at the helm as the squirrel continued to chitter. He squinted at it and then asked, "What want Three Toe do?"

The squirrel banged on the helm several times and the old ogre stumbled over and picked it up. Somehow it was still cool. Below it was something rolled up. The squirrel began chittering again so he took that too. He headed for the tunnel and the squirrel scampered up his leg and back to perch on his shoulder.

The old ogre headed up a ramp, muttering to the squirrel. "Youse no bees boss me."

———————————————————

Three Toe looked into the chamber the Tribe kept prey in to slaughter. He saw his nephew tied up within. The squirrel leapt to the floor and disappeared inside. The old ogre wandered in to give his nephew the bad news and then headed up the forbidden ways to hide in the shadows. He found a place where he could watch the ramps and sat. He watched and waited and a small tear rolled down his face.

Much later, the old ogre moved as softly as he could behind his nephew as the boy moved up the ramps of the forbidden tunnels. Three Toe followed as his nephew went outside. He was glad to see Hunter's sword sticking up over the boy's shoulder. From just inside the tunnel, he watched his nephew stare for a long time at outside. It was dark so Three Toes' eyes did not hurt. After a while, the boy moved off down a trail around the mountainside.

The old ogre crept out and placed the rolled thing on a large rock. "Dere little pest. Done. Now youse ken leaves me lone."

He wandered over to the trail that his nephew had taken and stared down it, longing to go with the boy. He resisted the temptation to follow. The squirrel had promised he would see the boy again.

He heard the rustle of feathers behind him and turned to see a large night bird sitting on the rock with the rolled thing in the talons of one foot.

Three Toe the ogre shook his head, looked one last time at his nephew's path, and headed back into the tunnels where it was safe and animals were for eating.

Author Bio

Major Ursa's love of fantasy and science fiction began as a child lost in the worlds created by Andre Norton. Her characters were true heroes. They walked the paths of honor even when it came at a price. That lesson became a part of Ursa's own life.

Major Ursa made his first forays into fantasy gaming in 1980. Soon, he was creating worlds and adventures to entertain friends and family. The games became stories to entertain his children and grandchildren. Somewhere along the way, entertainment turned into teaching about honor and sacrifice and ways to persevere when things were hard. Now, the old bear is putting his favorite tales in print. The world needs heroes, even fictional ones, that are willing to put the needs of others before their own desires.